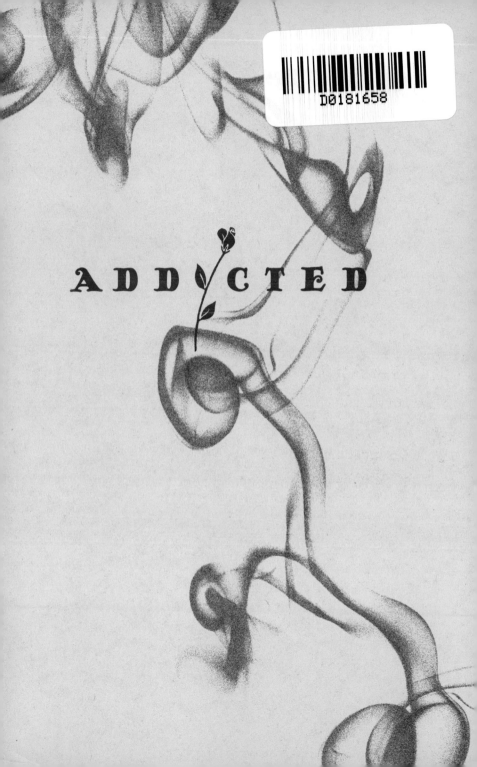

ADDICTED

ADD CTED

CHARLOTTE FEATHERSTONE

Spice

Spice

ADDICTED

ISBN-13: 978-0-373-60528-6
ISBN-10:   0-373-60528-5

Recycling programs
for this product may
not exist in your area.

www.Spice-Books.com

Printed in U.S.A.

To Joe and Olivia, who have sacrificed so much for me to fulfill my dream. I love you more than words can say, and I thank you for being supportive, understanding and easygoing when the house looks as if a bomb has gone off, and we have frozen pizza or hot dogs for yet another dinner. I swear, I'll make it up to you at Disney!

And for my sisters who make up The Line of Pigs.
Donna "Double D," a kindred spirit, and Tinker. Gisele, whose brown eyes are always full of laughter and mischievousness. Lynda, who shares my "trashy romance" fetish, and Rhonda, who is fast becoming another romance junkie—told you Edward was hot! To Amy, the quiet one of the bunch, whom I hear giggling when we talk about "swords," and another Edward groupie. Last but not least, Joanne, aka Daisy, the lady of the group. Where would I be without you to make the shifts tolerable? Thanks for the 4:00 a.m. chats and giggles. Please know that you're more than friends, you're family, and I could not imagine going to work and not having you there with me. Shift after shift, you keep me going, but more important, you keep me laughing, and isn't that what life is all about?

Opium unites the souls of smokers who recline around the same lamp. It's a bath in a thick atmosphere, a reunion in one bed with heavy covers, a veritable coupling that one can't resist. There is, certainly, in each opium addict an unhappy or unsatisfied lover.

—Robert Desnos, *Le Vin est Tiré*

Prologue

Slave. Minion. Fiend. The others who have come before me have been called such things, but I prefer to think of myself as a disciple; a devout follower of my voluptuous mistress.

They say my lover is a sinister beauty, and perhaps they are correct. But when caught in her heady embrace there is nothing sinister about her. How can she be evil, when she bathes my body in a thousand raptures? How can she be anything but a radiant sorceress when she takes me to heights never before experienced?

No, my mistress is many things, but not a succubus in a gossamer cloak. True, she demands much from me, but I know how to coax and coddle her so that her black flesh responds to my skilled hands. Between my fingers, she melts like a woman in the throes of climax.

I warm her, care for her, wait patiently for her to cloak me in her sensual and supple embrace.

I worship her.

My relationship with my mistress is uncomplicated. I know

what she desires of me; at the same time, she understands and fulfills my needs. As any mistress she is, at times, demanding to the point of suffocation, always wanting more—needing more. But when I come to her, she loves me like nothing—or no one—ever has.

All she wants is my return to her, night after night, hour after hour. And I do return with eager anticipation. She always welcomes my homecoming with outstretched arms and together, we make the sweetest, most decadent love, a love where two become one. Where I become so coiled in her powers that I never want to leave.

She is here now, I realize, as I see the gray fingers of her arrival begin to swirl up from the altar I have prepared for her. Soon she will be curling her fingers in my hair, caressing my face and covering my mouth with her evocative beauty. I will taste her heady fragrance on my tongue, inhale her bittersweet scent deep into my lungs. My mind will cloud, will begin to wander and float. I will fall back on my red velvet cushion, drunk with anticipation as I observe the couples surrounding me make love. I watch them like a disembodied voyeur. Not even the sounds and sights of an orgy surrounding me can arouse me so well as the thought of my mistress does.

Lush female bottoms, naked and pale, are before me. Breasts of every size and color attempt to beckon me. Quims, glistening, ready for the taking try to entice, but I wait for my mistress, as any dedicated lover would.

It is worth the wait, because when I am aroused and eager, my bewitching paramour will consume me with her fire and satisfy me with her skilled attention—ministrations that are

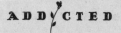

much more pleasing than watching the dreamy specter of couples naked and writhing before me. While they enjoy each other's bodies, I can only find satisfaction and pleasure in the arms of my enchantress.

Among the gossamer tendrils my mistress rises like Venus from the shell. She beckons me and I allow her to take over, her greedy hands swathing my body and mind in a frenzy of orgasmic temptations.

With a smile I forget about the women at my feet. I no longer hear their moans, the sounds of flesh hitting flesh. I no longer see them riding the staffs of men as they flick their hair over their shoulders and cast me glances that invite me to join their party.

Instead, I fall back and allow my mistress to fully shroud me until I feel smothered in her intoxicating perfume.

Soon her ethereal mist will begin to evaporate and part like the branches of a tree in the wind, revealing the flesh and blood woman my body desires. The flesh and blood woman who will never be found here in this den of pleasure.

This is the moment I live for with my mistress. This power she has to conjure up my most sacred, private fantasies. The beckoning enchantment she entices me with is the glimpse of the woman I crave, the woman who has ruled my heart for so long that I can see no others except her. Desire no one but her.

Through heavy-lidded eyes I will see my flesh lover, her pale skin tinted the color of cream, her long, golden hair glistening like corn silk in the sun as she stands before the candle and brass burner. Through the vapors, I watch her disrobe for me, her breasts spilling from her gown. Unbound, they are lush and full, the pale pink nipples pearled, waiting for my hands and mouth to show her pleasure. Slowly, as if to extend my torment, she waits to reveal the rest of her lovely form.

But patiently I wait, allowing my mistress to keep her hold of me until the beauty can walk through the twisting tendrils of smoke and fall at my feet.

She is always naked, my angel, and she always desires me. The real me. The man I am. Even though my mistress is there watching, whispering into my ear.

It is always a ménage, this coming together. Always my mistress comes between my flesh lover and me. But in this world of red smoke and dreams, the two who hold me enraptured, live harmoniously side by side. There is no anger. No petty jealousy for my attention. No demands that I give up the other.

For I couldn't. I need both like I need breath.

One rules my mind and my strength; the other, my heart, soul and body.

The one knows me as a man, an aristocrat with a secret.

The other knows me for what I am. An opium addict.

Slave, minion, fiend. I suppose I am. But I prefer to think of myself as a disciple. It is so much more palatable to believe that this path I walk is based on devotion and faith—not the bonds of slavery.

1

Bewdley, Worcestershire, England
1850

"Up and at 'em, milord."

The valet's gruff voice reached through the thick fog in his brain, disturbing the peaceful slumber and the lingering effects of the red smoke. "Sod off, Vallery," Lindsay groaned.

His valet, ever the dutiful gentleman's gentleman, groaned under Lindsay's weight as he pulled him up from the brocade divan. "Any other time I would, milord, but Lord Darnby and his chits will be here within an hour and I've got a day's debauchery to rid you of."

Lindsay felt his arm being thrown around Vallery's thick neck. His head lolled just a bit, forcing him to open his eyes. He was in his pleasure den, the remnants of last night's bacchanal still surrounding him.

With his valet's steadying hand and a few blinks of his burning eyes, Lindsay found himself slowly acclimating to the world around him. From the windows, he saw that the sky was not bright with the sun, but dark, the color of twilight. Bloody hell, what time was it?

"'Tis nearly seven, milord," Vallery answered as he saw Lindsay's confused gaze focus on the darkening skies. "You've been asleep all day. Now 'tis time to clean up."

Yes. A bath and shave would set him to rights. It always did.

"Now then, will you bathe in the waters or do you wish me to take you to your apartments via the servants' stairs?"

"My mother is around, then?"

The coarse visage of his valet came sharply into the line of his vision. Vallery was no effeminate Frenchman who clucked over him and his clothes. His unorthodox background and upbringing was what had made Lindsay desire him as his most trusted servant. It was Vallery's steadfast loyalty that Lindsay appreciated most, not the intricate folds of a starched cravat.

"Would I be traipsing up those rickety old stairs carrying you if the marchioness was not about, flying high in the boughs?" Vallery grumbled.

Lindsay chuckled and removed his arm from his valet. He was sober as a monk now, although he could tell from the look in Vallery's gaze that his appearance still lingered with a hint of debauchery.

"I think my mother is probably clucking about like a mother hen. She usually does when company is expected."

"Thought you might like to know that the Duke of Torrington has already arrived."

"And Wallingford?"

"Not yet, milord."

Lindsay snorted as he pulled the already untied cravat from

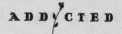

his neck. "I'm not surprised. Wallingford has made it his solemn vow to never be in his father's company. Why would things change today?"

Vallery said nothing as Lindsay continued to strip out of his clothes. Like the dutiful servant he was, his valet reached out for the wrinkled garments, draping them carefully over his arm. "So, it's the baths then, is it?"

With a nod, Lindsay draped his trousers over Vallery's arms and headed for the mineral bath. He stepped into the hot water and allowed it to engulf his body and soak his muscles. With a sigh, he looked up at the arched ceiling above his head, then back down to the water that bubbled around him. A hot mineral spring ran beneath the house, allowing him this small luxury. Naturally, he had designed his pleasure den around the baths, which now resembled a Middle Eastern hammam. It was something straight out of the Arabian Nights. The only thing it lacked was a lovely odalisque.

Lindsay smiled to himself. He knew exactly who he would like to have in that particular role. She was going to be there in his home tonight. Already desire swirled in his veins. He had denied himself for too long. It was time, far past time in actuality, to see if the lady desired him in the same manner.

"You'll need to be quick about it this evening," Vallery called over his shoulder. "You will not want your Lady Anais to see you in such a state."

Lindsay closed his eyes against the prick of pain in his chest. He did not want her name soiled with his other vice. How well Vallery knew him, for the last thing Lindsay wished was for Anais to know how he dabbled in opium. Anais would not understand.

"You place your arrows well, Vallery."

"I intend for them to wound, milord. Never kill."

"And wound they have." Lindsay knew what Vallery thought, but his valet was wrong. He could stop. He was not a habitué. He could and would stop. Once he had Anais in his life and in his bed he would have no further use for the opium.

He dunked himself beneath the water, no longer desirous to see his valet looking at him with what Lindsay knew was concern. When he arose he wiped the water from his eyes, shook his curly mane free of wetness and pulled himself out of the bath. Vallery was there, holding out a black dressing gown.

"I wanted to tell you last night, before your...celebration," Vallery said awkwardly as he glanced at the elaborate spread, "how thankful I am for you allowing me into that stock sale. I made a bundle, and I wouldn't even have been allowed in the Exchange if you would not have placed my bid for me."

Lindsay slapped his long-suffering valet on the shoulder. "We both made a packet, my friend. Besides, knowledge is to be shared amongst men—amongst all classes. You frown now, Vallery, but mark my words, you'll see in another twenty-odd years how the middling classes will supersede the aristocracy. Like the dinosaurs on display at the British Museum, the aristocracy will one day weaken and become extinct."

"If you say so, milord."

"You doubt me, but I believe what I say."

"Your thoughts will get you kicked out of parliament once you gain your seat."

"There are others like me, Vallery. There is a whole class of men who think just as I think."

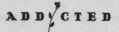

"That was university, when you were young and idealistic. Every young man at that age wants to change the world. Everyone thinks they can. Then they get out into the real world, and they then decide that the privilege of their birth is more important to fight for than the miserable lives of those born below them."

"Idleness and indolence. That is what you always say of my class."

"I do not mean to insinuate that you are always indolent, milord."

Lindsay reached for the towel Vallery held out to him and dried his hair. "But you do think my wealth could be better spent than on lavish opium dens."

"You have been known to be gone for days, milord."

"Let me worry about that. You worry about what I've said. The world is changing, Vallery. Slowly, but surely. I know it can change. I know it *will* change."

"The haves will continue to have, and the have-nots will continue to go without. It is the way of things. The foundation of our empire."

"I see the failures of our aristocratic forebears. No longer can our huge estates thrive and survive on the backs of the working man. In time, Vallery, we aristocrats will be working men, too."

"You already do, milord. Making money is your full-time vocation."

Lindsay grinned. "I do have a knack for it, I'll admit. But what I find just as thrilling is teaching others how to double, triple their income."

"You've the heart of a merchant, hoarding your treasures and counting your money, you've the mind of a mercenary who strategizes every move. You will forgive me for saying, my lord, but you are unlike any aristocrat I've ever met."

"And that's why you jumped at the chance to be my valet once your soldiering days were over." Vallery, the taciturn man, rolled his eyes. Lindsay threw the wet towel at him. "You may accuse me of many things, but never of withholding knowledge from the everyday man. They, too, deserve a chance. I'm only seeing to it they get it. Why should it only be blue bloods who are given the chance to increase their fortunes? We're born rich, the untitled man is not. He is the one who needs the chances in life."

"You're a good man, my lord. I wonder when you'll see it? You are not your father, nor are you likely to become like him."

Lindsay grimaced. "Good God, Vallery, don't go all sentimental on me now. It gives me hives. I'd rather you call me a stupid ass for my behaviors than talk this melodrama. I've told you time and time again, I'm a dabbler. A dilettante, if you please. I am no rookery addict."

"Of course, milord."

Lindsay knew the man was lying. Knew his manservant was worried. But there was nothing to be worried about, because he could throw out his pipe whenever he damned well pleased. He did not have a habit.

"I am always available to you, Vallery. Lord knows you've put up with enough of my shenanigans since Cambridge. The least I can do is see to it that your retirement will be prosperous."

"There is no denying your skill at the 'Change. You've certainly saved this place from demolition," Vallery muttered as he looked around the lavish Moorish architecture that surrounded them.

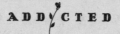

"My father has wallowed in his cups for too many years. He hasn't seen to the proper running of this place for decades."

"I hope he knows to whom he is indebted."

Lindsay laughed as he tied the sash around his middle. "My father is too busy drinking and whoring to notice what has gone on around him. Hell, the walls could crumble about our heads and he'd be too drunk to notice—or care. No, my father worries about his hounds and his drink, my mother and her comforts have been gone from his mind for many years."

Running two fingers over his chin, Lindsay felt the growth that had erupted since last night. He bent and looked at the shadowed reflection in the mirror. "What do you think? Too much?"

"I think you will frighten off the ladies, milord."

"Really?" He doubted Anais would be frightened of a little beard. Not her. She was not a silly chit. Perhaps she might even like it. He grinned, running his fingers over the stubble. Perhaps Anais would care to learn the benefits of a little facial hair. With the proper tutor, Anais might very well welcome such lessons. Certainly she would enjoy the scrape of his chin against her soft, fleshy thighs. He knew he certainly would.

"It is not my place to ask, milord—"

"When has that ever stopped you?" Lindsay interrupted as he took a chair and allowed his head to be tipped back in preparation for a shave.

"You do allow me unheard of freedoms, milord."

"Yes, well, I'm a Renaissance man. I keep telling you that, Vallery."

"And I keep telling you I don't know what that means."

Lindsay saw him reach for the silver blade and swirl it in the water of the blue ceramic basin. "It means I am rather liberal and my way of thinking is new and perhaps a bit nonconformist."

Vallery grunted and brought the blade to Lindsay's throat. "What I was going to ask, milord, is if you wanted the blue jacket and the ivory waistcoat this evening."

Lindsay could almost hear his valet finish his question with "you know, the new ones you've been saving for just the right evening."

"You must have found the box I hid in the waistcoat."

Vallery flushed. "I did, indeed, milord."

"What did you think of it?"

"I think you shall have to get the lady some sort of support for her hand. That gem is the largest I think I've ever seen."

Lindsay smiled. "It came all the way from India. Cost me a packet, but what does that matter when I shall have the privilege of seeing it every day on her finger. I think of it as my brand, Vallery. I hope to claim her with that ring."

"I think any woman would be claimed by such a bauble, my lord."

Lindsay chuckled. The diamond was very big, but not garish. He hoped it said devotion and undying love, not greed. "Do you think tonight would be a good night to ask her, Vallery? Is that what you are suggesting?"

"It is not my place to suggest, milord."

He laughed. Bloody hell, his bossy valet was always suggesting. Just last night he *suggested* that he'd had enough of the red smoke. Lindsay had spited him by blowing another cloud.

All finished with the shave, Lindsay stood and strolled over

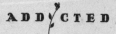
to the divan where Vallery had prepared his evening clothes. The new blue jacket and ivory brocade were there. Lindsay wondered if his valet had been kind enough to put the brown box containing the emerald and diamond ring in the pocket.

"You've the look of the cat that just ate the canary," Vallery muttered as he cleaned up the shaving things.

"It's obvious, is it? And how am I to help it?" he asked. "I'm going to ask the most beautiful woman in the world to be my wife."

"What a relief," his valet taunted. "Now I won't have to listen to ye bellyache anymore over the girl. 'Tis unnatural how you're lovesick for her."

"No," Lindsay whispered as the image of Anais came to mind. "It's the most natural thing in the world to love her as much as I do."

"Well, you had best get yerself out of this wicked pleasure den and make your way to your mother's salon. You're late."

Lindsay dressed quickly and left the den, which had, at one time, been his mother's sorely neglected and run-down conservatory. When he'd come into money from his business investments, he'd claimed the crumbling monstrosity for his own and made it into an escape. Designed like the Alhambra in Spain, it was the height of decadence. With its Moorish influence, and the hot spring bath, it was a world within a room. An escape he craved at the end of the day.

He thought of it as his harem. And he'd decorated it as such.

"Ah, here he is at last," his father, the Marquis of Weatherby said in a voice that was already slurred by drink.

"Good evening, sir." Lindsay nodded in the direction of his father, then reached for the gloved hand of his mother.

"Mama, you look lovely this evening."

Her gaze drifted over his, as if taking stock of his appearance. There was nothing left in his eyes for her to catch on to. Nothing but the dutiful and loving son standing before her, kissing her hand. The stains of his mistress were washed away from his body. He was clean. For how long, he didn't know. It didn't matter, for tonight he was not thinking about *her,* and when he would next require her services.

He made quick work of the introductions, all the while resisting the urge to search out Anais. It was a game he liked to play, to see how long he could endure it, not seeing her.

His body was now as tense as a bow. His mouth dry from talking. His eyes hungry for a glance of her ripe body and lovely face. As if the dinner guests knew of his need, they parted, revealing Anais standing by the hearth, talking to her younger sister.

She must have felt his burning gaze, because she stopped talking and turned to look at him. Her smile went all the way to his core, hitting like a rush—like that first great inhalation of opium.

If a man's future was truly preordained—his destiny written while still in the womb—then he was looking upon the woman who was his fate, the woman he knew had been created solely for him.

He had always known that someday Anais would belong to him. She would be more than his friend. He'd always believed it, but never more than this moment as their gazes collided together, and their bodies became aware of each other.

She always took his breath away. They'd been friends forever, since young childhood, but his feelings were no longer chaste

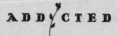

or platonic. No, his feelings and desires were hot. Passionate. Erotic. And the perfumed dreams he had of Anais last night had been the most erotic yet. The things she had let him do to her...

One day, they wouldn't be just dreams and fantasies.

"Good evening, Lindsay."

Her soft voice washed over him like a caress, and he felt himself grow aroused. It was so hard to hide his feelings from her. He doubted he could for much longer.

Her gloved hand felt so right in his palm as he raised her fingers to his lips. Her eyes, those beautiful, mesmerizing pools, captured his attention, watching as his lips slowly descended to her fingertips. He lingered there, inhaling her perfume, watching the rise and fall of her breasts in the tight bodice. She moved in, just a hint, and the cloud of her rich perfume rose up to coil around him.

She had scented her breasts with the French perfume he had purchased for her.

Desire gripped him, and lost to everything but need, he closed his eyes and inhaled the heady scent. In his mind, he could see the golden liquid trickle between the cleft of her breasts. He saw the cut crystal bottle stopper in her hand as she trailed it along her cleavage. One day, he vowed, he would lay negligently in their bed, which would be rumpled from their love making, and watch her at her toilette. One day, he would come and stand behind her and take the stopper from her hand and trace her breasts with it. One day, she would look into the mirror and see him standing there, desire in his eyes.

"Lindsay?"

Slowly, his eyelids opened and there she was. Her head was bent, her lips ripe for his mouth to plunder. It would be no trial—and highly arousing—to pull the little puffy sleeves of her gown down her arms and expose her. He knew she would be wearing a corset, but in his dreams, she would be naked beneath, bared to his eyes and hands.

His gaze swept over her face, which was so lovely to him, then down her throat, which he longed to brush his lips over, down to the pulse that fluttered like butterfly wings. Every inch of her was as luscious as a sweet from the candy shop. And God above, he was beyond wanting a taste of her.

"Good evening, my angel," he said over her hand. "You look ravishing, as always."

"You have been practicing your flattery, my lord," she said with a little laugh that was too high. Nervous? Aroused? Her laugh seemed unnatural. "The ladies in London must swoon at your skill, sir."

"I do not know. I do not share any compliments with ladies other than you, Anais."

Her eyes told him she was dubious about his sincerity. "Truth," he whispered in her ear.

She bristled at the sudden contact of their bodies. He was forgetting himself, forgetting where he was. Forgetting that in Anais's mind they were friends, not lovers.

Yet, in his mind they'd been lovers for years. Carnally, he was very well acquainted with every inch of her enticing body. What man wouldn't dream of a woman like Anais? Plump and womanly, she would feel so damn good beneath him with her hair, that was golden blond and long, draped over his chest. Her breasts, large

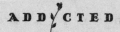

and firm, would cushion him, would beckon him to taste and play—would amuse him for hours. Her décolletage, which was always so elegantly but tastefully displayed in her gowns, never ceased to capture his notice, nor his imagination. Hell, there wasn't a part of her body that didn't entice him. He wanted to span her hips with his hands and crush her to his pelvis, grinding into her. He wanted to feel her soft belly cushion his cock, he wanted to fill his hands with her firm bottom, and knead as he plunged his tongue between her soft lips. He wanted to strip her down and study the body that held him captive for so many years.

His hands, he knew, would worship her curves, and he would lose himself in those lovely blue eyes that reminded him of a clear sky. Her shy smile would be his undoing—it always had been.

Anais was built for loving, for the type of bed sport be enjoyed. With Anais he wouldn't have to feel as though he were going to break her. He wouldn't have to treat her like a fragile flower. He could indulge in that luscious body for hours.

But more than her body, Lindsay lusted for her heart, that piece of her she guarded so carefully. He wanted to mean something more to her than friend. Lover, confidant, he wanted Anais for her body, her sharp mind, and the friendship he had always relied upon.

Of course, seeing her tonight, friendship wasn't on his mind. Her décolletage, and the elegant line of her throat covered with his lips had suddenly rushed to the forefront of his thoughts.

One day, he knew he was going to see her naked, and that visual would be a hundred times more arousing than it was in his dreams.

"I think that was the bell for dinner," his mother announced over the drumming of voices that filled the salon.

"Allow me?" Lindsay held his arm out to Anais. She slipped her hand so easily around his forearm and pressed into his side. His body hardened as he felt her hips contour against his. He wished he could drag her off to his den and confess all to her. But first he had to do the pretty and be a gentleman.

"You look different somehow," she said as she looked up at him.

"Oh?"

She nodded and a curling strand of golden-blond hair slipped from a pin, only to land on the crest of her breast that was exposed by her low-cut bodice. God help him if that strand was going to lie there all evening long. He couldn't drag his gaze away from it, nor vanquish the image of his lips brushing it aside.

"I'm not sure what it is. You just seem…different. It's in your eyes."

Heat. Longing. Desire. He knew what was reflected there. He couldn't hide it.

"Lindsay, are you all right? You've been acting strangely ever since you arrived back from London two weeks ago."

Yes, he was perfectly sound. Just needy for her.

"Meet me tonight, Anais. At the stables."

She cocked her head to the side, studied him, and he felt the compulsion to shrink back in horror and shame. Was it not his amorous feelings she saw reflected in his eyes, but something else? The other side of him he hid from the world.

"I'm worried about you."

He smiled and clutched her fingers. "There's no need. Now, after dessert, tell your mother you're going for a ride. We'll ride into the forest and I might even let you beat me."

She laughed then, her eyes sparkling. "Oh, how you delude yourself. For I am going to trounce you. Just you wait and see."

God willing he thought, as he led Anais into the dining room. Although he had the feeling that they were both thinking two different things when it came to trouncing.

Something was afoot. Anais stole another sidelong glance at Lindsay, who sat to the right of her. There was a feral intensity about him this evening, one she had never seen before from her longtime friend.

Whatever had brought on his bizarre behavior this evening had obviously been beleaguering him for the past fortnight. Lindsay had simply not been himself these past two weeks.

Perhaps it was the extraordinarily lovely Lady Mary Grantworth who had made his wits addled. Mary certainly stared enough at him from her spot across the table. She had also engaged him in conversation for the better part of the dinner.

What man wouldn't become addled in the presence of Mary's violet eyes and lithe figure? A figure that was trim, unlike her own dumpling body.

Did Lindsay prefer small, pert breasts and narrow hips? If so, Anais knew she hadn't a hope, for her breasts were much too big, and her hips wide. Hers was a body that was soft and curvaceous. The type she had told herself that men desired in a woman whom they were about to make love to. But perhaps she had erred in thinking that a man would desire such things.

She couldn't help the way she had been created. She had always been well endowed, even from a young age. She had accepted herself, and her body, and had even grown to admire her bosom in a low-cut bodice, and the flare of her hips from her waist that dipped in like an hourglass. It had been aeons since she had wished to change her body. Until tonight. Until she saw what she perceived as her rival sitting across the table from her, looking at her smugly. Mary was beautiful, thin, fashionable. Anais, while pretty enough, with her long, blond hair that was given to curl, was neither slim, nor fashionable, thanks to her mother's belief that a body like hers was best left in plain clothes.

What did Lindsay think? Was it Mary's little bosom, rising above her bodice like two firm apples, that enticed him? Or was it hers, soft, warm, inviting in its display of perfect peach skin, which she had so carefully scented.

Which woman would Lindsay want to feel beneath him? She had always dreamed it was her he desired. But now, sitting across from the perfect Mary, she wasn't so certain.

"You scowl," Lindsay suddenly whispered to her, startling her.

"Merely in thought," she replied, refusing to look at him. His face was close to hers. She could feel his breath, the way it caressed her neck. She couldn't look into that beautiful face and show every feeling she possessed.

"Are your thoughts so unsavory, then?"

Oh, they were! They were thoughts of the beautiful Mary and Lindsay together. There was no doubt about it, Mary Grantworth wanted Lindsay, and for more than just his title.

All Anais had ever wanted was him. His title be damned. It was the man she desired. The childhood friend who had grown into a strong man, a man of good standing and intellect. A man

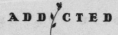

who was not an idle gadabout waiting to come into his title and inheritance.

Lindsay was so much more than a viscount and heir presumptive to a marquisate.

"When you pout, angel, every man looks at you, wishing he could kiss away the sadness from those lovely lips."

Yet how could she or any other woman resist him? With his dark good looks, he was everything a young woman dreamed of in a man. He was tall, broad and well muscled, yet he walked with a predator-like grace that held a woman's gaze and captured her imagination. His clothes were immaculate, well tailored to accentuate his shoulders and toned legs. His hair was onyx colored, and he wore it long to his shoulders, where it hung in loose waves she had longed to run her fingers through. His eyes, the color of Irish moss, were fringed with long, black lashes that were utterly wasted on a man. He was beautiful, the very epitome of a brooding poet, but with his hair worn long, and the sinful curve of his mouth, which was usually shadowed with a night beard, he reminded Anais not of a poet, but a fallen angel, the sort who would tempt any woman into an indiscretion with a smile and a flash of his eyes.

That was what made Lindsay so alluring. He was a mix of romantic sensitivity, with an underlying aura of sinful masculinity. There was a part of Lindsay that called to the romantic girl, and the other part that called to the womanly needs she kept so carefully hidden from him.

Her gaze strayed to his hands, long, elegant, artistic, she shivered as she imagined those beautiful hands traversing her body; and his lips, good God, she could not look at those strong lips and not shudder as she thought of him kissing every inch of her.

It was no wonder that Mary had set her sights on him. Anais herself could hardly bear to look away from his hansome profile, or stop herself from imagining what he must look like beneath his waistcoat and jacket. She had no doubt, though, that what lurked beneath his clothes would be every bit as perfect as his face.

She had no doubt that sharing a bed with Lindsay would be beyond what she could ever possibly think of while she pleasured herself. As if he knew her thoughts, he looked at her, his gaze burning, his lips lifting in a secret smile.

Yes, wicked. Wanton. She wished he would lean into her and whisper into her ear all the naughty things he whispered to her in her dreams. Instead, she swallowed and broke the spell of his gaze holding hers.

Her gaze lifted, landed, as she suspected they would, on his face. There was no teasing in his eyes. No smile.

"You attempt to flatter me," she said as she stole a look at Mary Grantworth. She was watching them with unabashed venom.

"No, Anais. I would never speak false words to you. You know that."

Of course she did. They were friends, after all. *Friends.* How the word began to feel like a noose around her neck. She did not want to be friends with Lindsay. She wanted more. She wanted the same things she dreamed about. The same feelings coursing through her body as when she pleasured herself, while dreaming it was him touching her.

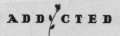

She felt her face warm and glanced away. If Lindsay knew what thoughts she had of him. How erotic. How unchaste and unmaidenly those thoughts were, he would run as fast as he could in the opposite direction.

While he might not speak falsely to her, he certainly could not mean anything by his words. They were meant to be kind, to help a friend. She mustn't read more into them, or into the scene they had shared in the salon. She must not think it anything of import, how he had pressed closer to her, how his mouth had lingered over her hand and he had seemed to inhale her essence deep within his chest.

No! She was being fanciful. Allowing her bedtime wishes to become real. Lindsay did not desire her the way she desired him.

"My lord, shall you be attending the agricultural fair next week in Blackpool?" Mary Grantworth asked, drawing Lindsay's attention away from Anais's face.

"I had not considered it, Lady Mary."

"No? You should. My uncle has entered his Belgian Warmbloods to be judged. I know he plans to sell a few of his stallions. As you are known around town as the most accomplished horseman, as well as a connoisseur of flesh——"

"Flesh?" Lindsay asked with a raised brow.

Mary colored prettily, but it was far from innocent. "A connoisseur of *horseflesh,* Lord Raeburn. I thought perhaps you would be interested in the sale of those stallions, since you are interested in starting a breeding program here in Bewdley. At least, I assumed that was what you meant when you spoke of breeding during our walk last week."

Mary shot Anais a look of triumph from across the table as

she waited for Lindsay's reply. With a stern nod that bordered on impolite, Lindsay shifted his focus to his plate and the piece of prime rib that sat on it. He gave no answer to Mary's inquiry and Anais saw a look of pure menace cloud Mary's beautiful expression.

Anais's appetite abandoned her at once. She couldn't possibly stomach anything, not when her insides had turned to lead. Anais struggled for composure, for inner calm against the tumultuous thoughts running with abandon through her mind. Just when she thought she'd go mad with her thoughts, she felt the softest of caresses against the top of her hand as it rested on her lap beneath the table. It was followed by another, then another. The tingling rose up her arm, covering her skin in gooseflesh. The caress reached higher, until it wrapped around her wrist.

Lindsay.

She looked up at him, saw the way his gaze had darkened; saw the way he looked down at her. Then he took her hand in his, entwining his fingers with hers, and placed their hands on his thigh. With his free hand he traced her knuckles and the veins beneath her skin in such a tender way she began to tremble.

It was singularly the most erotic thing ever done to her. To be holding hands and touching beneath the supper table while two dozen guests sat around them was the most scandalously wicked thing.

"I want to kiss your lips," he murmured for her alone as his gaze slipped to her mouth. "I want to have you all to myself—alone," he clarified. "Do you want that, Anais? To be alone with me?"

He'd taken his hand off hers and rested it on her leg where

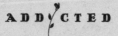
his fingers traveled lightly over her thigh. She could barely think, couldn't breathe as his hand slid inexorably closer to the apex of her thighs.

"Be with me, Anais?" He rose from his chair, carefully removing his hand so no one would see. He dragged his palm across the taffeta of her gown, the motion slow and teasing. He made a show of bending down, a pretense of reaching for his napkin, but instead he took that moment to whisper in her ear.

"Come to me."

He straightened, made his excuses and left the table. Anais finally let out her breath. *Come to me...* The words tumbled through her mind for the next half hour.

2

Blue eyes flashed at him from behind the veil of her curling golden hair. Her lips parted, taunting him with innocence. Lindsay's gaze slipped to those red, plump lips, telling him of the sinful delights that could be found in her mouth. Sweet innocence mixed with forbidden sensuality.

She was a lady born and bred. His childhood friend, although a child no more. She was a woman, with a woman's mind, a woman's body. But had she the appetite of a woman? Did she hunger for him? Would she allow him to appease the ache— the same damn ache that had gnawed at his insides for years?

The way they had touched, their hands hidden beneath the table, had told him that she might just welcome an advance from him. He had felt her tremble as he made the caress more intimate. There was no mistaking his intent. No more denying what he wanted.

"You're falling behind, Lindsay," Anais called as she looked over her shoulder and through the long curls that waved and flapped in the cold evening air. "You should have ridden the

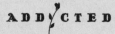

chestnut bay. Now I'm going to beat you to the stables and you are going to lose our wager," she said with a laugh. Urging her mare forward, she bent low over the saddle, her full, lush bottom perched in the air as she brazenly rode astride.

Desire curled in Lindsay's belly as his gaze strayed to the roundness of her bottom. He should have stayed in London, should have kept himself buried in Tran's opium den, numbing himself to these wanton appetites. In truth, he could no more keep his distance from Anais Darnby than a moth could keep from flying into a flame.

A familiar ache settled in his gut and he gripped the reins in his gloved hands, urging his mount forward as he closed the distance between him and Anais.

He should never have offered this evening ride. Should never have tempted himself by touching her beneath the table. Bloody hell, he should have known not to ask her to accompany him— alone. He knew better. He had been unable to take his eyes off her during dinner. Had watched her eat, studied the erotic play of her tongue on her lips, the fork. He had hungered and lusted through the entire damned meal. He'd been humiliatingly erect watching her, his blood heating with the desire to make Anais more than just a friend. Damn it, he should have known that a bruising ride through the woods would not assuage the dangerous desire he had flooding his veins.

Again, she glanced over her shoulder, her eyes widening when she saw how he was coming up hard on her heels, preparing to overtake her mare. She smiled in challenge and his blood heated more.

He couldn't think when she looked at him like that, like a seductress with pouting, skillful lips. She was his friend—his best friend. He treasured their easy friendship—the rarity of it. What he was contemplating, what he desired, might very well ruin any feelings she held for him.

But he needed—*had*—to have at least one taste of the pleasure she could give him. *One taste. One simple, forbidden taste...*

He should have been thinking about the ring he'd left in his den. Thinking about how he should be proposing marriage before taking their relationship further. Anais was a lady, after all, not a demirep. He was a gentleman who knew how to treat a lady. Except, at this moment, all he could think about was how much he needed Anais sexually.

The stable was now in sight and Anais's mare galloped full speed toward the open doors. His heart was pounding a furious pace. It always did when he was riding. But there was something else there. An irregularity; a skipped beat when he thought of turning his relationship with Anais from innocent friendship to an intimate session of shared delight. *Pink, flushed skin. Swollen lips, parted in pleasure. Her fingers digging into his shoulders as their bodies heated and glistened with desire...* Yes, that was what he wanted, the shared delight of flesh.

He wanted her as a companion. A wife. A lover. He didn't think he could stand the agony of enduring another day, another month, another year of dreaming and longing. How damned torturous it was to have her near him and not be able to touch her. Had she any idea what he wanted to do to her as they sat by the pond and twirled the blades of grass between their fingers? Did she know how much control it took for him to resist

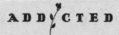

lying atop her as she stretched out onto the grass and gazed up at the sky?

The bay snorted heavily as they tore into the stables. He heard the hard snorting breaths of Anais's mare and he urged the bay to the stall. Before him, Anais was dismounting, the toe of her half boot caught in the stirrup. A flash of a stocking-clad ankle met his eyes and his cock hardened again. The hunger he had kept tightly reined in over supper broke free of his restraint.

Within seconds he had his hands around her waist, lifting her free of the stirrups. She gasped, a womanly, husky pant, and he didn't think. Didn't care that she might not want him like he wanted her. This was the moment he had been waiting for. The moment of truth. The destiny that had been ordained for him.

"I can go no longer, Anais." His breathing was deep, his words husky as he brought her up against the stable wall. "It's agony watching you from afar. It's bloody torture thinking of you in the night when I am alone and wanting the feel of you against me. For so long I have needed and wanted you."

Her eyes widened. Shock? Passion? He didn't know, but the uncertainty ate at his belly. "I can't look at you anymore with only friendship in my mind. I want your body beneath me. I want you flushed and hot in my arms. I want to be inside you."

He didn't wait for her answer. Didn't want to hear it if she told him his feelings and desires were one-sided. He only wanted to feel her wind-chafed lips beneath his. One kiss. He would stop at a kiss if she said so. But to deny himself that, to resist the temptation, was a torment he could not withstand. If she allowed him any liberties, he would confess his love. He would sweep her away and marry her. He would make love to her in all the ways he knew how.

"Do you know what I want you to give me?" he asked, lowering his mouth to hers.

"Yes," she whispered breathlessly.

"Will you give me what I want?" He pulled his gloves from his hands, dropping them to the stable floor. Unbuttoning her cloak, he let it fall from her shoulders, before he smoothed his palms down her arms and the delicate silk of her gown.

"If you say no, Anais, I will not press you." Their gazes met, and he saw the war waged in her eyes. Waiting for her answer was a lesson in agony.

Another frigid blast of north wind howled angrily from the snowcapped hills. The shutters on the window flanking the wall behind Anais creaked against the bricks as the wind gusted yet again, sending icy air through the cracks of the old, weathered casement window, the sound distracting her from her thoughts.

She should have been shivering with cold after being out in the elements for so long, but she did not feel the sting of the bitter winter air, only a ravaging heat that enveloped her in a fevered warmth.

"Anais, I shall go mad if I deny myself any longer," Lindsay's deep voice whispered in her ear. *"Please,"* he pleaded, sliding both her dress and chemise down her arms, baring the white stay beneath her shift. "Say yes," he implored as his long fingers sought the ties of her corset. "Or tell me to cease these attentions before I cannot stop."

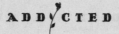

What was she to say? She knew what she should say, but the word would not come forth. *No* had never felt so impossibly hard to say as it did now. She did not want to speak the word, for she knew that Lindsay would honor her refusal. Refusing him was something she didn't want to do. She wanted this, despite the fact it was against everything she had been taught. She wanted his lovemaking, regardless of the fact she could find herself ruined in the eyes of society.

"Anais?"

"Don't stop," she said on a gasp. "Oh, Lindsay, please don't stop."

With masterful skill, he undid the bow on her corset, pulling on the strings before releasing her straining breasts into the cool air. She shuddered, feeling the sexual awakening flooding her hot blood like a glass of fine champagne.

Lowering his mouth to the valley of her breasts, he trailed his lips along her flesh, making her burn hotter. Raking her hands through Lindsay's thick, curling hair, Anais clenched her fingers in the silky strands as his lips trailed openmouthed along her skin. Her breath froze as his mouth descended lower. Closing her eyes, she allowed her held breath to pass in a soft exhalation of yearning—a desire she knew was forbidden. No woman of her class would do such a thing without the benefit of marriage, and in a stable no less! Only common strumpets would allow a man such liberties where anyone may happen upon them. But the forbidden was the most succulent of fruits, especially when it was Lindsay offering the illicit taste.

She didn't think, only felt as his mouth followed the descent of her gown. It was followed by the slow slide of his fingers hooking beneath the waist of her petticoats as he drew them over her generous hips till they lay in a lace heap around her feet.

Gasping, Anais pressed further against the cold stone when Lindsay dropped to his knees and began to nuzzle the damp flesh between her thighs. His hands cupped her breasts as his mouth moved eagerly—*hungrily*—over her wet sex as he lapped at her.

How was she to deny him? How was she to deny herself this sinful pleasure, especially when she had desired—no, loved—this man her entire life? It was neither fanciful thinking nor melodrama in the heat of sexual frenzy, but the truth. She had loved Lindsay for...well, forever. To be here with him now, in the stables of his estate, to feel his mouth caress her in forbidden places and exotic ways was beyond what she had ever dared hope for. And she had hoped and longed for this moment for so long...

Blood pounded fiercely in her ears as Lindsay's hot mouth covered every inch of her flesh. She heard the rapid fire of her heart mixing with the erotic sounds of his tongue laving her. The way he pleasured her made her wish for him to devour her whole and she encouraged him on with her husky breaths and the way she instinctively gripped his hair.

"I knew you would be this responsive," he said in a guttural voice as he sunk his finger deep inside her, coaxing more wetness from her. "My God, you're beautiful," he rasped, suddenly standing up and studying her naked body as she stood vulnerably before him.

"You know that isn't true," she said through trembling lips, even though she wished it was.

"It is." His voice was forceful as he stroked his fingertip along her swollen nipple. "Haven't you ever noticed how I can't keep from watching you? Haven't you ever wondered why I need to be near you? You're an angel, Anais. You're my angel. You're perfect."

Lindsay was looking at her like a man starved, like a man possessed by the power of lust. She knew that he *had* to finish what he had started. She could think on things later. When she was alone in her room she could try to understand why now, after years of friendship, he had decided to turn their relationship into something more.

The feel of his hands stroking her breasts chased her thoughts away. He swirled his thumb along her nipples until the buds were hard pebbles and her womb was clenching in longing. Over and over he teased her with his thumbs, plucking at her nipples until little tremors raced down her back.

"I want to feel you tremble like this when I'm buried deep inside you." She met his gaze and he smiled slowly—sensually. "Let me make love to you."

"Yes," she hissed as he ran his tongue along her nipple before slipping it between his lips, *"Yes, I want this—so much."*

Picking her up as if she were light as a feather, he carried her to the corner of the stable where bales of hay were stacked. He lowered her to stand beside him. Pulling his shirt from his shoulders he placed it atop their makeshift bed. Picking her up again, he placed her on the linen, which was damp from his sweat.

They had ridden hard on their ride through the woods. Even now she could see the rivulets of perspiration trickling down his chest as the silver moonlight filtered through the window and reflected on his chest. She loved the masculine texture of his damp shirt beneath her and the scent of him—male and musky—surrounding her. She didn't care that she was going to be tumbled on a bale of hay in a stable for her first time. She didn't care, because this was Lindsay, this was his world—the world they had always shared together.

Sitting back and resting on his heels, he studied her, all the time running his hands along her body. "So soft, so beautiful and pale," he said, sounding awed. "I want to remember you like this, stretched out, waiting for me to take you for the first time."

Her thighs trembled. She shoved aside the awkwardness. Now was not the time to be gauche. Now was the time to indulge her deepest, most private fantasy—making love with Lindsay.

He ran his hand over her nipples, then down her ribs till he reached her hip. He caressed and kneaded, watching her response, listening to her sounds of pleasure before he ran his fingertips along the inside of her thighs, eliciting a flush of gooseflesh along her skin. He played there for a while, touching her, heightening the anticipation until she was clutching at his shoulders and urging him down. She had liked his mouth between her thighs, and greedy as she was, she wanted it there again.

He knew what she desired, and with a wicked smile that made her toes curl, he lowered his head and set his mouth against her sex. She arched at the intimacy, brushing her damp flesh against his cheek and lips. She heard his groan, a sound of approval and delight before he raked his tongue against her.

She cried out his name as she felt his tongue part her folds and she covered her mouth with the back of her hand, silencing her wanton pleas. He only teased her more by flicking his

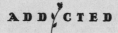

tongue slowly up the length of her before circling the sensitive bud of flesh. She tensed and looked down, only to see him looking up at her as he slowly raked his tongue around the hood of her sex. That sinful visual was enough to stop her heart.

"I've always wondered how you would taste coming in my mouth. Now I know."

Wicked, wicked man! But the words would not come, only the uncontrollable shaking of her body beneath him as she climaxed into his mouth. When she could utter a sound, it was in hushed, stuttering breaths, pleading with him to stop. He would not listen. He pushed her on. His tongue hungrily, forcefully licked her until she clutched at his head and raised herself on her elbows. She watched as he tormented her with his tongue.

Her hips moved in time to his probing tongue. She heard him growl, watched as his gaze lowered to her breasts, which were swaying with her efforts as she climbed the hill to orgasm once again.

Lindsay continued to study her breasts as she cupped one in her hand, stroking her nipple with her thumb, just as she did at night, hidden beneath her bedsheets, pretending that it was Lindsay doing all those wicked things to her body and not her own hands.

"Little minx, you've done this before, haven't you?"

She smiled a slow half smile and continued to palm her breasts, teasing him, delighting in his husky growl when she rolled her nipple between her thumb and finger. "It was you that I dreamed of when I brought myself to orgasm, Lindsay. But it never felt like this. This intoxicating."

Sitting up, he pulled off his boots and tossed them down to the flagstone floor. He tore at the flaps of his breeches, pulling them along his hips, allowing her only a glimpse of black curls and his rampant erection before he pressed his hot, damp body on hers.

Holding out her arms, she reached for him, allowing his chest to cover hers as he buried his face in her neck and the hair that spilled out over the hay. He pressed inside her, filling her so full that she could only slide up and away from the intrusion, but he reached for her hips and held them firm in his big hands.

"I'm full of you," she breathed, feeling the thick length of him still sinking farther into her. He groaned, still clutching her hips, holding her still so that he could surge up inside her.

The pain she expected did not come. A brief, stinging sensation made her wince, but it was quickly soothed away by the exquisite sensation of Lindsay buried deep. They were one now. She could no longer tell where she left off and he began.

He reached his hands around to her bottom, gripping her tight, stroking her deep, quickening his thrusts as he watched her breasts dance and sway. She arched her back, feeling the pressure building inside her once again. He kept thrusting until she felt his shoulders stiffen beneath her fingers.

"Anais," he groaned. "Angel."

She held his gaze steady as he thrust into her slowly at first, then steadily deeper and faster. *My beautiful, beautiful Lindsay, how I love you…*

A draft crept in through the barn boards, caressing their naked bodies. Anais shivered, snuggling into Lindsay's warmth. He reached up and pulled a woolen blanket down from an iron hook.

"You don't mind, do you?" he asked, covering them up with the tartan wool. "I know it's not silk brocade, but I confess I'm

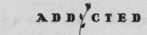

not ready to let you up. I want to feel all this against me," he murmured, running his hand over her body.

She pressed up against him instead of slapping his probing hand away. In truth, she couldn't get enough of his compliments, or the way his hands seemed to continuously stroke her body in the most reverent of ways.

"How many more times do you expect to do this tonight?"

He chuckled and pressed his chin against the top of her head. "I don't know. I can't get enough of you. I have a lifetime to make up for, you know. So many years of watching you. You don't know the tortures you've put me through. Tonight in the salon, when I first saw you standing by the hearth, I nearly carried you off then, I wanted you so badly."

His fingers reached out, capturing a curl that lay over her shoulder. She watched as he studied the blond strands in the golden light. "I'm so bloody glad I finally got up the courage to take you to bed," he murmured, before dropping her hair and smoothing his fingers down her shoulder.

"So am I." *It was about time he saw her as a woman.*

He caught her hand and slowly entwined her fingers with his. "I don't want this moment to end, but I suppose it's getting late and I shall have to give you up. No doubt your mother and father are waiting to go back home. We've been *riding,*" he said with a grin, "for an inordinately long time."

She nodded, knowing he was right, but wishing he wasn't. She didn't want this moment to end, either. She had waited too long for a sign from Lindsay that he desired her as a woman, not just a friend.

"Are you going to the Torrington masquerade on Tuesday?"

"Yes," she groaned, hating the very thought of having to dress up.

"I thought you loved Valentine's Day. What better way to celebrate it than with a masquerade?"

"I do love Valentine's Day. I just don't care for masquerades."

"Why not?"

She sat up and the blanket slipped down, baring her large breasts. "You would not like them, either, if you had a mother who forced you to wear a shepherdess costume."

His green eyes turned darker. Reaching out, he circled her pink areola with the tip of his finger. "I think you should go as an odalisque. I can't imagine anything more arousing than seeing you dressed as though you had just stepped out of a harem. Would you do that for me, Anais?" he asked her, looking up at her through his impossibly long black lashes. "Would you dress as a houri? *My* houri?"

Anais decided she would move heaven and hell to make a costume that would please him. She would indulge him in his penchant for anything Eastern. She would play the part of the harem girl if that was what he desired.

He smiled and wrapped his fingers around her neck, bringing her closer to him. "Will you let me have my wicked way with you, my houri? Will you find a way to come to me that night and make love with me?"

What could she say? This was simply a dream come true. "Yes."

Lindsay lowered his mouth to hers, kissing her in a soft, lulling, almost drugging kiss. His hand moved to her breast and he caught it in his palm before running his hand along the side of her body in a slow, sweeping manner—*a loving manner.*

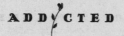

"Can you feel how hard I am growing against your warm belly? Just the thought of you makes me this way, Anais. I want you again, to spend inside you once more so that you can feel me inside you for the rest of the night. I want you every night for the rest of my life."

How many years had she waited for such a declaration? "Are you asking me to marry you?" she asked incredulously. She had almost given up any hope that Lindsay might return her affections. Yet here they were, naked in each other's arms, talking of forever.

"We *will* marry. But as to the asking, I have plans. When I propose I want it to be special. Be assured you're mine. You will be my wife. Trust me in this, Anais."

A crash echoed outside the stable window. Anais smothered a squeal as she reached for the blanket, covering her nakedness.

"Just some barn cats that have gotten into the old tin milk cans, that is all," he murmured. "Don't worry, sweeting. Now then, put your pretty legs around me and ride me like you do your mare." He brushed his hands down her backside and sought her sex between her folds. "I've watched you riding, wishing those lovely thighs were wrapped around me and not Lady."

Anais rose to her knees and peered out the window, fearing she saw the shadow of someone running from the stable. "Perhaps we should be getting back."

"How can I convince you to stay with me?" he asked, coming up behind her and holding her tight in his arms. "What could change your mind?" He pressed small kisses along her spine, sending gooseflesh down every nerve as he cupped her breasts from behind. "What if I were to beg you? Or coerce you with pretty words? What if I just took you?" he suggested darkly. "Now that is an interesting thought, me just taking you—"

"Where the hell are they?"

Anais straightened as if she had been lashed with a whip. It was the booming voice of the Marquis of Weatherby—Lindsay's father. "I'll whip that son of mine if he hasn't kept that cock of his in his trousers."

"Get dressed," Lindsay commanded, helping her down from the bale and turning her so that he could tie her corset strings. "Hurry," he whispered, helping her into her chemise. "Now then, hide in the hay."

"Lindsay—"

"Do it," he commanded, as he tossed her gown to her.

"Boy!" his father called from outside, his voice loud and sounding very drunk.

Anais shot Lindsay a nervous look before hurriedly stepping into the heavy taffeta gown.

The marquis was a drunken sot. As useless as the day was long, and nothing but a whoring drunkard, her father always said. The man was capable of anything while in his cups. She feared for Lindsay and what his father might do.

The stable door was flung open. Frigid February air gust in, followed by swirling wind and snow that caused the horses to whinny nervously. Anais peered through the slats of the barn board walls, seeing that the marquis loomed large in the doorway with his hands fisted at his sides. His head turned in her direction and she whimpered before dropping down beside two bales of hay.

"Where are ye?" the marquis growled, prowling into the

stable before slamming the door firmly shut. He tripped over a footstool in his drunkenness and with a violent kick, he sent the stool flying down the length of the stable.

"Ah," Weatherby snarled when he fixed his gaze on Lindsay. "There ye are. Fixin' your shirt, I see. This isn't the time to be diddling with the staff, my boy. If you wanted a go with one of the maids, you should have waited till our company departed."

Lindsay shrugged into his shirt then reached for his boots, ignoring his father.

"You weren't prickin' that Darnby chit, were you?" Anais saw Lindsay's broad shoulders go rigid, but he said nothing as he reached for his second boot. "Lord knows that girl—*Anais*—" Weatherby snorted "—needs a good, sound tupping. Far too above herself, that one. Forever looking down her nose at me like I was nothing but a common slug. But your mother, you know. The idea of you defiling the sweet and innocent Darnby chit—plain, nothing little thing that she is—would send her to bed for a week. I can't have that. I've a party of gents coming at the end of the week. I've got a large packet riding on this and I can't have your mother skulking about, confined to her bed. I want her gone to London, with you. So, if you've been amusing yourself tonight with Darnby's girl, it's high time you put your cock back in your trousers and made yer way back to the house."

Lindsay finally turned his attention to his father, his face showing barely restrained contempt. "Lady Anais returned to the house immediately after our ride."

Lord Weatherby snorted. "Didn't want to raise her skirts for the likes of you, eh? No doubt she thinks of you the same way she thinks of your sire. Fat lot she knows, the frigid little shrew.

Don't know why she's so high in the instep. Her mother was nothing before she married Lord Darnby. Came from nothing, she did. Only had her looks, and I can tell you—" Weatherby leered "—her mama did not come to her marriage bed a virgin."

"Father!" Lindsay snapped, glancing in her direction for a brief second before returning his gaze to his insolent father. But Lindsay knew as well as she that her mama was far from a saint. In fact, her mother was nothing but a hypocrite, preaching one thing and doing the exact opposite. Anais harbored no grand illusions about her mother. She had long ago come to terms with her mother's behavior.

She'd been eight years old when she first saw her mother flirting with her father's friend during a picnic. That night, as she snuck out of the house toward the lake to watch the fireflies with Lindsay, she had seen her mother, dressed in a white wrapper, running across the lawn to the orangery. Her father's friend was there, waiting. Her mother had fallen into his arms before the door had even closed behind them. The last thing Anais heard was her mother pleading with her lover. "Take me away from all this hell," she'd begged. "Erase the touch of my husband, a man I despise. Treat me like a woman, for my husband never has."

Even at eight, Anais had known what her mother was. A social climber. A fraud. An adulteress. That incident, Anais had admitted, was unlikely the first for her mother. It was certainly not the last.

Years later, when Anais had been in her early teens, she had discovered her mother in the attic with a young, handsome footman who had just been taken on. Anais hadn't run away like

the other times she had seen her mother betraying her father. She'd confronted her.

That was when her mother had told her the truth she'd long suspected. That marriage to her father had brought her riches and social status. That was the only reason she'd married him. His money brought her happiness and lovers. His physical affection made her ill. So, too, did looking at the children she had to produce in order to keep her husband appeased. She hated her children for what they had done to her body. She loathed the time she was forced to spend with them, even though it was minimal. And she despised Anais the most, she had told her, because she out of her two sisters most resembled her father, both in looks and personality.

Morality, her mother scoffed, was not a trait worth a pence. It gave you only misery, and the feeling of a noose closing ever tighter around your neck.

Anais had left the attic room, which at one time had been her nursery, a thought that disgusted her. Seeing her mother engaging in such debauchery in a room where she and her sisters had slept as children sickened her and made her realize just what sort of a heartless tart her mother was.

She had not confided the news to her father because it would destroy him. She had not told her oldest sister, Abigail, because in truth, Abby was more like their mother than any of them. Ann, the youngest, had still been a child. So she'd turned to the only person who she trusted. The only soul she had ever confided in. And like always, he'd been there waiting for her at the stables, her horse had already been saddled and both Lindsay and her mare had watched patiently for her arrival.

Anais had fallen into his arms sobbing, just like her mother had fallen into the arms of her lover all those years ago. Lindsay kept her safe. Had held her close to him and allowed her to dampen his shirt with her tears. He'd been eighteen then. More man than boy. He could have left her; she was, after all, still considered a child, even at sixteen. But he hadn't, and she'd clung to him like the ivy on the walls of her home as he stroked her back with his palm that she recalled felt so strong and warm along her spine.

Confiding in Lindsay had taken the pain away, but the realization that her mother's cold and ruthless blood swam in her own veins was something that always terrified her. She still had not made peace with the knowledge.

She did not want to become her mother. She would *not* become her mother, she vowed as she listened to Lord Weatherby spew his venom. Venom she knew was the truth.

"What exactly is it you don't want to hear, boy?" his father taunted, drawing her gaze away from the muscle that flicked in Lindsay's jaw. "What is it that makes you so irate? The fact that I can't stand that little bitch you call a friend, or the fact I pricked her mother?"

"Stop it," Lindsay demanded.

His father chuckled and slapped Lindsay's shoulder. "Don't act all honorable, son. You're not, you know. I know all about you and your habits. So, tell me, how does it feel to be a chip off the old block—nine and twenty and friggin' all the household help?"

"Thirty," Lindsay snapped before reaching for his evening coat. "What's that?"

"I turned thirty last month. But you cannot be expected to remember that. After all, you've spent the last years in a drunken haze in London with your mistresses and your cronies."

"Well, thirty, then," his father said unrepentantly. "How does it feel to be a man, to take some comely little maid in here and give it to her hard against a wall?"

"I have been a man, with a man's responsibilities for many years, Father," Lindsay growled as he shrugged into his jacket. "While you have been whoring and drinking the years away, I have grown up. I have become something you are not—*a gentleman.*"

His father leaned forward and winked, unaffected by Lindsay's rebuke. "Was it that buxom little Sally? I had her the other day. Lively little thing, and skilled, too. Beautiful wide mouth. Oh, come now." His father grinned wickedly when he saw Lindsay's scowl. "You were doing what comes natural. At least what comes natural to you and me," his father teased, elbowing him in the ribs, then staggering to the left. "What man doesn't enjoy a woman's mouth around him from time to time? Best damn release you can find, my boy, a willing mouth eager to please. A mouth—" his father sneered "—you won't have to marry or have harping at you for the rest of yer days."

"You disgust me," Lindsay said with a snarl.

"I'm happy, boy," his father declared, heedless of Lindsay's censure. "I'm right happy with the reports I've been getting from Town. Seems it's true, apples really don't fall far from the tree."

Anais watched the color drain from Lindsay's face. He was now a ghastly, ashen color. She had never seen Lindsay looking so discomposed. Was it because his father had talked of his previous conquests, and she was present to hear it? Was Lindsay concerned for her feelings, especially after what they had shared?

She knew, that at Lindsay's age, he had knowledge of other women. She wasn't naive to believe that he had saved himself for her. Besides, she'd known his skill by the first touch of his hands on her body. And while she felt jealous and hurt, she believed that what they had shared was more than what he had with other women.

She had to believe that, because to believe anything else would be too painful to bear.

"Well, then, I'm off, back to the house to tell that pompous ass Darnby that his shrew of a daughter is not out here with you—I knew you had more taste than to go tupping someone like that—but your mother," he scoffed as he staggered away, "your mother wouldn't be appeased until I left my port and hand of cards to search for you. That damn woman, I don't know what I ever did to deserve her. And," Weatherby snapped as he whirled around, "you might consider being a trifle more civil to the Grantworth chit. She's worth a fortune and far prettier than the Darnby girl. She's got one of the biggest dowries on the marriage mart this year and she fancies you. See to it you make arrangements to go driving or attend that blasted fair. I want an heir from you before I die. Do I make myself clear?"

When the stable door closed, Lindsay looked back at Anais, an expression of shame marring his handsome face. "He was drunk," she murmured quietly while pulling stray bits of hay from her hair. "He didn't know what he was saying."

It was the same excuse she had heard Lindsay use for his father

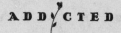

since they were small children. She despised the words even as
she said them. There was no excuse for such a wastrel. The
marquis was always in a state of grotesque inebriation. She had
seen him falling down drunk and groping women who were not
his wife more times than she cared to admit.

But then Anais could not fault Lindsay for trying to soften
the embarrassment of having such a father. She did much the
same with her mother. Anais had dealt with the shame, not by
defending her mother's actions, but writing her out of her life.
Anais dealt with the disgrace by pretending she had no mother.
And her mother couldn't have been happier for her absence.

"After what we've just shared, you must know that I hold no
liking or desire for Mary Grantworth." Anais smiled, happy to
hear it. "She wanted you to believe that we had gone on a walk
together and spoken intimately. The truth, Anais, is that I met
her coming out of the apothecary, and I talked with her for less
than a minute."

"Thank you for telling me, Lindsay. Not that you needed to."

"Yes, I did. I was worried the whole time he was going on
about women, and about Mary Grantworth, that you would hate
me and believe what my father was saying. I was terrified that
when I finally was able to come to you, you wouldn't believe
me when I told you that you've been the only woman I've ever
wanted permanently in my life."

The coldness that had suddenly gathered inside her melted
away and she reached up on her tiptoes and brushed her mouth
against his. "I believe you, Lindsay."

"I'm not like him, Anais. I'm not my father. I don't share
his vices."

She cupped Lindsay's face, forcing him to look at her. He told her he would never speak a false word against her, and she believed him. "You don't?"

"No. I…" His eyes turned unreadable and he tried, tried so very hard, she knew, to hold his gaze steady. In the end he couldn't and he was looking over her shoulder at a spot on the wall behind her when he said, "I swear it. I'm not like him."

Something in her began to hurt, but it was soon replaced by the great love she had for him, and the need to believe in him. She could handle whatever he was afraid to tell her. Nothing could stop her from loving Lindsay—nothing. At this moment, everything was too new. They needed time to adjust to the way things were now between them.

"Then everything will be all right, won't it?"

He nodded as he ran the pad of his thumb along her lips. "This *is* right," he said emphatically, as if he were trying to convince himself and not her. He clutched her face, peering down into her eyes as he rested his forehead against hers. "This bond we have, it must never be broken. Promise me," he said, cupping her cheeks in his hands. "Promise me that this chain that binds us will never come unlinked."

"I have always been bound to you. My heart will forever be yours, Lindsay. Never forget that."

"I need your goodness in my life, Anais. I need you to keep me from becoming my father."

"You won't, Lindsay."

"Swear to me, Anais. Swear you will always be there for me. Say you will never change."

"I swear, Lindsay."

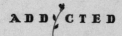

"And will you remember me tonight?"

"I will. And will you think of me, Lindsay?"

"I have your scent on my hand. The taste of you on my tongue. *I will never forget, Anais.*"

3

"You're keeping secrets!"

Anais looked up from the purple-and-gold silk that lay in her lap. Rebecca, her closest friend in Bewdley, sauntered into the room, looking more radiant than what was fair. Rebecca was so exotic-looking, with sable-colored curls and amber eyes that were almond-shaped and fringed with lush, sooty lashes.

Anais watched as Rebecca flopped down on the bed and propped her chin in her delicate doll's hand. Her friend was everything she was not. The only virtue Rebecca lacked was fortune and family connections. But that fact hadn't seemed to deter the numerous swains that had attempted to court Rebecca over the years. There had been many times as Anais stood on the peripheries, alone and unnoticed, watching her friend smile charmingly at the latest rogue pursuing her, that she wished she possessed a fraction of Rebecca's beauty. Anais would have handed over her dowry for only a pittance of her friend's charms and smoldering looks.

"Well," Rebecca challenged, raising a perfectly shaped brow.

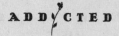

"You were gone riding for a very long time. What in the world did Lord Raeburn do with you after he all but stole you from the salon?"

A small smile lifted her lips upwards. She had almost completely forgotten that Rebecca had been in attendance at dinner.

"Come, now, Anais, spill your secrets! I know you must have had an impassioned tryst in the stable."

"And what makes you think that?" Anais thought back to the moment when she had heard a crash outside the stable, and had seen a figure fleeing through the window. Had Rebecca been spying on her? But why?

"Anais, we have been friends much too long. All the signs of a torrid embrace were there on your person when you arrived back in the salon. Your color was high, and your lips," Rebecca teased, "were as pink and swollen as anything. Either you were stung by a bee in February, or you were utterly and pleasurably ravished! Now do not keep me in suspense any longer. I am positively dying to learn what happened between the two of you!"

Anais flushed and stabbed her needle through the purple silk, trying to prevent her hand from shaking and making the hem uneven. She wanted this costume to be perfect.

"Anais," Rebecca said teasingly, "we've been friends too long, you know. You cannot hide the truth from me. He kissed you, didn't he?"

"Perhaps," Anais said, unable to hide the huge smile that parted her lips.

"*You fiend!*" Rebecca cried, coming off the bed and tearing the fabric from her hands. "Two days you've kept this from me! Tell me all of it. Was it divine? Does he have strong lips?"

"Rebecca, I'm quite certain you already know that it was heaven. After all, you've been kissed many times before."

"But never by anyone as deliciously wicked as Lord Raeburn."

For some reason Anais did not want to discuss Lindsay with Rebecca. It was not that she didn't trust her friend to be discreet and keep her secret. She trusted Rebecca implicitly. But she realized that what had happened between her and Lindsay was meant to be kept just between them.

"Well?" Rebecca prodded.

"I'm quite certain Lord Broughton is just as deliciously wicked, Rebecca. A fact I'm certain you shall discover when he proposes marriage to you."

"Oh, I'm afraid Lord Broughton is the most pious of gentlemen. *Deliciously wicked* are two words I would not use to describe him."

Anais frowned and thought of the man who had been courting Rebecca. Garrett, Lord Broughton, was a gentleman. Handsome and rich, Garrett was much sought after by the marriage-minded girls and their mamas. He was a gentleman and given to quiet introspection, true, but there was no disputing that Rebecca had captured his attention.

"What are you making?" Rebecca asked suddenly, running her finger along the gold cording that Anais was busy sewing to the purple silk.

"My costume for the masquerade tonight."

"You told me you were going as a shepherdess. I thought your mother already had your costume made up for you."

"I'm not wearing that hideous monstrosity." Anais glanced at the costume that hung on the door of her wardrobe. "I'll look as wide as a frigate in that hooped skirt."

Rebecca's gaze roamed over the costume. "It is revolting, isn't it?"

"I'm not wearing it."

"So then, what are you wearing?"

"I'm going as an odalisque."

Rebecca's mouth hung open before she snapped it closed again. "You do know what an odalisque is, do you not? You're aware that you're going to be baring a great deal of..." Rebecca swallowed and looked pointedly at her. "You'll be baring a great deal of your person, Anais."

"Oh, I will incorporate the appropriate modifications that will allow me to be presentable in society—never fear that. But I have it on good authority that I would look rather fetching dressed as an odalisque. Lindsay suggested the idea and I want to please him."

Her friend's eyes went round with disbelief. "I cannot believe that of Raeburn. Well, not that he shouldn't find you attractive," Rebecca said in a rush. "It's just that after all these years...after years of being...well, seemingly uninterested in *that* sort of relationship..." Rebecca murmured before trailing off altogether.

"I can hardly believe it myself. Oh, Rebecca, I do believe he loves me. He says we're going to be married."

"Are you certain, Anais? I would so hate for you to be disappointed."

Something in Rebecca's words made Anais's blood freeze. The sinister coils of doubt began to unfurl, slowly choking out her new self-confidence, but she shoved it aside. Lindsay did want her. She had seen it in his eyes, heard it in his voice, *felt* it in his touch.

"Come, now. Let us not dwell on gloomy thoughts. Of course he loves you, Anais. How could he not? You've been traipsing in his boot tracks for years. It was only a matter of time before Lord Raeburn tripped over you and took notice of your presence."

Is that what had happened? Had Lindsay merely relented? Was he tired of always having her near? Had he just resigned himself to the inevitable and finally given in to his mother's fondest wish—a desire his mother had taken no pains to disguise?

"Anais," her sister Ann's voice rang out. "You have a letter."

"Quick." Anais jumped up from her chair and scooped the purple-and-gold skirt from the bed. "Help me hide this."

Rebecca helped her tuck the costume into a coarse muslin sack seconds before the door was flung open and her fourteen-year-old sister came rushing into the room, her ringlets bouncing and her cheeks flushed pink with excitement.

She looked like an excited little pixie, with her gently upturned nose and sparkling, pale blue eyes. Ann was slight and petite, her hair was paler, more silvery than gold and straighter than Anais's curls. Her skin was like porcelain and her features, while aristocratic, held a certain fragility that made her seem almost ethereal. But her bubbly personality stopped her from being untouchable.

One day, Ann Darnby was going to be stunningly beautiful and the most sought-after woman in England, and Anais suddenly couldn't wait for her sister to find the man of her dreams.

"A valentine," Ann announced, her voice breathless with her exertion.

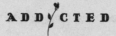

Anais reached for the red wrapping and tore it out of her sister's hand. Turning her back, she stripped away the wrapping to find a heart-shaped piece of vellum tucked neatly inside.

Your pasha awaits, you. At midnight, on the terrace.

"Well?" Rebecca asked, excitedly. "Who is it from?"

"An admirer?" Ann said coyly. "Do you have a secret admirer, Anais?"

"Ann, do stop being a pest," their mother said from the door. Her mother's expression suddenly sobered as her gaze fixed on Anais. "Of course your sister does not have an admirer, don't be a goose, Ann." Her mother's lovely eyes raked over her and Anais saw the familiar emotion of displeasure shining in them.

Anais was well aware she was a disappointment to her mother. *Such a lovely, passionate name, quite wasted on that plain creature.* She had heard that remark many times, most of which had been uttered in her mother's bitter voice.

How many times had Anais overheard someone say at a ball that there had to be at least one plain one amongst all the beautiful Darnby women? However, the truth of that statement wouldn't hurt so much had she not had the misfortune to be the plain one.

Her older sister, Abigail, who had been the belle of the ball and was now the Countess of Weston, had been the raving beauty of the family, not to mention her mother's favorite child. Her mother never failed to remind Anais of Abigail's beauty or cachet in snaring a most sought-after husband. Now Ann, her youngest sister, was poised to be a great beauty—even more beautiful than Abigail, and much less conceited about it, too—*thank heavens.*

"Now then, girls, it is time to get ready for the Torrington masquerade. You will require much time, my dear, if we're to get you presentable. Marriage, Anais," her mother lectured while she waved her perfectly manicured finger before Anais's nose. "You must remember that an advantageous marriage is a well-bred young lady's primary goal in life. You're already at a disadvantage. Now with your age—well, it's going to be impossible to find someone suitable, what with the debs coming out this Season."

"Mother..." Lord, she hated when her mother talked so in front of Rebecca.

"Well, it is true. You'll be eight and twenty next week and you've little to recommend you beside your dowry. In my day a woman was firmly upon the shelf at your age. Why, I had already bore my husband two children by five and twenty."

"Mother..."

"Look at Rebecca, here. Poor as a church mouse and with little in the way of family connections. Had it not been for your father and I, as well as her uncle, she would have amounted to nothing more than a governess. Despite all that, she has made a splash in society, even capturing the attentions of someone who is notorious for being most discerning. Rebecca's charm and beauty have made Lord Broughton forget that she hasn't any money or family connections. You will forgive me for speaking so frankly, dear," her mother whispered remorsefully to Rebecca. "I'm just trying to make Anais understand, you see, that it is not enough to be rich, one must be beautiful, as well."

"One cannot help if they are beautiful or not," Anais muttered, twisting her fingers in her apron.

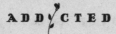

"True enough," her mother said, patting her flaxen curls. "But one can at least make an attempt to work with what attributes one has."

"I think Anais is pretty," Ann said, coming to her defense.

"Come, Anais," her mother said with a superior tilt of her chin. "Rebecca, dear, your uncle has sent his carriage to fetch you. It's waiting in the lane. Do not keep me waiting, Anais," her mother warned with a pointed look as she reached for the door latch.

"I think you're lovely, Anais," Ann said proudly. "Furthermore, I overheard Lindsay remark to Lord Wallingford that he thought you were a perfect blend of beauty and brains. He called you his angel. I think he's going to propose. I truly believe—"

"Enough, Ann," her mother said with a glare. "Good Lord, I'd love nothing more than for him to marry her and take her off my hands, but we haven't a chance now for that. If he hasn't proposed after all these years, nothing will induce him to now."

"Mama, I heard—"

"Enough of this nonsense. There will be no custard for you after dinner."

"Mama!" Ann cried.

"You're getting a bit thick in the middle, Ann. One night without bread pudding will serve you well. You must be conscious now of maintaining your figure. A man will go a long way before seeing a figure like yours. You must guard it most carefully," her mother lectured as she promptly left with Ann, who was protesting loudly over the loss of her pudding.

"Well?"

"He wants to meet me!" Anais said excitedly, forgetting about her mother's nagging, she showed Rebecca the valentine Lindsay had designed for her.

Rebecca read it and when she looked up at her, she had a strange intensity to her amber eyes. "How lovely."

"What are you wearing tonight?" Anais asked excitedly as her gaze strayed to a sack by the door. "How will I know you in the crowd?"

"Never fear, you will find me," Rebecca groaned, reaching for the muslin sack she had dropped on the floor when she came in. "Mrs. Button informed Uncle that she had the perfect costume for me. Of course, as you know, my uncle bows to every one of Mrs. Button's wishes." Rebecca pulled out an old brown cloth and held it out to Anais.

"A nun?" Anais croaked, laughing at the image of Rebecca wearing the brown sack.

"Hmm. I'm certain that this costume will not inspire Lord Broughton to dare enter the realm of wickedness."

"You never know," Anais teased. "The night could bring anything."

"How right you are, Anais," Rebecca said quietly, gathering her sack that lay atop the bed. She shoved the brown tunic inside before smiling brightly. "One must work with what fate hands them."

Lowering himself onto the red velvet settee, Lindsay spread his arms wide on the back of the wooden frame as he surveyed the small room that had become a means of escape from the theatrics of the ballroom one floor below.

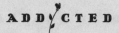

The air in the salon was thick with curling smoke, heavy with the perfume of spilled claret and Turkish tobacco. Numerous pillows had been strewn about, while braziers were lit with incense, emitting a heavy, almost sensual aroma he was all too familiar with. The heady perfume of fine Turkish opium clouded the room, blanketing him in an intoxicating aroma.

In the center of the room, dressed as a pasha, sat the Earl of Wallingford. The eldest child of the Duke of Torrington. Wallingford was an indolent wastrel of the highest order—he was also a very good friend.

"I wondered when you would escape the clutches of those marriage-minded debutantes my father insisted on inviting to his masquerade," Wallingford said with a grin. "Virgins are so damn insipid and tiresome. Give me a courtesan with the knowledge and talent to rouse me over a simpering, blushing virgin."

"It was a trial avoiding their snares, but I managed," Lindsay said, laughing as he thought of the numerous young ladies that had tried to corner him in one of the many dark alcoves of the ballroom. Virgins might be inexperienced in the bedroom, but they were master manipulators when it came to seeking an advantageous marriage.

"Well, then, what do you think, old boy?" Wallingford asked, making a sweeping gesture with his hand, indicating the decor of the salon that had recently been redecorated in the Eastern style. A style that was currently all the rage amongst artists and poets who thought themselves Romantics in the manner of Byron and Shelley.

"You've managed to convert me at last, Raeburn—I've

turned Turk," Wallingford said with a sharp satirical laugh. "Oh, I know it doesn't quite scratch up to that room of yours, but it is a start, wouldn't you agree?"

"It is indeed," Lindsay said, inhaling the heady fragrance from the incense stick that was suddenly lit beside him. He leaned over and inhaled the smoke, sighing appreciatively as he sank farther into the plump cushions of the settee, feeling the gnawing hunger in his belly slowly uncurl and subside.

"I was quite pleased with the results. It will no doubt serve adequately as we pursue our pleasures. Of course, when I saw how it enraged my father, I became even more enamored of it," Wallingford drawled, his smile wolfish. "Makes him wonder what I will do with this gothic monstrosity once he goes to his just reward. I confess, I do enjoy torturing him with glimpses of what may be. Perhaps I'll turn the place into a bordello, or better yet, an opium den where the wicked and idle may sprawl out and smoke themselves to sleep. Of course we shall have ladies lying about, makes the scene that much more debauched, don't you think? That ought to make the old goat twist in his grave. But enough of my father, the duke. Come and have a drink, old boy," Wallingford slurred drunkenly. "We'll only have so much longer before we shall have to return to my father's insipid ball. We'll need fortification."

"I'll pass." Lindsay watched as Wallingford reached for the hand of a young serving girl dressed in silks and veils. He pulled her atop his lap, his claret sloshing over the rim of his goblet, landing on the young lady's exposed cleavage.

"Oh, look," Wallingford drawled, his eyes glistening wickedly. "A new way to sip your evening tipple."

Male laughter erupted in the room as Wallingford bent his

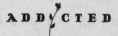

head to the girl's bosom and licked the trickling red liquor as it dribbled between her breasts. Instead of acting shocked, the girl, obviously a professional courtesan, giggled and clutched his face to her décolletage.

"Come, let us see what else we can have dribbling between these," Wallingford purred as he raised himself onto unsteady feet, his gaze never leaving the large ivory mounds of the courtesan's breasts.

Lindsay looked away from the departing couple. He had witnessed more drunken debauchery at his father's hands than he cared to recount. He had no wish to see Wallingford make an ass of himself—nor had he a wish to follow him down the drunken path of nothingness.

Searching the room and seeing that several other men had sequestered themselves with other willing women, Lindsay sighed and plucked the incense stick from the wood-and-brass holder. Waving it under his nose, he let the curling tendrils caress his skin before inhaling the scent, dissecting the pungent fragrance like a connoisseur. The aroma was rich, earthy with a touch of moss and sandalwood. Definitely Turkish. Nothing smelled quite as potent as Turkish opium.

Closing his eyes, he rested his head against the settee, glancing at the clock. It was not quite midnight. He had a bit longer yet before he would meet Anais on the terrace. He thought about her and how she had looked standing naked before him in the stable. What a beauty she had been with her honey-blond hair lying loose around her shoulders and her wide blue eyes, eyes that were always full of life and mischief. Mentally he conjured up the memory of her full, rose-tipped breasts and the delightfully rounded mound of her belly. He had not spent enough time worshiping her belly, nor had he allowed himself to linger over the soft space between her thighs.

He had stared at the soft triangle of space where her lush thighs grazed together and the downy curls of her mons connected. It was a mysterious space, a place where he was drawn, a place for his mouth, his fingers, *his cock*. Lord, but he was hungry for her. He'd had her twice two nights ago. Instead of abating his desire, it had only fuelled his need for her.

How long it had been since he'd desired to have her in his bed? He'd been sixteen. That was how long he'd been fantasizing about Anais. Fourteen long, agonizing years—seeing her, hearing her, being next to her. So many years of yearning, of imagining her face on the women he'd bedded.

He'd waited too long, he sighed, tossing the used stick atop the table. He'd wasted too many years. But he'd been uncertain—of her and himself.

Up until two nights ago, he hadn't known what she truly thought of him. Her letters to him while he was away at Cambridge had always been warm and personal while staying just on the side of propriety. He hadn't been able to glean what truly lay inside her heart, although he had spent many a night rereading every letter she had sent him, searching for the slightest sign that she returned his affection.

He in turn had started countless letters, declaring his love for her, his physical need for her. But he'd only balled them up and flung them into the fire, afraid of alienating her from his life with his lustful thoughts and actions. So he had bided his time, trying to make certain that she returned something of his regard.

But it hadn't only been her he'd been unsure of. He'd been worried about his own worthiness.

Anais might be a shy, and somewhat self-conscious woman, but she was also a gently bred lady who knew what she was about. She wasn't like the other women of his acquaintance— overblown and concerned only with money and fashion. That was the beauty of Anais. She didn't have any idea how damn desirable she was or how to use her voluptuous body to get what she wanted. Anais was not *that* sort of woman. She was strong in her convictions with unwavering loyalty. Anais thought only in black and white, good and evil.

For Anais, there weren't any shades of gray in her life—and so much of his life was nothing but a gray veil of mist. And yet, as unbending in her views of right and wrong were, she was kind, thoughtful and sweetly innocent. Simply put, Anais was the angel to his demon.

Her friendship had meant the world to him. He treasured it as if it were the rarest of gems. He had told her things that he'd never told another soul. She knew him more intimately than anyone did, or, he thought, anyone ever would. There was something about Anais that allowed openness and honesty. She had a way of making him feel calm and peaceful and loved.

Whether she realized it or not, she had carved out a place in his heart, settling herself so deeply inside him that she would be forever entrenched in his soul. She had stood by him through thick and thin, despite her obvious distaste for his father and his libertine ways.

How many times had he spoken of his father? How he feared for the way he might grow up? How often had she reassured him that he was not his father? That his father's weaknesses and excesses would not be his?

She had such faith in the man he was, in the man she knew he could be. He would never do anything to harm that trust, because Lindsay knew that if he lost Anais's faith in him, he had nothing. Without Anais, he would be his father's son in more than just blood.

"Evening, Raeburn."

Lindsay opened his eyes in time to see Garrett, Lord Broughton, flick his dress tails out behind him and sit on the cushion beside him.

"Evening, Broughton."

"An interesting little scene of debauchery, isn't it?"

"Hmm," Lindsay murmured, before lighting another incense stick and passing it to his friend who shook his head. Lindsay shrugged and waved the opium beneath his nose, inhaling the curling smoke.

"I don't know how you abide that stuff." Broughton coughed. "I damn near suffocated the instant I walked into the room. It makes my head feel damned strange and I nearly always purge my guts into the nearest potted palm."

Lindsay shut his eyes once again, allowing his senses to slow. "Nothing like a little quality Turkish Delight to facilitate the mind, Broughton. It is supposed to elevate the senses and carry you to another place and time. It's like living out a dream," he murmured, remembering all the wicked dreams he had of Anais over the years. Passionate, carnal dreams of making love to her in every conceivable way. Dreams of passionate lovemaking and heated, carnal fucking.

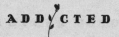

"I'm afraid the only Turkish Delight I indulge in is covered in powdered sugar."

"Stop being such a stick in the mud and light up. Blowing a cloud would do you wonders, you know. The Magic Mist hinders melancholy, begets confidence, converts fear into boldness and makes the silent eloquent. You'd be amazed at the things you can imagine when the smoke is caressing your face. Hell, you may even discover a hidden poet inside that dutiful breast of yours."

"I haven't the imagination, I'm afraid," Broughton grumbled.

Lindsay was no poet, but he certainly had a healthy imagination. Even now, with his blood slowing and thickening in his veins, Lindsay could imagine Anais on her knees, loving his cock with her mouth. He wanted to see that lovely pink mouth taking in his thick shaft. He wanted to see it glistening from her wet mouth and pulsating with the urge to spend freely along her full, high breasts.

"I don't need anything to facilitate my mind, thank you. Furthermore, neither do you," Broughton lectured. "Have you seen enough?" he asked, suddenly sounding perturbed. "You look as though you're about to fall asleep."

"Mmm," Lindsay smiled, feeling languid and relaxed. He could fall asleep, right in Anais's arms—and he would, tonight, as a matter of fact, right after he had thoroughly made love to her. Tonight he was going to take her home—to the divan that was filled with pillows. He would carry her, his odalisque, off to his harem. He was going to disrobe her, licking, devouring her for hours.

He had planned it all, right down to the valentine he had

waiting for her and the way he was going to propose to her. He thought about holding her in his arms as she lay spent from her release. He imagined himself leaning down and kissing her softly as he asked her to marry him. But then the image of plunging into her open, waiting body took hold. He could see himself thrusting deep inside, claiming her and watching her lips part in pleasure. He would sink into her again and whisper his proposal. Yes, definitely that, he thought, feeling his cock thicken. He would propose as he was filling her with his body and as she shuddered in release. As he spent his seed inside her, she would agree on a husky pant that she would be his wife.

"My lords?" a soft and feminine voice demurred.

"No, no thank you," Broughton grunted, stiffening beside him.

Lindsay opened one eye, peering down at a pair of ivory breasts that were spilling from the bodice of an exquisite beaded top—a houri's bodice he thought, taking in the gold shimmer of the silk cording that edged her overflowing bodice.

"Try it, Raeburn, old boy. A Turkish delicacy," Wallingford taunted from across the room as his evening's entertainment slipped her hand down the front of Wallingford's trousers.

Lindsay opened his other eye and saw that the houri held a silver tray before him. He looked up into her eyes and saw them gleaming. He had seen those eyes before, but where, he couldn't quite remember.

"Come, Raeburn," Wallingford jeered. "Have a taste. The Greeks have their grape leaves, the Turks their Passion Lips."

With a shrug, he reached for the pale yellow circle that resembled a poppy seed cake.

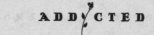

"I think you would find the red more to your liking," the houri purred seductively.

"Very well," he said, taking a red cake from her tray. He popped it in his mouth and chewed the tough texture. "Bloody awful," he mumbled to Broughton. "The Turks may keep their Passion Lips. I'd take a grape leaf any day."

"That girl looks very familiar," Broughton said thoughtfully as his gaze followed the houri's progress through the room.

"Perhaps she will look even more familiar as the night progresses?" Lindsay asked with a grin.

Broughton shot him a disgruntled look. "May I remind you that I've been courting Miss Thomas?"

Lindsay shrugged and looked away. As far as he was concerned, Rebecca Thomas was no damned good for his friend. There was something about the girl he couldn't quite put his finger on, but that unsavoury feeling was there nonetheless. He had never cared for Rebecca. She was manipulative and uncaring. Calculating coldness was always blatant in her eyes. Furthermore, he did not care for the way the conniving Rebecca had wormed her way into his gentle Anais's friendship.

Anais, he thought, searching through the thickening smoke for the clock. "Well, then, I'm off," he said when he saw it was nearing midnight.

"And where are you going?" Broughton asked as he stood, straightening his already immaculate waistcoat.

"I'm off to meet a charming young lady on the terrace."

"Take care of her." Broughton's voice held a hint of warning that Lindsay did not particularly care for.

"I love her, Broughton."

"I know, but sometimes…" Lindsay knew what his friend was going to say. *Sometimes you're not worthy of someone as good as Anais Darnby.*

"My Cambridge days are behind me, Broughton. I am no longer the neck or nothing youngblood you knew in university. Then I was searching for what I wanted in life and I know I was reckless. I no longer need to do that. I know what, and *who,* I want."

Broughton reached for his arm and stayed him. "Do not make the mistake of thinking you're the only one who cares for her. Anais has been my friend as long as she has been yours. I would not want her feelings trifled with."

"What are you implying?" Lindsay asked with a glare.

"I think you know what I mean, Raeburn. If your intentions are not honorable toward her, then do not pursue her."

Lindsay brushed Broughton's hand off his arm. "I would never dishonor her."

"I would hope not. I would hope that you would strive— *always*—to be the sort of man she needs and deserves."

With a brisk tilt of his head and the clenching of his teeth, Lindsay turned and made his way to the door, slightly disoriented from the heavy vapor of smoke hanging in the air. Opening the door, he let himself out, waiting for the fresh air to clear the cobwebs that were suddenly taking root in his brain.

Anais, he thought, reaching to the wall to steady himself. *I'm not like my father. I'm worthy of you. I can be the sort of man you need. I swear it.*

"Good evening, Lindsay."

He whirled around. The corridor narrowed sharply, making him experience a nauseating bout of syncope. The candle flames

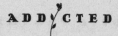

flickered madly, almost as if they were leaping from their wax stands and he reeled back as he watched the flames jump out at him, threatening to land on his clothes. The vision was gone as soon as it appeared, replaced by a kaleidoscope of bright swirling colors that clouded his vision.

Blinking, Lindsay looked up from the black-and-white floor that seemed to ripple like a ribbon in a breeze beneath his feet. And then he saw her, Anais, standing at the end of the hall dressed in a wonderfully seductive purple-and-gold gown.

"Anais?" he asked in a disbelieving voice. He tried to step forward but couldn't. He could barely see straight or focus his gaze on her.

Bloody hell, what was the matter with him? The Passion Lips, he suddenly remembered. What had the houri fed him? Certainly nothing he recalled ever dabbling in before. He had never imbibed anything quite so potent.

"Lindsay," Anais cried, calling his name and running toward him.

He caught her in his arms and pressed her against the wall. He ran his hands along her curves, delighting in her soft skin, in the flare of her hip above the low-slung skirt. His fingers became tangled in the filmy purple chiffon and he growled appreciatively, suddenly as randy as he had ever been in his life.

"Kiss me," she purred in a low, hypnotic voice that made his already hard cock rear in his trousers. "Kiss me, Lindsay," she said, over and over again, as if she were chanting a Siren's seductive call.

He searched for her mouth and kissed her, slow at first, then more carnally as she slipped her tongue between his lips. He groaned as she rubbed her mound against his throbbing arousal. He couldn't make himself stop. His blood was humming. His body felt languorous, as if he had all the time in the world, as if they were already back in his bedchamber and not standing in a hall where anyone may happen upon them.

She moaned and reached for his bulging trousers, stroking him boldly. Bloody hell, where had she learned that? "Touch me, Lindsay. Take me into your mouth as you did in the stables."

"Mmm, yes," he said, feeling the floor shift again. He lowered her bodice and cupped her. Opening his eyes, he struggled to focus on the pale breasts in his hands. But instead of two full, round breasts, he held four blurred globes, with nipples that danced and swayed before him. He blinked, trying to still the image so he could fasten his lips onto her and suckle her, but the more he blinked, the more his vision seemed to swim.

"Taste me, Lindsay," she encouraged, filling his hands with her breasts—breasts that he had thought felt much bigger two nights ago. But then, he wasn't in his right mind now. Something was ruling him. He was certain it wasn't just the power of lust he felt rushing through his veins.

He tried to push the doubting thoughts aside. It wasn't right to take her like this. He had taken her virginity in a stable, for heaven's sake, she did not need to be taken against a wall. But he could not tell his prick that. He needed her, to be buried deep inside her. He needed to hear his name on her lips as she cried out in her pleasure. He needed to hear that she loved him.

Old fears crept into his mind. He shoved them away, but they came back, more demanding, clearer and more persuasive. No,

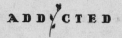

he was not like his father. He would not destroy her in the manner that his father destroyed his mother. He loved her. He would love her forever.

Needing to show her, he lowered his head to her breasts and took her nipple into his mouth, suckling her greedily till she raked her hands through his hair and panted his name wantonly against his temple.

"I need you, Anais," he murmured in a harsh voice. "I need you so much."

Something was wrong. He could not keep that thought from snaking in and out of his head, despite the magic in Anais's touch. There was definitely something about Anais that was not right. She didn't feel *right* beneath his fingers—she was too thin. He wanted her to feel the way she had the night in the stable—all soft and curvy and voluptuous.

"Give me the words," she coaxed, gripping his cock so that he groaned in pleasure and pain. "Tell me how much better this is than the first time."

He couldn't deny her, not with the way she was stroking his shaft through his breeches. He was ready to explode; yet his mind kept resisting. But he wanted to please her. He wanted so damn much to be the sort of man she desired. And he needed release. God, he needed that. To spill himself in her hand and press his face into her sweetly scented throat.

She unfastened his trousers and slipped her hand into the front of them, finding his cock and swirling her finger around the wet tip. "How aroused you are. You're wet already and leaking your seed."

His cock stiffened further and he shoved his hips forward encouraging her to stroke him. He was unable to believe that his shy little Anais was being so bold. But it excited him. The more she stroked him, the more aroused and reckless he became. "You're a little cock tease," he murmured as she cupped his cods in her palm.

"And do you like how I tease your cock?"

"I should think you know the answer to that, especially after the other night."

"And am I better than the other night?" she demurred, inflaming him further. "Am I a better cock tease?"

He raised her skirt and stroked her bare backside. A backside that felt much different from the delightful heart-shaped derriere he recalled. But this *was* Anais. He sensed her as he always did. It was this damn thing that had poisoned his brain, making him think such crazed thoughts.

"What do you want me to do with this?" she asked boldly, cradling his shaft in her hand.

"Suck it," he groaned, the words spilling out in a long rush of breath as he gave voice to his deepest fantasy. And then almost violently he captured her lips with his and kissed her, needing her in a desperation he had never felt before. "I have to tell you. I can't wait. I love you," he said passionately between long, hard, drugging kisses. "I always have. I can't hide it anymore. I don't want to hide it. It's only ever been you—it will forever only be you."

A heartrending gasp shattered the sound of their breaths. He looked up at the woman in his arms and blinked, his vision still swimming before him. And then, the image slowly danced into focus and he felt the contents of his stomach threaten to come up

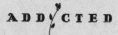

and spill onto the floor. He looked from the woman who was pressed against him to the sound of the frantic breathing he heard coming from beside him. His mind whirled with the impossibility.

Anais stood frozen, shocked, horrified. The implications of what she was witnessing spun with dizzying speed in her head. Her chest began to rise and fall too rapidly and she felt as though she were being choked by the blue ribbon around her throat. With shaking hands she tore the bonnet from her head. How could Lindsay have done this to her? How, after what they had shared with each other in the stable, could he so easily fall into the arms of another?

"Jesus, how long?" She wasn't certain if Lindsay knew he said the words aloud.

"Long enough to see you with her and hear that you love her," she whispered, choking back a sob. She looked away, sickened by the sight of him and saw, for the first time, the woman who was pressed against him.

"Why?" she asked in what was little more than a half-strangled whisper. But she could not finish the sentence. She could not look at Rebecca pressed against Lindsay, her breasts glistening from Lindsay's mouth. She could not stand to see the woman who had been her trusted friend wearing her costume—the only thing she had ever owned that had not been designed or ordered by her mother. The only thing she had ever wanted Lindsay to see her wearing. Oh, God, what a stupid trusting fool she had been to think that Rebecca had picked up her muslin sack by mistake. It had not been by mistake, but by design—a cruel, ugly design.

"It was you I said those words to. I thought she was you, Anais," he stammered. "Let me explain—"

"I don't think the words are necessary, darling," Rebecca purred, reminding Anais of the snake her friend truly was. "I think what Anais saw speaks for itself. We needn't hide it anymore."

"Don't touch me," Lindsay snapped, shaking off Rebecca's hold on his arm. "Goddamn you, what have you done?"

"It's what you have done, Lindsay," Anais replied. "You have done this."

"Let me explain," he muttered, staggering closer. "I was with Wallingford. I was…slipped something…that is, I took something that made me confused. I thought Rebecca was you. I *believed,* Anais, that it was truly you."

"How could you think such a thing? We look nothing alike."

"Nor are we the same size." Rebecca's voice dripped with venom.

Lindsay shot Rebecca a murderous glare as he held on to the wall, supporting his wavering frame. "Anais, listen to me. It was a drug. I'm not drunk. I swear it. It was a mistake. I thought it was you. Believed it was you…believe me, Anais."

"Lies," Anais whispered brokenly as she fixed her blurry gaze on Lindsay. "Everything you said, everything you told me…it was nothing but lies. What we did, that was a lie, too. You were just amusing yourself with me—God, how you must have laughed at me, falling for your seductions so easily."

"Don't say that, Anais."

"What, that you were bored silly that night so you thought you'd take me—plain, undesirable spinster that I am—out to the stables for a little amusement? You probably thought you

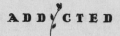

were doing me a favor by sleeping with me. You must have really felt sorry for me that night to put up with such an inexperienced wallflower like me—especially when you could have had..." Anais glanced at Rebecca and felt her throat squeeze shut. "When you could have had someone beautiful, someone as desirable as *her*."

"I wanted you—I want *you*," he corrected with a frown. "You know that. Just remember how it was, Anais."

"I remember all too well. I remember a woman who is not beautiful, a woman with a round body that is too full in the belly and the hips, a woman who thought she was beautiful enough for someone like you. Obviously I was an evening of sport until you could move on to better and prettier things." God, to think of the way she had blindly believed him. Never questioning his sincerity, actually believing that he had not proposed after making love to her because he wanted it to be special like he claimed. And she had fallen for it.

"No, this is a mistake. It's not what it seems," he began, taking a staggering step toward her while using his hand against the wall for support.

Anais felt her lips twist with disgust. He looked so very much like his father, stumbling toward her, fumbling with the fastenings of his trousers, his curling hair in disarray, his shirttails hanging outside his trousers. She could hardly look at him without wanting to vomit. This was not the Lindsay of her childhood. This was not the man she had lain with two nights ago. This was a stranger—a dissipated wastrel she had never seen before.

"No, please. Don't look at me like that, Anais. Don't look at me like you do him. I'm not like *him*," he roared, staggering toward her. "Listen to me and let me explain. I don't want Rebecca. I don't want anyone but you."

Anais was suddenly aware of a strong presence beside her. Without looking, she knew that it was Lord Broughton. His arm around her waist was strong and comforting and she sagged against his side.

"Broughton! Thank God...tell her—tell her about the drug..." Lindsay pleaded, lurching toward them. "Broughton knows...he was with me—"

"For as long as I live I shall remember you this way," Anais gasped through trembling lips as she tried to stem her sob of pain. "Never have you resembled *him* more than you do now. You've broken my heart." She covered her mouth once more, praying she would be able to leave before she completely broke down. "I wish I had never let you touch me."

"No, Anais," he said, his voice pleading. *"Christ, no, don't say that!"*

But she turned from him, and Garrett, who was just as shocked by Rebecca's betrayal, reached for her and took her into his arms.

"I'm sorry," Lindsay cried. "Christ, don't leave!"

Anais closed her eyes, blocking out the sound, hating the words she had heard him say so many times before. Such meaningless, empty words. Such a meaningless act. What a fool she had been. A hopeless, romantic fool.

"I will not lose you!" Lindsay roared as she turned and walked away, still holding fiercely onto Garrett's arm. "You cannot run from me, Anais. I will find you. *Anais!*" Her name, ripped from the depths of Lindsay's tortured soul, echoed throughout the hall and Anais shivered, still hearing him calling her name even after the carriage wheels had set into motion.

4

Ten months later

"Anais, you must come downstairs, at least for a cup of tea. It is Christmas Eve, you cannot possibly spend it up here in your room, *oh*——" Ann's voice broke off when she came waltzing into the room and spotted Anais lying in bed with Robert Middleton's ear to her breast.

"I'm sorry," Ann mumbled, clearly horrified that she had walked in on her sister in such an intimate position.

"Don't be silly, Ann. Dr. Middleton was just finishing with me, were you not, sir?"

"Indeed I was, Lady Anais." He straightened away from her. "I shall check in with you tomorrow to see how you are faring."

"Surely you do not need to call on me tomorrow? 'Tis Christmas morn, and you have a wife and child that you will not wish to leave."

He reached for her hand, clasping it tightly in his warm one. "I shall see you tomorrow, Lady Anais. Sleep well and remember you are not to exert yourself." He snapped shut the wooden cylinder he had used to listen to her chest. "It's utterly amazing.

Your heart sounds much stronger than it did two days ago. If you keep this up, you shall be wandering about the woods in no time."

"Thank you, Dr. Middleton."

"Just Robert," he murmured as he placed his hat over his dark blond hair. "We have, after all, known each other since we were in swaddling clothes."

"Thank you, Robert," Anais replied, knowing he would not be happy until she did so. And truth be told, she did feel silly acting so formal around him. She had known him all her life. He was Garrett's younger brother after all.

"Send word to The Lodge if you need me. And remember, you are not to be near drafts or the cold air. The cold makes it harder for the heart to pump the blood. Your heart doesn't need the strain. I'm afraid you shall have to miss out on the church service this evening. Your condition is delicate, you must not take any risks."

"Mother says that she believes you are much too young to attend me," Anais said, laughing at him and his boyish pout.

"No doubt she puts more stock in that old physician of hers, the one whose medical books were written in the time of the Bible."

"She's threatened to send him to me."

"Whatever you do, don't let him bleed you, Anais."

"I won't, Robert."

"Well, then, if that is all, I shall be on my way. The weather, it appears, has taken a turn for the worst."

"Never know what winter will bring in Worcestershire."

He nodded and reached for his brown pigskin bag. "It's much

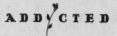

the same in Edinburgh. Well, then, good night, Anais, and happy Christmas to you."

"To you, too. Wish Margaret the same and give your daughter a kiss for me."

"I shall," he said, beaming a wide smile at the mention of his child. "I certainly shall. Happy Christmas, Lady Ann," he said, inclining his head as he passed her sister.

Ann came over to the bed and sat down beside her after Dr. Middleton had closed the door. "I'm sorry. I didn't realize he was still here. He was up here for a very long time."

Anais shrugged and picked at the loose thread of the woolen blanket that covered her. She couldn't help but notice how pale her fingers still looked and how her veins, so blue and cold, could be seen through her skin, as if her flesh was nothing but transparent tissue that was used for papier-mâché.

"You are improving?" Ann captured her gaze. "You must be, for you look much better than you did a month ago when you returned from France. Lud, you looked on death's door when Lord Broughton carried you in. I vow, it was providence indeed that you met up with him in Paris, for Aunt Millie would have been in hysterics had she to deal with you alone, and in a foreign city."

"It was very fortunate that I met up with his lordship," she muttered, not wanting to talk about Garrett and the events that had taken place.

"Has Dr. Middleton told you what your delicate condition is? He's mentioned it several times to Mama and Papa, but he is rather vague to its cause."

Anais let her sister see her impatience. "I have told you, Ann, that it is nothing more than a bit of fever and malaise."

Ann arched an intelligent, blond brow, clearly not believing what she was hearing, but letting the rebuke slide. "Mother told Father that it is most likely your womanly organs rotting away in spinsterhood that is causing your heart to fail. But father believes that you've caught some sort of virulent brain fever from the French."

Anais smiled and reached for Ann's hand. "I vow, Ann, my womanly organs are just fine. And I am not allowing that quack, Dr. Thurston, to talk Mother into believing that my condition is nothing more than hysteria caused by my woman's parts."

Ann chuckled. "When you say it, Anais, it sounds like such flummery. How can a woman's organs make one hysterical?"

"They can't. Dr. Thurston just despises women, that is all."

"Louisa has come to me." Ann sobered. "I thought you would want to know that your maid is concerned that your last flux lasted nearly two weeks. It was rather…er…according to Louisa, it was rather heavy."

"For heaven's sake," Anais groaned, blushing all the way to her scalp. "Is nothing sacred in this house?"

"Of course not," Ann said with a grin. "In a house filled with women, how can a subject like monthlies be kept quiet? Still, Louisa fears that it may indeed be your womanly organs that are making you ill after all."

"The humiliation!" Anais said with mock horror. "What? Do all the maids line up in a row while they gather our monthly padding and discuss our courses? Does the entire house know when one is early, or one is late?"

"I should think the late bit would be most talked about," Ann said, sticking out her tongue in a cheeky manner. "Imagine the

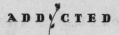

gossip if one of us were to miss our monthlies. Mother would interrogate us for hours if she ever found out."

"Mama cares only about Mama. I doubt she'd care a tuppence about something as mundane as monthlies."

"True," Ann agreed. "But still, I thought you would like to know. And *I* want to know that you are on the mend. The bleeding has stopped, hasn't it?" Ann asked, concern once again creeping into her eyes.

"It has."

"Father said there was nothing wrong with you that rest won't cure. He always takes up your side, you know."

"You are right about Father having a soft spot for me. And thank heavens for that, because if it were up to Mama, I would be in the care of Dr. Thurston, being bled every day and confined to bed with my womanly organs while he contrives to find a way to keep them from making me mad."

"Yes," Ann said, laughing. "Papa adores you as I know very well that you adore him. Every man you have ever met is held up to him, aren't they? He is the pinnacle that your suitors must strive for."

Anais felt herself blush. It was true, no matter how silly the notion sounded. Her father was a good, kind, honest man. Was it so wrong for her to desire that the man she choose to marry and commit her life to, be nothing short of the sort her father was?

"And then there is Mama," Ann said with a groan. "She is forever making me fuss over my appearance. She is only interested in me when I am looking pretty and am dressed in frilly gowns with layers of flounces and bows. She never bothers to read my poems, and furthermore, I don't believe she listens to me when I sing, unless of course I'm surrounded by potential beaux. Then she uses it to her advantage to inform everyone, most embarrassingly, I might add, what a wonderful wife I shall make. I vow, Mama never has a substantial thought in her head. She never thinks of anything other than fashion and her toilette. How could father have married such a shallow person?"

"Love is blind, I suppose." Anais thought of how she had been blinded by love. Love had stopped her from seeing what Lindsay was truly like. Naiveté had prevented her from realizing that Rebecca was not truly her dearest friend. She had been so blind to many things this past year.

"Anais," Ann asked, her tone suddenly somber. "I wish to know if anything happened between you and Lindsay. You both left Bewdley so suddenly. I never heard a word about you going off to France with Aunt Millie and her companion, Jane. And suddenly, you were gone. Then Lindsay arrived and I heard him yelling downstairs in Papa's study, demanding to know where you were being kept. He was distraught. I could not help but think his choice of words was rather bizarre."

"Perhaps you misinterpreted them."

Her sister frowned. "I did not. And do not pretend to believe that you don't think Lindsay's sudden disappearance is not odd. I don't believe that he just *poof*—" Ann puffed between her lips as she waved her hand as if she held a magic wand in her fingers "—he just disappeared into thin air without a word to anyone. Not even his mother, Lady Weatherby, knows precisely where he is. He has been gone over ten months, Anais, with no news of him. Are you not concerned?"

"I'm tired, Ann." She *was* feeling weak and fatigued, but most

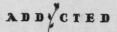

of all she did not want to talk about Lindsay and what had happened between them the night of the masquerade ball. She had told no one, not her father, and most certainly not her mother. She had to divulge a few of the details to Aunt Millie. Aunt Millie's companion, Jane, knew a bit more than her aunt, but Anais had convoluted the truth to suit her needs. The only person who knew the full truth was Garrett, and he had been remarkably supportive, not to mention silent.

"I'm very disappointed in Lord Raeburn," Ann said, stroking Anais's hand with her fingertips. "I thought for certain he would propose to you. How wrong I was."

"It's all right, dearest," Anais said, trying to smile for her sister's benefit. "It wasn't meant to be."

"But you loved him, Anais."

"In truth, it would not have been a sound alliance."

Her sister shot her a dubious look. "And an alliance with Lord Broughton would be more sound, then?"

"Ann," she warned. "I am not talking about such things with you."

"I'm fifteen now," she wailed, "and Squire Wilton's son kissed me beneath the Maypole. I'm a woman, Anais. I know about such things as love and marriage."

"Really? Then you are much more educated than I, for I understand none of it. Now, off to church you go. I think I hear Mama calling your name."

"What of Lord Broughton, Anais, are you going to marry him?"

"Garrett is a friend, Ann. A very dear friend."

"Just like Lindsay was your very dear friend?"

Anais looked toward the window, to the black night beyond

and the white snow that fell in a straight, heavy line. "Lindsay was a dear friend. But that was before."

"I'm sorry that Lindsay ran off instead of proposing to you. I would have liked to have him for a brother-in-law. He is much more sporting than Lord Broughton."

"Lord Broughton is a very kind man. He is very loving, very forgiving."

"And what has Lord Broughton to forgive you for?" Ann asked, immediately pouncing on the little slip.

"For not marrying him despite—" Anais looked away and brushed a small tear that escaped unchecked from her eye. She did not finish her thought. Could not finish it, despite the very great need she had to confide in someone. She felt so alone, so empty inside. But then, she had made her own choices and the consequences were hers alone to live with.

"I hope someday you shall be able to tell me the truth of what happened between you and Lord Broughton in Paris, Anais. Perhaps you have convinced Mama and Papa that this mysterious illness of yours is nothing but a trifling fever, but you have not fooled me. I would hate to think you could not share confidences with your own sister."

"Confidences can be such burdens, Ann. I contracted my illness while traveling abroad. Lord Broughton returned me home to convalesce, there is nothing else to say."

Ann's blue eyes swept along the covers that shielded Anais's form. Anais could not help but draw her knees up farther, hiding deeper beneath the blanket. "I suppose time will tell us, won't it?" Ann said with a sad wistfulness. "Good night, Anais."

"Good night, Ann."

Her sister smiled and let herself out. Sighing heavily, Anais looked about her room, feeling tired and drained. Her body was tired, her mind and the worries that constantly plagued her further drained her of what little strength she still possessed. She wondered if she would ever be free of the worries she harbored. Perhaps it was her penance to live every day in fear that her secret would be found out and exposed to the world.

The clopping of horse hooves on the cobble lane outside broke through her thoughts and she slipped out of bed, watching as her sister and mother were handed into the carriage by a footman dressed in his blue-and-silver livery. Where was her papa? she wondered. Perhaps he was already in the carriage. But it was not like him to not wait for the ladies of the house to enter the carriage first.

The carriage door slammed shut and within seconds, the four white horses were in motion, carrying her family the short ride into the village and the Christmas Eve church service.

Reaching for the book that sat atop her bedside table, Anais reached for it only to have it slip from her fingers and land with a loud crack against the floor. She startled in surprise. It was a loud, ringing sound for so slim a volume, and the resonance echoed throughout her room. The echo, she noticed, was followed by a peculiar thudding on the stairs below.

Strange. Who could be running up the stairs in such an undignified manner? Shrugging, she bent at the waist to retrieve the book and straightened in horror. The almost overpowering scent of smoke wafted up between the floorboards and she ran to the door, breathless despite the minute exertion. Throwing open her chamber door, Anais saw that the hallway was engulfed in fire.

The staircase, that only minutes before Ann had descended, was swallowed in black smoke and orange flames. Shutting the door as the wind came from below and licked the flames into a soaring giant tower, Anais scrambled to her dressing room, praying she could escape down the stairs before the fire consumed that portion of the staircase. But as she reached for the latch, she realized it was locked and the key missing. Squelching the panic that arose in her breast, Anais fought to clear her head of the dizziness and the burning sensation in her chest. She was trapped.

The house, nearly two centuries old and built entirely of wood and plaster, would be engulfed by fire in no time. She did not have minutes to waste in panic.

Anais looked to the window and ran to it, flinging open the sash and ignoring the bitterly cold air that rushed in. Tearing the velvet draperies from the wooden rods, she ignored the heaviness in her chest and went to work tying them together before she reached for her blankets and drew the coverlet from the bed.

There was no recourse left, the window was her only means of escape.

5

The wind howled through the forest and down the mountains, only to whirl around the lumbering conveyance. The chill air somehow found a way through the tight seams of the carriage frame, plummeting the temperature inside so that the interior felt like an icebox. Burying his chin into the folded depths of his greatcoat, Lindsay felt another chill race down his spine.

"Damn cold," he grunted, burrowing deeper into the warm Yorkshire wool of his coat. What bloody timing to arrive back in England during a snowstorm.

As the rhythmic rocking of the carriage continued, Lindsay fought to stay awake, but soon his eyes grew heavy until it was impossible to hold them open. Within minutes he was dreaming. Dreaming of dry, arid heat and the scent of Arabian spices that sifted through the waving branches of cypress trees.

In his dream he was back in Constantinople, where the saffron-colored sun hung heavy on the azure horizon, illuminating the cobalt and gilt tiles of the Islamic columns of the *Kapali Çarsi*. The sun burned hot on his cheeks. The scarf he used to protect his head from the heat rippled in the breeze as the salt-scented air rolled in from the Sea of Marmara. That salty, spicy breeze was the only reprieve from the scorching heat of the midday sun and the sea of humanity that swarmed inside the covered bazaar.

Inside the *Kapali Çarsi,* viziers and pashas smoked their hookahs while their slaves and attendants bartered for goods for their richly furnished homes. It had been there, in Constantinople's covered bazaar, that Lindsay and his traveling companion, Lord Wallingford, found themselves meandering through the hundreds of stalls that sold everything from spices and nuts to hashish and beautiful women who were bought by rich men as new acquisitions for their harems.

Constantinople's voluptuous exoticness was so different from his genteel England. He was so very far removed from the glittering ton and the fancy town houses in Mayfair. Far away from his responsibilities to his family and the estates in Worcestershire. Yet Constantinople had not been far enough away from the reaches of his past. He still remembered how Anais had fled from him the night she'd discovered him in the hall with her best friend. No physical distance could make him forget that strangled cry of shock and hurt, nor the distraught look in her eyes.

Now semiawake, he struggled to find his way back to his dream—to a time where nothing had mattered but the warm, lazy days spent in decadence. To the days when the hookah and a beautiful concubine had been all he needed to wile away the hours and deaden the pain of his failure.

But damn him, the dream would not return. It remained elusive and he was faced once more with remembering how

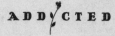

Anais had seemed to vanish into thin air after she left the Torrington masquerade. He had looked everywhere for her, but she had evaded his pursuit, denying him the chance to explain that he had not set out to seduce her friend or to destroy her faith in him.

After searching throughout England he'd traveled across the channel to France. He had learned from Anais's mother that she had gone abroad with her aunt—a trip, Lady Darnby had told him, that had been planned for some time. But he knew better. She'd gone to France in order to be free of him.

He had immediately set out for the continent, but hadn't been able to locate her in Paris. It was then that Wallingford grew frustrated with him and his obsession with finding Anais. After weeks of fruitlessly searching Paris, Lindsay had allowed Wallingford to persuade him into accompanying him to Constantinople where Lindsay had been seduced, not by beautiful women, but by the allure of opium. Opium, that heavenly demon.

The carriage swayed sharply, pitching to the right. Lindsay found himself fully awakened, and he shook his head free of the memory of his time in Constantinople, as well as the bitter memories of Anais.

"You were dreaming," Wallingford said, tossing him a fur for his lap.

The temperature had dropped again and the carriage, despite its cushioned silk and thick blinds, could not keep out the chill from the violent winds.

"I was remembering how warm the breeze was when it blew in from the Bosphorus. Perhaps we should not have left the warmth of Constantinople," Lindsay muttered, lifting up the blind and seeing nothing but the blinding whirl of snow outside the window. "I had almost forgotten how damn cold England gets in December. Although, this amount of snow is quite rare so early in the season."

Wallingford nodded as he puffed on his cheroot. "It is bloody cold. But three months ago we were not thinking of winter when we left Turkey. We were thinking of other things—like the beauty of the woods in the fall. The sound of the wind howling through the forest as it blows from atop the Malvern Hills. We had had enough of traveling, had we not? We were anxious to see England again."

"Indeed." But had he not experienced that dream of Anais all those months ago, he might still be in Constantinople, wasting away his days in lavish Eastern decadence. He had been lost for days at a time, the opium his only companion in a world of silk veils and velvet pillows. Where he had only had a taste for opium before, he now had a consuming hunger.

"Sir," one of the footmen called, rapping his fist against the back of the carriage. "We need to stop, milord."

With a tap of his walking stick against the trap door, Lindsay signaled for the coachman to bring the team to a stop. As the six grays came to a prancing halt, Lindsay threw open the door and covered his face with his arm as snow, wild and angry, gusted inside the carriage.

Lindsay could not help but notice how red-cheeked and shivering the footman was, despite the beaver hat and numerous layers of thick woolen capes. "The stallion is rearing in the box carriage, milord. Jenkins says that the animal has begun to suffer from the cold."

"Not acclimated yet," Lindsay called over his shoulder to Wallingford. "I'll ride him the rest of the way. That should warm him up."

"Bloody fool," Wallingford yelled after him after Lindsay disembarked from the carriage. "You'll get yourself killed riding that animal in this weather."

"I spent a fortune on him. I'll be damned if I allow him to die from the cold. He's going to stud my stables and he can't very well perform when he's frozen, can he?"

"Damn it, Raeburn," Wallingford grunted as he tossed his cheroot into a drift of snow. "You know I won't let you go alone. Not in this weather. Bloody hell, man."

Lindsay tossed his friend a smile. "Come, it will be like old times, when we were neck-or-nothing youths galloping at breakneck speeds down the mountainside."

"Our bones were not so easily broken in our youth," Wallingford grumbled as he raised the collar of his greatcoat to protect his face from the biting wind. "Nor were our heads, for that matter."

"You sound like Broughton when he used to chastise us for our foolish recklessness."

"I'm coming to believe that our dear friend was the more intelligent of the three."

"Come," Lindsay said, not wanting to think of how he had betrayed Broughton, as well as Anais. Instead, he stalked to the box carriage to where his prized Arabian stallion was snorting and stomping.

"Lead on, Raeburn," Wallingford said, following in Lindsay's wake. "And if we are so fortunate to make it home alive, the first to enter the stables may buy the other a warm pint of cider and a hot woman."

Lindsay gained the stallion's saddle and took up the reins, turning the Arabian in the other direction. Through the snow, he ran the animal as safely as he could while ignoring the biting wind. On instinct, Lindsay guided the horse down a path he had followed countless times in his lifetime.

As the familiar sites came into view, Lindsay slowed the stallion as it pranced along the icy path that overlooked the town of Bewdley nestled snugly in the vale below them. Ice pallets floated aimlessly atop the black waters of the Severn River, reminding Lindsay of the paintings he had once seen of the remnants of an iceberg after it had crumbled into the sea.

Tossing its sleek black head, the Arabian's billowing breaths misted gray and evaporated amongst the snowflakes that were circling about them. Tightening the reins, Lindsay settled the rearing animal before casting his gaze to the roof of St. Ann's Church that dominated the view of the town.

Below the ridge lay the sleepy village he had called home since birth. But tonight, the quiet little village of Bewdley was coming alive. Its residents were strolling down the cobbled streets, candles in hand as they made their pilgrimage to church. To the west of the town center, huddled in the valley where a small tributary broke away from the Severn and formed a creek, lay the first of four prominent estates that anchored Bewdley's aristocratic society. Wallingford's family estate bordered the forest. Broughton's was to the east and only minutes down the ridge. His own home, Eden Park, rested on the other side of the

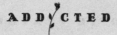

bridge. And directly below him lay Anais's home, which he had not seen in nearly a year.

Scouring the Jacobean-style mansion from high above the valley, Lindsay blinked back the snowflakes that landed on his eyelashes. The earthy, acrid smell of wood burning in the cold air drifted up to meet him and he inhaled the scent, so familiar to him, yet so long since he'd been home to smell its aroma.

It was Christmas Eve and the coal was replaced in the hearths of the faithful with a Yule log that would burn throughout the holiday. Lindsay watched the smoke billow out of the three large chimneys that loomed above the peaked roof. The calming scent took him back to the time when he was young and carefree. A time when he once sat beside the hearth and ate plum pudding and custard with Anais after the Christmas Eve service.

His gaze immediately focused on the last window on the right side of the house. A gentle glow from a lone candle flickered lazily. He could almost imagine Anais sitting on her window bench staring out at the sky with her chin propped in her hand. She adored winter. They had sat side by side so many times watching the snow falling gently to the ground. No, that wasn't entirely the truth. *She* had watched the snow, he had watched her; and he had fallen more in love with her than he had ever thought possible.

He slid his gaze from her window and allowed it to roam over the land where the verdant green fields were now covered in a thick white blanket that shimmered like crystals in the silver moonlight; where the hawthorn and holly hedgerows that marked each farm were weighted with snow. Only the occasional red bunch of holly berries could be seen peeking out beneath its white winter blanket.

Again the wind began its low moan through the branches of the forest behind them, and Lindsay brought the collar of his greatcoat around his chin, staving off the cold and the chilling wail of the wind. It was a melancholy sound that somehow resonated deep within him.

"Beautiful, isn't it?" Wallingford asked, reigning in his mount to stand beside his. "The wilds of nature are unparalleled here, are they not? Nowhere can you appreciate her more than in the Wyre Forest. I shall have to paint this view when I get home," he said, scanning the grounds below them. "I've never seen the vale looking so desolate and untamed, yet so hauntingly beautiful."

"Spoken like a true artist," Lindsay drawled, unable to keep his eye on the hedgerows. Unfortunately, he kept stealing glances at the lone candle in the window, wishing Anais would appear; hoping the dreams he had of her were not the omen his soul believed them to be.

"When shall you call upon her?" Wallingford asked quietly after noting the direction of Lindsay's gaze.

"I don't know."

"When we left Constantinople you were hell-bent on finding her. For the three months it's taken us to arrive in England you've been having nightmares about her. You've feared the worst. Now you lack the conviction to see for yourself if your vision was real or merely a deception of the sultan's hookah?"

Lindsay recalled the crippling fear that had lanced through him as he awoke from his startling dream. "It was real."

"The hookah is a magical thing," Wallingford said, watching

him curiously. "It makes us see ghosts in the vapors. It makes us feel things that are not there and the things that are there no longer matter. It is so easy to run from our ghosts with the hookah as I think you discovered."

"It is never easy to run. I shall never outrun this ghost."

Wallingford pursed his lips tightly together and studied him, his expression growing somber. "This particular ghost has an otherworldly hold on you, Raeburn. I'm afraid she always will. She is going to destroy you."

"I already am. I brought about my own demise when I foolishly allowed myself to be weak. I should have resisted the lure that bitch Rebecca offered me. Had I resisted temptation instead of pursuing it, Anais would have been my wife by now. I would not be standing here on Christmas Eve, longing for her, wishing I could find a way to magically erase the past."

"What did you see?" Wallingford asked. "What was so terrible that you had to race back here to the woman who would not even allow you to defend yourself? A woman whose love is so fleeting that she cannot allow you an ounce of forgiveness?"

In the vision, Anais arose amidst a veil of gossamer smoke, her beauty unveiled amidst curling tendrils that cloaked the air. Her softly rounded body and her rose, taut nipples were clearly visible beneath the pale pink gown that hugged her body. Her long blond curls were unbound and her arms outstretched, beckoning him to come to her, and like a slavish disciple he had gone to her. In that moment, she had taken him in her arms, whispering absolution.

He had lowered her onto the silk pillows that were scattered about the floor of his room. He could smell her—the scent of her petal-soft skin—despite the heavy and sensual cloud of incense that hung like a haze above the divan.

She had felt warm and alive in his arms until suddenly she grew stiff and cold. Her beautiful, sparkling, cornflower-blue eyes grew dim and distant as she stared unseeing at him. And then he saw the crimson liquid that slowly began to engulf them. It glistened in the candlelight from the lanterns that hung above them as it began to cover her pale skin. And she kept looking at him with those cold, lifeless eyes. He could not bear it, could not stand to watch her taken from him. As he pushed himself away from her, her lips parted and she softly said the words that haunted him for months. "You did this to me, Lindsay, you have killed me."

He had awakened, shaken by the vision, terrified that it had been a sign that something was wrong—a sign that he had to come back to her and make amends. A sign he could not ignore.

"Raeburn, look," Wallingford commanded, drawing him from the horror of his mind. "There are flames coming from the side of the house."

Snapping to attention, Lindsay focused his gaze on the level below Anais's window. From his position above the house he saw the brilliant orange flicker that was reflected by the glass.

"That is Darnby's study," he said, setting the stallion into motion. "And the hearth is next to that window. Come, Wallingford," he yelled, racing down the path that led to the vale.

Lindsay wondered, as he blinked back the snow from his eyes, if this was not the reason he had felt compelled to come back home.

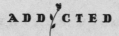

Jumping off his horse, Lindsay ran up the manor stairs and threw open the doors. The house was in a state of chaos with servants rushing here and there, screaming and running wild and frightened with buckets of water. He watched as two burly footmen emerged from a thick cloud of smoke, dragging a coughing and sputtering Lord Darnby from his study.

"Oh, Lord Raeburn," Anais's lady's maid gasped when she saw him through the smoke. "You've come back."

"Where is your mistress, Louisa?"

"Trapped upstairs. Roger and William have gone to fetch her, but they canna see or breathe for the smoke."

"See to Darnby," Lindsay ordered Wallingford who had followed him inside. "Bring him to Eden Park. I shall meet back up with you there."

Lindsay could see the blood running in rivulets down Darnby's balding head. "He's injured," Wallingford called. "He'll need a physician."

"Then do it, man," he barked, shrugging out of his greatcoat. "I shall find Anais."

"What the bloody hell is going on?"

Lindsay whirled around and came face-to-face with Broughton. The last time he had looked into his friend's face, he had been standing before him with a brace of dueling pistols in his hands.

Broughton had called him out the next day, after the debacle with Rebecca. The duel had not been about avenging Rebecca's honor, or Garrett's. No, Broughton had called him out to defend Anais, and Lindsay had agreed to it, hoping to gain some measure of his own honor back. Only they had not been able to go through with it. Putting a bullet in each other would never satisfy, could never wash away the pain that Lindsay had brought to everyone he had ever cared about.

They had both fired their shots in the air, then turned their backs on each other.

"What the devil are you doing in here?"

Lindsay did not miss how Broughton's face went white as his gaze furiously raced back and forth between the burning staircase and him.

"Anais is trapped up there. I'm going to get her."

Garrett glared at him, "You cannot possibly manage the task on those stairs, Raeburn. It's unsafe. If you don't get yourself killed first, then you'll hurt her on the way down. No, the only way is from outside."

"No," Lindsay barked, already racing for the stairs. "It's thirty feet at least to the ground. She cannot possibly lower herself out the window from that height."

"The stairs will be gone by the time you find her. It will be the only way down."

Ignoring Broughton, he rushed up the stairs and saw that the flames were already licking their way up the door of Anais's chamber. "Anais," he shouted through cupped hands. But there was no sound save for the cracking and splintering of wood and the roar of the flames.

Shouldering through the door, he saw that he was in Anais's dressing room. Running over to the door that connected to her bedroom, he prayed he would find it unlocked. He was not so fortunate. By the time he was able to thrust it open with his shoulder, she was dangling outside the window, the gigot sleeve

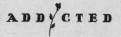

of her muslin wrapper caught on a wire hook in the curtain she had used to make her escape.

"It's all right, angel," he said, fear eating at him as he saw the delicate fabric begin to give way beneath her weight. Her fingers, blue and trembling, would not be able to sustain their hold on the curtain rope much longer. Her eyes were round as saucers as she slipped farther. There was no recognition in those familiar blue eyes, just terror, he realized as she looked blankly up at him.

"My wrapper...I'm pinned," she gasped, choking as the smoke filled the chamber.

"Don't look down, Anais. Here, reach for my hand. Trust me, love. I'll save you, Anais. Have faith in me."

She looked down at Garrett who was standing below, his arms outstretched. Lindsay knew what thoughts were running through her mind. Garrett could be trusted to catch her. Lindsay feared that he was just a specter she saw through the growing smoke. The distrust he saw in her eyes, the hurt and pain made him realize the depth of the destruction he had caused. Never before had she chosen Garrett over him, but it was clear to Lindsay that Anais was going to put her trust—and her life— in Garrett's waiting arms.

"Damn you, reach for my hand," he ordered, leaning out of the window as his shirtsleeves billowed in the wind. Terror was ruling him now. There was no way that Broughton could catch her from this height. His arms would not bear the weight or the force of her fall. She would be crushed and broken, and Lindsay could not stand to think that he would bear witness to it.

"Anais, reach for my hand. Do it," he commanded. *"Do it now!"*

And then he saw the delicate muslin cuff give way. Saw her eyes go round and her pale mouth part on a silent sound. "No!" he roared, heaving himself forward in a desperate bid to reach her, but she slipped through his fingers, and he was forced to watch her fall backward, her arms stretched out to him. Her hair, loose from its pins, floated about her. Her name was ripped from his soul as he saw his vision being born before his eyes.

He watched her, helpless, frozen in time as his gaze stayed locked on her wide, frightened eyes, and he swore he could almost hear her say, *You've done this to me, Lindsay. You've killed me.*

6

Racing out of the chamber, heart pounding, Lindsay lunged for the stairs, heedless of the flames that were busy devouring the wooden banister. Reaching the main level, he ran outside and froze on the step, his breathing coming in hard gasping pants. Before him, Broughton stood with legs braced wide and Anais draped in his arms, her long golden curls cascading over the sleeve of Garrett's black greatcoat.

For what felt like minutes Lindsay could say nothing as his gaze stayed riveted on Anais, waiting for some sign that she had made it through the ordeal unscathed. When he saw her chest rise and fall, he fought the urge to sink to his knees in relief. At that moment, he didn't care that it was Broughton she had chosen.

"I've got Darnby," Wallingford called from his horse, jolting Lindsay out of his stupor. Anais's father was in the saddle in front of Wallingford, barely conscious. Lindsay could see that the man had suffered a deep wound to his head and that it was bleeding heavily.

"I've sent one of the stable boys to Broughton's estate," Wallingford called over his shoulder as he took the reins in his gloved hand. "Broughton says Robert is in residence. I shall meet you back at Eden Park, then?"

Lindsay nodded, his gaze straying back to Broughton, who continued to hold Anais in his arms. Still he was unable to slow his breathing or the shaking of his hands. He felt like a damn weakling, but Christ, he had nearly lost her. The thought was more than he could endure.

"The carriage," Broughton yelled as he brushed away a mass of curls from Anais's face. "Somebody get me a bloody carriage—*now!*"

Something inside Lindsay snapped as he watched his friend bring Anais's body closer into his. "Give her to me," Lindsay begged as he ran down the steps. "I will take her on horseback and be there much quicker than the time it will take a carriage to make its way through the roads."

"You'll do no such thing. She's been ill—*gravely ill*. She can't be out in this weather. Jesus, she's turning blue as we speak," Broughton snarled, clutching her hard against his chest, shielding her from the biting wind and cold just as a loud crack exploded through the roof. Seconds later, the attic of the house caved in, sending sparks and flames jumping up into the sky that resembled black velvet.

"Now is not the time to argue, Broughton." Lindsay eyed the tower of flame that erupted through the opening that was once the attic. The wind was up, making a dangerous situation that much more. "For God's sake, the entire house is engulfed in flame. We have to get away from here, and get Anais to safety. Give her to me!" Lindsay was prying Anais, who was in the midst of a deep swoon, from Broughton's arms. "For the love of God, man, my stallion can have her at Eden Park in minutes."

Broughton looked down at Anais, who was still asleep in his arms. Lindsay didn't care for the possessive, familiar look in Broughton's eyes. Nor could he tamp down the fierce jealousy that pierced his breast. Bloody hell, Broughton was far too comfortable with a half-dressed Anais draped in his arms.

"Smith," Lindsay called, beckoning Darnby's groom. "Bring me the black Arabian."

The stallion was brought round. Lindsay gained the saddle swiftly before snatching a cloak from a maid who had run outside to check on her mistress.

"Give her to me, Broughton."

"What the devil do you think?" Broughton snapped, his angry expression glowed in the orange glare of the flames. "That you can come traipsing back here as though nothing has happened, like you're some goddamned knight in shining armor?"

"Give her to me," Lindsay thundered. "It's cold. She shouldn't be outside any longer than needed."

Broughton continued to clutch Anais protectively against his chest. "Do you actually think I'll sit back this time and allow you to hurt her once again?"

Lindsay narrowed his gaze. They were no longer talking about Anais's safety and getting her out of the cold. It was very clear that Broughton was staking a claim to the woman Lindsay loved. "I don't deny I was wrong. I don't deny that I have very little right to expect anything from Anais, but that is not the most pressing detail now. I've been on the roads in a carriage, Broughton. It's slow and icy, and frankly, treacherous. I can be there faster on horseback. Put aside your anger with me, to realize it's in Anais's best interest. After, if you want to call me out again and put a bullet in my chest, then be my guest. Right now, I'm thinking only of Anais."

With one last look at her face, Broughton reluctantly placed her into Lindsay's outstretched arms. "I'll be right behind you," he muttered, turning to his carriage, which had just been brought around.

Covering Anais from head to toe with the cloak, Lindsay sunk his stirrups into the Arabian's sides, tearing off into the blowing snow for the short ride to Eden Park.

By the time he reached his estate, the house was rife with disorder and shouting. His father, irritated and inebriated, was bellowing obscenities, irked to have his home descended upon by unwanted guests and in such a haphazard fashion.

"Bloody hell, boy, is that you?" his father grunted as Lindsay emerged through the door carrying Anais. "Or am I seeing visions?"

"It is me," Lindsay grumbled. "Where is Mother? I will need her help."

"Church, where else would she be on Christmas Eve?" his father snapped. "You might have sent word that you were coming home. Christ, you might have sent word that you were still alive."

"Might you lecture me later, Father?"

His father, who looked jaundiced and haggard, narrowed his eyes. "What the devil are you going to do with her?"

"Might I suggest the guest wing?" Worthing, their butler, announced.

"You may not," Lindsay grumbled. "She will stay in my

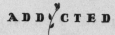
chamber until she is well enough. I want her close in case she requires anything. I will use my sitting room."

"That isn't wise, boy," his father bellowed. "Things have changed since you've been gone. I've a feeling your friend Broughton will raise hell when he finds out."

Lindsay stopped on the top riser, his gut turning to stone as he pivoted on the heel of his boot to glare down at his father. "Broughton can go to the devil. She is in my care now, and I will say what is to be done for her."

Ignoring his father's grunt, Lindsay stalked down the hall and flung open the door of his chamber. Placing her atop his bed, he pulled the cloak from her face, his fingers tracing her cheeks as he whispered for her to wake up.

"I'll tend to Lady Anais first."

It was Robert Middleton's voice. "In here, Middleton. She's breathing, but still in her swoon."

Robert passed him and turned to shut the door, but Lindsay stayed him. "Your brother said she's been ill. What the devil does he mean? She's never been sick a day in her life."

"Now is not the time, for God's sake," Robert snapped. "Many things have changed since you've left, things that are not of your concern. Now, get out of my way and let me attend Anais."

The door to the room slammed shut, and Lindsay had the horrible, gut-wrenching sensation that he'd just been shut out of Anais's life. As he stared at the glossed cherry wood, he saw himself on the outside, looking in. No longer was he welcome. Now, he was just a ghostly image standing on the peripheries, no longer wanted, no longer needed.

* * *

The door to Lindsay's sitting room clicked shut. Tension—taut and pulsing—filled the atmosphere. A year ago the three of them—Lindsay, Broughton and Wallingford—would have taken their leisure amongst the pillows and divans scattering the room.

Now they stood separate, shoulders squared, jaws locked. Striding to the window, Lindsay clutched the casement frame and watched the blinding whirl of snow on the ground below. His gaze immediately strayed to the left, searching for Lansdowne farm, to the scene of his duel with Broughton and the decimation of their friendship.

No honor had been gained in that duel. No satisfaction for the wrongs he had caused. He wondered if Broughton now wished he had not wasted his shot and instead, shot him dead, only to leave him bleeding on the damp grass.

God knew, men had been killed on the field of honor for less weighty trespasses than what he had done.

"She cannot possibly stay here," Broughton snapped as he started pacing, his wet boots grinding into the delicate threads of the gold-and-blue Persian carpet.

"Where would you have her go?" Wallingford asked, reaching inside his jacket for a cheroot. "Perhaps you haven't noticed, but there is a bloody blizzard outside and the girl is lying unconscious in the bed next door."

"It would be an insult for her to have to spend any length of time in this house. Not after what *he* has done to her."

"For the love of God, Broughton," Wallingford mumbled as he lit his smoke. "Where else would you have the girl go?"

"She could have come to The Lodge. Robert and his wife are

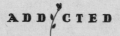

in residence for the winter. He could oversee her care from there. Margaret could have acted as chaperone."

Lindsay's fingers tightened on the wood. *Anais at Broughton's estate? Never.* He may no longer deserve a spot in her life, but he couldn't swallow the idea of Anais staying in Garrett's home. Christ, he'd rather be dead than to think of Anais together with Garrett. With anyone but him.

"Think of the scandal, Broughton. No one will bat an eye at the Darnbys staying with the Marquis of Weatherby. Everyone in the county knows of the longstanding friendship between Anais's father and Raeburn's mother. But to have Anais staying with you, while her parents are with the Weatherbys—it just wouldn't work, you must see that."

"And what is a bit of scandal to you, Wallingford? It is not as though you've ever batted a moral eye before," Broughton barked.

Wallingford arched a mocking brow. "So— " he shrugged "—I have the morals of a tomcat. Everyone knows of my proclivities. I make no secret of them. As willing as I am to discuss my numerous affairs, I don't think that is really the issue here. Unless, of course, you wish to follow in my boot steps."

"Damn you, Wallingford! You think this is amusing? While you've been off traipsing through Europe and the East, whoring and drinking and doing God knows what, things have changed since you and *he* decided to indulge in your vices."

"I see, so you and Anais have become so intimate in the past months that the villagers would think nothing of her residing with you?"

Lindsay's entire body tightened. He did not want to hear

Broughton's answer. He did not want to think of Anais in Broughton's bed.

"Why were you not at church, Broughton, with the rest of your family? It was apparent from what I saw that Anais was not dressed for entertaining. What had you at the Darnbys' when Anais was dressed and ready for bed?" Wallingford inquired. Lindsay silently thanked his friend for asking the very same question Lindsay wanted answered.

"Since when do I need to answer to you?"

Wallingford shrugged. "It's the elephant in the room. Curious minds, and all that."

"If it was your concern, I'd tell you. But since it's not, I'll keep to my own council. I fail to see what is so damned amusing, Wallingford," Broughton muttered as he paced the width of the room.

Wallingford was grinning. "Christ sakes, Broughton, you're being a prig. Keep your council, then. I don't give a damn, but realize that for Anais's reputation, it is far more logical for her and her family to stay here."

"He betrayed her!" Lindsay caught Broughton's gaze in the glass. "He betrayed *me*."

"Do you actually think he was the first?" Wallingford asked, his lips curving into a mirthless smile. "I will not believe you are that naive. Blinded by righteousness, perhaps, but not green."

"Explain."

"Rebecca Thomas." Wallingford smiled as he blew a circle of smoke into the air from the cheroot he had just lit. "Do you think Raeburn was the first man she attempted to seduce?" Broughton sputtered and curled his fingers into fists. "Oh, come now,

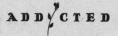

Broughton, don't play the Prince Valiant with me. You know as well as I what sort of woman Rebecca is. You told me yourself the day before you found her with Raeburn that you were not certain she was the one for you. You will recall I told you that you were correct in assuming she was not the sort of female you would want as your countess or the mother of your children."

"What are you saying?"

Wallingford made a grunt of disgust and reached for his tumbler. "I'm saying that she wanted an heir to a dukedom before she ever wanted an earl."

Broughton reeled on his heels. "I do not believe you."

Wallingford shrugged. "Believe what you want, but she came to me a week before she drugged and seduced Raeburn. She was a grasping, manipulative creature and she was willing to bed your friends for the promise of a superior title. She was plotting and waiting, willing to spread her thighs in the hope of one day being a duchess or—" Wallingford inclined his head toward the window where Lindsay stood "—a marchioness."

"Did you sleep with her? Jesus, you did, didn't you? You can never keep your prick in your trousers."

"What man can when a woman is so damn eager for it?" Wallingford taunted.

"Did you know she had set her designs on Raeburn? Good God, were you aware that she was traipsing about that pleasure den of yours pretending she was a servant?"

"I was as ignorant of that as you, Broughton. She was disguised, and if you will recall, I was enjoying the delightful hand of a most skilled courtesan. In that, I may assure you, I did not keep my prick in my trousers."

"You don't give a damn about anything, most certainly not women."

"Not if that woman is Rebecca Thomas," Wallingford growled. "I told her what I thought of her. I informed her she was a conniving slut. She no longer found me to her liking. Apparently she took umbrage at my honesty. She left before I could get my prick out of my trousers," Wallingford jeered.

Lindsay continued to keep his back to his friends, preferring to watch the exchange from the window, which acted like a mirror. He did not trust himself to confront Broughton. He did not understand the emotions coursing within him. He was not a coward, nor was he ashamed to meet his friend. It was something more. It was beyond jealousy what he was feeling.

The feeling he had lost everything that had ever mattered to him began to suck him under. All he could think about was Anais in the next room and how she had blindly thrown herself into Garrett's arms. The pain that knowledge caused him was savage, and the urge to light up his bamboo pipe and smoke until he could feel nothing but numbness began to fire at the base of his brain.

But he fought it, the urge to succumb to his weakness. It was Anais he needed to think about. Anais who needed him. He had failed her that night at Wallingford's. He had not returned from Constantinople only to fail her again.

"I don't give a damn about Rebecca," Broughton muttered, running his hands through his hair. "It's Anais I care about. Raeburn vowed never to hurt her and he went out and did such a thing not half an hour after giving me his word."

"Then you should have put a bullet through him when you had the chance instead of firing it into the air and wasting a per-

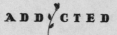

fectly good shot," Wallingford said with an air of superior boredom. "Then we would not be quarreling over where the girl belongs and whose bed she should be lying in."

"You think you can ride back here and pick up where you left off, Raeburn?" Broughton thundered as he confronted him at the window. "You think that nothing has changed since you left? Well, I assure you, a great many things have changed. I shall not allow you to ruin someone as good as Anais."

"Who can find a virtuous woman? For her price is far above rubies," Wallingford mumbled.

"How dare you! Anais *is* a virtuous woman."

"Really?"

"I assure you, *sir,* Anais is quite above the sort of woman you deign to entertain."

"Oh, I entertain any sort of woman, as you very well know," Wallingford said with a leer. "One quim is the same as any other. The Haymarket whore, the expensive courtesan, the merry widow and the unhappy wife—not a virtuous one in the lot. They're all only good for one thing, and it isn't a damn bit virtuous, I assure you."

"Enough," Lindsay growled as he rubbed his neck. "Wallingford, as much as I appreciate you picking up the gauntlet, I am fully able to defend myself against any accusations our dear friend might wish to cast. Broughton, you may address your concerns to me—man to man. Wallingford need not be our intermediary."

The dressing-room door opened and Robert poked his head in. "Enough of the bellowing. It is time to put the past behind you, at least for tonight."

"How is she?" Lindsay asked, no longer caring about the quarrel between himself and Broughton.

"Cold. And her heart is beating very slowly. We must get her warmed."

"Anything. Whatever you need."

"Of course," Broughton said, glaring at Lindsay. "Anything you ask."

"I shall need someone to get into bed with her. It is the fastest way to restore warmth. A bath will take too long, not to mention it will expose her to the cold air, which will, in turn, make her colder. Warming pans are inefficient, not to mention they cool precipitously. I'm using the pans now, but they are not proving even remotely effective. What she needs is the warmth that flesh and blood provide. Her heart cannot afford the stress—it's too weak."

All three stared at Robert as if he'd lost his mind.

"Good God, is that what they've taught you in Edinburgh?" Wallingford chuckled. "I fear I should have listened to my father, after all, when he told me to quit chasing skirts and see to putting my head to my studies. I could have then gone to medical school and hopped into bed with scores of naked women, and all in the name of medical science."

"It is the science of physics, to be precise. It is the most expedient manner in which to heat a body. What I am asking for is not sexual," Middleton snapped. "I am merely asking for a body to supply the girl with heat while I attempt to see to her father. Nothing more sinister than that."

"I will do it," Broughton muttered. Already he had discarded his jacket and was in the process of tearing off his cravat.

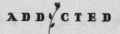

"No, *I* will." Lindsay felt the tension in the room tighten. He had no right to crawl into bed with Anais—not after what he had put her through. But damn it, he would not have Broughton crawling into bed—*his* bed, with Anais.

"I would prefer it if the three of you raced back to the village and retrieved her mother and sister from church. Anais is calling for her and Ann will no doubt be anxious to aid me in her sister's care."

"Let Wallingford and Raeburn go," Broughton mumbled while he removed his cuff links. "I will see to Anais while they are bringing her sister to her. If she is in danger it is not prudent to put off what might save her. I will not have any treatment delayed only to have something happen to her, do you understand me, Robert?"

A silent warning passed between them and Lindsay felt his senses sharpen. There was a shared confidence there, and he didn't like it. Didn't like it any more than Broughton's easy agreement to get into bed with her.

"Come, brother. I'm not going to allow any one of you to do such a thing. The only person to see the job through shall be Lady Ann. You will not argue further, Garrett," Robert warned his older brother when Broughton frowned deeply. "You will ride into the village with Wallingford. Lord Raeburn shall be kept far away from my patient, I assure you."

Lindsay glared at Robert. Who was he to try to prevent him from seeing Anais?

"If he hurts her further I will show him what hell is truly like," Broughton muttered as he swung open the chamber door and walked into the hallway.

"He has already seen hell," Wallingford said in answer. "He has been living in it for the past ten months. I don't believe there is anything more you can show him."

"You're wrong." Broughton shot a menacing glare at him from over his shoulder. "There is more than even he can imagine."

"You will excuse me, Lord Raeburn," Robert Middleton murmured. "But I must return to my patient."

"Middleton," Lindsay asked, forcing aside his scrambled thoughts. "You mentioned her heart. What has happened?"

"I'm not at liberty to say."

"We are friends. You can tell me."

"Things have changed since you've been gone, Raeburn. That is all I am prepared to say to you. You are not her husband, nor even her intended. I owe you nothing in the way of explanations."

Lindsay reached for Robert's arm, preventing the doctor's departure. "I will accept all fault for what has happened. But I will not allow anyone to think it was because I intended to deliberately hurt Anais or Broughton. I ask because I care, Middleton. Am I not even allowed that? Am I so undeserving that I should be kept in the dark about Anais and her illness? I love her," Lindsay couldn't help but say. "Seeing her like this, knowing she's ill cuts me like a knife."

"Then perhaps you shouldn't have left."

Lindsay struggled for a comeback just as Middleton brushed Lindsay's hand off his shirtsleeve.

"She has a weak heart. Such stress as she has suffered this night might very well set her recovery back."

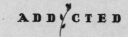

"What do you mean a weak heart?"

"Her condition is delicate," Robert said, but he steadfastly avoided his gaze. "And that is all I'm prepared to say on the matter."

The door to the bedroom closed once again, leaving Lindsay alone in his sitting room. Bloody hell, what the devil was happening here? Something was afoot, and he was not going to rest until he discovered what secrets the doctor shared with Anais.

Anais, he thought as he gazed at the connecting door that kept him out, *how am I ever going to get you back?*

7

Smoke, warm and scented, misted along Lindsay's mouth and cheeks, transporting him to a place where nothing mattered—where he felt nothing but numbness.

Inhaling the curling vapors, he awaited the pleasure that would soon allow him to leave this world and the relentless desire he had for Anais behind.

It was in this world where he was at peace and, he feared, in a state of irredeemable despair. For he needed to be without sensation. He could not withstand the torture of feeling, of needing and never having.

To feel was hell. To be numb, heaven. It had been this way for him since he had left England on his fruitless search for Anais. Everything always came back to this, to opium and Anais.

Closing his eyes, Lindsay waited for the physical lust to abate—it always did when his mistress took over. While awaiting the pleasure of the opium, Lindsay focused on the slowing of his blood and the sleep that would free him from the pitfalls of his mind.

The feeling did not come. He was still awake. Still feeling. Still aching.

Drawing the smoke into his lungs, he took the heavenly demon deep into himself and exhaled with slow precision, watching the smoke twine up like clawing fingers, only to disappear in the light of the flickering candle. He had not been able to resist the lure of his mistress or the hours of pleasure and escape she gave him. He had sought her out tonight, needing her skill, hating her for the power she held over him. While in Constantinople he had succumbed to her charms, allowing her to enchain him with a beauty that was at once so evocative, yet soul stealing.

He was dependent now. While in the throes of the red smoke, he could admit the horrible truth. He was as dependent upon opium as he was food and air.

While lucid, he could not bring himself to admit that terrible truth, that weakness in his character. He denied his dependence, even as his mind fired and throbbed with the need for more, even while his body cried out in pain he denied he needed it. He always told himself he could stop, whenever he wished, even as he was rolling the black gum between his fingers and placing the paste on the scales. Even as the anticipation coursed through him as the flame from the spirit lamp flickered to life, heating the opium until those glorious gray vapors began to rise from the pipe. Even then, with the eagerness ruling him, he told himself he didn't need the drug.

It had always only been a lark to him. Used in hours of idleness with his friends. He was a dabbler, he told himself as he lay back on his cushions and luxuriated in the wait for that first inhalation of smoke.

It was denial, right up until that very moment when the opium would slow his blood and make his eyes heavy. In that moment, when his mind fractured from his body, he no longer denied the call of the opium. The pleasure it gave was like nothing he had ever known. To feel…nothing was a peace unto itself. That peace he could not deny.

Even now, inhaling the smoke from his favorite pipe, he told himself he could stop, if for nothing else but another chance to make everything right with Anais.

What a bloody farce, for he was inhaling another cloud of the smoke as he told himself that, knowing it for a lie.

He hated doing this, knowing Anais was lying in the next room. Hated the thought of her seeing him like this. Shame had never been a part of smoking opium for him before. He had always thought it decadent, mystical, erotic to be in a den with naked bodies and dreamy smokers. It had never been sordid. Dirty. Yet he felt soiled and guilty tonight smoking with Anais so close to him.

But you need me, the vapors seemed to whisper in a voice that drew him in. *You need me far more than you need her.*

It sickened Lindsay to admit it, but it was the truth. He needed to feel the opium in his veins. Yes, he needed the opium, but he wanted Anais. Wanted her more than opium.

You cannot have both.

He shut out the voice with another slow draw on the bamboo pipe. He didn't want to dwell on those thoughts. He didn't want to feel tonight. Didn't want to think.

The door in the next room closed, jarring his body into alertness. The opium, for the time being, was forgotten, his pipe

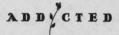

resting on the silver tray that held the items of his ritual. His gaze found the door and he imagined Anais asleep in his bed.

Fleetingly he wondered if Robert Middleton had finally left Anais's bedside. Robert had been a constant guardian to her throughout the evening. Because of that, Lindsay had found himself pacing his dressing room like a caged beast. More than once he had pressed his ear to the door, listening for sounds, half expecting to hear Broughton's deep voice rumbling above Robert's. But Garrett had not returned with Wallingford and the Darnby women. Lindsay wasn't sure what he felt more, surprise or relief.

His own mother had accompanied Lady Darnby and Ann home, and she had immediately sought him out. He had not relished the uproar that had ensued when his mother discovered he had returned from his absence. He hadn't wanted the fussing that came with her affection. But his mother had insisted that she settle the Darnbys and their servants into the house and that he join her in the salon once their guests had settled for the night.

After so long an absence, he had indulged his mother. He loved her, but he could not keep from glancing up at the staircase, half expecting to see Anais gliding down the steps in her shimmering gauze wrapper. His mother had known, of course, about his feelings for Anais. But what his mother didn't realize was that nothing had turned out as he had planned. Nor did she know that he'd buggered it up by his own excesses. He had destroyed Anais's faith in him. The last thing he wanted to do was pull the veil from his mother's eyes as he had from Anais's.

Perhaps he was just like his father. What if he had found

something other than alcohol to lean on when he was confused or wishing to escape the pressures of his world? He supposed that did make him just like his father, for those were the reasons his father had sought solace in the bottom of a brandy decanter—escape.

Sighing, he closed his eyes and listened to the soft ticking of the clock that sat upon his writing desk. It had been hours since the house had settled and Lord Darnby's wounds had been dressed. Hours since he had lain in this room, ignoring his mother's pleas that he take one of the other chambers. He had told her he was too tired and the silk cushions and the divan would provide him with the rest he needed. But the truth was, he wanted to be close to Anais.

Listening in the quiet, he tried to think of anything other than Anais lying in bed—*his bed*. He knew he was being a pathetic wretch internalizing all this angst and acting like a beardless boy after losing his first crush. He should have listened to Wallingford when he had given him advice. *Find yourself a woman, Raeburn. Willing, available flesh is the best cure for your affliction.*

He had tried, despite the sickness that settled in his stomach whenever he touched his mouth to another. But those women never tasted right, never felt the way he wanted them to feel beneath his hands. He had left more than one Turkish beauty bewildered and unsatisfied during his time in Constantinople.

There was no other woman for him. No other could replace her in his heart. No other woman came close to Anais.

The muffled sound of the bedroom door opening and closing once again made his body stiffen, knowing it was likely Ann had left the chamber this time. His suspicions were confirmed when

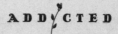

he heard Ann and Middleton whispering in the hall outside his
sitting room. Middleton was ushering Ann to her own chamber.
It seemed that the good doctor was confident his patient was
safe enough to spend the night alone.

Alone. Hunger uncurled in Lindsay's belly and he rose from
the cushions and walked silently, if not a touch unsteadily, to the
connecting door. Reaching for the knob, he twisted it and let
himself inside the room. A fire burned low in the hearth, casting
peach-colored shadows on the walls. He stood by the bed and
felt his chest grow tight when he saw Anais curled up in a ball,
her face so white he was hardly able to discern where the sheets
left off and her skin began.

As if in a trance, he continued to watch her sleeping as he
shrugged out of his jacket, then reached for his cravat. Her
breathing was shallow. He counted the movements of the
blanket and knew that she was breathing slow, but easy.

He had tried his best to keep her warm on the ride to his
estate, but not even the thick flannel nightgown and the heavy
wool blanket had been enough to protect her from the snow and
wind. He had done everything he could think of, even covering
her with his own cape, but the wind had whipped about them,
ruthlessly penetrating the layers meant to protect her.

He should have done more to care for her. Perhaps he should
have listened to Broughton's command that he wait for the carriage, but damn it, he hadn't been thinking straight. The only
thing he had thought of was saving Anais.

Lindsay stood there studying her, his eyes unblinking,
drinking in every facet of her white skin, every golden curl that
lay in disarray on his pillow. She was where she belonged. In his

bed. But she should not be pale and cold. She should be warm and aroused—*restless*—her legs tangling in the sheets while she watched him disrobe for her. She should be studying him hungrily with bright sensual eyes as he drew out the minutes before he would come and join her in bed.

He wondered if she would have raised herself on her knees and reached for him, hastily helping him disrobe. Or would she have smiled secretly and allowed her gaze to rove along his body, taking in his torso and waist as he pulled his shirt over his shoulders. Would those shining eyes have boldly slid down his naked body and fixed on his cock? Would she have looked away in shyness, or would she have reached out to him and captured him in her hand, *her mouth?*

He closed his eyes, imagining such a welcome. His fingers curled into fists at his sides as he imagined what she would look like lying beneath him, his ring glinting on her finger while she traced her fingertips along his chest.

Hearing her whimper in her sleep, Lindsay strolled to the door and locked it, then removed the key. The candle flame blew out when the door closed, and he used the shaft of silvery moonlight filtering in from the window to guide him to the side of the bed. Pulling his shirt over his shoulders, he let it drop silently to the floor. Reaching for his trousers, he freed the buttons, feeling his shaft fill as it escaped the confines of the wool.

His mind was filled with innocent images of providing Anais with heat. His body, on the other hand, was preparing itself for the feel of Anais's supple curves against him. He was a man. He had needs. He could not hide those needs—needs that not even

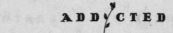

the opium could take away from him. Perhaps his mistress had robbed his body of its sex other times, but never when Anais was near him. When she was close, nothing could dampen his ardor.

Naked, he reached for the blankets and placed his leg on the mattress. It creaked beneath his weight. His gaze shot up and he saw that she still slept. He did not want to awaken her. He wanted her lying beside him, weak and still so that he could smell her and wrap his arms about her.

With a moan she brought her knees up to her belly, burrowing her chin into the blankets. He scoured her hair, rumpled against the pillow, concealing her unnaturally pale face. He did not dare to look beneath the covers. If he stole a glance he knew he would not be strong enough to resist her. Temptation was something he found so difficult to defy, especially when it was Anais offering it.

Swallowing hard, he lay on his side and allowed his hand and arm to snake beneath the covers. His fingers hesitated only briefly above her shoulder before they lightly grazed her alabaster flesh. The thick flannel gown she wore had slipped down, leaving her upper arms exposed. She was so cold. So still. Suddenly he could not stop himself, he reached for her and placed his arm along her breasts, moving her so that her back met his chest. He flinched at the coldness of her body as it curled into his. Even through the flannel he felt the chill that gripped her.

Holding her tighter, he squeezed his forearm into her breasts, wrapping his thigh along her legs while he pressed his face into her hair and smelled her—country flowers and skin. Anais's scent.

She moaned, a weak, husky sound that came from the depths of her chest. He felt the vibrations of it against his arm. Fitting his body even tighter around hers, his erection swelled and his scrotum drew up in pleasured agony as his body absorbed the chill from hers. He ignored the urgings of his cock, focusing instead on supplying her with the warmth she needed.

Turning suddenly in his arms, Anais crushed her breasts against his chest and wrapped her cold arms along his waist, seeking more of his warmth. It felt so damned right to hold her like this, as if they were man and wife and had shared the same bed for years. But he knew that it was not the right thing to be in bed with her. He had just smoked opium, something he had never done before coming to her. He had never wanted to be with her while the opium ruled him, had never wanted to love her body while his mistress swam in his veins. Excluding that extraordinary lapse in judgment the night at Wallingford's, Lindsay had never come to Anais high on opium.

Besides, even if he had refrained from smoking, Anais was not aware of what she was doing. She only craved the heat he could provide.

Christ, she was such sweet torment. The way her belly cushioned his erection—an erection that was painfully engorged and throbbing was a pleasure his body had not experienced since that night in the stables with her.

How many times had he thought of that night? How many other nights had he dreamed of?

Her flesh began to warm beneath his hands and he pressed the side of his face to her chest, listening to the dull thudding of her heart. His mouth was so close to her nipple, and he

squeezed his eyes shut, blocking out the image of his tongue flicking it.

"I need you," he whispered, unable to silence the words. "Will you ever need me again? Will you ever see what sort of man I could be for you?" he asked, giving voice to the fears he had harbored for months.

"You're just a dream," she mumbled sleepily. "This isn't real."

He lifted his face and looked down into her sleeping face. He brought her closer to him, his cock pressing impatiently into her soft belly. The reality of the hardness—he was certain—would awaken her. But it did not. Instead, she snuggled closer and pressed her cheek against his neck. He could feel the moist heat from her mouth as he curled her hair around his hand, trying to fight the physical need he felt swimming in his veins.

He groaned softly. Losing the war against his honor, he brought her face up from his neck. She did not open her eyes, but her lips parted as if she were waiting for the touch of his mouth against hers.

He should not be doing this. He had taken her virginity, then had broken her heart. They needed to talk, there was so much to be explained, so many things to be said, but he needed *her*, as well. He was not strong enough to resist her. Not the way she was now, sleepy and disoriented, soft and supple, the faint arousal of her sex drifting up between their bodies and the sheets.

"Do you ever think of me?" she asked sleepily.

He watched her lashes flutter, then slowly lift. Her gaze was unfocused. It would be so damn easy to take advantage of her, of the situation he now found himself in. But it would be dishonorable. He had already dishonored her once before.

"Do you ever dream of me, Lindsay?"

He traced her lips with the pad of his finger. "Every day," he whispered against her mouth. "Every night."

He kissed her, a slow, savoring kiss with an open mouth that captured her lips. She softened and placed her palms on his chest. *Stop,* his mind called, but he could not. He could not end something that felt this right.

She opened her mouth, enticing him to possess her and he submitted to her, sliding his tongue into her mouth and rubbing it against hers. A kiss that had been slow and loving was now frantic and erotic.

She mewled, he clutched her hair in his hand, angling her head so that he could penetrate the depths of her mouth. She breathed deep and he stole her breath, pressing her back so that she was lying beneath him. His hand, which had come free of her hair, was sliding down the smooth column of her neck toward her breast.

Tearing his mouth from hers, he set his lips to her throat at the same moment he felt her heart begin to pump faster beneath his palm. His fingers slid down the crest of her full breast so that he could cup her. He was desperate now, too far gone with passion.

"Love me, Anais." He captured her mouth, kissing her hungrily as he cupped and squeezed her breast. It was full and much heavier than he remembered and so perfect for what he wanted to do with her. Shifting his palm so that her nipple grazed the center of his hand Lindsay watched her as she arched beneath him, enjoying the sensation of having her nipple teased. She was sensitive, and he repeated the action, slowly arousing her until the nipple had furled.

He moved away from her in order to slide down her body. His own was shaking with sexual need, but she reached for him, her nails digging into his shoulders.

"Don't leave me," she cried out. "Don't end this dream."

"I won't ever leave you again," he said against her silken navel that was covered by her nightgown. Her belly contracted as the warmth of his breath penetrated the fibers. Setting his mouth to her, he kissed, then sucked at the rounded mound as he reached for the hem of her night rail that had ridden up to her thighs.

He paid homage to her belly, just as he told himself he would. He mouthed her, kissed her, nipped at the tender skin and felt it quiver in pleasure. Her belly was lush, rounded, tempting him to imagine how soft it would feel beneath him. His hand stroked her thigh while he rubbed his erection along the tops of them until he could feel the silky hair of her mound tickle his cock. He felt the hot, silky length of her coat his cock and he pressed his eyes shut, struggling for control, fighting the urge to sink himself between her lush thighs.

In the still functioning part of his mind he knew that he was bringing disaster upon himself. With the light of morning his actions would cease to be pleasurable. In the morning he would be the defiler once again. Lindsay knew that he could not make love to her like this—when she was not fully awake. But he couldn't stop touching her. She needed release if the restlessness of her body beneath him was any indication. And God, how he needed release. And she was so wet. Her nipples hard, pointed little buds, and her breaths were aroused pants that told him she needed to feel passion.

He pressed the head of his erection between her swollen sex

and her breath got caught up in a husky pant. He looked up at her, her neck arched back, her swollen mouth parted in ecstasy. He was about to spread her thighs with his knee when suddenly they fell open and he felt her sex part and capture him. He looked down then, saw his hand—tanned from the hot Turkish sun—between her white thighs. He smelled her arousal. His finger sought her opening and he ran his fingertip along the edge of it, teasing her with the lightness of his touch, with the possibility that he might enter her with his finger, or possibly two. Could she accept three?

He studied her sex as he spread her wide, seeing that she was glistening and her clitoris was swollen and pink. It was begging to be tongued and worked with his eager fingers. He was aching to oblige her.

Her body was ready. He felt it. Could almost taste it. And then he lowered his mouth and flicked his tongue along the erect little nubbin and listened to her wanton moan. He placed his fingers so that they ran along the edge of her clitoris and then he stroked her, running his fingers along the raised bud while he swirled his tongue in a slow circle that made her buck wildly beneath him.

So beautiful. So perfect. He studied the way his fingers glistened in the folds of her wet, silken sex as he brought her higher and higher. What a gorgeous little cunt she had, too gorgeous not to taste once again.

Grasping handfuls of his hair, she held him to her and she came for him so easily he thought he might have imagined it until he tasted her. He plunged his tongue into her quim and sucked until he tasted more, until she was gasping and shaking and he

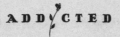

felt the vibration of her clitoris beneath his fingertip. He felt the
first drops of his seed begin to seep out from the swollen head.
With a growl, he held his cock in his hand, pressing it against
her pulsing clitoris until he could stand the torture no longer.
Needing to find release, he stroked himself until he came,
pouring his seed on her silken belly while he sucked the crest
of her breast in an attempt to muffle the sounds of his shatter-
ing climax.

Slowly he came to his senses as his body accustomed itself to
the languor of orgasm. He held her close, breathing hard against
her breast while he slowly laved the little mark he had created with
his mouth. She soothed him with her gentle fingers in his hair.

"It's never felt this real—my dreams," she clarified in a whisper. "I've never felt so complete after dreaming of you. Garrett
must never learn of my dreams," she murmured in a broken
whisper as she clutched him to her. "Never..."

No, he could not have heard her say Broughton's name. Not
while she was lying with him. She could not be thinking of
Broughton. It was *him* she had shared her body with. It was *him*
in bed with her.

Much has changed since you have left...

Broughton's words ran through his head and he wondered just
how much had changed. Was Anais now Broughton's lover? He
thought of the way she had willingly allowed herself to fall into
Broughton's arms—implicit trust. He had seen the faith in her
eyes when she'd looked down to see Broughton waiting for her,
his arms outstretched. He remembered the wariness in her eyes
as she had looked up at him. She had not reached for his hand.
She had not trusted him.

He looked away from her face and saw a brown bottle and spoon that lay atop her night table. Laudanum. His gaze returned to hers. She was once again asleep. How had he mistaken the glistening in her eyes for sleep and sensuality? Awareness had not rendered her eyes glistening—laudanum had. Damn it, she truly would think that she had dreamed what happened this night if she even recalled it in the morning. Perhaps she would even attribute it to Broughton, this completion she felt swimming in her veins.

Flinging back the blankets, Lindsay untangled his limbs from hers, wondering if he would ever feel warmth in his body again, or would he forever be cursed with the numb coldness that had settled in his veins when he realized that Anais might very well be lost to him.

He scoffed at the absurdity of his thoughts. For nearly a year he had been consumed with the desire to be numb, until now, until he had felt his body come alive with Anais.

8

Anais squinted against the bright beam of sunshine that bathed her cheeks with warmth. The mattress sagged with the weight of the person beside her. Tension made her jump as she felt her nightgown being raised, felt the slow rise of the hem slide along her calves and shins, then over her knees to rest along her thighs. In a bid to forget what was happening, she lifted her face to the warm sunbeams and pretended she was anyplace but there.

"Part your legs, and try to relax. It may be uncomfortable at first, but I will do what I can to lessen the pain."

Swallowing hard, Anais nodded and squeezed her eyelids firmly together until she could see tiny bright floating sparks. Her breathing slowed and she tried to let her body go limp, tried to think of something other than the fact that Robert Middleton was examining her most intimately.

After several minutes, the mattress creaked again, even louder than before. Anais felt his weight shift away from her. The sheet—cold and smooth—slid against her skin, exposing her thigh. He righted it so that she was covered and she felt the mattress lift as he left the bed.

The sound of water being poured in a basin reached her ears and she opened her eyes, seeing that Robert's back was to her as he busily washed his hands. Taking a cloth, he dried them, then tossed the towel onto the commode before turning to face her.

"You understand that I cannot say, with any reasonable certainty, what damage has occurred?"

"Yes, I understand."

"The opening to the womb is closed and there doesn't seem to be any further bleeding, which greatly pleases me—I was most worried about the bleeding—it lasted too long before. Your heart can not afford to lose more blood. But only time will tell us what the future holds."

"Must I still eat the kidneys and the rare beef? I truly cannot abide them. I feel ill just thinking about having to endure another meal of it."

"I'm afraid you must, for a few more months, at least. You bled significantly, Anais. You must restore the humors in your body. Your heart must have rich blood."

She nodded and swept her gaze from the window to him. "Of course, you are right," she said with a smile. "I will take your advice. Tell me," she murmured as Robert set his stethoscope to her breast, "did you speak of any of this to Garrett?"

"He is my brother," he said quietly as he pressed his ear to the tube where he could hear her heart beating. "He has been consumed with worry. Under the circumstances, I felt I needed to tell him. You are not cross with me, are you?"

"No, of course not." She looked away so that Robert could not see the deceit in her eyes. For some unfathomable reason she was miffed that Robert had discussed her with Garrett. But why? Was it because she worried that perhaps Garrett still held out some measure of hope? Did these past months spent with Garrett entitle him to know her most personal business?

Witch, she chastised. Garrett had been nothing but kind and compassionate since Lindsay's betrayal. Their friendship had grown and deepened and she had relied on him in the past months more than she had relied on anyone in her life. What a heartless soul she was to feel uncharitable toward him now. How could she when he had sacrificed so much for her?

Lindsay.... The answer came to her in the blink of an eye. Would she be feeling any of these terrible emotions—thinking any of these cruel thoughts if he had not arrived home? She stirred beneath the sheets, her body becoming restless and warm. She had experienced such vivid dreams about him last night. She remembered seeing him standing inside her room, his hand outstretched to her as he implored her to reach for him, to trust him. She had wanted to trust him, had wanted so desperately to believe in him like she had before, but then she saw Garrett, standing below her dangling feet, waiting for her and she knew which man she could trust with her safety. That vision had been replaced by the one with Lindsay in her bed, touching her with beautiful hands and a hungry mouth. It had not been Garrett she had imagined loving her body, but Lindsay. It was always only ever Lindsay.

When she had awakened from her dream, it was to find her maid, Louisa, sitting beside her, and to discover that she was not in her own bed, but that of Lindsay's. Her house was gone, taken by the fire. She and her family were now dependent upon Lindsay's family for shelter and the necessities of life.

Lindsay, Louisa had informed Anais while she brushed her hair, had taken the servants under his wing, finding them shelter and seeing that they were fed. He had even gone so far as to order up numerous carriages to take the servants to their families for the holidays. The others, who had elected to stay on, and the ones who had no other family, he found shelter for in the available rooms in the servants' quarters.

"He is a very good man," Louisa had said, beaming. "He offered me a carriage and a few shillings, but I could not accept, miss. My place is here by you. I only wish you had allowed me to travel with you to France. I might have been able to prevent you from becoming ill."

Anais had allowed Louisa to chatter on. Her sweet Yorkshire accent had filled her mind, driving out thoughts of Lindsay and the very great dilemma she now found herself in.

"Garrett is waiting outside the door, Anais," Robert announced as he folded his instrument and placed it in his bag. "Shall I bring him in—for just a moment? He hasn't slept all night for worrying about you."

Anais cleared her head of the discussion with her maid. "Please."

Without preamble, Robert strolled to the door and Garrett rushed in, looking tired and tense. "How are you?" he asked, coming to the side of the bed and sitting down beside her. He reached for her hands and clasped them in his, squeezing them tightly. "My God, all I was able to see whenever I closed my eyes was the image of you falling from that window."

Anais placed a caring hand on the side of his face and ran the tip of her finger along the scar of his top lip. "I'm completely well, Garrett. I have heard that it is to you I owe my thanks."

He flushed and squeezed her hands in both of his before kissing the tips of her fingers. "No, say nothing of that. But— *my God*—" he said in a rush before clutching her about her shoulders so that he was embracing her tightly while pressing small kisses along her temple. "You gave me a fright, Anais. I've still not recovered from it."

"I'm well."

He set her back and looked at her while he held her hands. "You're still pale, but you have more color to your cheeks than before. Are you positive you're well? Robert," he said, turning to his brother. "You're certain that you've thoroughly examined her? You've thought of everything—checked everything?"

"I have."

Garrett met her gaze and she saw a strange emotion flicker in his brown eyes. It was almost…she dared not say the word, but it crept into her consciousness anyway…*hopeful*.

"I am very glad. I shudder to think about what might have happened if I had not decided to come by before church to check on you. I had to see you, Anais, to make certain there was nothing you needed. I thought…well, that is, I thought perhaps you might have need of me."

Anais squirmed beneath that forthright gaze, hating herself for the dream she had last night. As much as she wanted to believe she was not such a weak creature or at the mercy of her own sexual needs, she knew she could not deny the truth. Not with the actions of her past confronting her. She had been weak, and once again, it had been Lindsay who had stripped away her self-control. Even her dreams were not her own. They, along with her memories, belonged to Lindsay. And try as she might to forget him, she couldn't.

"The house is gone, you know. Burnt to the ground. Only the outbuildings survived. Weatherby's stables are large enough to accommodate most of the horses. I had Lady brought here. I knew you would not want to be without her."

How very thoughtful he was. Anais wondered why she could not bring herself to admit that any woman with half an ounce of sense would jump at the chance to accept this man's marriage proposal.

"I hope you do not find me presumptuous, but with your father indisposed and your mother unable to...well, I think you understand your mother's failings. I don't need to speak of them, do I? Well, someone needed to take charge, and as we've become...close," he said awkwardly. "Well, I thought it should be me."

He was so very good at taking up the reins of command. He was a good man, a handsome man. *Why, why, why* could she not bring herself to accept his suit? Why must she keep him waiting for an answer? Why was she being deliberately cruel to him? She had accepted what he'd offered readily enough, why now could she not give him what he needed?

"I'm not sure if they've told you yet, but Raeburn has returned. He's here in the house, Anais."

"Louisa told me. She says that he's been organizing transportation for the staff who are desirous to go home for the holidays."

Mouth grim, Garrett nodded. "I am afraid you shall have to

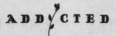

stay here at Eden Park with your family. Of course, I should prefer you to be in my home, but until…" He swallowed and looked to see where his brother was. *"If,"* he whispered for her ears only, "you agree to wed me, then it might be seen in a better light—with proper chaperones, of course—for you to reside with me. Until then, and given your father's friendship with Lady Weatherby, it is reasonable that you would stay here until your father's health improves and new accommodations can be found until the house is rebuilt."

"Of course," she replied, fearing he was going to press for an answer.

"We will need to discuss matters. We cannot put off our conversation forever."

"Robert cannot be certain that, that is to say, perhaps in another month we will know more—"

"I was prepared to wait another month to allow you time to think about matters," Garrett muttered, interrupting her with a firmness he had never used with her before. "But with Racburn's return, well, you must see we must make our decision."

"I am not feeling very well, I am afraid. Can we continue our talk later?"

It was what she always said when she was afraid to disappoint him and terrified to commit to something she was not certain she wanted. What sort of wife would she make him? They had shared intimate moments together and he felt honor bound as a gentleman to offer for her. He wanted to marry her despite the fact she had never offered him more than her friendship and gratitude for easing the pain of Lindsay's betrayal.

Covering her with the blankets, he rose from the bed, kissing her atop her head while running his finger down her cheek. "I am here for you, Anais. Never forget that."

"You are very good to me," she said, smiling into his troubled face.

"But not good enough, it would seem."

She watched him walk away and cursed herself for hurting him. She should agree to marry him, to be thankful that he wanted her; that he was willing to do the honorable thing, but she couldn't stop thinking, *what if . . .*

"Good morning, sleepyhead," Ann said as she peeked around the corner of the door. She stopped dead in her tracks when she saw Garrett and Robert in the room. "Oh, beg pardon, am I interrupting something?"

"Not at all, Lady Ann," Robert said smoothly. "I was just finishing up my visit with your sister. Naturally my brother was worried for her and wished to see for himself that no harm has come to her."

Garrett nodded politely before letting himself out. He was followed by Robert, who closed the door behind him.

"It's about time you roused yourself," Ann said, smiling as she walked toward her. "It's Christmas morning. Surely you are not going to laze about in bed all day!"

She had forgotten it was Christmas. Anais shook her head and attempted to clear the haze in her brain.

"Lord Raeburn has returned home, you know," Ann said coyly. "He's been asking about you, almost every hour, in fact."

Anais blinked against the light streaming in through the windows and saw the image of her sister's narrow shoulders outlined in the sun's beams. "Papa suffered quite a wound to his

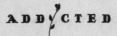

head, but Dr. Middleton has assured us that he will recover completely. Mama is at his bedside even now. He was asking for you. He was quite distraught thinking about you trapped in your room."

Anais slid out of the covers and steadied herself with her hand against the wooden poster. "I should go to him."

"After." Ann caught her about the waist and held tight. "First you must take care of yourself. You've had nothing to eat. You must be famished."

Anais felt the queasiness that always accompanied the dizziness surge up through her belly, and she feared her face had turned a ghastly shade of green. "I'm afraid I'm not up to eating right now."

Ann studied her quizzically. "Surely you must be starving. You barely ate anything yesterday and here it's already past noon. You must at least have a bite of toast and a coddled egg."

The image of runny egg whites and rich yellow yolk made Anais retch. Wildly, she waved for the chamber pot. Ann reached it with no time to spare. What little contents remained in Anais's stomach rose up with a vengeance and by the time she was done retching, she was left with the bitter taste of the laudanum that Robert had spooned down her throat the night before.

"You're an awful color, Anais. Lud, you're the same shade of yellow wax that Lord Weatherby is," her sister prattled on as she took the chamber pot from Anais's shaking hands. "You won't believe the site of him, his eyes are as yellow as lemons."

"Not now," Anais whispered, wiping her mouth with the cloth Ann held out to her. She didn't want to hear any reminders that they were now indebted to Lindsay's father for food and shelter. She had too many things to think about. How would she prepare herself for that first glimpse of Lindsay since that dreaded night at the masquerade? How would she conceal the secrets she steadfastly clung to?

No, staying here was much too dangerous. Not only were her secrets threatened by staying under the same roof as Lindsay, but her heart, as well. Despite everything that had happened, her damnable heart still beat for him. Why couldn't it have beat for Garrett? Things would have been so much simpler then. But nothing had ever been simple where Lindsay was concerned. Anais feared it would always be like this for her. She was the type to love only once, and that love had always belonged to Lindsay. It still did, no matter how much she wished otherwise.

"Shall I call for Louisa?" Ann asked. "Perhaps a warm bath will make you feel better."

"That would be nice."

Ann pulled the red velvet cord, ringing for the maid. "Geraldine went home. Lord Raeburn sent a footman to escort her into the village."

"That was very kind of you to allow your maid to return to her family."

"Mother was horrified, of course."

"Mother is self-absorbed. She looks only as far as the end of her nose. If Geraldine wished to return to her parents, then you were right to allow her, Ann. Now, what of the other staff?"

"Most have gone home, to their families. Lord Raeburn has collected their locations so that they can be notified when to return. He's also gone back to the house, or what is left of it.

He brought a cart with him, but he was unable to salvage anything. It's basically all ash. He's really been rather good at organizing everything."

Yes. He had always been very good at that sort of thing. When it came to taking care of people, no one was more dedicated than Lindsay. Too bad he had never actually seen to taking care of himself.

"After he returned from the house, he came back only long enough to change his clothes. Even now, I'm afraid, he is out waking the local architects from their warm beds. He's determined to start rebuilding our home as soon as possible. What a gentleman he is, Anais."

Anais's mind was swimming, not to mention her stomach was still reeling from her bout of nausea. She couldn't seem to think straight knowing that at some future point in the day she would come face-to-face with the man she had loved all her life. What would she say?

"What design should we encourage father to build? I am rather fond of the new gothic style. But then again, I am something of a romantic—"

"Dearest, you're prattling." Anais shot her sister a placating smile. "Just give me a few minutes. It is somewhat daunting to awaken to memories of falling out one's bedroom window and discovering that one no longer has a home in which to live. I fear I'm having some difficulty taking it all in."

"Sorry. I guess I forgot. I've had all night and morning to assimilate the happenings of last night. As the house is we are going to have to stay here until Aunt Millie arrives from Town and takes us back with her to live, but that won't be till the holidays are over. How I wish Papa had not sold our town house," Ann said with a sigh. "I'm afraid that I don't really like it here."

Ann looked up into Anais's face and kissed her cheek. "I'm so very glad that you have finally awakened. Mama has spent the entire morning with Papa and, well, Lord Weatherby has done nothing but grumble about the whole unexpectedness of our household descending upon him. Lady Weatherby has been busy organizing her staff and overseeing preparations for Christmas dinner and I feel as though I'm only in the way. Frankly, there is no one about to talk to with Lindsay gone into the village. I was hoping you would soon awaken so that you could keep me company."

"Yes, dearest," Anais said, lowering herself back onto the bed. "Perhaps I might do so now. Let me have my bath. And then after that we will figure out what clothes I shall wear—for I cannot go about wearing my night rail and wrapper—and then we will go together and see Papa."

Ann left in search of a servant to fill the tub, while Anais stood before the cheval looking glass that was beside a dressing screen. Untying the satin ties of her night rail, she let it slide down her shoulders until her large, swollen breasts were revealed. Her nipples were darker, more sensitive and perhaps a bit more plump than before.

Atop her left breast was a purple bruise that marred her nearly translucent flesh. With a gasp, the memory of her dream came to her. Lindsay had sucked her there, lost in the throes of his climax. Her fingers shook as she traced the mark that had been left from Lindsay's greedy, sucking mouth. Her knees felt curiously weak as she traced his mark with her fingertip. That

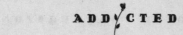

beautiful dream had been real. He had come to her, and she had allowed it—welcomed him.

Oh, God, how was she to face him this morning? How had she allowed herself to be intimate with him? This—Lindsay's reappearance—was something she could not afford. Everything would be ruined if he discovered things about her and Garrett. And that was the one thing she would not allow. She could not allow Lindsay to come between her and her secret.

Her gaze scanned the bruise once more and the dream came back, every vivid, beautiful moment. A memory she would clutch to her breast. A beautiful night that could never happen again. She had to promise herself that she would not weaken and allow him in. She must not.

How would she ever manage it, for she was a weakling and a fool when it came to Lindsay and her love for him.

After dressing in a gown that Robert Middleton's wife had sent for her, Anais searched out her father's sickroom. She found her father dozing, propped up on pillows, his head wrapped in white bandages that were shadowed with blood. Robert had dosed him well with laudanum owing to what her father said "was like gunfire going off in his head." She sat for long minutes, holding his hand, watching his stubbled cheeks sink in and out with his snoring breaths. Her mother's impatient sighs mingled with her father's peaceful breaths, and Anais found she could not sit in the chamber with her mother any longer, watching the wretched woman sitting beside her father, knowing that her mother had never cared about her husband.

"We have nothing now," her mother cried, despair ringing in

her voice. "All my gowns, my jewels," she wept. "The new furniture and the rugs. All of it gone. What shall become of me?"

"The house and its contents were insured, Mother," Ann said sharply. "You should be giving thanks that Lord Raeburn talked Papa into taking out the new policies that Lloyd's began underwriting. Very forward thinking, if you ask me."

"Yes, but how long will the business take to settle?" her mother cried, glaring at her daughters over her shoulder as they stood at the foot of the bed. "What if Lord Raeburn was wrong about this business of paying for insurance? What assurances do we have that they will come through with the money to replace what I've lost!"

"What *you've* lost?" Ann asked incredulously. "What we have all lost. And furthermore, I have heard you complain of nothing but the loss of material possessions, things that can be replaced very easily. It could have been much worse, Mother. You could have lost your husband. You could have lost Anais."

Her mother's eyes settled on her. There was no love lost between them, she knew, but Anais was confronted with the harsh reality of the truth when she saw the way her mother looked at her. In that instant she knew her mother would have gladly thrown her into the flames if it would have saved her jewels.

It should have hurt her—cut her to the quick—to see what very little a child could mean to its mother. But the truth was, it did not. A year ago, she could not have believed, let alone understood, how someone could be so utterly mercenary. She understood now, she comprehended the workings of the world. Her naiveté was lost, replaced by life's lessons.

"Now I shall be forced to live with your father's sister," their mother snapped as she looked away and glared at her sleeping husband. "Why did your sister have to go scampering off to Cádiz for the winter? We should be staying with her. She should be taking care of me."

"Mother," Anais chastised. "Abigail is newly married. You cannot fault her for deciding to honeymoon someplace warm."

"She has already been gone two months! She doesn't need to be gone till spring."

Anais sighed. "Even if Abigail were home for the winter, there is no guarantee we could travel such a distance and in such weather. The north of Scotland is not an easy trek. No, it is much more prudent to go and live with my aunt until Abigail arrives home in the spring."

"I suppose it is impossible to think that the house will be rebuilt by then."

"No, Mother. The house will not be rebuilt. It will take nothing short of a miracle to have that happen in four months."

Her mother snorted, disgust marring her considerable beauty. "Then I am stuck with her, my sister-in-law. Lord, I cannot abide that woman—not a fashionable ounce in her over-flabby body. There will be no balls, no dinners, no excursions to the pleasure gardens. Just intolerable afternoons and evenings spent in her drab little house in Portman Square."

"Mother," Ann retorted. "We are indebted to Aunt Millie for her kindness to our family. She has never been anything but generous and loving toward us."

"I cannot live *there*," her mother snapped. "I cannot abide her small home and her silly society of women. I cannot stand that unfashionable creature she calls her companion—*I will not* be seen in that girl's company."

"Jane has been a support to Millie," Anais challenged, hating to hear her mother taint the merits of her aunt's companion. Anais had always thought of Jane as a friend, and listening to her mother abuse her friend's name set her teeth on edge. Her mother wouldn't know a true friend if it hit her over the head.

"Millie has supported that...that *nobody* for years. That girl has taken everything away from Millie—it should have been yours, girls. It could have bought you a duke," her mother said with a menacing glare. "All that money that Millie keeps hidden could have been yours if not for that conniving girl. And now, hamfisted as Millie is, I will have to suffer her small home and poor furnishings and penny-pinching ways. I cannot begin to know how I shall show my face in society. What will my friends think? Oh, why did Abigail's husband have to steal away to the wilds of the Mediterranean? No one considers my thoughts or my needs."

"I will not listen to another word of this," Anais snapped. "Abigail is off on her honeymoon. Be happy for her. She has caught herself a rich lord. Was that not your goal?"

"It was my goal for each of you, but *you* will not achieve it."

Anais felt the familiar barb, though the sting was much less than it was a year ago. "You may send word to me when Papa awakes. I will come to visit when you have vacated the room. I can't imagine it will be too much longer as compassion and caring for your family was never high on your list. We could never come before a new ballgown or an invitation to a prestigious soiree, could we?"

"Ungrateful, spoiled child. I should have thrown you to the streets."

As her mother glared at her, Anais felt the unexpected nausea

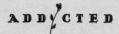

rear in her belly. How easy it would have been for her mother to toss her aside, and the reality cruelly gripped her middle.

Anais couldn't help but wonder if the numbness she had felt settle in her soul these past months was because she was turning into the same sort of selfish woman as her mother. As she looked from her mother to her father lying asleep in bed, the vision changed so that she saw Garrett lying there, and herself sitting beside the bed, pining away for another man while the one who loved her lay helpless in the bed before her.

Suddenly she felt very weary—tired of inflicting pain on a man who had never been anything but kind and compassionate to her. It was time to let the past go. It was time for her to seek her future. That future, she told herself over and over again, could not include Lindsay.

9

The waning sun slipped behind a heavy, gray cloud, casting the salon in shadow and snuffing out the melancholy memories of Anais's afternoon visit with her mother. It was early evening and supper was to be served as a buffet for the guests that had come to partake of the Christmas festivities with Lord and Lady Weatherby.

Anais wished to be anywhere but the salon. She would have asked for a tray to be sent to her room, but she could not in all conscience leave Ann alone on Christmas. It was bad enough that her mother had made no attempt to show some Christmas spirit, despite the fact it was obvious their father was not in any danger of succumbing to his wounds. No, Anais could not leave young Ann alone, so she found herself seated on the settee closest to the fire, arranging her hands in her lap, praying she looked tranquil and at ease.

Nothing was further from the truth. Inside she was a mass of knots and jangled nerves. She told herself that she could do this, she could act composed and as though her heart had not been trampled through. She had done that, during her years as an unnoticed debutante. Certainly she could summon the skill once again.

Looking down at the borrowed emerald silk gown she wore, Anais allowed her fingers to fidget with the lace ruffle on the flounce of the bell-shaped skirt. Taking what she hoped was a calming breath, she pretended interest in the occupants of the room.

Lord Weatherby was drunk. But that was nothing out of the ordinary. He was playing a hand of whist with Lord Walling-ford and Dr. Middleton, as well as Mr. Pratt, the minister from St. Ann's parish.

A roar of laughter erupted from Weatherby's lips and he patted Wallingford's shoulder before taking a large gulp of port. "A good man, you are, my boy," he commended Wallingford drunkenly. "Never dreamed you were holding back that ace."

"I am a man of secrets," Wallingford said with a sly smile. Wallingford's dark gaze found hers over Dr. Middleton's shoulder and he winked at her.

Anais liked Wallingford despite knowing he was a rake—and a heartless one—or so she had heard from the numerous ladies he had loved and left. The four of them, Lindsay, Garrett, she and Wallingford, had all grown up in the district, playing together, attending the same social activities and assemblies. But her friendship with Wallingford had not withstood the years that hers with Lindsay had. By the time she turned fourteen, Wallingford had distanced himself from her, never allowing himself to be the sort of friend to her that Lindsay and Garrett were. He was always a bit aloof, but he had never acted the rake with her. She had seen him act the part when he'd been prowling about the ballrooms, but he had been nothing more than the man she had known since childhood when he was in her company.

"You are looking very lovely, Lady Anais," Wallingford said as his twilight-blue gaze assessed her. "The firelight becomes you."

She blushed at the comment and saw that Weatherby's eyes suddenly traveled over Wallingford's broad shoulder and landed on her, sending her own gaze fleeing to the group of women who sat at another table playing lottery tickets. There was something in Lindsay's father's scrutiny that disturbed her. It was penetrating, knowing. It was a look that told her he might well know of the secret she was trying desperately to keep.

Before, she had only seen drunken debauchery shining in those eyes. But tonight she saw something much more frightening in them—*clarity.*

"Come and join us, my dear," Lady Weatherby called gently. "Mrs. Pratt is beating us soundly. Mrs. Middleton and I shall quite be under the hatches if you do not come and save us."

"Thank you, no," she said, forcing a smile to her lips. "I'm afraid the fire has too great a hold of me."

"Shall I ring for another blanket? Your shoulders are trembling."

In unison, every guest's attention was directed her way and she felt her face flush crimson. The bodice of the gown was comprised of an off-the-shoulder lace collar that exposed her throat and much of her full décolletage. Anais was certain that the tight bodice hid very little of her flesh that was glowing hot, and most likely red, beneath their inquisitive stares.

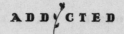

How she wished Lady Weatherby was not quite so observant.

"Lindsay, darling," Lady Weatherby called. "Bring a blanket for Anais, won't you? That window is so terribly drafty. I'm certain she'll take a chill."

Horrified, Anais turned to find that Lindsay had just entered the room and was now pulling a thick cashmere shawl from the back of a winged chair. Her spine stiffened as he started to make his way toward her. It was the first time she had really seen him since the night at the Torrington masquerade. He had been walking toward her that night, too, but looking much different than he now was.

His face was impassive. She saw that his green eyes, which had always reminded her of rich Irish moss, held a watchfulness about them. They were also glistening with a strange flicker she had never seen before. His hair, which had always been given to curl, was in desperate need of a cut, for it hung to his shoulders in onyx-colored curling locks that made her fingers itch to run through the thick, silken mass. She remembered how it felt to have the silky strands slide through her fingers. She didn't understand why, but there was something about Lindsay's wild, unfashionable hair that had her looking at him more intently than she should.

Finally, her gaze slipped to his lips and she shivered, unable to conceal it when she saw that she had not imagined his chin covered with black whiskers. Anais could not stop her body from remembering the feel of his face, covered with a thick beard, against her thighs and belly. How erotic it had been to feel the abrasive brush of his whiskers paired with the silky feel of his tongue. She had thought it all a fevered erotic dream last night. Looking at him now, knowing it was real made her tremble visibly.

She could not allow him to know that she remembered every heated moment in his arms nor learn what truly lay in her heart. She must keep to the performance she had written and act the part she had scripted for herself.

What she needed to do was act as if she did not remember that she had been with him in his bed. Pretend not to care about him or their friendship. She could do it. She had become rather skilled at pretending. So skilled, in fact, that she was able to pretend that she had not given Lindsay her virginity in a stable, or that the past ten months of heartache had never really existed.

She had washed all the hurt away in an emotionless void that felt cold and lonely and empty. She was blank inside. A hollowed-out shell of herself. But preservation would do that to a person. It left a person cold.

"A shawl." He came to a stop before her. Instead of handing it to her, he dropped to his knees and wrapped the paisley cashmere around her shoulders. His gaze met hers, and he unabashedly stared at her despite the fact his parents' guests were there to lay witness to it.

But then, as far as the guests were concerned, they were the very best of friends. No one outside of Lindsay and Garrett knew that she had given her innocence to Lindsay. No one knew that they were no longer friends because she'd caught him in an indecent act with someone she thought was her friend.

What the guests saw was a man and woman—childhood friends—sharing a moment of privacy after a long absence from each other.

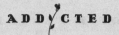

"Better?" he asked, rubbing his large palms up and down her shoulders. Gathering the shawl in her fingers, she brought it tighter around her arms so that it covered her bosom.

"Yes, thank you."

"They tell me you've been ill," he said quietly.

She let her gaze flit away when she saw there was more than curiosity shining in his eyes. "I am on the mend now."

"You're as pale as a ghost. You do not look yourself. I've been told your heart is failing."

"I'm well on the way to being recovered."

"Was it a broken heart?" he asked in what could only be described as a whisper. Anais could not help but look at him. She saw pain in his expression and she wanted to spare him the thought that his actions had anything to do with her ailment. For he had nothing to do with it. It was the result of her own folly.

"I contracted an illness while I was in Paris. It affected my heart."

His eyes scoured hers and she shrunk back, bringing the shawl tighter around her, pretending that she could hide everything from him. "This is a very lovely wrap," she murmured as her fingers wound around the braided fringe.

"It's Persian. I purchased it for Mother at the covered market in Constantinople."

Looking down at the pale green-and-rose pattern, Anais steadfastly avoided his eyes and the questions she knew were burning in his brain. "It's lovely."

"Not as lovely as you."

She was not that lovely, else he would not have turned so eagerly to Rebecca.

"How did you like Constantinople? I believe you've always had a desire to see it."

He stood abruptly and peered down at her. "The city was everything I expected it to be. It is vibrant and rich, full of culture and exotic tales. I did not, however, enjoy the circumstances that brought me there."

She refused to look up. He was baiting her. She was not to engage him in a war of words. The past was the past, nothing about it could be changed. Neutral ground was what she needed to find with Lindsay.

"You must have taken great interest in the culture, for you look very much like one of those Eastern despots I've seen in my books. Sort of like the count in Dumas's book." Anais attempted a jovial tone as she indicated his attire, but her voice sounded jaded and she winced when she saw his eyes narrow.

"A despot?" he inquired. "Or am I the Count of Monte Cristo? I believe the count found himself betrayed by his lover and his friend, is that not right?"

Her gaze slid away from his face and landed on his shoulders. His long, black, velvet coat was opened all the way down the front, revealing his silk waistcoat that was the color of a rich claret. Gold embroidery edged the cuffs of the evening jacket and the unusual collar was folded down in the style reminiscent of the Mandarins. It was a strange style of jacket, but she admitted that the cut suited his long body and broad shoulders. The color especially was starkly vivid against his dark hair and tanned skin. There was certainly an Eastern wildness about him. His untamed hair and sun-kissed skin, not to mention the beard—something no self-respecting gentleman would grow,

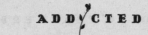

let alone wear before women—all smacked of untamed Eastern decadence. But if any Englishman could carry off looking like a seductive sultan, it was Lindsay.

The tenseness about his eyes seemed to lessen and he grinned, a slow, sensual smile that began to churn her insides. "Does the beard offend you? Mother was aghast when she first saw me. I was reminded of how very unfashionable and ungentlemanly it is to wear facial hair in the presence of a lady. But then, I've never been that good at playing the gentleman, have I?"

Swallowing hard, Anais steadfastly refused to tilt her head to look at him. Instead, she studied the hearth that was decked with evergreen swags and bunches of holly and laurel. She watched the orange flames in the hearth leap and dance, crackling in shooting sparks as the Yule log burned bright and hot. She feigned interest in the hearth so that she would not have to answer that leading question. She would not allow him to draw her into a conversation that was best left unspoken.

She sat as such, wondering when, or if, he would tire of her silence and move on to other more talkative guests. In the end, he stepped to the right and took the cushion next to her on the settee.

"Why did you run from me?"

The question was uttered softly, but in the darkest of tones, in a manner that spoke of barely tethered anger. The sound slithered along her nerves, fueling her own anger.

"I searched everywhere for you. Do you know that?"

Yes. She had known. He'd come nearly every day to the house, and finally, when she'd convinced her maid to tell him she had left for London, he had followed her there.

"Why did you run, Anais?"

"You know perfectly well the answer to that question. And I would beg you not to talk about such things here," she said, smiling at Lady Weatherby, who was watching them intently.

"Where shall we have this conversation?" he asked, pressing closer to her. He was so close that his breath whispered along her ear. "For we will have it, Anais."

"There is nothing to talk about. Nothing more to say. I witnessed the act. I saw the truth. No explanation is necessary."

"Look at me."

Oh, how she wished Garrett was here. He could extricate her from this very uncomfortable confrontation. He was excessively good at saving her. He could save her now, from Lindsay's sensual gaze and the memories of those beautiful lips kissing her body.

Lindsay's hand slid on the brocade cushion. His fingers found hers and he entwined them with her trembling ones, shielding his inappropriate touch in the folds of her skirt. "Please, look at me."

She fought against the need she heard in his voice, but felt herself slowly weakening as his fingers pressed urgently against hers. She was saved, however, by Worthing, the Weatherbys' ancient butler.

"If you please, ma'am," he said, addressing Lady Weatherby. "Mrs. Jennings and her shopgirls are in the front hall, desirous to see Lady Darnby and her daughters."

"Lovely," Lady Weatherby said. "Put them in the crimson salon, Worthing. We shall be with them directly. Why doesn't everyone wander into the ballroom?" she announced, rising from her chair. "There is a hot buffet set up and we shall have

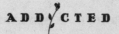

some dancing later. Ann," Lady Weatherby said, motioning for her to take her hand. "Come along with me. We will see you settled first and allow Anais a few more minutes with my son. I'm certain they are both desirous to catch up on these past months of absence."

"That would be lovely, Lady Weatherby," Ann said before casting an apologetic glance in Anais's direction.

"Well, come along then," Lady Weatherby commanded as she clasped Ann's hand with hers. With Ann in tow, she left the room, closing the door firmly behind her.

"I shall have to kiss her for that."

Anais turned on her cushion, only to see Lindsay grinning rakishly down at her. "I believe I will leave. I really cannot afford to miss the opportunity to have Mrs. Jennings fit me with a new wardrobe. I certainly cannot keep borrowing Mrs. Middleton's gowns, now, can I?"

"Indeed not." She saw his eyes skim down the column of her throat to the white swells of her décolletage that could not be contained behind the bodice. "Obviously Mrs. Middleton lacks the bosom the gods have graciously bestowed upon you."

"It was the only gown that was suitable to be seen in," she said on a gasp as he suddenly pressed forward. The scent of him washed over her and it brought memories of last night racing back. She had smelled the same scent of him as he lay atop her— spice and man. Her body began to shake, reawakening to the sensations he had woken inside her, and she pressed back from him until she could feel the rolled arm of the settee between her shoulder blades.

"I need you." He followed her movement. His chest was so

close to her she felt the muscled contours of his belly rising and falling against the rounded mound of hers. "I want you back— I *need* you back in my life." His arm reached out past her shoulder and his fingers curled around the settee, caging her. "I have never needed anything more, Anais. I cannot stand—"

"I forgive you."

She had blurted that out in a hurried breath she feared sounded much too husky. Her breathing was rushed, her bosom threatening to spill completely from the ill-fitting bodice of her borrowed gown. A log cracked and snapped, sending Lindsay's shoulders tensing as his gaze burned—unwavering— at her.

"I beg your pardon?" he asked, enunciating every word with precision.

"I have forgiven you."

Behind her, she could hear his fingers curling into the silk of the settee. "Forgiven me?" He looked perplexed. His gaze slid to her trembling lips, then back to her eyes. "How is that possible when we left off under such wretched circumstances? You have not even allowed me to apologize, and yet you forgive me?"

"Forgive, and you will be forgiven."

She had not meant to say those words, but they had slipped out effortlessly. How many times had the vicar preached the gospel of Luke? How many times had they heard those words growing up? Those words had become her mantra. She so desperately wanted to believe in the validity of those words.

"What have you to be forgiven for, Anais? It is I who seek forgiveness from you."

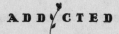

She needed to leave before she made matters worse. He would be relentless. He would pry, would try to wear down her defenses until he learned what he wanted. She couldn't let him.

"You have my forgiveness, now let me go."

"Why, when I have not done anything to be worthy of your forgiveness? How is it you can easily accept what I have done?"

"Because I must," she whispered, closing her eyes. "Because it is not for me to judge you and set your punishment. I do not mean to say that because I have forgiven you I have deemed your actions acceptable, for I do not. Rather, I mean to say I understand why you did what you did."

"Just like that." He snapped his fingers before her nose. "In a blink of an eye, and without a word, you forgive me for betraying your trust and the bond we shared together? How can that be? How can you forgive me so easily? Hell," he raged, "I haven't even come close to forgiving myself for what I've done."

"I have moved on with my life, Lindsay. The past is the past. It is forgotten and forgiven."

"Forgotten?" He clutched her face in his palms and forced her to look at him. "You cannot mean that. You have not forgotten me. Your body has not forgotten me."

She held his gaze, forcing aside the weakening resolve of her body. "We shared a past. It was lovely and passionate. But our futures are separate."

She tried to slip out from beside him, but he caught her about the waist. "Is there nothing left, Anais? Of us?" He placed his palm over her breast and smoothed his index finger back and forth along the apex of her bounding heart. "You don't feel me here anymore?"

She fought to summon the strength to lie to Lindsay. The first of many to come, she told herself. It would get easier after the first time. It was for his own good, but she knew it was a lie. It was for *her* peace of mind.

"There is nothing left, Lindsay, but memories. It is best, I think, to leave the past where it belongs, behind us."

"No, I won't. *I can't!* Damn it, I do not belong in your past, I am your future, Anais. I've always known it, and furthermore, so have you."

"Things have changed. It is too late to drag the past out into the light."

"That's not true—it can't be true."

"I am afraid there is more going on here than you and I and what happened almost a year ago."

His fingers sunk deep into her shoulders, biting her skin. "What the hell are you saying? Have...have..." His face paled and he made a strangled sound deep in his throat. "Have you found someone else? Are you in love with another man? Broughton—" He bit off in a strange choked breath.

It should be easier to lie the second time. So why couldn't she? Why could she not bring herself to meet Lindsay's wounded eyes and tell him she no longer loved him?

Anais took advantage of his slackened hold and slipped out from beside him. "I'm sorry if I have caused pain to you, Lindsay. It was unconsciously done. I never meant to hurt you, as I know you never intended to hurt me."

His eyes darkened and he rose from the settee, stalking her so that she stepped back from him. Step for step he followed her until she found herself backed up against the door.

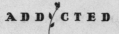

Towering above her, he stared down at her with his penetrating gaze.

"You were made but for one man," he said fiercely. "Born for one man. *You're mine.*" His voice was a painful whisper as his arms shot out and his hands rested flat against the door, effectively caging her. "You were made for me to love, Anais. And now you are trying to tell me that the glimpse I had—the taste of you— that you *gave* to me is what I can never have?"

The heat in his eyes singed her and she looked away. She had never seen him in such a volatile state. She was unnerved by the fierceness in him.

"I'm cold," she said, shivering. She was lying and hating herself for acting as if she was timid and weak. But she had to get away from his intensity and the need she saw in his eyes—a need she was certain would be shining in hers if she allowed herself to tarry with him.

"You're shivering, yes," he murmured as he lowered his face to her neck and inhaled her scent. When he spoke she felt the faintest brush of his lips against her earlobe. "But it is not trembling from cold, but hunger—sexual hunger."

"No," she protested. Closing her eyes, she rested her head back against the door.

"Yes. Your body is reawakening to mine. Just as it did last night. You remember, don't you? The feel of me atop you. My mouth moving along your skin, the roughness of my tongue laving your silky quim as you shuddered in climax beneath me."

Her eyelids flew open. Too late, she saw the realization flash in his eyes.

"Of course you remember. You're trembling because you

recall what I did to you, and how you felt. You're shaking because you remember what it is like to be filled with my cock, the pleasures of it thrusting deep inside you. You want that again. You want what I can give your body. You want what only *I* can give you."

"I do not recall a thing." Her breathing was heavy and her nipples were hard buds that rubbed against her corset, sending her womb clenching in excitement.

"I marked you," Lindsay murmured darkly, making her toes curl in her slippers. "Remember how I allowed myself to spend on your belly? I sucked your breast as I lost myself in climax. Tell me, how will you hide my mark, Anais? When the village seamstress wishes to measure you, how will you shield the mark of my mouth—my passion?"

Anais covered the swell of her left breast with her palm. Lindsay smiled wickedly, triumphantly, as he peeled her fingers from her flesh and lowered the lace collar of her bodice so that crest of her breast, which strained above the ill-fitting corset, was exposed. But he did not stop until he hooked his finger along the edge of the linen corset, shoving it lower until the small purple bruise beside her areola was exposed.

"There is no denying last night." Lowering his mouth to her breast, he kissed her so softly she could have whimpered. "Are you going to deny it? Are you going to pretend we weren't on fire for each other? Will you try to claim that while you were lying beneath me and I was marking you, that you were thinking of whoever you misguidedly think will replace me in your heart?"

"I forgive you," she breathed heavily, struggling to right her reeling senses and reaffirm her mantra. "Let that be enough."

"It is not enough," he growled, flattening his hand on the door behind her. "I don't want this easy acquiescence. I want your anger. I want to feel it. I want to see it. Don't you understand? I don't want your submission. Submission means I have defeated you. Hate me, yell at me—*hit me*. But do not stand before me and pretend as though your heart is not racing and your body is not crying out for my touch."

"Please don't do this," she whispered afraid of succumbing to the temptation that was Lindsay. His fingers trailed down her flushed cheek and he leaned in farther so that she could feel his breath upon her lips.

"Make me work for you, Anais. Make me earn your forgiveness. Don't just hand it to me. A year ago you would have hung me by my bollocks for abusing you so terribly. Where is your sense of right and wrong?"

"What is it you want?" she cried. "What more can I possibly give you?"

"A chance to redeem myself in your eyes. Another chance to earn your love. Another chance for a future together."

Anais held his gaze and tried to ignore the way her chest rose and fell in hard, gasping breaths. "I do not want a future with you. I don't want your love."

Lindsay's head snapped back as though she had hit him. She bit her lip, fighting the urge to brush back the lock of hair that had fallen onto his brow. How easily she had once reached out and touched him. She had forever straightened his cravat and ran her hand through his hair in order to brush the unruly locks from his brow. How normal it seemed now, to reach out and feel him beneath her fingers. They had, at one time, been so intimate with each other. Now they were only strangers.

Sighing, Anais smiled sadly at the man who, at one time, had been her knight in shining armor; her savior, her lover. There were still glimpses of that man beneath the troubled shell. She saw him, the old Lindsay, trying to crawl out from under his darkness and she tried not to see his struggle—tried to pretend that what she felt was indifference. But indifference should not have felt this warm in her blood.

"You say you forgive me. Yet you do not want me in your life?"

"I understand why everything happened. You no longer have to pretend, Lindsay. I know your secret."

"What could you possibly know?"

"That you had not set out to seduce Rebecca that night, but that you merely mistook her for me." His face paled, and she saw his hand ball into a fist. "*You* did not betray me, did you? Your habit did."

"And what habit is that?" he snapped, pushing himself away from her, but she saw the fear shining in his eyes.

"Opium. I know all about it."

"Opium?" The word was a strangled cry from his mouth.

"You don't have to lie," she whispered. Reluctantly, she met his gaze and started at the hungry, haunted look in his eye. "You needn't worry, Garrett explained everything."

"Just what has he told you?"

"While you were away at Cambridge you discovered the lure of opium."

"Well, who the hell hasn't?" he thundered. "In case you haven't heard, smoking opium, eating opium, *drinking opium* is

the thing to do. There isn't a fashionable salon that doesn't have a smoking room. There isn't a poet or a writer that has not used it to elevate his senses from time to time in order to allow the words to flow through his quill—Byron, Shelley, Dickens, Dumas, they have all dabbled in it. There isn't a man of my acquaintance that has not experimented with it from time to time, and that includes Broughton."

"Opium is a very false friend. It may be a useful servant, Lindsay, but it is a dangerous master."

"It is not *my* master!"

"Garrett says you have developed a...a...sort of dependence."

He clung to her, cupped her face in his hands. "I *don't* have a habit."

Tilting her chin, Anais eyed him defiantly. "Before you were to meet me on the terrace at the Torrington masquerade he was with you, and you were smoking opium—"

"I was *inhaling* opium-laced incense. There is a difference."

"Smoking it, inhaling it, what does it matter," she hissed, "it is still something that I cannot condone." His face reddened, he was ashamed that she knew his secret, but she plunged on, knowing she was wielding a weapon that would likely destroy him. "I don't want a future with you, Lindsay. I will not stand by and watch you stumbling about in the state in which I last saw you. I am repulsed whenever I remember the way you staggered toward me."

"I was drugged that night—I didn't know what was in that cake when I took it. I truly believed it was just cake. But it wasn't laced with opium. It was hashish—I never imbibe that. I never did before that night, and I haven't since, I swear that to you."

"But you have used opium since, haven't you?"

His face fell and he looked away, unable to meet her eye. His expression confirmed her suspicions. "It does not matter, does it? I cannot be a party to your habit. I will not ignore it like your mother has ignored your father's failings. I will not allow myself to be tied to a man who might mistake another woman for his wife when he is wandering about with his mind in an opium haze. I could never live like that, nor would I subject a child to that. A father is someone a child should look up to, not be ashamed of."

"And this is what you think of me?" he asked, his voice sounding defeated. "You think I'm some dependent like De Quincey? Do you think my life is what is portrayed in his book?"

"I have not read *Confessions of an English Opium Eater*. I have no desire to. I have seen enough of opium and what havoc it caused that night on the terrace."

"You think opium rules my life? That I *have* to have it? That I can't stop using it?"

She couldn't stand to think of Lindsay infusing his body with opium all these years. She did not wish to see him as his father and she looked away from him, from the man she had loved all her life, unable to admit the harmful truth to him.

"Look at me, Anais," he pleaded as he held her face in his palms. "Do I look like a man with a habit?"

The pain in her breast was excruciating, almost as much as the pain she was witnessing in Lindsay's expression. To deny him the truth of her love was like a knife stabbing her in the heart. Over and over she felt the blade of guilt being pulled deeper and deeper until she could barely breathe.

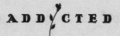

"Tell me, Anais, that I have another chance to win you," he whispered, his words shaky and hushed. "Please tell me I haven't lost you."

Had she no secrets to hide, had she no shame to turn from, she would have thrown herself into his arms and cried—held him—begged him to hold her. She could forgive him, even those transgressions in the hall with Rebecca she could forgive, but she could not forgive what she had done. There was no magic wand to erase the past. She had made her bed. Now she must lie in it.

With a heavy heart and eyes that stung bitter tears, Anais raised her gaze to Lindsay's, held it steady and boldly lied to him. "The love is gone, Lindsay. Now, if you will excuse me, I will leave before someone comes in search of me."

He studied her through narrow eyes. "You haven't forgiven me. You're torturing me instead."

"I have no wish to torture you, Lindsay. I have forgiven you and accepted you are not the man I thought you were. I have moved on. I suggest you do the same."

He reached for her like a man struggling for life. *"I made a mistake!"*

Evading his touch, Anais opened the door and stepped into the hall. As she closed the door, something pummeled the wood, then smashed.

"Damn you!" she heard him cry through the wood and she closed her eyes, envisioning him with his palms to the door in barely tethered anguish. "Damn you for never knowing what it is to be weak."

Unable to stop herself she placed her cheek against the wood and raised her palm to the door, imagining that she was resting her hand against his. Closing her eyes, she became aware of his harsh breathing on the other side of the door. The tears spilled down her cheeks. The heat from them was the first warmth she had felt since Lindsay's touch last night.

"Come back to me, Anais," he pleaded through the wood. "I will stop. I can stop. Just…give me something to stop for."

I have made mistakes, too. And I pray that it is a mistake I can hide while I am staying in this house. I can't be yours, she wanted to scream, but instead she smoothed her hand down the door and walked away, sickened by the fact she was no longer the sort of woman he needed—that she wanted to be. She was a fallen woman, a weak woman, and soon, Lindsay would know just how far she had fallen.

10

Ignoring the gay voices and merry laughter of the departing guests, Lindsay stirred the embers of the Yule log so that flames once more engulfed the stone grate. It was past midnight, yet he felt restless, not weary. His mind was racing, replaying every facet of his conversation with Anais.

He had not expected to be forgiven. Nor had he expected to be forgotten.

Christ, he grumbled, flopping inelegantly onto the wingback chair before the hearth. What the hell was he to do? What sort of strategy was he to use when the woman he wanted— the woman he loved—claimed to no longer love him?

She might not love him any longer, he thought savagely, but she sure as hell desired him. He had seen that yearning in her eyes, had sensed her desire flaring up between their tense bodies. She remembered him, remembered the feel of his hands, recalled the way he could bring her to orgasm after orgasm. She could not deny *that.*

But she repressed that desire. Those sexual yearnings were

locked up tightly behind her considerable self-control—a control she had always clung to, except for that one incredible night in his stables.

How the devil was he to proceed in getting her back? Anais had never been weak. Had never known what it was like to be chased and tempted by demons. She could never understand the reasons he found solace in the opium.

Bloody hell, but Broughton had grievously misled her. He was no rookery addict spending his days and nights in a tumbledown room at the end of a filthy alley. Hell, he'd only discovered it in Cambridge because he had been looking for a way to cool his raging lust for her. Even then, in university he had a physical need for her, but she was not of an age to indulge his pleasures. He used the opium so that he could dream of her, so that he could see her when he was fucking other women. There was no guilt that way. With the opium, the remorse was deadened. In his hazed mind it had been as if he was faithful to her because he had seen her face atop him and his mind had called her name when he had found release.

It had all seemed so simple and rational then. *He* ruled the opium, not the other way around, despite the lies Broughton had spewed to Anais. But how was he to convince her of that when she believed Broughton. His friend was more creditable than himself. After all, it had not been Broughton who had destroyed her faith. How could she think otherwise? Anais had witnessed the effects of the hashish, had witnessed him in a drugged stupor ravishing her friend. Bloody hell, how was he to erase those memories so that she could once again trust and believe in him?

And what of Broughton? To what end did he speak of his

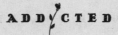

opium use to Anais? To further discredit him? No, Broughton had never been the vengeful sort, but damn him, Lindsay was beginning to think otherwise. A healthy case of suspicion and jealousy were clouding his thoughts. He didn't dare allow himself to think of the possibility that one of his best friends had taken Anais away from him. He couldn't travel that path, to see Anais lying in Broughton's arms.

The door opened and a shaft of yellow light stole across the carpet, followed by the sounds of gently padding feet.

"Oh!" a woman's voice shrieked. "You've scared me out of my wits!"

Lindsay looked up from the flames and saw a petite blonde standing before him, her large blue eyes round as saucers. "Forgive me, Lady Ann, I should have announced my presence."

She let out her held breath and he noticed that the candlestick she held in her hand shook tremulously. "Yes, you should have," she said tartly.

"I thought the household was settled for the night. I did not expect to be found."

"I came for a book. I thought you had already gone to bed."

"That would have been a complete waste of time. I would only spend it tossing and turning and cursing away the hours."

"Hmm," she murmured before turning to scan the bookcase before her. She held her candle higher as she read the gilt spines. He noticed how her hair was highlighted with pale yellow streaks, not the gold that Anais's was. He also noted that while Ann was ethereally beautiful and her figure lithe and trim, it did nothing to stir his blood. Unlike Anais's voluptuous curves that made his blood run hot and his groin throb.

Anais had the sort of body a man could spend hours exploring and savoring—the sort of soft warmth that cushioned a man and made him feel loved. Frankly, Anais had been the image of his ideal for as long as he could remember.

"Any suggestions?" Ann asked over her shoulder. "There are so many books here I don't know where to begin."

"What is your pleasure?" He thought he saw her cheeks flame red, but she averted her face and concentrated on picking out a volume.

"I prefer novels."

"With romance in them?" he teased.

"Possibly. I am, after all, a woman. What woman does not dream of romance?"

"A woman?" he said, enjoying baiting her. "You are all of what, thirteen years?"

She shot him a scathing look over her shoulder. "I am fifteen now, my lord."

"So soon?" he mumbled, studying her as she rose onto tiptoes to reach for a book. "When I went away to Cambridge, you were nothing but a child."

"I really despise being thought of as a child," she snapped. "Everyone forgets that I no longer am."

"My apologies. Do you still enjoy those gothic tales of foggy nights and mysterious vampires that roam the Carpathians?"

She whirled around, her eyes bright with excitement. "Those are my favorites."

"Two tomes to the right. The book with the green spine," he directed as her fingers touched each volume with reverence. "I think you would enjoy it. I have it on good authority

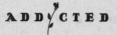

the dark and brooding villain of the work was based on Lord Byron."

Ann pulled the book from its spot on the shelf and when she turned to face him, she had the book clutched to her breasts and a huge smile on her face. "Thank you, my lord. Dark and brooding heroes are my favorite."

He laughed. "Then happy reading, Ann."

She made to pass him, then stopped. He looked up and saw that she was studying him with an expression that could only be described as quizzical. "Why did you not come and join us in the ballroom?" she asked. "It's Christmas day and you've spent it all alone."

"I am not feeling very merry," he replied with a shrug. In truth, he had spent the rest of the evening in his hideaway, smoking opium after his talk with Anais. He had not wanted to feel the pain of her dismissal, or accept the reality that she might very well be lost forever to him. So he had smoked away the pain, reveling in the disembodied numbness of the mistress he tried so hard to hide.

"Why aren't you in good spirits?" she pressed. "Is it because my family is here?"

"Don't be a pea-wit, Ann. It has nothing to do with that. Besides, how many Christmases have our families shared together? It is not as though it is strange to be sharing the holidays with you and your parents."

"Then it is about Anais, isn't it?"

He stilled in his chair, forcing his expression to remain impassive. What had Anais told her sister? Had she confessed to her sibling that he'd taken her virginity? Had she told Ann that he'd taken her in the stable and then run off?

"Why did you leave?" Ann asked, lowering herself to her knees and resting her hand on the arm of his chair. "You were going to propose—I heard you," she rushed on when he tried to speak. "I overheard you talking with Wallingford. But then you left. I couldn't understand it, how you could be so earnest with your friend and so careless with the woman you loved."

"We had a…disagreement."

"She went to France. Anais claims it had been planned for months, but I had never heard word of it. I discovered the fact the morning she left. I found her standing at the front door with her trunks surrounding her. Louisa, her maid, did not even accompany her."

"Who did she go with, pet?" he asked, pressing forward and curling his hand around Ann's slim fingers. "Can you tell me?"

"She went with Aunt Millie and Jane, our aunt's companion. You remember Jane, do you not?" He furrowed his brow, trying to place Jane, the lady's companion. "Red hair, freckles and spectacles," Ann provided.

"Ah, yes," he groaned. "The young lady who is organizing the women's Suffrage Society. I recall her all too well, now."

"Yes, that one," Ann said with a laugh. "Well, she is a good sort. Anais has always considered her a dear friend. The three of them went to France." Ann frowned, then looked up into his eyes. "I'm not certain when exactly they met up with Lord Broughton there."

"I beg your pardon?" he asked in a deceptively calm voice, feeling as though he'd been hit in the middle with a hammer. Every instinct he possessed was on alert, every fear he harbored came to a rearing head.

"Oh, yes, Lord Broughton was there in Paris with them. Didn't you know?" she asked, sounding puzzled. "It appeared to me like he had stayed with them for an extended period of time. I'm not sure how long, of course. It was Lord Broughton who brought Anais back home when she was so ill. In fact, he's been a constant fixture at our house for the past six weeks at least."

Things have changed.... Anais's words filtered through his mind and he fought the urge to throw something. *Broughton in Paris with Anais? Broughton and Anais? Doing God only knew what.*

His fingers dug deep into the leather arms of the chair as he fought to control the feelings that were threatening to drown him. "Tell me about Anais and Broughton, Ann."

"There really is nothing to tell," she said with a dainty shrug of her shoulders. "My sister no longer confides in me. We don't talk—not about anything important, that is. Lord Broughton is now her confidant."

He had once been her confidant. It had been him that she had turned to when she needed to talk. Hearing that Anais had turned to another made him feel cold inside. But then, it had all been his own doing. Through his own excesses and weakness he'd brought on this disaster. As much as he would love to blame it on his friend, or to rail at Anais for turning against him, he could not. Through his poor choices he had lost her, and that truth had never been a more bitter pill to swallow.

"I see them whispering when they think no one is watching them. I know there is something very secretive between them. Something happened in France, I'm sure of it. But Anais won't tell me. She won't speak of any of it."

"Her illness?" he asked. "What of that?"

"I'm as in the dark as you, I'm afraid. I don't know anything other than what Anais tells me and it is the same thing over and over. She contracted an illness while in France, and the sickness, whatever it was, left her with malaise and a bad heart."

"And Dr. Middleton, what does he say?"

"That's what is so frustrating. He repeats the same thing, almost word for word. It's as though it's all been rehearsed for everyone's benefit. But I know my sister. I know there is more going on than just a case of fatigue. She's not herself."

"How so?"

"Well, for one thing, she's eating kidneys and liver for almost every meal. Surely you remember how much she loathed organ meats."

He nodded, recalling how Anais used to push such foods around on her plate, never eating them, but making it appear as though she had at least tried them.

"And there is the fact that Dr. Middleton visits her every day. *Every day*," Ann said with emphasis. "How can that be when it's apparent that she is now on the mend? And furthermore, I've heard him asking about her bleeding—" Ann's hand flew to her mouth and her eyes went round with embarrassment. "That was far too bold of me. Mother would lock me away for a month if she knew what I've just said, and in front of a gentleman, too."

"Shh, pet," he soothed, trying to unruffle her feathers. "I will surely not tell your mama anything that is said in this room."

Ann flushed a brilliant shade of crimson, but bravely carried on. "I know I should not be speaking such things to anyone, but

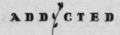

you're different, my lord. You won't judge me and find me lacking, will you?"

"No, I will not. Society's rules can be so silly in regards to the matters of women and men." He pressed his side against the chair and looked down into her lovely upturned face. What an innocent she was, but beneath the naive expression was an intelligent and curious mind dying to be let free to discover the wonders of the world. He knew a true gentleman would not allow himself to be found in a room alone with a young woman, let alone discussing what he was with Ann, but there was something in her eyes, something that made him think of Anais, and he suddenly remembered all the intimate conversations he and Anais had shared together over the years. It had been him to explain the facts of life to Anais—him that spoke of kissing and the intimacies of love and passion. With Anais, no subject had been off-limits, nor had he judged her harshly for her natural curiosity. He had never found another person whom he could talk to as easily as he had talked with Anais.

He had given her his heart and soul, never thinking that one day she might hand them both back to him.

"This is why Anais loved you so much, why she treasured every minute she spent in your company," Ann said as she smiled brilliantly at him. "I can't imagine there is anything one cannot talk to you about."

"I wish your sister felt that way."

"I told Anais you were much more sporting than the very proper Lord Broughton."

Lindsay smiled indulgently. Ann had always been such a sweet innocent. It was amazing to see her now, all traces of the little girl who had followed Anais and him about was now gone, replaced by a young woman in the first blush of womanhood.

"Tell me more of Lord Broughton, pet."

"I don't know. She will not talk of him. I see the way he looks at her, though. I'm well aware that everyone thinks of me as a child, my lord, but I know what it means when a man looks at a woman such as the way Lord Broughton looks at my sister. I also know that something of great import must have transpired between them because Anais thinks nothing of allowing Lord Broughton the intimacy of whispering to her. Anais has never been one to throw the rules of propriety to the wind, but when Lord Broughton is around, it is as if only the two of them exist, even if the salon is full of people. It is as if..." Ann trailed off and looked at the book that lay in her lap. "You will forgive me for saying this, my lord, but I know that you will not think ill of my sister if I voice my feelings."

"Go on, pet. I will keep your confidence."

Ann looked up and he saw that her eyes were misty. "I fear...that is—" she licked her lips and allowed her fingers to grip the corners of her book until her knuckles turned white "—I believe that Lord Broughton and my sister have...they have become close."

"Close?" he repeated, hardly able to say the word.

"Intimate," Ann clarified before she reached for his hand and squeezed tight. "But she cannot love him. She cannot. I don't believe she can love him the way... Oh, why did you not prove yourself and ask her to marry you, my lord? You loved her, didn't you? I did not mistake that, did I?"

"I would bleed myself dry for her, Ann."

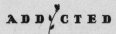

"Do not give up, my lord," Ann whispered as she rose from her knees to stand before him. "There is much I do not know about Anais and Lord Broughton, but I do know this—she has never forgotten you. I don't believe that Anais could stop loving you."

"You have grown into a woman," he said, looking at Ann with fresh eyes. "A lovely, insightful woman." She blossomed under that comment and he could not help but tap the sweet tip of her nose with his fingertip. "One day you're going to make a man jump through hoops to have you. Just as your sister has done with me."

"Oh, I do hope so, my lord," she said gaily as she walked from the room. "Oh, Lord Raeburn?" she called before she left.

"Yes?"

"Lord Broughton has proposed to my sister. I am not sure of her answer. I only know that she has not given it yet."

He will not be marrying her, Lindsay silently vowed as he watched Ann turn and leave. After Ann closed the door, he stood up and tossed the iron poker against the wall. He was lost, so damn perplexed, bewildered. He could barely think straight, could only think of Anais and escape. An escape that would allow him to dream and hope. An escape that was fast becoming his daily life.

11

It was late when Anais slipped into her wrapper and tiptoed out of her bedroom. It had been hours since the last of the noises from the party had quieted down and the guests had departed. Finally, silence had descended, blanketing the house.

Clutching the soot-covered leather-bound book to her breasts, Anais made her way down the curving staircase. In her hand, a candlestick wobbled as she held it high to light the way.

What she was doing, she didn't care to think about. She was playing with fire, seeking out Lindsay. She should not be doing this. They had left off that afternoon in the salon precisely where they should have, with him believing she no longer wanted him in her life.

She had told herself that she needed to remain aloof and indifferent, but had known the pretense would be so much more difficult after she had returned to her room from visiting her father. When she'd found Lindsay's Christmas gift to her on the bed, wrapped in a pretty red velvet shawl, she'd known the struggle would be near to impossible.

She had debated about whether or not to open the gift. After all, she did not want to encourage him. In the end, it called to her and she'd pulled the tail of the silk bow and allowed the wrapping to come free.

Inside the folded shawl was an exquisite matching night rail and wrapper that was adorned with a lavish amount of fine lace. Anais had never owned anything as lovely as that. Where he had purchased it, she didn't know. The blackened book beside the wrapper was entirely too familiar.

She put on the wrapper and studied herself in the looking glass, noticing how the fine spun silk hugged her curves. The firelight shone through it, throwing the silhouette of her figure into relief. Something as seductive as this could not be found at the village modiste.

Anais knew she couldn't accept a gift like this, especially from Lindsay. But the child inside her hugged the gown to her chest, afraid to have it taken away. She had never been allowed to wear lovely things. Her mother made certain of that. It was something her mother enjoyed doing to punish her. She always ordered Anais's dresses with no lace or other adornments. Her figure, which had always been full and womanly, always looked dowdy and dumplinglike owing to the stripes and heavy fabric her mother insisted she wear.

No, she could not possibly give this up. So instead of giving the gift back, she had donned it with the intention of thanking Lindsay. She did not particularly care to give voice to the other intentions that continually tried to creep into her mind.

The sound of the ticking grandfather clock in the hall drew her out of her musings and told her she was nearing the study.

When she arrived at the open door, she peered in, holding the candle higher. There was no one inside.

Perhaps he was sleeping in one of the other chambers?

"May I be of some service, miss?"

Anais whirled around. When the candlelight revealed a square face and nose that appeared to have been broken several times, she covered her mouth, certain she was ready to scream at the top of her lungs.

"None of that, now," he said, reaching for her hand. "You're safe enough with me."

She had been a part of Lindsay's life long enough to know the servants of the house. It was Vallery, Lindsay's valet. With a great exhalation, Anais blew out her held breath. "Forgive me, I didn't recognize you right away."

He cocked his thick brow and looked her over. "Well, now, Lady Anais, what would you be doing up at this time of night and in the dark?"

He watched her carefully, his eyes never leaving her face. She couldn't very well tell him that she was searching for his master. Not this late at night, and dressed in her wrapper. As she fumbled for an excuse he reached for her elbow and steered her toward the staircase.

"Lord Raeburn is indisposed, my lady. I shall tell him I saw you and he will seek you out tomorrow. Will that suffice?"

Digging in her heels, Anais stopped before the servant could lead her to the stairs. "I wish to see him."

"But he doesn't wish to see you."

Anais felt her mouth drop open and her eyes blink in surprise. "I beg your pardon?"

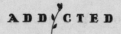

The servant colored and cleared his throat. "It's not that he doesn't want to see you, Lady Anais. What is more accurate is that he doesn't want you to see him—that is, not as he is now." Vallery backed away and stepped into the shadows. "I will tell my gentleman you came by tonight. Take care going back up the stairs, Lady Anais."

Anais watched the valet disappear into the darkness. She wished she could pretend that she didn't understand what he was trying to tell her. She knew what he meant. Lindsay was off somewhere smoking opium.

Glancing at the stairs, Anais knew she had just been given a reprieve. She should take it. But the thought of Lindsay alone, smoking that horrid stuff pushed her into motion.

Silently, she followed the steps of the valet, careful to keep to the shadows. She had blown out her candle so that he wouldn't see her following him.

Through the cavernous halls of the large country house, she followed the servant, down through the portrait gallery and the ballroom, then through a narrow hall that led to double wooden doors, which he opened wide and stepped through. Anais waited a moment, then opened them, stealing through the opening. What she entered was a pleasure den straight out of something from the Arabian Nights.

The room, which she knew had once been Lindsay's mother's conservatory, was done in the Moorish style. Vibrant silk veils tented the ceilings in reds and oranges and pinks. Marble pillars stood from floor to ceiling in a square around a bath with steaming water. It was a mineral bath, like the hot springs in Bath and Tunbridge. Only Lindsay had made it into what the Arabs called a hammam.

"I came across your lady," came a disembodied voice.

"Oh?"

"She was looking for you."

"You had the good sense to put her off, didn't you?"

"Aye. I knew you wouldn't want her here."

"No, I do want her here, that is the problem, Vallery. Sick bastard, aren't I, for wanting her here in my little harem while I indulge in my opium and my lust."

The servant said nothing. Anais tiptoed farther into the room and peered around a tall potted palm tree that stood on the corner of the bath. Beyond it lay what she would call a tent room, an exotic creation of veils and scarves that acted like curtains. From the ceiling, Moroccan lanterns were suspended with chains, while on the floor a silk divan, fit for a sultan, was covered with tasseled pillows and silk scarves. In the middle of the divan, his back against the wall with one knee bent, was Lindsay. To his left was a table with a silver tray, a lacquered box and a pipe that had smoke curling from a raised brass burner.

She should have been repulsed by the fact that Lindsay was in this room smoking opium. It was a vile thing that turned good men into sinners. But repulsion was the furthest thing from her mind. All she could think about was the mystique, the decadent languor that surrounded her.

The visuals alone were a feast for her senses. She felt as though she really was half the world away in Constantinople or Morocco, wandering through the covered bazaars.

Everything was so sensual, right down to Lindsay, who was

sitting negligently on the divan, dressed only in black trousers and a white shirt that was fully opened. His head was tipped back and his lips parted as a cloud of smoke escaped them. He was the very picture of a dreamy smoker, and the image of him, so beautiful and seductive, posed like this, beckoned her.

"Why don't you take to your bed," Lindsay drawled. He kept his head back and his eyes closed as he spoke. "I'll be up for a while yet."

The valet said nothing, but walked to the side of the room and slipped through another door. Lindsay lifted his head, shifted his position so that he was lying on his side and reached for the pipe. Through the dancing vapors, their gazes collided.

"You're here early," he said, sitting back against the wall. "I usually need much more to see you so clearly."

Stepping closer, she walked along the cold tiles toward the tented dome where Lindsay sat. His eyes, now a different color of green, were more jade as they seemed to glow amongst the smoke. They appeared to dance, too, as his gaze roved over her body.

Anais didn't dare speak lest she break the spell that seemed to be weaving itself around them.

"I've often tried to imagine you in that gown and wrapper. I bought it last year, you know. A modiste created it from my specifications. I had planned on giving it to you for a wedding gift. Perhaps that's why I've never been able to see you in it. I couldn't bring myself to think of never having a wedding night with you."

Her breath caught as the implications of his words settled in. He'd designed this for her and had it made, especially for her.

"I see you've brought the book, too. You like it. I'm glad."

He reached for the pipe and brought it to his lips. Closing his eyes, he inhaled the fumes. Anais found herself walking slowly over to him, as though she were in a dream. His body called to hers. The sensuality in the room hung heavy, blanketing her in a desire she had tried to forget.

Putting the pipe down, he winced and clutched his fingers. Anais saw then how red the tips were—blistered, filled with water.

"You've burned yourself." Standing over him, she reached for his hand and held it up to the dim light. The lanterns were not lit. Only one candle provided light, and that was the candle Lindsay used to heat his opium.

"It's not from the pipe, you needn't worry about that." Anais felt his hand go to her hair. Slowly he pulled her hair free of the ribbon she had used to tie it back. The thick mass cascaded over her shoulder, and he reached for it, running his fingers through her curls. "I burned them today, going through the rubble of your father's estate. I tried to salvage the volume of Keats, but it was beyond hope. I didn't realize how hot it would be when I saw it lying amongst the rubble."

Her heart leapt at his kindness. He had always been so caring and thoughtful toward her. It had been his sensitive nature that had drawn her in the first place. Sitting down beside him, Anais held his hand gently in hers. "You need to take care of this, Lindsay. It'll grow infected if you don't."

"I don't need anything." He cupped her face. "Just you here in the quiet with me."

She saw how sleepy he appeared. How much had he smoked? she wondered.

"Angel," he said as his hand reached for the tie of her wrapper, "come to me."

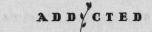

She wanted to. Oh, God, how much she wanted to.

He sat up, leaning a little closer to her as he ran his hand down the curve of her breast, which pressed against the silk. "Rise up from this bed and walk to me amidst the smoke. Crawl atop me, just like the smoke does, Anais."

She didn't move, only closed her eyes against the wonderful sensation of his gentle touch. "Are you real, angel, or are you just anther figment of my mind? I can hardly tell anymore. Yet you feel so very real. So warm and alive. I can feel your heart beating against my palm. I can hear your breaths. Yet I know I must be dreaming, seeing you like this."

She was weakening, feeling herself moving into him. What sort of creature was she? Some stranger in her own skin, a wanton who could not stop her gaze from roving along his sculpted chest and chiseled abdomen. A hussy who secretly hoped that he would tear the silk from her trembling fingers and finish what he had started? A fraud who wanted him to just take her, regardless of her ineffectual protests so that she would not have to admit that she truly wanted this—with him?

It would be so much easier to deny her desire and absolve herself of her own willing involvement. She could do it now if he would only prove himself the beast she tried so hard to believe he was. If he would only push her back on the divan and cover her body and protesting mouth.

But he denied her. He did not force his mouth on hers and ruthlessly plunge his tongue between her lips, but instead reached out with a finger that trembled, and stroked her flushed cheek, his eyes softening in the candlelight as he scoured her face.

He pressed into her, inhaling her skin, the scent of her hair.

She felt him nuzzle her riotous curls with his lips, and when he pulled away he took with him a handful of curls that he allowed to slip through his fingers, all the while studying the strands that glistened in the flickering light.

Her breath was rapid, short pants and her mouth parted when he pressed his lips against her face and grazed them, featherlight, along her forehead only to skate down to her cheek and over the bridge of her nose and finally down to her lips. He said not a word, not a sound. She only felt the barest brush of his breath against her tingling lips, felt the heat of his gaze as he searched her face, willing her to raise her gaze and meet his burning eyes. But she stood firm, pretending she was not moved, that she was not affected by his mastery.

His touch became more insistent and she refused to look at him and instead turned her face in an attempt to show abhorrence. But he was not persuaded to believe her disgust of him. Instead, he cupped her throat and ran his thumb along her bounding pulse, discovering for himself the extent of her deceit.

"How sweetly you enslave me, Anais." Her lips quivered as he stroked them with the pad of his thumb. "With one glance from your beautiful eyes, one shy smile from your lush, welcoming mouth, I have, and always will be, your slave."

He tilted her face upward so that she was looking into his eyes, eyes that were glazed with opium and passion, a heady, alluring mixture that called to the very depths of her soul. Never had she thought to have wanted him like this. Yet she could not deny the desire, the heavy pulse and throb in her blood. She wanted him, right here in his pleasure den. She

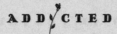

wanted this Lindsay, the secret side of him she hadn't known existed. There was nothing to guard against his feelings for her, no safety net of propriety. The opium had freed him, made him uninhibited, and she wanted that. The sharing of bodies and pleasure without anything between them.

"'I have been astonished that men could die martyrs for religion—I have shuddered at it. I shudder no more—I could be martyred for my religion—love is my religion. I could die for that. I could die for you.'"

Keats. He had quoted the famous poet, recalled every word, even through the opium. After all this time, he still remembered that day by the river, when he had presented her with a volume of Keats's poetry. He had read it to her as they lay on a blanket, surrounded by the remnants of their picnic lunch. He had kissed her, a tender, slow burning kiss that had promised so much as they had said their goodbyes. The next day, he had left for Cambridge, leaving her with the memories of that late summer day by the river. It seemed so long ago, yet her mind relived it as though it were yesterday.

"I just want it like it was, before I hurt you," he whispered as he ran his hand down her side and along her hip. "I am so very, very sorry, Anais. I would tell you a thousand—no, a million times—if I thought it would ease the pain."

"I know you are, Lindsay." His heart was in his eyes. She could not deny him that or pretend that he didn't mean it. It was there, shining down at her.

"How can I make it up to you? What words can I say to make it better? What can I do? Can I show you with my body?"

She weakened. There was no shame in desire. She was a

woman who had experienced pleasure, then it was gone. She had not forgotten the passion or the way her body had felt. She longed to feel that again.

It was so very, very wicked to do this. She was, in fact, using him. He was under the influence of opium. He might very well not even recall what he had said, or what they were about to do. But then, if there was a chance she thought he would remember, would she be contemplating this?

No, she would not. It was only knowing that the opium was inside him that made her bold enough to risk this.

What a flawed, horrid woman she was. So weak. But she needed to feel the passion, the way her body seemed to light up beneath his hands. She wanted sexual fulfillment once more.

"I have told you with words how sorry I am, now let me show you with my body, angel."

Anais opened her mouth to him, allowing him entrance. He pushed her back onto the cushions, crushing her with his weight, reassuring her with his heat. It was silent acceptance of what they both wanted.

There would be no guilt or remorse. Tonight was just pleasure. A man and a woman sharing their bodies. In the morning she could remind herself how much of a fallen woman she was. How horrid she was. Because come the morning she would deny him—she must. But tonight, she would accept him just as he was.

His hands undid the sash of her wrapper. His fingers, trembling, unbuttoned her night rail until it parted over her body. The single light from the candle that sat on the tray had dimmed, the wick had burned low, creating an atmospheric curtain around them. It was a perfect setting for this dark seduction.

Unable to help herself, Anais raked her hands through his long hair as he bent over her, his tongue trailing a line from her navel to the valley of her breasts. Instead of licking her nipples as she expected and hoped he would, he nuzzled them with his lips, moistening them with his breath, then blew gently against them until they were so tight and erect she moved restlessly against him.

Her hands continued to slide through his silky hair while he held himself above her, bracing his weight on his forearms. He was still teasing her and Anais opened her eyelids a fraction— just enough to watch his bottom lip toy with the very tip of her nipple. His eyes, still glazed from the opium, met hers, and with deliberate strokes he flicked her nipple with his tongue. He continued to hold her gaze while his tongue crept out again. This time though, he circled the erect flesh in a slow, delicious swirl.

Her fingers continued to tangle through his hair, clenching when arousal coiled and tightened in her belly. She watched him lave her breasts, and whenever he looked up at her, he watched her face while wickedly swirling his tongue around her nipple, sending sharp pains of desire deep within her.

"I could feast on you for hours, angel," he said while his fingers stroked her thigh. Drawing little circles on her skin, he made his way to her knee. With little encouragement, she let her leg drop so that her mound was exposed. He studied her there, not touching her. Then lifted himself off of her and pulled his shirttails from his trousers. Flinging his shirt down beside them, he undid the front of his pants. She met his gaze, then leisurely let her eyes roam the expanse of his chest, which was broad and heavily sculpted. The muscles of his belly were taut and chiseled. A silky line of black hair swirled around his navel only to disappear below the waist of his trousers. How breathtakingly beautiful his body was.

As if he knew her thoughts, he smiled, a wicked, lusty grin, then slowly pushed aside the fabric. He grasped his erection in his hand. Anais felt her eyes widen at the size of him, but also at the way he intimately and shamelessly stroked himself. Impossible to believe, his shaft actually thickened and widened, and Anais looked up to his face and saw that he stared at her.

"Do you think I've never done this before while thinking of you? Always, only you, Anais."

Empowered by his confession, Anais watched as his erection slid between the space between his thumb and index finger. Slowly at first, he stroked, up and down, reaching only as far as the pink tip. His grip was loose and slow, his hips moving in time with his hand. But soon his breathing increased, as did his hold. Soon he was gripping his shaft, working it hard and assuredly, watching her as she studied him. The sight was so erotic, that Anais could not help but reach out and glide her finger along the rigid length of him. Suddenly he stopped, deprived her of her feeling him and stood. Lindsay removed his trousers and stood naked before her, his shaft thick and throbbing between his thighs.

"Sit up, angel," he commanded before walking behind her. When he was seated on his knees, he brought her knees up and spread her thighs wide. "Have you touched yourself, while dreaming of me, Anais?"

She nodded as he entwined their hands and placed them on her sex. "Show me, Anais, and let me watch," he asked, kissing

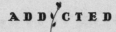

the hollow below her ear. He slid his fingers along her sex and parted her. She felt his hot gaze there where his fingers played in her folds. "You're already so wet, angel," he said, touching her ever so softly. Then he stopped, brought his finger to his mouth and licked, "and you taste every bit as good as I remember."

Lost in him, Anais luxuriated in the feel of Lindsay's hand gliding down her side to her thigh, his gaze moving with the motion of his hand as it trailed along her pale skin, assessing her like a slave at a bazaar. His lashes flickered, then lifted to meet her face while his hand skated over her rounded belly.

"I have dreamed of this, Anais, this physical reunion between us. It was at once my torture and my salvation."

Before she knew what was happening, her night rail and wrapper were pulled from her shoulders and Lindsay was lying on his back, urging her on top of him.

"Let me look at you, angel," he whispered as she sat astride him. Anais crossed her arms over her breast and belly. The shadows, she was afraid, would not hide everything she wished. He forced her arms to her sides, and Anais noticed how his gaze hungrily devoured her breasts in one glance. With his palms he traveled along her body, cupping her breasts before sliding his fingers over her waist and allowing them to follow the curve of her hips. Over and over he repeated the action until Anais was moving slowly, gliding her hips back and forth. She was restless. Hot. Her back was arched and her arms were behind her. Her own hands were tangling in her hair as she began her dance of seduction.

Lindsay was whispering encouragement as he plucked at her nipple with one hand. With the other, he gripped his erection and was brushing the silken tip along her plump buttock. She felt the warm wetness against her skin. He was already wet, leaking his seed.

It made her more wanton, and she writhed a bit more seductively, her movements less stiff, more sensual and undulating. She had lowered her arms and caught her breasts in her hands, massaging them as he watched. Pressing them together, she squeezed, then parted them in invitation.

With strong hands, he gripped her hips and lifted her up, bringing her higher onto his chest. "Lower yourself onto my mouth, Anais, and let me taste you."

With a whimper of surprise and excitement she did. Her fingers clutched onto his shoulders, his hands anchored her hips, tilting them until her mound was angled toward his mouth. Then the sensation of his hot tongue brushing the length of her made her moan long and deep.

The thin beard on his chin abraded and sensitized her skin, making the sensation so much more consuming. Soon her fingers were pressing into his shoulders as she moved atop him, showing him with her hips the direction she wanted his tongue to move.

Anais looked down to find Lindsay's black head between her thighs. A strangled sound escaped her and he looked up, his eyes wickedly gazing back at her as he slowly licked, showing her his tongue on her. She reached down and touched herself, sliding her fingers up to her clitoris, allowing her fingers to glide against Lindsay's tongue. He licked her wet fingers while she played with her sex.

"God, you're so beautiful," he murmured as he watched her

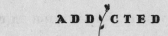

fingers stroking herself. The pressure was building deep within her when suddenly she felt his fingers inside her. It was too much, he held her tight, pressing her sex to his mouth, trembling as he sucked—drinking all of her in.

"Lindsay!" Anais rocked shamelessly against him. When at last she stilled, she pulled away from him, sliding down his body and burying her face in his hard chest.

"Anais," his voice was soft and soothing, much like his fingers as they raked through her tousled hair. "You were so beautiful and passionate. I'll never forget the way you looked on top of me."

She blushed and pressed her face into his neck. She hoped he forgot, or at least thought it was a fantasy induced by opium, for if Lindsay remembered this night, her plan to feign disinterest in him would be ruined. How could she reasonably tell him she no longer desired him after what she had done tonight?

Lindsay held her tight as he smoothed his palm along her spine. Their breaths merged, syncing in time with each other. Anais felt a peace still over her and she closed her eyes, allowing herself to stay for just a moment longer in Lindsay's arms.

"I'm sorry, angel," he murmured against her. "So sorry for everything. If you were here now, I could tell you, but you're just a figment of the smoke. The smoke, it's always so real, but I know when I open my eyes I will be all alone." Lifting her head, Anais could not help but kiss him. If circumstances were different, if she had not turned to Garrett for help, if she had not done something so terrible, then they might have been able to be together.

"You'll be gone. Won't you?"

"Yes, Lindsay. I will be gone."

"Then I shall smoke more, and you'll come back to me. You always come back to me, walking out of the smoke and into my arms."

12

Morning sunlight streamed through the frosted windowpane and glinted brilliantly off the highly polished silver tea service that sat in the middle of the dining table. Sounds of cutlery eagerly clanking against bone china shattered the quiet of the breakfast table. Conversation was at a minimum and Anais could not have been happier for it. The sooner she laid waste to her plate, the sooner she could leave the room and not have to feel Lindsay's bold gaze boring into her from across the table.

Keeping her eyes downcast, Anais forced herself to swallow a bitter bite of the deviled kidneys a footman had placed on her plate from the sideboard. Her stomach lurched as her teeth bit into the tough texture. Choking the bite down, she reached for her napkin, shielding her repulsion behind the white linen.

Confident that she was not going to disgrace herself by retching, Anais reached for her teacup and drank the entire contents in one long swallow, washing down the acerbic after-taste of the kidneys.

Finally feeling composed, Anais looked up, straight into

Lindsay's quizzical gaze. With an arch of a questioning brow and a glance at her plate that was laden with kidneys and a slice of stuffed beef heart.

She looked away, resisting his blatant stare.

"Have Lord and Lady Weston no room for you?" Lord Weatherby grumbled.

"My daughter and her husband are in Cádiz. They are not expected to return until the spring. We shall stay with my sister-in-law in London, just as soon as we are able to send word to her."

"When shall you write to your husband's sister?" Lord Weatherby slapped his folded news sheet atop the table. "Soon, I hope. Darnby looks to be out of imminent danger. I'm quite certain he will survive his mishap and will no doubt linger for years to come, delighting in being a damned thorn in my side."

"I have agreed to undertake the correspondence with my aunt, my lord," Anais replied after clearing her throat. "If I may bother Lady Weatherby for some paper and nibs, as well as a pot of ink, I shall write to my aunt directly after breakfast."

"You may have a ream of paper and a half-dozen pots of ink if it will get you out of my house faster," Weatherby growled before shoving a forkful of eggs in his mouth.

"My lord, *really*," Lady Weatherby murmured discreetly, but Anais could see the stain of embarrassment tinting the marchioness's ivory cheeks.

"Well, what am I to say, Eleanor? That I am pleased to have the entire Darnby household thrust upon me? Shall I pretend to be enjoying their company when any fool with eyes and half a brain knows that I wish for nothing but to have my home to myself?"

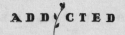

"We are very thankful, my lord, for your generosity toward our family," Anais murmured, hoping she sounded contrite enough to placate an obviously surly and hungover Lord Weatherby. "My family and I will make every attempt to vacate the premises as soon as may be."

"You may thank my wife, not me. It is her hospitality and her damnable, annoying friendship with your father that keeps you here. Had it been up to me, I would have shut the door and not looked back. Damned inconvenient, the lot of ye."

"Father," Lindsay growled in warning from down the length of the table. "That is enough."

"Enough?" Weatherby snorted. "I have been roused from my bed at the god-awful hour of ten when everyone in this house, including my blasted valet, knows that I do not flutter my lashes till at least noon, let alone actually get up out of bed. And if that is not enough, I am ordered, during my morning ablutions, to behave myself in a manner befitting a host by not only my wife, but my son, a son, I may add, who has frigged off to parts unknown for the past year. Oh, no, my boy, I have not yet begun. Perhaps I may start right now, with your unexpected return after months and months of bloody silence. Months of not knowing whether my son was alive or dead. Months of wondering if any day some damn Eastern infidel would arrive on my doorstep with your dead body."

"Charles," Lady Weatherby whispered softly and Anais watched as Lindsay's mother placed a gentle hand atop Weatherby's wrinkled fingers. To Anais's shock, the old marquis clutched his wife's hand.

"The Darnbys are like family, are they not?" Weatherby

grunted. "Is that not what you are forever telling me? Well, damn me, Eleanor, they can listen to our family squabbles. I'm certain that even a woman like Lady Darnby here would feel some inkling of maternal instinct if one of her chits squandered off for parts unknown without a damned word to anyone."

I wouldn't bet on that, Anais thought silently, as she looked at her mother's bored expression. Her mother was completely lacking in the finer female sentiments. She had conceived her children, carried them and delivered them. After that, she had promptly given her daughters over to a nanny, washing her hands of them until they were of an age to shape into perfect china dolls in order to catch the perfect son-in-law. A son-in-law who would prove perfectly useful in furthering her prestige in society, while generously giving his money to his ever spending mother-in-law.

"Damn me, boy," Weatherby said with a scowl, "who the devil is to run this place when I am gone? Have you no inkling of responsibility?"

Anais's gaze swung to Lindsay, whose expression had turned hard and unyielding. His father's accusation was cruel, for Lindsay had been responsible for overseeing the running of Eden Park since he was sixteen years old, thus allowing his father to spend his days in London, whoring and drinking and frittering away his life. In that, Lindsay had never shirked his duties. Lindsay may have gotten caught up in opium. He might have hurt her, albeit unwittingly, but he was not a gadabout. He did not evade his responsibilities. Without Lindsay's head for investments and his tireless work ethic, Eden Park would have crumbled into the ground.

And the way Lindsay had always taken care of his mother was something to be commended, and his father, too. A father who had always been too drunk, too indifferent to his son to see him raised in the manner of a gentleman. Despite all that, Lindsay had grown into a respectable man of influence and wealth. And even though his father hadn't spared a second of his time on his son, Lindsay still provided for him, making certain both his parents were comfortable in their homes. The sudden recollection of Lindsay's childhood made her realize how soon Lindsay had been forced to grow up. Sadly she wondered who had seen to Lindsay's needs and happiness.

Their gazes met across the table, and Anais felt her insides twist as Lindsay's expression, still glazed from the smoke he had imbibed in last night, held an emptiness that tore at her heart. It was then that she had her answer. Opium gave him what he needed.

"Well, what the devil have you to say for yourself, boy?"

"Charles, you're upsetting your digestion."

"Hang my damned digestion, Eleanor!" Weatherby thundered. "I am dying Any simpleton can see that. I am dying and I want to know if my son, my *only* son, is prepared to stick around and see to his duties. Or does he plan to run off the next time a muffed piece of tail decides to hold him captive by the short hairs."

"Your language would make an old roué blush, Father. This is not the sort of talk considered polite or appropriate for the table, not to mention in front of mixed company," Lindsay said, glaring at his father. "Might we adjourn this conversation until another time?"

"Coward," his father taunted, "she still has you by the bollocks."

Lindsay threw his napkin to the table as if it were a gauntlet. Sliding his chair back, he began to rise, like a cobra uncurling itself, preparing to strike an unsuspecting victim. Anais had seen that implacable look in Lindsay's eyes before.

"That is quite enough," Lady Weatherby demanded, her voice shaking with rage. "It is the Christmas season, and we have guests. Can you not behave yourself, Charles? For once, will you please refrain from doing your utmost to humiliate me? Our son is home, safe and sound. Should we not be rejoicing such a fact? I despise this fighting...this constant needling between the pair of you."

"My pardon, Mama, I seem to have forgotten myself," Lindsay murmured, nodding to his mother in apology. He slowly regained his chair, but his hands were fisted tightly. Anais knew he was raging inside. She knew, too, that Lady Weatherby was close to tears, and her own mama was smiling that grin that was smug and haughty, a grin that let everyone at the table know how far above them she thought she was.

"I am aware how very difficult it is to have one's routine upset," Anais said, avoiding the uneasy glances of her sister, as well as that of Lady Weatherby. "I assure you, my lord, that I will inform my aunt, in the most ardent terms possible, that her immediate assistance is required. In the meantime, sir, we shall endeavor to stay out of your way and attempt to make certain that our presence here will cause the minimal of upset to your routine. I promise you, my lord, that we will not overstay our welcome."

"Ye already have," Weatherby muttered as he continued to shovel his breakfast into his mouth. Lady Weatherby shot her an apologizing look that spoke of too many years of shame. Anais could not imagine having to live with such a boor for a

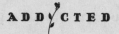

husband and for some reason her gaze shot to Lindsay, whose own eyes seemed to cry out to her, *I'm not like him.*

"Tea?" Anais inquired politely as she held the teapot up, hoping to break the considerable tension at the table.

"Please." Lindsay held out his cup and saucer to her.

"Do you still take sugar?"

He shook his head and raised the steaming cup to his mouth. "Scandal and love are the best sweeteners of tea. We have had a bit of scandal, now what shall we do about love?"

Anais colored and shot him a warning scowl, but he only arched his brow in return. Try as she might, she was drawn to him. Perhaps she was as addicted to Lindsay as he was to the opium.

"I have had a missive from the vicar, Mr. Pratt," Lady Weatherby said as her gaze volleyed between Anais and Lindsay. "He's asked permission for the villagers to skate on the little creek that runs from the village through the estate. Might I inform him, my lord—" she turned to ask her husband "—that the villagers may do as they please? It is Boxing Day, after all."

"I don't give a bloody damn what the villagers do, as long as they pay their rents they may skate and slide about all the way to London for all I care."

"I shall inform Mr. Pratt," the marchioness replied. "Immediately after breakfast. I am taking Lady Darnby and Ann into the village to Mrs. Jennings's shop. She promised to have at least a day dress ready for each of them. The rest of their trousseau shall be ready within the week, I hope. Anais, you must come, too. Mrs. Jennings was not able to see you for a fitting. But before all that, we shall make the vicarage our first stop."

Weatherby grumbled and continued eating, and Anais felt her

lips curl in distaste. How had Lindsay's mother borne the weight of being a wife to such a worthless man?

"Shall you go into the village today, Lindsay?" Lady Weatherby asked. "We would be happy for a male escort, you know."

"The village modiste holds little allure, Mama," Lindsay said with a chuckle and an indulgent smile for his mother. "However, the notion of a sleigh ride and skating does hold some appeal. Who can I talk into such a pastime?"

"Excuse me, my lord, my lady," Worthing, the butler, said with a bow. "Lord Wallingford and his sister are here and are desirous to speak to Lord Raeburn and our guests."

"Do send them in, Worthing." Lady Weatherby's smile lit her face, taking away the sadness that marred her lovely green eyes.

"Christ almighty," Weatherby spat viciously, "I thought he'd have more sense than to bring that irritating half-wit sister of his."

Anais heard, as well as saw, her mother's smile and little chuckle. Her gaze shot to Ann who was seated next to their mother. Shock and disbelief tore through Anais as she watched Ann laugh and mimic the wringing, agitated hands of Lady Sarah, Wallingford's sweet but simple-minded sister.

"Aye, you've the right of it," Weatherby laughed. "Damned irritating, the chit."

The door swung open, revealing Wallingford and a nervous, fidgeting Sarah. Catching Ann's gaze, Anais narrowed her eyes in a message that was unable to be misinterpreted.

"Good day, my lord, Lady Sarah," Lady Weatherby said with a kind smile. "Do have a seat. Have you dined, yet?"

"Good day," Wallingford said with a nod. He did not take the chair that was offered him, but instead placed a protective hand

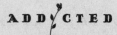

between his sister's shoulders before sending a black glare down the length of the table toward Weatherby and Anais's sister and mother. Obviously, he had heard what had been said of his sister, and Anais had never felt shame more acutely than she did now.

"You are looking very lovely, Lady Sarah," Anais said, waving her over to the empty chair beside her. "Pray, how does your maid get all that lovely hair of yours up into a bun without having any curls escaping?"

"With pins that hurt," Sarah said with a childish pout. But she smiled and took the chair beside Anais before looking at her brother for reassurance. Wallingford, Anais noticed, nodded. His dark and usually unreadable eyes softened with emotion.

"We have come to give your sister some clothes," Sarah said in a quiet voice. Anais could not help but notice how Sarah began to rock back and forth while she wrapped and unwrapped her fingers in her lap.

"How very kind of you," Anais said, resting her hand reassuringly across Sarah's wringing hands. "Nothing survived the fire."

Sarah's dark blue eyes went wide and her little bow mouth parted in shock. "Nothing? Not even your clothes? What of the house?" Sarah asked.

"Oh, of course the house survived, only the clothes went up in flame," Ann muttered in a chiding, snide manner.

Anais sent her sister a quelling look and didn't care that Lindsay had witnessed the silent threat before she turned her attention back to a nervous Sarah who was rounding her shoulders and trying to withdraw into herself. No doubt the poor girl was wishing the floor would open up and take her, chair and all, far away from such insolent people.

"I'm afraid not even our home survived, Sarah. We are dependent upon such kind people like you to help us get back on our feet. We are quite without anything, that is, until you came today."

"I don't have anything for you," Sarah stated. "I'm afraid you're too big to wear my clothes. And my sisters that still live at home with me are much skinnier than you."

Anais felt her face flame red. When she heard Ann's gasp of outrage, she knew the entire room had heard Sarah, but she could not belittle the sweet creature. Sarah simply didn't know any better, and Anais knew the girl didn't have a malicious bone in her body.

"Sarah," Wallingford muttered in a deep warning voice, but Anais smiled and silently told him she had not taken any offence.

"I fear that is what eating too many puddings and custards do to a woman," Anais whispered to her as if they were sharing a secret.

"I will remember that, Lady Anais," Sarah whispered back.

"I thought I heard something about a sleigh ride and skating," Wallingford said, peering down at her and smiling with affection—affection Anais had never seen so openly displayed by him before.

"What do you say?" Lindsay asked. "Who is game for a little sport this morning?"

"Oh, will you come, Lady Anais?" Sarah asked, clutching Anais's hands as if they were a lifeline. "Say you will."

"Anais won't be going, she has letters to write," Ann said while she rolled her blue eyes. "Plus, she can't skate. Anais is a chicken when it comes to skating."

"Is that true?" Sarah turned to her and studied her with wide,

innocent eyes. "Even *I* can skate, Lady Anais. I can teach you," Sarah cried with the exuberance of a seven-year-old child, and Anais felt her heart soften. Sarah was fifteen years old, her sister Ann's age.

"Well," Anais hesitated. She didn't know how to skate, and falling down with her skirts landing above her knees in front of Lindsay and Wallingford was something she didn't care to partake in. Not to mention the fact she had planned on avoiding Lindsay for the next weeks until Aunt Millie could come and retrieve them.

"Coward," Ann goaded.

"I am not." Anais glared at her sister. "Come along then, Sarah. Now, I have not been feeling up to snuff these past weeks, so I can make you no promises, other than I shall try to skate. And if I am unable, we shall have to be satisfied with a sleigh ride. Is it a deal?"

"Oh, goodie," Sarah said with a laugh, followed by a little skip that carried her to where her brother waited. "Lady Anais is coming, Matthew! Oh, this is going to be the bestest, funnest day ever."

"Yes, it will, sweeting."

"I am so happy I came with you, Matthew."

"I am glad, too, pet," Wallingford said with a soft smile. Anais felt herself grinning when Wallingford's eyes, which were warm with emotion, peered over Sarah's shoulder and found her gaze. *Thank you,* he mouthed before offering his arm to his sister. "Come along, pet, we've got to get you bundled up if we're to be skating. We wouldn't want you getting your little fingers and toes bitten by the frost."

Anais watched as everyone filed out of the dining room. When Ann made to leave, Anais reached for her arm and held her back, smiling at Lady Weatherby as she passed by. "I've just been reminded of something I need to discuss with my sister. You will inform our party that we will be a moment longer?"

"Of course, dear. Take your time. I'm certain it will take the grooms a few minutes to harness the sleigh to the horses."

When the door closed behind Lindsay's mother, Anais reeled on her sister. "Your behavior was beyond the pale. It was one thing for Mama to laugh and find humor in Lord Weatherby's jest, but it was beneath *you*," Anais hissed as she ruthlessly clutched her sister's slender arm. "It shamed me to the core that my sister could act with such blatant disregard for the feelings of others. That girl cannot help the way she is. The world at large would seek to make fun of her and misunderstand her. She need not hear the same from you."

Ann's blue eyes immediately began to water. "Badly done, Ann," Anais chided. "Very badly done. That was childish and inexcusable behavior from you. Our mother is that sort of person, don't let me have the pain of knowing that my beloved sister is following in her footsteps."

"I didn't mean for her to find out. I didn't want to hurt her," Ann said through trembling lips.

"For the past months you have professed to be a woman, Ann, but I can assure you the behavior you displayed is not the behavior of a well-bred young woman."

"I'm sorry, Anias. Do you hate me now? Like you hate Mother?"

"I don't hate you. But God's truth I am sorely disappointed in you. You have it in you to be a very kind person, Ann,

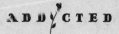

remember that. It is a mark of a woman of breeding to be kind and indulgent to those weaker than themselves. I'm only telling you this because you are so beautiful and lovely. You are quite the most popular girl in the village. People will want to emulate you, they will look to you to be guided in their actions. Whether you want to believe it or not, it is the truth. If people see you belittling someone as innocent and defence-less as Sarah, they will deem it the right thing to do. When they look to you, Ann, is that what you want them to see, a mean, spiteful, beautiful girl, so haughty and uncaring that she delights in hurting the feelings of someone who cannot change who she is?"

Ann sobbed as the tears fell from her eyes. "No, I don't want to be that person. But I don't know what to do. What to say to Sarah."

"Perhaps you should seek to get to know her. Maybe if she felt secure in the fact that she was amongst friends, she would let her guard down and her nervousness and awkwardness would not show so much."

"I will, Anais, for you."

"Do not do it for me. Do it because you want to be that sort of person. It's pointless if you seek only to be kind to better yourself in someone else's eyes. Be kind because you are, not because it is desired of you."

Ann sniffled and wiped her eyes with the back of her hand. "I am sorry, Anais."

"I know, dearest," Anais whispered, folding her sister in her arms. "I was harsh, perhaps too harsh. Everyone makes mistakes."

"Not you," Ann whimpered into the silk shoulder of Anais's borrowed morning gown.

"Oh, I have made mistakes, Ann. Believe me. They are far more painful than what you have done today. Now then, on you go and dry your tears."

Ann reached for a napkin from the table and blew into it with vigor. Opening the door, her sister rushed out and headed for the stairs. When Anais stepped forward, Lindsay's body blocked the door. Anais's head shot up and she saw that he was looking at her, his eyes assessing her, roaming over her in a most disconcerting fashion.

"It's true then." He reached for her hand and brought her fingertips to his mouth.

"What is true?"

"That she still lives."

"Who lives?" Anais asked, confused and more than a little befuddled when Lindsay placed her palm against his cheek.

"My Anais."

He tugged her forward and pressed his mouth to her temple. "I knew she couldn't just die, she was too strong for that. But I admit, I feared she was locked away, but she got out today, didn't she? I saw her, the Anais of my youth. The Anais who stole my heart with her fiery temper and her staunch support of those less fortunate. You protect those you care about, like a little tigress. You tried to protect me, too—from my father."

"You are making more out of this than it needs to be."

"No, I am not. You aren't the cold, indifferent ice princess you have been pretending to be. You haven't changed as you wish me to believe. Your game is up, Anais."

"Lindsay, please, someone will see."

"She lives. And as long as she does, I have a chance to get her back."

She looked up pleadingly into his face. "Do not try to gain me back. It can never be, Lindsay. Please…just believe me, and accept that it is over."

He reached for her wrist as she walked past him and pulled her back to whisper in her ear. "This will only be over when both of us draw our last breath, and even then I am not convinced my desire for you will end. I want another chance, Anais, and I will have it."

13

The morning passed pleasantly, and Anais could say with all honesty that she had not enjoyed herself so well in months. Wallingford and his sister Sarah had taught her to skate, and seeing Sarah laugh was enough to make Anais's embarrassing stumbles and flailing arms bearable. She had only been able to skate a few short minutes before fatigue and heavy breathing made her rest at the side of the riverbank. She probably should not have ventured out at all, but she needed a reprieve from the house. She also didn't want to appear too ill, otherwise Lindsay might take it upon himself to investigate her condition; something that would lead to the proverbial Pandora's box. Lindsay simply could not learn the root of her illness.

Thankfully Lindsay had occupied himself with his mother and Ann, touring them about the village in the sleigh. He had offered to take her, as well, but Anais had flatly refused. Sitting that close to him would be far too tempting.

The hours spent in the village seemed to go by in a blur. Before Anais knew it, she was back at Eden Park, sipping tea with Lady Weatherby while Wallingford and Lindsay went riding. After tea, Anais made her way upstairs to check in on her father.

When she arrived at his chamber, she was surprised to see Lindsay was with him, sitting in a chair at her father's bedside. They had been deep in conversation and Anais had not been able to hear any of their words, although she had tried. Lindsay's expression when he rose from his chair was a look of concern. She glanced at her father and saw that his face looked tired and drawn.

"I have your word, son?" her father grumbled.

Lindsay nodded. As he passed her, his fingers brushed hers. Without a word, he left the room.

"What were you discussing?"

"Nothing of any import, child," her father said, motioning her over to him. "Now then, why don't you read to me? I am bored to tears just lying abed all day."

Anais spent most of the afternoon with her father, reading to him and playing cards. She had tried many different tactics to get her father to talk of his conversation with Lindsay, but he avoided the topic and refused to speak of it, leaving her even more intrigued.

Hours later, when Anais returned to her room she was utterly exhausted. She had pushed herself hard, trying to appear as though nothing was wrong. Instead, she felt weak and had every intention of lying down and napping, but she heard the thundering of hooves and was drawn to her window by the sounds of a galloping horse. Below, she saw Lindsay astride the most magnificent black mount she had ever seen. Sleek and fast with graceful turns, she watched as Lindsay pressed forward in the saddle, encouraging the horse to run faster.

Clouds of white snow shot out from behind the horse. Billowing gray vapor puffed from the horse's long muzzle and Anais swore she could hear the snort of the Arabian's labored breathing as Lindsay pressed the mount forward. Her eyes followed them until they passed beneath her window then swiftly turned direction, disappearing around the stables.

Anais stood at the window for a long while, watching for Lindsay to emerge, but he did not come out. She knew Lindsay well enough to know he would not entrust such an animal to one of Weatherby's grooms. He had always saddled and cared for his own mounts, cooling them down as he thought they should be. He had showed her how to care for her own horse, too. She smiled, thinking of those lessons, how they had laughed and teased. They had been the best of friends then.

Horses had been their shared passion. It had always only been the two of them whenever they went riding, and she realized with a strange wistfulness that she missed those times—those hours of freedom and lightness. Of being nothing more than friends who could talk about anything.

It would not do to dwell in the past. That part of her life was over. She was no longer that person who indulged in midnight rides and stolen moments of passion in a stable. She was now an actress, performing the most important role of her life. Anais hoped with all her being that she could act her part and convince Lindsay she didn't want him in her life. Yet she couldn't stop thinking of the previous night—of being drawn into the mystique of the room and the sensuality that had clouded her.

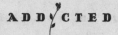

Her body wanted what her mind knew she should not desire. Lindsay once more. To be taken on those luxurious pillows in a heady dream of passion and abandon.

Turning from the window, Anais forced herself to forget her desires. Lindsay was the past. She must look now to the future.

Despite a significant nap, the evening was long and arduous. Anais pled fatigue in order to extricate herself from the hours spent listening to her mother bewail her misfortune to anyone with a sympathetic ear. Ann had retired at the same time as she, and Lindsay had remained curiously absent through not only supper, but the evening, as well.

Sitting on the window bench in her room, Anais curled her feet beneath her legs and stared out at the moonlit snow. Bringing her arms around her knees, she sighed as her gaze skated over the blanket of snow toward the stables.

The brick building called to her, like a Siren calling to sailors, and without thinking the matter through, she rifled through a trunk Margaret Middleton had sent over and pulled out a brown woolen gown.

Devil take it! She was tired of sitting in her room feeling sorry for herself. It was about time she found some of the spirit she used to have.

After hurriedly donning the serviceable gown, Anais hunted in Lindsay's wardrobe, searching for the pair of riding boots she knew were hidden in the cupboard. Slipping her stocking feet inside, she lowered her flounced skirts. The hem dragged on the carpet without the bell-shaped crinolines to hold them out.

But she did not need them to support her skirts for what she had in mind.

Silently, Anais crept down the stairs and into the pantry. Sliding the bolt free of the lock, she stepped outside and ran for the stables, streaking across the frozen ground. She slipped through the door, making her way to the stall that housed the black Arabian. She had not been able to resist a meeting with the sleek stallion, not after glimpsing him running wild and free with Lindsay this afternoon.

Two lanterns hung from thick wooden beams and the orange flame danced behind the glass shield, casting shadows along the stable walls. A soft whinny erupted from the lighted corner; it was returned with the deep throaty snort of the stallion.

Drawing her cloak around her, Anais stopped before the giant beast whose head hung over the gate and whose huge brown eyes studied her intently.

"Shh," she soothed, reaching inside her cloak and pulling out two cubes of sugar she had pinched from the pantry. "Here you go." She held her hand, palm out to the stallion. He sniffed her gloved fingers then tilted his head, staring at her.

Running her hand down the long, proud line of his muzzle, she brushed back the coal-colored forelock from his eyes. "Your mane is as unruly as your owner's," she said, smiling when she saw the lock had slipped back over his one eye. "But you are a magnificent animal. I bet you run as fast as the wind." The stallion continued to stare at her as if he could understand her words. "You're wonderfully muscled and sleek," she purred, running her hand appreciatively over his strong neck. "Spirited, too. I know how he likes his horses."

The stallion tossed his head and she swore she saw the

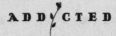

breadth of his chest increase. "You're puffing yourself up, are you?" she laughed. "You know you're the most beautiful creature in the world and I would give anything to ride you, don't you?"

He tossed his head again and pressed his mouth into her hand, taking the cubes from her as she studied his high tail and the refined narrow head that made him the perfect Arabian specimen. The stallion's back was covered with a thick blanket and his mane had been brushed until his coat shone to a spectacular gloss.

"You could not have found yourself a better master," she whispered, and the horse whickered in response. "He shall take very good care of you, you know."

A whinny erupted in the quiet and the stallion pranced back in his stall, away from her so that he was facing the line of stalls to the rear of his.

"Lift your leg, Lady," Lindsay's voice spoke in a gentle tone. "God, but you're a bloody mess." Startled, Anais looked about the stable, but could not see him. Only the line of lanterns hung from the walls told her where he would be. "What is it, Sultan?" Lindsay asked over the sound of the curry brush he must be pulling through Lady's coat. "What has you prancing about?" The stallion snorted and stomped, tossing his head in agitation. "She is a pretty little thing, isn't she? But I'm afraid she's not for you."

The Arabian snorted louder and stomped his foreleg against the stall door.

"What a bloody mess you're in, my girl," Lindsay muttered. "Darnby's grooms should be whipped for taking such atrocious care of you. I should imagine your mistress has not yet seen the state of you."

No, she had not seen Lady in months. How was it she had so easily discarded everything in her life that had ever mattered—Lindsay, Ann, her horse? Maybe she was just like her mother. Perhaps the same selfish blood of her mother did flow through her own veins. She had cared only for herself these past months, never thinking of what others might be going through. It was only her pain she had been concerned with.

"You haven't been ridden in months. Look at you, yer as plump as a maid," he laughed, slapping what Anais thought was Lady's haunches. "She's forgotten you, has she, just as she's forgotten everyone else?"

He stood then, and Anais could see Lindsay's head overtop of the stall. Could see his hair, so enticingly disheveled, sweeping across his brow. She sucked in her breath and was nearly overcome with the scent of hay and horse that served to trigger her mind to the last time she had been in the stable with Lindsay.

She turned to leave, hoping to keep her presence unknown. The Arabian snorted and stomped again and she used the noise to her advantage to creep along the aisle to the door. She was just passing the row of stalls when something strong manacled her wrist.

Her gaze flew up to see Lindsay standing before her, wearing a linen shirt with the neck gaping open and an unbuttoned greatcoat that was the color of deep moss.

"You're the reason for Sultan's frustration, are you? He has a roving eye, that one. He always spots the most beguiling fillies." The smile in his eyes contained a sensual flame.

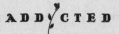

"He is a beautiful animal," she said, glancing away from his lips. "I saw you riding him this afternoon. I had to have a glimpse of him."

"Where did you see me riding?"

"My bedroom window," she confessed in a whisper.

"Were you spying on me?" he asked, stepping close to her so that his coat brushed her thighs.

"I...I heard the pounding of hooves...I...thought mayhap some visitors..."

"You knew it would be me, didn't you? No one runs at full speed into this stable except me, and at one time, you."

He was right. She had known that the mad pounding of hooves so close to the stable would be Lindsay. He was a highly skilled rider, so adept with his mounts that no one other than him would dare to go charging through the stable at such speed. He was always one with his horses.

"I thought of you on my ride. I was wondering what I could do to get you alone." He lowered his head to hers. She looked away, biting her lip. "You wouldn't let me close to you this morning at the village. Had I a pistol, I would have shot Wallingford for monopolizing you. It is such a damned agony having to watch you from afar. It never used to be that way, Anais."

She kept her face averted while she gnawed on her lower lip. But her indifference did not stop him from stepping closer to her. "You must know how I feel. God, Anais, I burn for you, and what is more, you burn for me. Why must we go on like this? Denying our bodies, our hearts? Instead, you shun me, keep me at arm's length, pretending that you don't want me."

"We cannot go back to the past. The way it was for us, what was between us cannot be. How can I make you understand?"

"What was Broughton doing here today?" he asked, his voice holding a dangerous edge. "Is that how you intend to make me understand? By parading him in front of me?"

"You don't realize," she murmured, unable to concentrate on anything but how close Lindsay's lips were to hers. She could smell the minty aroma of tooth powder and the scent of horse and sweat. Many women would have been repulsed by such scents, but Anais found her knees beginning to liquefy.

"You give so much of your time to Broughton that you have very little left for me. You always had time for me. I want that back. Tell me how and I will do it. Anything, Anais. Just tell me how."

"He truly is a lovely animal," she said, changing the course of the conversation as she kept her face averted from him. "Beautiful definition and perfect Arabian features."

"Every time I look in that corner I can see you flushed and naked beneath me. In my mind I can still hear the way you said my name as you found release. I can feel the cascade of hot tears against my lips—the tears you wept when you shuddered beneath me during your pleasure."

She was weakening, so much so that she did not dare look up at him. He was too close. "I must be getting back. I only came to check on Lady and I thought I might have a glimpse at the Arabian while I was here."

"You still appreciate horseflesh, then? That hasn't changed?"

"Not everything has changed."

"Only the most important things," he murmured. "Kiss me, Anais," he said, brushing his thumb against her bottom lip. "Lift your face and look into my eyes. Touch your lips to mine."

She fought to act as though she felt nothing for him. "Are you

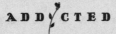

breeding him?" she asked, suppressing a shiver as he bent closer to her, his breath caressing her lips.

He raised his mouth slightly from hers, but his finger continued to brush her tender flesh. "Is this all you will allow, this polite conversation? Very well, I will take it, for now.

"I would like to breed him, but I'm afraid that he has taken a fancy to your mare. I had intended to start a pure Arabian breeding program, with Sultan as the founder of his dynasty, but it seems that his roving eye has settled on a warm-blooded bay, instead."

"I would not mind a foal from Sultan."

"Would you care to ride him, Anais?"

The sparkle in Anais's eye told him he had done the right thing. Everyone was tempted by something, and if *he* couldn't tempt her then perhaps an invitation for a moonlit ride on his prized Arabian would be enough temptation for her to spend more time with him. And more than that, she would be seated before him, astride the animal, with his arms protectively encircling her.

Lindsay grew pleasurably aroused thinking of his hand resting atop her belly, then slowly sliding down the mound of her sex where she would feel hot, and no doubt, damp against his palm. He had not been able to get the memories of his vision out of his thoughts. Couldn't stop thinking how warm and wet she had been on his mouth. How erotic it had been to ravish her in his opium den.

He had been in misery all day, waiting for this chance to be alone with her once again. On horseback, in his den, the stable, he didn't care where he was, as long as he was with her.

"I am not suitably dressed for riding," she said, indicating her gown beneath the cloak.

"When have you ever resisted the urge to raise your skirts and ride astride?" he challenged. "You did that night we made love. You answered my challenge in the drawing room and you were already raising your skirts by the time you entered the stable."

"I shouldn't, I…I haven't been well," she croaked, looking longingly at the stallion, then to him as she nibbled on her lip. "I really shouldn't be out riding."

"Admit you want to."

His challenge hung in the air. As the seconds ticked on, he wondered if she would summon the strength to say no. The Anais he used to know would never have turned down an offer of a midnight ride. The woman he had loved would have answered his challenge and met him wearing a pair of his breeches and his shirt, the ones he would have sent over to her wrapped up in brown paper. She would have donned her boots, the ones he had Talbot in London make for her—the pair he kept hidden in his wardrobe so that her mother wouldn't discover them.

Did she remember those midnight rides in which they ran until they were breathing hard and their mounts were huffing and sweating? Did she remember how they would climb down from their horses and walk them, allowing them to graze while they sat beside the Severn River, watching the stars twinkle atop the black waters? Did she remember the first kiss he had stolen? She had looked so damned beautiful—so damned much like a woman. He had read romantic poetry to her, and finally had given in to temptation and reached for her, pressing his mouth to hers as they sat watching the sun set in the tall grass.

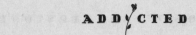

It had been so pure, so innocent, that kiss. He had relived it a million times, heard her gasping breath and saw her eyes close as he slowly penetrated her mouth with his tongue. He had watched her during that kiss. A part of him knew he could have pressed her back and had his way with her, but he'd been trying to be a gentleman. Trying to be anything but his father. So he had ended the kiss and gone to Cambridge with the taste of her on his mouth and the need for her in his blood.

And then he had discovered something that took the edge of his need away. The same something that had now begun to rival even thoughts of Anais.

"Someone could very well see us," she finally said, drawing him away from his memories.

"Someone could have discovered our rides years ago. It never stopped you then."

"Still, I could not risk it now." Suddenly she looked up at him and slowly a small grin curled her lips. "Let's go."

Within minutes he had Sultan harnessed and saddled and was atop him with his hand reaching out to Anais. She accepted it and vaulted up into the saddle, settling her bottom before him into the juncture of his groin. Lady was also harnessed and saddled, waiting obediently at the gates of the stable. Reaching for her reins, he wrapped them around his hand and led Sultan out of the stable, Lady trailing diligently behind the stallion. Once they were outside, he let Lady free and urged Sultan into an open run across the frozen snow beneath the black velvet cover of night.

Anais's hair came loose of its pins and whipped back, brushing his face. He smelled the soap she had used and he pressed his face against the heavy mound so that he could inhale more of her scent. Her body soon matched the rhythm of Sultan's movements, and he didn't need to hold her any longer, but he could not bear to break his hold, and instead shifted his hand so that it rested against her belly.

She stiffened and brushed his hand away, allowing him to rest it against her hip. He felt keenly deprived of the intimacy he had felt when his hand cupped her belly and he fleetingly wondered how a woman reputed to be so ill for over a month could have such a deliciously rounded belly—a belly he found very erotic.

"Your body is lush, full—ripe with womanhood," he whispered as his gloved hand sought her waist once again. "I like you this way, Anais. You have a body made for making love to a man. I will be that man again, Anais. *I will.*"

14

Sultan pranced along the edge of the ridge, tossing his sleek head as he snorted. Below, in the snow-filled vale, the last wisps of smoke from the pile of rubble that was once her home curled up into the black night, fading once they reached the heavy snow clouds in the sky.

"Are you cold?" Lindsay asked. "I can feel you trembling."

Anais tried to stem the flow of tears as she looked down at the destruction. "I do not know why I am tremulous, only that I cannot control it."

He pulled her close, wrapping both arms tightly around her waist, warming her with the heat of his body. "I wasn't thinking when I brought you here. My apologies."

"No, I'm glad you did." She turned slightly in the saddle and looked up at him. "I needed to see for myself—to know that there is truly nothing left. Everything we had—"

"The most important things are still here. Ann. Your mother and father. The servants and the horses—you. *God,* I could not have lived had you died in that fire, Anais."

She shuddered, remembering what it was like to be holding on for dear life to the curtain. Things could have been so much more deadly than they had.

"Did Papa say what happened?" she asked, her gaze straying once more to the pile of blackened wood. "I thought perhaps he might have discussed it with you this afternoon."

Lindsay shook his head and glanced away, but not before she saw the lie in his eyes. "You know as well as I that fires can start anytime, Anais."

Anais knew both men so well, that it was impossible for them to keep anything from her. Something had passed between Lindsay and her father that afternoon, something her father did not want to share with his family. "Lindsay—"

"Shh, don't ask me." He pressed his face into her hair that was blowing in the wind. "Let it be, Anais. Nothing can be done to change it. Let it go."

Just like their past. For the first time in weeks, Anais allowed herself to think *what if.* What if she had not allowed Broughton to comfort her after Lindsay's betrayal? What if she had never run from Lindsay in the first place?

But what-ifs had no place in real life. What-if was just a frustrating game that made one doubt everything they had ever believed in and every choice they had made. Even when, deep down, they knew the choice was the only one available to them.

"I have been wondering, Anais, you said you have forgiven me, but what of Rebecca?"

Stiffening in the saddle, Anais's spine became as rigid as an iron rod. Her old friend's name, spoken in Lindsay's voice, had an odd effect on her, making her feel as though she was going to be ill.

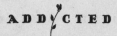

Pinching her lips together in distaste, Anais replied, "She has gone to live in Town, if that is what you are asking. Word is rife that she is now the mistress of a rich gentleman who keeps her in a town house in Trevor Square."

"I don't give a damn where she has gone or what she has done with her life," he growled. "What I want to know is if you have so easily forgiven her for her part in this sordid affair. After all, she was the one who disguised herself so that she could drug me and make me believe it was you I held in my arms."

Anais closed her eyes against the remembered pain. "I have not forgiven her. I cannot be that kind. I hate her for what she did, but I understand why she did it. What other avenues are open to women of suspect birth and little money? They have their bodies and their allurements, that is all. If they are to succeed in this world they must be ruthless. I cannot condemn Rebecca for not wanting to spend her life as a governess. But what I can't condone is that she ran roughshod over our friendship and my feelings in order to avoid such a life."

"The Anais I knew would never have condoned such a mercenary thing as a woman resorting to seduction to trick a man into gaining her fortune."

"The Anais you knew was nothing but an innocent, naive girl who had no real knowledge of the world or the hardships in life. I was always sheltered from those stark realities. I never knew what it was like to face an unknown future. Because of that, I thought only in absolutes—the fixed ideas that were taught to me by my father, my governess and by society's dictates. But I have grown up, Lindsay, and that innocent girl has left me. I have had to make choices…difficult choices," she whispered. "Those decisions have shaped me into the person I am today. I have become wiser and perhaps more sympathetic than I was a year ago. I am no longer blind nor ignorant to the ways of survival."

"Was giving me up one of those difficult choices, Anais?"

Sliding from Sultan's saddle, Anais expected Lindsay to reach for her and stay her, but he let her go and she looked up at him through her curls that waved in the cold breeze. "Yes. Giving you up was one of those decisions."

"What are we, Anais? Are we friends? Acquaintances? Or are we each other's regret?"

"Each other's past," she said simply before walking away and reaching for Lady's bridle. "One last ride, Lindsay," she said, gaining the saddle and spurring Lady forward. "For tonight, let us be friends once again."

Moonlight shone silver on the new-fallen snow and filtered between the leafless branches that were now shimmering in the glow of the moon and ice. The glistening above their heads and the iridescence at their feet illuminated the paths through the woods, providing enough light for them to safely maneuver their mounts in a canter along the path. Anais would have liked to break out in a liberating run, to feel the wind push back her hood as she allowed Lady to gallop. But she would settle for a quiet canter and the chance to enjoy the woods in their snowy slumber.

It would have been a forbidding place if not for the snow and the full moon that hung heavy in the black sky. But with the wilds of winter surrounding them and the sparkling branches, the Wyre Forest was transformed into some mystical realm where fairies lived and magic prevailed.

Lady whickered softly, the sound was followed by a heavy cloud of vapor. The air was crisp and clear and Anais's lungs burned with heaviness as she breathed deep of the night. Sultan stomped, irritated by the slow pace Lindsay was setting. Effortlessly, he pulled Sultan in with the tightening of his thighs and a gentle tug of the reins. The Arabian was as antsy as she to break into a run—to taste freedom and the liberating rush of the wind.

"You may put that thought right out of your mind," Lindsay grumbled as he pulled Sultan in alongside her.

Anais tilted her head back and looked up at the magnificent display of iced branches that creaked above their heads. "And what thoughts are those?"

"Of breaking stride and running."

"How did you know?"

He chuckled. "I have seen that particular expression on your face many times. You get a certain look in your eye. I always thought of it as a craving to be free. To shun the world and run unbridled and do what you please."

"Yes," she said, laughing softly. "I did that enough, didn't I? How many times did I force you to accompany me on my wild escapades?"

"As I recall, it wasn't too terribly difficult to talk me into anything, especially when it provided me time alone with you."

She glanced at him, watching the way his curling hair blew softly around his face. She studied his strong chin that was now devoid of the facial hair he had returned home with. He was simply Lindsay, looking as he now was—the man she had loved all her life.

"Tell me about Constantinople."

"It was lovely. Rather warm at times, but beautiful. The nights there are particularly decadent. The breeze that blows in from the Bosphorus is balmy, making the night less sultry. From our rooms we could smell the scent of frankincense and myrrh from the spice bazaar as it wafted in through the windows."

"Sounds lovely and exotic."

"It was."

"I'm certain the women were just as exotic." She couldn't help but say that and she saw how he grinned at her barb.

"I suppose they were. Wallingford certainly thought so."

"Oh, you didn't?" she asked archly.

"My penchant runs to blue-eyed blondes, and I may assure you, Turkey is grossly lacking in that."

"I suppose it was all very decadent and opulent there."

"It was. Much like something out of the Arabian Nights. I think you would have liked it."

"And the opium?" she couldn't help but ask.

"Yes," he answered quietly, "there was opium there."

"And you used it," she finished for him.

His gaze flickered to hers. She saw nothing that told her he was lying to her. "Yes. I smoked wherever I could. I smoked so much that I could do nothing but sleep and dream. I did not dream of the women in Turkey, Anais. I dreamed of you."

"But I was not enough, was I?"

"I have never chosen opium over you, Anais."

"It doesn't really matter now, does it?"

He reached for Lady's bridle, pulling her to a stop in the middle of the path. "Let us speak freely, Anais. I did not go to Constantinople because of the lure of opium. After that night

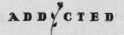

with Rebecca, I couldn't find you. You'll never know what an agony that was. The opium took that pain away, but it never took away my love for you, or my desire to find you and right the mistakes I had made. You may believe whatever you want, I have never preferred opium to you, nor would I allow it to come between us."

"It already has, Lindsay. Don't you see that?"

"There is more than opium between us, Anais. You are hiding something from me. What has made you so ill? Why are you so pale and fragile looking?"

"It is nothing."

"Tell me," he urged, pressing closer to her.

"Lindsay, some things are of a private nature."

"Private? What is private between us? We've been naked with each other—we've made love. Anais, there is nothing you can't tell me."

"I…I don't really know what it is," she murmured, looking away from him.

"Consumption?" he asked.

"No."

"Pleurisy?"

"Lindsay, please. It is nothing. As I've told you, I am on the mend."

"You never used to hide anything from me. We shared everything, didn't we? But now your confidences seem to be shared with Broughton. You're settling, Anais. You don't love Broughton. I'd bet my life on it that you feel nothing but friendship for him. So why now? Why after all these years would you settle for a man that does not make you feel passion?"

"You know nothing about Garrett and me."

"I know he can't make you happy. He can't give you what you need. I don't believe he even knows what you need. He doesn't even know the real you. Not the person you show to the world, but the true you—the person you were with me. Does Broughton indulge you as I indulged you?"

Nudging Lady with her knees, Anais attempted to move Lady forward, but Lindsay reached for the reins and pulled them to a stop.

"Does he?" he asked, his voice harsh. "Does Broughton bring you riding? Does he encourage you to be free of all of society's silly little rules that govern what a woman should be and how she should act? Do you wear his breeches like you used to wear mine?" He leaned forward and she felt his heat. "Do your breasts fill *his* shirts?"

She bit her lip, refusing to lose her composure. "Does he lay with you in the grass? Does he stare up at the stars, speaking of his dreams, wishing he could roll over and kiss you and run his fingers along the breasts that tease him beneath the shirt—the shirt he knows he will carry home with him and smell and, God help him, sleep in, just so he could be close to you?"

The barest hint of his lips brushed intimately against the corner of her mouth, and her lips instinctively parted. "The shirt he could not bear to have washed," he whispered, "so he kept it hidden and brought it back to Cambridge with him, only to drag it out every night and smell it, fearing that one night he might not be able to smell you still clinging to the linen."

He raised one hand from the reins and brought it to her hood, slowly pushing it back over her hair. Her eyelids fluttered open and she found herself gazing into his searching eyes. "Does he wish it could have been his body your scent clung to instead of his shirt, because I vow to you, Anais, I would have given my soul to have you wrapped around me, covering my flesh with your scent. I dreamed of it every night. I still dream of it."

The whinnying of approaching horses made her pull back from him. Her heart, she feared, had stopped pulsating altogether during his speech. Anais felt herself gasping, trying to break free of the gossamer threads he was weaving around her.

"I will do anything, *anything* to get you back. Tell me what I must do, who I must be—"

"*Anais?*"

Her gaze snapped from Lindsay to the clearing of trees where Garrett was steadying his mount. Seconds later, Wallingford emerged from the woods and reined in his horse alongside Garrett.

"Good evening," Wallingford drawled. "Splendid night for a ride, don't you think? Couldn't resist the lure, myself. Had to drag old Broughton out here, didn't I?"

Garrett was not listening to Wallingford. His attention was directed solely upon her and she felt as guilty as a child caught stealing a sweet by the governess. Should she feel guilty? She was only out riding. Yet she did feel shame.

"Should you be riding?" Garrett asked, his voice clipped. "Is it at all safe? Has my brother given you leave to be doing such a thing?"

"I'm fine," she said, feeling blood rush to her cheeks, especially when she saw how Lindsay's gaze volleyed back and forth, studying both she and Garrett.

"You shouldn't be riding in your condition."

"Should I not?" she asked, bristling at the accusatory tone of his voice. He opened his mouth to say something and she feared that in his present state he would give far too much away. But then his mouth shut firmly and his eyes strayed from her to Lindsay, whose position so close to her left little to the imagination.

"Enjoy your ride. I trust that your activities this evening will not alter your plans to attend dinner with me on Friday."

"Garrett—"

"Good evening," he muttered before turning his mount around and tearing off down the path. Nodding goodbye, Wallingford galloped off after Garrett.

As she watched Garrett and Wallingford race along the path, their greatcoats billowing out behind them, she said on a strangled breath. "Take me home."

"Why can't you give in to what I see in your eyes, Anais?"

"I told you, people change. *I have changed.*"

"And along with that so have your needs? Your desires? Don't deny what you feel. I see the same desire in your eyes as that night I made you mine in the stable. The hunger is there. The yearning is there."

She knew it was. Knew she could not hide it and so she spurred Lady into a run, racing back to the stables, trying to outrun the man she feared she could never leave behind her. He wasn't what she needed in her life. He wasn't the right choice. Yet she could think of nothing but feeling him deep inside her. Even as she hated herself for hurting Garrett, she could not stop herself from desiring Lindsay.

15

Anais was struggling to free her boot from the stirrup when Lindsay's strong hands wrapped around her waist, dragging her from the saddle. Her breasts brushed along his chest while she waited impatiently to feel her boots touch the ground. Instead of setting her down, he wrapped her leg around his hip and cupped her bottom in his hand, silencing her outraged gasp with his hungry, demanding mouth.

He was ferocious in his kiss, in the way he sought and captured her mouth. Not breaking the kiss, he stepped to the side, taking her with him until he pressed her up against the stable wall, tearing the cloak from her shoulders. Flinging it to the ground, he continued to kiss her wildly as he rubbed his tented breeches against the apex of her thighs.

Gasping for air between his demanding kisses, Anais felt his fingers seek the fastenings of her gown. With a mastery that stole her breath, he shoved the bodice away from her shoulders, revealing the thin shift she wore beneath.

She tried to release her death grip on his shoulders and cover her breasts with her arms, but he reached for her hands and kissed a hot path down her throat. Releasing one of her wrists, he thrust aside the chemise, baring her swollen, sensitive breast. Greedily he fastened his mouth to her nipple, which was curled into a tight little bud, and sucked, pulling the tender flesh deep into his mouth until she could feel his tongue curling around it.

Anais cried out, a keening moan that came from some place deep inside her. His roughness, his commanding aura, called to all her secret fantasies. Her womb tightened in response to his hands and mouth, and arousal dampened her thighs. He felt it, too, he must have, for he raised her skirts higher and pressed closer, stimulating her with his pelvis as he broke the seal of his mouth on her breast and looked up at her.

"You're aching for it as much as I."

The embarrassing rush of her wetness directly against his breeches jolted her into awareness. She squirmed against him, not knowing if she wanted to run or push herself wantonly against the hard phallus that was pressing urgently against her sex.

Shifting his hips, he rubbed her—in the right spot—between her swollen sex so she could feel the shape of him combined with the friction of the material working her into a frenzy.

She moaned, unable to do anything but arch her back and rest her head against the stable wall, still trying to fight her desires. But her strength was evaporating and she could not even speak let alone gather the might to struggle out of his grasp.

"Touch me, angel."

The haunting need she heard in his voice made her open her eyes. The need was there, shining in his eyes. The need for her body, the need for her.

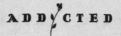

Lindsay reached for her hand. Anais felt the contact of his face beside hers, the warmth of his breath caressing her cheek. "Touch me."

With trembling fingers she grazed his cheek, watching her fingertips touch his sun-kissed skin that was warm and covered with the faintest dusting of stubble.

"I need your touch..." His breath was harsh against her ear and she felt the tips of his fingers glide down her throat and along the tops of her breasts. Sighing, she clutched his hair as he took her nipple into his mouth and sucked slowly, erotically, in a rhythm that was unhurried and sensual.

"Oh, God," she panted shakily when she felt his finger slide up her thigh and over her garter until it reached the cleft of her buttocks. She was trembling in anticipation. She wanted his hands all over her, caressing her, loving her.

"I can make it so good for you. Let me, Anais."

"Yes." The word was a hushed whisper, her agreement issued before she could stop it spilling from her lips. She was at the mercy of her own needs now.

He unfastened the facings of his breeches, her hand slipped down between them, stroking his phallus as it parted the fabric and stretched against her hand.

"Do you ache for it?"

"Yes," she answered on a shaky breath.

He brought the head against her curls, rubbing it slowly against her slick flesh. Their gazes were locked in a way that was far more intimate than even the way their bodies were touching. Their need—their souls—were exposed. Every aching desire, every thought, every inch of hurt was mirrored in their eyes.

"Invite me in, Anais. Invite me to join you inside your body."

She felt strange, as if she were floating. As if the weight of the past months had magically been lifted from her shoulders.

"Come to me, Lindsay."

Slowly he entered her, angling her hips forward and up so that the moonlight shining through the stable window illuminated their bodies. She watched in the silver glow, Lindsay's body sinking into hers. His thick shaft glistened as he retreated before slowly pressing forward again. She had never seen anything more wondrous than Lindsay's body becoming part of hers.

Over and over she watched him thrust into her. She heard her heavy breaths, knew she was breathing too heavily, too fast, and he looked up from their sex and watched her. Unable to hide her response, she looked away and raised her arms above her head so that she could wrap her hands around the beam at her back. Closing her eyes, she stopped thinking of everything except the feel of the rhythm of their bodies together.

So damn beautiful... Lindsay kept saying the words over and over, chanting them as he watched Anais's little quim sucking him into her body, milking him with its silky, tight walls until he could not keep up the slow, unhurried pace.

How wanton she looked with her round breasts, covered in a damp chemise, thrusting forward, bouncing with the rhythm of his hips. Her head was thrown back and her lips parted with each thrust of his cock.

The dance of cock and cunt enticed him and he thrust harder. She took him, telling him with her little whimpers that she was aroused and enjoying—no, needing—what he was doing to

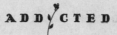

her. As he watched his cock, thick and hard, fill her quim, he felt a primitive possessiveness steal over him.

Beautiful, tight cunt, he thought, feeling his seed shoot up from his testicles. He was going to fill it full, to give her all of him. He felt her quim tightening around his cock, milking it. She screamed his name and he thrust again, but this time he parted her slick folds and flicked her erect clitoris with his finger in time to his stroking cock.

Immediately she bucked against him. Pressing forward, she wrapped her arms around him so that she could bury her mouth in the collar of his shirt.

Milk me. Let me spend inside this beautiful tight cunt.

She stiffened, reached for his hand to stop his assault on her clitoris, but he pressed harder, ignoring the way her fingers clutched his wrist.

"Please," she cried, her lips pressed against the bare skin of his throat, "please make this exquisite ache stop."

He sunk his cock deep inside her as he continued to circle her clitoris. She was panting against his throat as she cupped his neck. Her free hand was gripping his shirt as her body began to jerk in his arms.

Her quim contracted in pleasure, increasing his, and he came, his seed rushing out and splashing deep inside her. It was the most exquisite sensation to feel himself spending everything he had inside her. And then he felt it, the hot wetness from her eyes as her tears trickled down her cheeks and on to his.

"You were made for me. *Only me,*" he whispered harshly as he buried his face into the crook of her neck, not caring if he appeared weak or vulnerable, for he was weak. Anais was his weakness. "How beautiful you are during orgasm. How wonderfully perfect you are after it."

She let him hold her for long minutes as their breaths slowed, but then she tried to push him away. He only held her tighter to him and pressed his erection, which was still hard, deep inside her. "We must forget what we've done tonight, Lindsay. You must let me go."

Hysteria was slowly rising in her voice as the reality of what they had just done began to sink in. She needed to run, to get to her room and wash herself clean of his seed. Anais began to struggle in his arms, forcing him to break his hold on her.

"You want me to pretend that this never happened?" he asked, clearly perplexed. "You want me to let you go and forget about what you found in my arms? Forget how I watched your body taking me in?"

"Don't—"

"No, Anais! Don't you dare act like this was nothing to you. That you didn't enjoy every second of this—that you didn't need this—*need me.*"

"I can't be with you!" she yelled, trying to right her reeling senses. She needed to think. Needed a plan to make things right, but she couldn't think, so instead she raged at him. "Why do you refuse to listen? Why can you not accept that I cannot— that we cannot—be what we once were?"

"Why?"

"This—" she waved her hand between them "—was a moment of madness—a mistake—"

"Don't you ever call what happens between us a mistake. That night with Rebecca was a mistake. What we just did, the love we made, that was beautiful—too beautiful to regret."

She looked away, afraid that if she continued to look at the pain in his eyes she would ruin it all by throwing herself into his arms and weakening once more. "I was wrong to have indulged myself in this. I weakened to temptation and I will take the blame. But you must know that it changes nothing."

His eyes darkened. He was going to ask her why she couldn't be with him after allowing him to make love to her. She would have to remind him that the love they shared was gone. That she had given her heart to another. And it would be nothing but a scandalous lie.

"Is...is this because of Broughton?"

She nodded, crying. "Yes."

His grip slackened and she slid down his body. Her legs felt wobbly, but she flattened her palms to the wall and steadied herself. He must have seen the hesitation, the fear that flickered in her face, or perhaps he saw shame, for he reeled back and glared at her. "Christ, what hold has he over you?"

She should say it now. Confess. Repeat the lines she had rehearsed over and over. The words she was certain would turn him away from her forever. *I no longer love you, Lindsay. My heart belongs to Garrett. My body belongs to him...*

"Whatever has happened between us can be worked out. It will take time, but it can work."

"It can't because I am going to marry Garrett, Lindsay. My heart belongs to him. My body," she choked out, "belongs to him."

"What are you trying to say?" He gripped her about her shoulders. "Have you been letting him inside you?"

"We have nothing more to say to one another, Lindsay. This was a need in the night. It is meant to be forgotten."

She stepped away from him, but he reached for her wrist. "Tell me that my fears are not true, that you have not slept with Broughton, that you have not—" His words died, strangled in his throat.

"The truth, Lindsay, is that tonight meant nothing."

16

"You had no right to invite him to Lord Broughton's dinner party," Anais muttered to her sister as they stepped over the threshold of Broughton's front door.

"Are you Lord Broughton's event advisor?" Ann snapped. "I had no idea that the guest list needed your approval."

Anais glared at her sister. "You are putting words in my mouth, Ann."

"If you must know," Ann said with a haughtiness that would do a queen proud, "Lord Broughton made the suggestion that I might think of bringing someone. After careful consideration, I concluded Lord Broughton was absolutely correct. I do need an escort tonight."

"What he meant was, should he invite Baron Wilton's son, you pea-wit. He certainly did not mean for you to bring *him* along."

Anais was a little firebrand this evening, Lindsay thought, his gaze straying to her. Lindsay found himself grinning, enjoying this little spat between sisters. He doubted Anais knew her voice had risen so much that he could hear every word. Hell, he could almost read every thought running through her mind.

Lindsay knew unequivocally that his presence there tonight disconcerted her. The icy facade she had clung to after their dalliance in the stable had never cracked—not once—but tonight it was virtually crumbling into a thousand shards.

Was she worried he might spill the beans to Broughton? He thought of the immense pleasure he could derive by telling his rival such a thing. He would never do such a thing, of course. He was not out to harm Anais. His only goal was to win her back.

In truth he would rather eat glass than take a meal at Broughton's table, but he needed to know just what lay between his old friend and Anais. What secrets were the two of them keeping? He had to know if there was any chance—any chance at all—that he and Anais might be able to have a future.

"Unhand me, Anais," Ann muttered through clenched teeth. "Lud, you're making a spectacle of yourself."

Anais's hand slipped free of Ann's arm, but not before Lindsay saw her glare at her sister. "We will talk about this at home," she muttered, stealing a glance at him over her shoulder.

"I wonder what's for dinner," he asked, sneaking up behind them. "I'm ravenous. Although I hardly doubt Cook is serving up what I'm hungry for." Anais stiffened, obviously forgetting he was so near to her. "Do you know what I hunger for, Anais?" he whispered discreetly. "A glimpse of your pink skin beneath me, a touch of the pink silk between your plump thighs. Perhaps what I truly hunger for is you lying atop the table, legs spread— *helpless*—while I devour you for dessert."

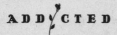

With a sidelong glance, she looked fiercely at him, but he refused to be drawn into her battle, despite the fact he felt like taking her in his hands and shaking her. Damn the little chit, she was making him crazed. How the devil could she so easily ignore him? How could she not possibly yearn for more of what they had shared in the stable? Bloody hell, he yearned for it—night and day—all the damned time he was yearning for her, and she didn't seem to give a bloody toss about him.

He still didn't believe she wanted to marry Broughton. Things might have changed, but Lindsay didn't believe that Anais had changed that much.

"Ah, Lady Anais, Lady Ann, Lord Raeburn," Margaret Middleton greeted them at the front door. The surprise in her voice when she said his name was not lost on Lindsay. "How good of you to come, Lord Raeburn, Broughton will be pleased."

"Will he?" he drawled, handing his greatcoat and hat to the butler. "I doubt that."

Margaret swallowed hard and she turned to Anais. "Mrs. Jennings has done a lovely job on that gown, Lady Anais. The color is simply stunning."

The velvet and fur-lined cape slipped from Anais's shoulders revealing the rose taffeta gown beneath. Lindsay felt his breath sucked from his lungs as his gaze hungrily took in the sight of the tight-fitting bodice and the gentle bell-shaped skirt.

The color was sheer perfection against her pale flesh. He studied the way it made her skin flush a faint pink, reminding him of the way her skin warmed beneath his hands. Her breasts were pushed up high in her corset, spilling elegantly over the ecru lace flounce that was draped invitingly off her shoulders.

God, he was a fool for a woman's naked shoulders, and Anais had the best set he'd ever seen.

Unable to help himself, his gaze strayed lower to the little coral cameo she had pinned to the middle of the flounce, directly below the valley of her breasts. Bloody hell, there wouldn't be a man at the table or the assembly tonight who could resist stealing a peek *there*.

Erotic images fluttered through his mind when he couldn't stop looking at the tight little crease of her décolletage. He imagined tonguing that seductive crevice, visualized his finger slipping between her breasts, saw the image of himself pressing his cock in that tight valley and stroking himself to the final release.

The rest of the gown was simple and elegant, free of all the annoying flounces and ribbons women were so fond of. Damn that Mrs. Jennings, she had turned a simple, unadorned gown into something decadent.

With one more sweep of his eyes, Lindsay took in her lush figure encased in rose taffeta and decided that he could very definitely devour her whole right there on the floor of Broughton's entrance.

"Shall we?" Margaret asked. Lindsay swallowed hard, mentally checking himself. Hell, he had the control of a damned gnat.

Ushering the ladies ahead, he followed behind, studying the swinging movements of Anais's hips. The image was only rendered more painful as he imagined peeling off the gown and finding her breasts inching above her corset. And beneath that corset he saw what was awaiting him—a warm and flushed curved body.

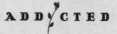
"Good evening," Robert Middleton called from his spot by the fire. "It is a fine night for a ball at the assembly rooms, is it not?"

Anais and Ann nodded and plunged into a long-winded conversation about the weather. Lindsay only halfheartedly listened and instead looked about the salon, wondering where the devil Broughton was lurking. He saw something squirm atop Middleton's lap and Margaret rushed over and lifted the white bundle from her husband's arms.

"Let me bring her to Nurse. I'm sure our daughter is hungry. And I am just as certain that the men will not wish to hear her bellows."

"A very good set of lungs, she has," Middleton chuckled. "She makes herself heard and very clearly understood."

Margaret attempted a smile, but Lindsay could perceive none of the warmth or enthusiasm she had shown when they'd first arrived.

"How old is she now?" Ann asked, pulling the blanket from the babe's face and grinning when a chubby little fist escaped the confines of the blanket.

"Nearly seven weeks," Middleton said proudly, but Margaret shut him up with a warning look conveyed by her narrowed eyes. "Well, yes," her husband grumbled. "I do believe you should bring her up, my love. She looks like she's about to wail like a banshee. I'm certain Raeburn could do without the recital."

He certainly could do without it. He'd never been around children or babies. Frankly he didn't know what to do with one. For instance, he didn't know if he was expected to look upon the child and make a comment, or was that the job of the women to fuss over the baby? Was his duty more toward Middleton, a sort of man-to-man congratulations, like a slap on the shoulder along with a "well done"?

In the end, he tilted his head and pretended he could see some of the child's features, which he couldn't as she had buried her face once again in the blankets. "A well-formed child," he murmured awkwardly, hoping it was the right thing to say. "And I'm certain you were happy to have her born at your ancestral home, Robert."

"It's a good thing you made it to Worcestershire when you did," Ann said with a mischievous smile. "Otherwise you might have delivered in some inn, or worse yet, in your coach."

"Ann," Anais scolded, but Ann carried on, heedless of her sister's warning. "It was much talked of in the village, how Mrs. Middleton had her baby less than a week after arriving from Scotland," Ann informed him.

"Traveling so far and so close to your day?" he asked quizzically. Weren't women confined to bed in the last months of their confinement—isn't that why they called it *confinement?* From his limited knowledge of childbirth he knew enough that men usually went mad those last few months worrying over the delivery. As far as he knew, husbands did not allow their wives to go gadding about in carriages halfway across Britain. He certainly would never let Anais travel about while heavy with his child.

The thought stopped him cold. He might never have the chance to make a family with her. Despite not having any experience with babies, Lindsay still desired a family of his own.

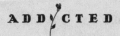

He had only ever thought of Anais having his children. The thought that dream might not come to realization had never occurred to him, till tonight.

"Her arrival was unexpected and early," Margaret murmured, and Lindsay saw her blush to the roots of her hair as her words drew him out of his melancholy thoughts. "Neither of us thought it possible that I would deliver early. Of course I was with Robert, he is...er...that is to say, he is well-versed in the art of childbirth. Now," she said with great relief, "I really must get her upstairs if we are to eat at the planned time."

The door to the salon opened and Broughton strolled in. Lindsay saw his gaze narrow at the same time the color drained from his cheeks. Barely glancing at Margaret and her baby as she slipped past him, Broughton stalked forward, his gaze pinning him with ruthless determination.

"What are you doing here?"

"Ann invited me to be her escort for the evening."

Broughton's expression appeared relieved, then his gaze slid to where Anais stood beside Robert, dismissing the fact he had an uninvited guest.

"You look beautiful tonight, Anais," Broughton said, stepping forward and taking her hand. "Very lovely, indeed."

She blushed for Broughton and Lindsay had the urge to drive his fist into his friend's face. Bloody hell, he could not stand to see her near him, nor Broughton's hands touching her.

"Shall we, then?" Lindsay saw the palm of his hand press against the hollow of Anais's lower back as Broughton guided her to the door that led to the dining room.

"Do see to Ann, will you?" Broughton told him with more than a hint of sarcasm. "And I shall see to taking care of Anais."

Accepting the assistance of a footman, Anais stepped up into the carriage and took her seat. Straightening her cloak, she pressed back against the velvet squabs, settling herself comfortably in the plush cushions.

An iron brazier had been heated and was in the process of being pushed into the carriage. Anais smiled appreciatively when she caught sight of the footman as he pulled his metal hook out from beneath the brazier.

"From his lordship," the servant announced.

"Lord Broughton is most kind."

"He is, ma'am."

Bowing, the footman took his leave and Anais saw to shaking out her skirts to prevent them from wrinkling and waited for Ann and Garrett to enter the carriage so that they could be off to the ball at the assembly rooms.

Lindsay could manage on his own, she thought bitterly. Lord, he had acted like an ass throughout dinner. More than once she had been forced to glare her disapproval, but he only hooded his eyes and maintained his brooding silence. Anais wondered if it had only been her that was aware of how darkly quiet and dangerous Lindsay had appeared throughout supper. Was she the only one to notice how he looked at her, how he refused to take his eyes off her? Bloody hell, he had made her feel like a spectacle and she wanted to throttle him for it.

The crunching of snow alerted her that someone was outside

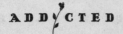

the carriage, but instead of it being Garrett's boot steps she heard, it was Lindsay she saw shouldering his way through the small opening. Without preamble, he took the bench opposite her and reached for the door, slamming it shut before rapping at the roof with his walking stick.

"Drive on!" he barked.

The wheels rumbled along the snow-covered gravel, sending the conveyance swaying from left to right as it traveled down the sloped lane to the road that would take them to the Bewdley Assembly Rooms.

He had not lit the lamps and the blackness that engulfed them was unforgiving in its depths. She could see nothing, not even the barest sliver of moonlight, for the window shades were lowered, blocking out every inch of light.

Since the night in the stable, Anais had not allowed herself to be alone with him. Now, after all her careful avoidance, it was only them in the unsettling blackness. How utterly unforgiving the quiet darkness was. *How completely unnerving.*

Now, completely blind, she realized her other senses were heightened—sound, smell. She heard his breathing—even and deep. Heard the heel of his boot scrape along the floor of the carriage as he positioned his long legs on either side of her feet. She smelled his cologne mixed with the scent of him—the scent of man and shaving soap and perhaps the remnants of opium smoke.

"Every night for the past week, I have lain awake in the dark waiting for you to come to me. But you never did."

She wanted to. Oh, how she wanted to search him out and feel his body against hers. Damn her for having these yearnings, for they were now a compulsion, an addiction she could not resist.

"I want it to be like it was, Anais."

Anais was relieved he had not lit the lamps, for he would have seen her tremble with awareness. He would know that she was eager for his touch, for the feel of his hands, and the sounds of his breath in her ear. She, too, wanted it to be like it was. She wanted him for her friend once again, and she wanted him as her lover.

Despite the threatening darkness, Anais had never been more aware of him as she now was, sitting across from her, unable to see him, only sense him. She could feel the sensual tension wrap itself tightly between them, drawing them inexorably closer to one another.

"I live in torture. Every time I see him look at you, every time he takes the liberty of reaching out and touching you, I feel ill. I live in anguish, picturing you together, him with his body atop yours, his hands fisted in your hair. It is my hell imagining you shivering for him."

The springs shifted again and Anais became aware of his presence before her. He didn't have to speak for her to feel the heat of his breath or smell the scent of him. Her body, so in tune to his, sensed how very close he truly was.

"I cannot sleep for thinking of you. Everywhere I look I see you. I watch you carry on, pretending you are oblivious to my suffering, but I know something you think I don't. I know you suffer, too. You just won't admit it."

Yes, she suffered. Yes, she wanted him.

***

Lindsay felt her shudder, heard the sound of the lace trim on her bodice brush against her fur-lined cloak. She was breathing fast, heard the air being sucked between her lips—felt it as she exhaled—the warm, moist air caressing his mouth.

"Do you know what it is like to constantly crave something you cannot have? To see it day after day, to dream of it night after night so that you are so consumed you would do anything for just a taste—a forbidden sampling—no matter how small? Can you imagine being willing to give up everything, including your soul to the devil, for just a stolen moment?"

He heard her swallow, followed by the slickness of her tongue wetting her lip. "You speak of opium, do you not?"

"No." He fought with every ounce of his being to resist pressing his mouth to hers. "You induce this fever in my body. I speak of you when I speak of my cravings. Only you have that hold over me, Anais."

He wanted nothing more than to wipe away the taint of Broughton's hand upon her cheek. He wanted Broughton's touch erased by his hands, *his* scent.

Reaching for the woolen blanket that was folded beside him, he tossed it to the floor then sought her hand and pulled her toward him. Country flowers and the scent of soft, feminine skin wafted up between their bodies, wrapping around him until he felt light-headed and his blood thickened in his veins as if he had smoked two pipes of opium.

"Release me from my torment," he whispered. He covered her mouth with his, tasting her, the sweetness of the wine mixed with her own heady taste. Her tongue curled with his and he deepened the kiss so that he was kissing her in slow, drugging, openmouthed kisses that made her mewl and writhe against him. Suddenly it wasn't enough. He wanted more.

Tipping her chin back, he ran his tongue down her neck, tasting her skin. She shivered and instead of seeing the goose-flesh covering her pale skin, he felt it against his tongue, leading him to wonder where else she was affected.

He raked the tip of his tongue along her throat once more and parted her cloak back over her shoulders. She trembled once again and he felt her skin pucker at the tops of her breasts. Even now he was imagining the delights of Anais's tight, glistening quim. Despite the dark, he could see her, her body anxious for his.

Wrapping his fingers along her nape, he brought her to him, crushing her lips beneath his so that he robbed her of breath. She did not struggle, but slackened against him as she gave in to her desires.

Her gloved fingers sought his face and traveled down his jaw where she brushed her fingertips against him. Her touch inflamed him—teasing him—and he could not stop himself from reaching for her hand and sliding it down his chest—then lower. When her hand flattened against his abdomen he groaned, his cock straining beneath his trousers.

"Put your hand on me," he commanded. Slowly he removed her glove and kept it in his hand, gripping it in his palm as she brushed her fingers along his tented trousers. Boldly she raked her nails down the shaft that was rigid beneath the wool. Unable to wait for her to fiddle with the fastenings, he reached between their bodies and tore open his trousers.

Unable to wait until she gathered her courage and touched

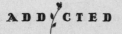

his naked flesh, he gripped his shaft in his hand and stroked himself, his breathing building in an echoing crescendo off the carriage walls.

She wanted this inside her. Anais wrapped her hand tighter around the silken hardness that was sliding up and down the length of her palm. Her sex clenched in yearning, recalling what it felt like to have this—Lindsay—deep inside her.

Was it the wine making her crave such things, making her so bold that she wanted to slide down his hard body and brush her lips against his velvet skin? Or was she by nature a wanton? There was no denying how easily she had discovered the joys of making love. Despite trying to talk herself into believing that she was ashamed by what they had done in the stable, she could not feel guilt. There was no ignominy in sharing your body with another, nor taking enjoyment in the pleasure given to you. Lindsay had filled her body and soul with a passion she feared she was becoming dependent upon.

"Lower your bodice and let me tongue your nipples," he whispered in the dark.

Instead, she kissed his neck and rubbed the head of his phallus with the tip of her finger, spreading the wetness so that it coated the shaft and his fingers. He groaned and nipped at the swells of flesh that inched above her bodice.

Closing her eyes, she realized she was entirely caught up in her own passion. It was the first time she had taken an active role in their lovemaking. Perhaps it was the wine liberating her, or the darkness that was making her bold. Whatever the reason, she didn't care, she couldn't let this moment pass. She had tried, no matter how briefly, to stem the desire, and she couldn't do it. Why couldn't she just enjoy the pleasures to be found in him?

Brushing his hand aside, she slowly lowered her mouth. The crinkling of her taffeta skirts mixed with his husky groan surrounded them. No light was needed for the other to know what was happening.

"Oh, God, yes," he hissed as if he were in pain.

She was kneeling on the blanket, her body pressed between his thighs. His hand raked down her spine, burning her through her bodice and she felt whatever inhibitions she still harbored slip away.

"Is this a craving?" she whispered, before she brushed her bottom lip against the vein that was pulsating in his shaft.

"Yes."

"Have you imagined me doing this?"

"Yes," he hissed again as she flicked her tongue along the length of him.

"Is this what you think of while smoking opium?"

He moaned, his fingers traveling up and down her spine. "This and so much more, Anais. I've thought of it in moments of haziness and lucidity."

"Then ask for it. Ask me just as you've always imagined."

Silence. Not a sound other than the coach wheels turning beneath them could be heard. She held her breath and knew he was holding his, too.

"Take my cock in your mouth. Let me feel how much you want it."

He reached for his phallus and brought it to her lips, brushing it against her mouth before she tasted him.

* * *

Lindsay had harbored many fantasies about Anais over the years, but the one that drove him to the brink—the one he had never allowed another woman to fulfill was this one. This primal, almost animalistic urge to watch her take his cock into her mouth as he held himself out to her; offering himself up to her.

"I want to feed this to you."

Without a word of protest, Anais parted her mouth and took the head of his cock between her lips, sucking and lapping at him so that he was gritting his teeth and squeezing his eyes shut in pleasured agony.

Becoming braver, she reached out and stroked him with her fingernails as she curled her tongue around him. Then she began to suck, the sounds, so electrifying, rippled through the air and he pressed his fingers into her neck and groaned, encouraging her to take him however she wanted.

His body jerked then twisted, shocks shuttering through his nerves. He was beyond thinking now, only conscious of the wave of pleasure that swam through him and the climax she was going to pull from the depths of his soul.

He tried to push her away, knowing that when he came it would be explosive and quick, but he couldn't move, and when he stiffened beneath her and felt the first rush of orgasm wash over him he was able to pull out, but she reached out and put the tip of her tongue to him, tasting the first drop. Then he was lost.

Anais was aware of Lindsay's stiffening, felt him searching for his greatcoat with groping hands as she sucked him, tasting the first drops of his essence. When he found his coat, he wrapped it around his shaft and she slowly allowed her mouth to slide up the length of him. As she did, she felt the pulsations swimming up his shaft.

"You've awakened me to such passion," she murmured, uncertain if she truly wanted to be speaking these words aloud. But there was something about his inability to see her, the depth of her emotion—her love—shining in her eyes, that compelled her to speak such things. "I never knew how much a body could yearn for the touch of another."

The carriage was slowing to a halt and she knew that any minute it would stop completely before the doors of the Bewdley Assembly Rooms.

"Don't go," he whispered, reaching for her wrist as she raised herself from between his knees. "Stay with me."

"I cannot," she murmured, settling herself back onto the bench and adjusting her cloak over her shoulders.

"Don't deny what we have, Anais. Not anymore."

"I could not even if I wished to," she said, her words so quiet she was not even certain he could hear her.

"You want me as a woman wants a man."

"Yes."

"Then take me, damn it. Take everything I am offering you."

She was so tempted to risk everything and allow herself to be caught up in such madness. Her body still trembled for him. She knew she would never experience the same sort of desire and pleasure with another man.

"Take what you want, Anais."

"Perhaps what we want and what is best for us is not the same thing."

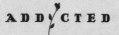

"You speak of the opium, do you not? You're afraid that I am my father. I can stop. I would stop for you."

She looked away and squeezed her eyes tightly, stemming the tears that sprung behind her lids. "I would never be able to trust you. I would live in fear that you would fall back into old habits. I cannot be with you for this reason, Lindsay. You're not what I need in my life." It was the truth and yet, she still kept so much from him—the real reason she could not be with him. What a faithless liar she was, making him feel as though it was all his fault they could never be together.

"You can't just throw away what we have. I won't let you—"

"It is best for both of us that we forget it."

"I will not." He gripped her wrist. "I don't give a damn what Broughton means to you. I don't care what part he has played in your life these past months. If you truly hated me, if you couldn't bear the sight of me, I would release you, but you don't. And that is the reason I will continue to pursue you. You don't love Broughton, I know you don't."

"No, I do not," she whispered, looking down at her hands, despite the fact she could not see them. "I do not love him. But I have an obligation to him."

The carriage stopped and the coachman's boots were crunching atop the gravel. The door was opened, allowing in the warm golden lights that blazed from the assembly rooms' windows. For the first time she saw Lindsay sitting across from her, looking fierce and handsome. Her gaze strayed to his trousers, and she could not help but think of what she had done not five minutes before.

He followed her gaze and then pressed forward, whispering in her ear as the coachman looked discreetly away. "You are a woman worth fighting for, Anais. I will fight for you. Never doubt it. I will show you that I can be worthy of you. You are an angel amongst women, Anais. My angel."

"No, I am not." She met his eyes and looked into them with an honesty she had not shown him since he'd arrived back home. "I am not an angel. I have sinned, and I shall have to live with it. We have both hurt each other. We will no doubt hurt each other again. Let it be over, Lindsay, please."

"I don't know what happened between you and Broughton when I left, but I do know that none of it matters now. I want you, and I will have you as my wife. I vow I am, and always will be, constant and faithful in my love for you, Anais. Nothing you or anyone else does shall alter these feelings. I am forever loving, forever waiting, forever yearning...forever yours."

"Oh, God," she whispered, smothering her tears. "You hurt me when you talk of love, for your love is all I have ever wanted, and now that I have it, I cannot accept it. It kills me to know I might have had your love. Oh, Lindsay, opium might have been your weakness, but you, you have always been mine. I cannot be strong around you. I can't...I can't be around you anymore," she said in a choked cry then flew down the carriage steps and into the assembly rooms, leaving Lindsay alone in the carriage.

17

Anais sat down on the bench in front of her dressing table, rubbing her feet. Never had she danced so much, not even during her first few seasons in Society. Lord, her feet ached! She groaned out loud when her fingers traversed over a particularly tender spot on her arch.

Closing her eyes, she continued to work out the cramps in her feet. In her mind she replayed every dance, every look and smile. From somewhere in the back of her mind the image of Lindsay standing alone in a dark corner watching her dance with Wallingford and Garrett flashed before her.

God help her, she had wanted him to ask her to dance, but he hadn't. In truth, he never danced and tonight was no exception.

"Look at poor Raeburn over there, marinating in his vinegar," Wallingford had murmured as he spun her around during a waltz. "I would wager my fortune he wishes he could navigate a dance floor now."

Lindsay despised dancing. She also knew that despite being known as a proliferate rake and a promiscuous lover, Wallingford quite enjoyed dancing. He never sat one out. It was also noted that he usually always graced his arm with at least one overlooked wallflower amongst the many beauties who usually hung on his arm.

"You know, when the four of us took dance instruction together, Raeburn used to pummel me soundly in your father's stables," Wallingford said on a laugh. "The man may have a deplorable sense of rhythm, but he has a fantastic set of fists. He would become irate whenever I danced the Sir Roger de Coverly with you. I could never understand it. But then during a particularly vicious attack on my person, he confessed it was because it was the longest dance of the set—nearly half an hour—and that I had monopolized you for most of the lesson, leaving him sitting on the peripheries, forced to watch me dancing with you."

She had sought out Lindsay then, and as their gazes collided across the ballroom, memories of their carriage ride ran rampant through her brain. Her heart had felt like a butterfly trapped in a glass apothecary jar—its wings fluttering in vain.

A soft click of the connecting door cut through her musings. Anais opened her eyes only to find Lindsay leaning against the door, his shirt unbuttoned to his waist. His hair was mussed and the faint shadow of his beard outlined his jaw, making it appear more angular and strong.

"You've brought me to my knees, Anais—again. You have consumed me."

She said nothing, fearing her words would betray her. Her lips—trembling and moist, were ready to betray her.

Stepping into the room he walked until he stood before her. "Forever waiting...forever yearning..." he murmured against her temple as he repeated the words he had said in the carriage. "Forever loving."

No man had the ability to entice her as Lindsay did. No man made her yearn for something that she should not, like Lindsay could. She feared that for her, everything would always come back to Lindsay. She was tired of denying it. Denying her wishes.

"Have you never had a failing, angel?"

Anais lowered her lashes. Yes, she had failed. He just didn't know it.

"I was weak that night. It was not weakness for sex or Rebecca. I was weak in my need for you. I willingly dabbled in the opium sticks. I allowed myself to imbibe the hashish. I could not resist the lure. Opium was my weakness, not Rebecca. I hope you know that."

His long fingers caressed her throat. Unconsciously Anais tilted her head, allowing his fingertips to graze her. She craved his touch, the familiar sensuality of his fingers along her skin.

"At Cambridge there were so many temptations—drink, whores, gambling. I felt it would be so easy to succumb to the temptations of my father. So I tried the opium instead. I was told it only made you sleep and dream. What harm is there in sleeping? What harm is there in dreaming? Especially when the dreams are passionate, erotic dreams of you?"

Slowly her lashes fluttered open and she gazed up into his face. Her body seemed to melt when she saw how he looked at her with a mixture of need and pain.

"After a while I used it because it took away the doubts, the fears, the desires I had. I doubted I would ever be good enough for you. I feared I would not. And I desired you. God, how much

I wanted you. You were everything I had ever desired in a woman. You were my best friend and I wanted you as my lover."

She gave in—just a little—to the temptation of pressing her cheek into his hand as he cupped the side of her face in his palm. "After I touched you during that first kiss we shared, I knew I would never want another woman.

"I love your smile, the sweetness of your face and the way your eyes crinkle when you laugh. I love the way your hair glimmers in the sunlight and how your curls look wild when you take your bonnet off and let the wind blow little wisps of hair into your eyes—I love brushing those wisps away, just so I can touch you."

"Lindsay," she whispered in a hoarse, pleading voice. She could not listen to any more. Truly, she could not withstand the torture.

"No more secrets. We have had enough secrets between us. I want to tell you everything, Anais. Have you any clue how long I've loved you? Do you know," he whispered, "that I still love you?

"Fear made me keep quiet about my love. I knew what you thought of my father. I never wanted your feelings for me to be like that. I wasn't sure how you felt, so I buried the longing and numbed the ache with opium. I was weak, I know that now. Have you never been weak?" he asked, his breath sweeping along her neck, the sensation curling around her nerves and finding its way into her belly. Her hand flew to her middle and she felt the butterflies circling madly—felt her breasts strain and ache against her corset.

Oh, she had been weak—unforgivably weak.

"Have you, Anais?"

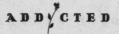

"Yes. I am weak now."

"Show me." He helped her up from the stool. "Be weak, Anais. Be weak for me."

Lifting her in his arms, Lindsay carried her to the bed where he sat down and held her in his lap. Running his hands through her hair, he dispelled the pins. Silently, they fell to the carpet.

Wrapping his fingers around her nape, he pulled her close, until their mouths were nearly touching. "Kiss me, angel. Love me."

Sinking his tongue deep inside, he stole her breath and gave it back to her. She allowed herself to give up the control she fought so hard to maintain. She was naturally weak where Lindsay was concerned. She could not deny him, nor summon the willpower to keep fighting him. Was it so very wrong to do this—to share her body with a man—a man she wanted? A man she needed?

He broke off the kiss and in one fluid movement, straightened so that his back was resting against the wooden poster of the bed. She was straddling his lap when Anais felt the warmth of his hand running up her stocking clad foot to her upper thigh above her garter.

"You are my soporific. It is you I need to feel swimming in my veins, not the opium." Slowly he undid the fastening at the back of her gown.

"You asked me about the opium." He bared one shoulder, then slid the silk down her arm until half of her bodice rested at her waist. "You wanted to know what I found in its powers." He slid the other sleeve along her arm, exposing her corset and the pale flesh that inched above the ruffled edge of the white muslin. His gaze slipped down to where his hands traced the front of her corset, running over the whale boning. "When the opium is swimming in my veins I feel euphoria, languor, passion—salvation." He reached for her hair and wrapped his hands around the silken length. Clutching the long strands, he brought her forward so that his lips were against hers. "I feel the very same things I find when I am making love to you."

Anais knew her eyes were wide with wonder and desire. Never had Lindsay been so open. When he gripped her hair she could feel, as well as see, his desire. "Loving you is the same feeling the opium gives me. Let me feel you now. Let me lose myself in you, Anais. Lust, passion, salvation."

"Yes."

Clutching her face in his hands, he let her see the desire in his eyes.

"You make me wish to be a better man. I *want* to be a better man for you."

Anais felt herself succumbing to a need she knew only too well. "I want you, too, Lindsay. Flesh and blood and warmth."

He came up on his knees, lowered his mouth onto hers. He swept his tongue inside and Anais, for the first time, allowed herself to stop thinking—to only feel.

Lindsay took his time exploring her mouth, delighting in the weight of her resting atop him. He kissed her, savoring her lips, coaxing her into kissing him back. Patiently he waited, entering, retreating, entering, until she mewled softly and let her body go limp against him.

His gaze strayed to her breasts, which were swollen and spilling over her corset. A blue vein ran from the little half moon

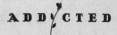

of her areola up to her neck. He traced it with the tip of his finger, inching the corset lower so that he could see more of her rose-tipped breast. She tossed her head back and sighed for him, the action pushing her breasts out in invitation.

"Offer yourself to me, Anais."

He saw her reach above his head, unfastening the ties of the shimmering silk bed curtains. The tieback dropped to the ground. Half the bed was bathed in shadow as the curtains swung into place.

The bed was now intimate, like a private harem. The sand-colored silk, combined with the golden candlelight, cast a warm glow upon Anais's skin—the sort of glow the setting Turkish sun would have cast upon her. In this harem, he had no need of a concubine, nor opium, not when Anais was here with him.

Capturing his gaze, she lowered her corset enough for her nipple to pop out from behind the muslin. As seductive as a professional courtesan, she pressed forward and brought her breast to his mouth, offering herself up to him.

He was lost. A deep hunger he had never known ruled him. Sucking, he drew her nipple into his mouth until she writhed atop him and brushed her petticoat-covered quim against his cock. He was going to make her come from just suckling.

"Lindsay!" she cried, trembling in his arms.

"You're so close," he said huskily as he brought her breasts together and tongued her nipples. "But not yet, I want to feed a bit longer."

She was already shaking and gripping his shoulders, sobbing into his neck. Without letting her recover, he placed her on the bed and stripped her so that she was naked. Despite the dark curtains, he could see the faint shadow of candlelight flicking up her legs, illuminating enticing patches of her skin and her womanly curves. Brushing the back of his hand along her downy curls, he delighted in her soft intake of air and the elegant arch of her back before he rolled her onto her belly.

His gaze traveled down her spine. The faint dusting of downy hair on her skin was illuminated by the candle's glow. He traced the length and curve of her spine with his fingertips, watching as gooseflesh erupted and feathered along her back, down to her rounded bottom.

She stirred restlessly beneath his touch and he watched the muscles of her derriere clench and loosen. He couldn't help but stroke her soft cheeks, cupping them in his hands while rubbing his thumbs along her supple flesh. She moaned, the sound muffled against the bedsheets.

So beautiful and lush, and all his.

Anais felt the air stir behind her, saw Lindsay's corded forearms on either side of her shoulders. She knew he was straddling her, could feel his muscled thighs riding against hers, could feel the heat of his body cocooning her. Yet he kept himself above her, his arms bearing his weight. Whimpering in anticipation, she sucked in her breath as his chest grazed her back and her hips moved restlessly, trying to ease the ache she felt between her thighs.

His tongue came out and raked her flesh, trailing along her spine and she curled her fingers into her palms, shivering with the heat of his tongue, then the coolness that was left behind when he moved his mouth lower. He repeated the action, moving up along her spine to her neck.

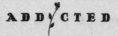

"I want my mouth on you." He pushed away from her and ran his fingers along her back and over her bottom as if he were assessing a slave. She shivered, imagining herself being his slave—his sexual slave.

His hand came around her waist and his fingers pressed into her belly as he raised her slowly to her knees. She was trembling now, not with fear or embarrassment, but desire.

"I want to see you—all of you." Anais felt his finger atop her bottom as it lightly traced her cleft, down to her slick sex.

"I want to watch." Parting her with one hand, he ran his finger along the edge of her folds.

"I want to taste."

"Yes," she said on a breathless whisper. Oh, God, yes.

Her fingers squeezed into tight little fists as his tongue came out and stroked her sex. She squirmed, made a strangled sound deep in her throat, but he held her still with one hand on her hip as he opened his mouth, capturing her sex. Tossing her head back, she flung her curls over her shoulder so that she could see Lindsay behind her. His fingers continued to stroke her sex while her hips undulated in a seductive, rolling motion.

"I can read the signs of your body, Anais. It's telling me it's mine. Let me see your lips say the words. Let me hear those words in your voice."

Anais was a slave to her desire. For just this night she wanted to be anything Lindsay desired. Everything he would give her, she wanted.

"I'm yours," she whispered brokenly before silently adding, *For tonight my body and soul is yours...for tonight....*

Their gazes met and his eyes burned with an intensity that made her stomach clench.

"Are you ready to feel me inside you, angel?"

She nodded, felt something far thicker and firmer than his fingers begin to stretch her. Closing her eyes, Anais tossed back her head and rested her weight on her hands, savoring the tremors that licked through her body, as Lindsay's thick phallus filled her in one possessive thrust.

His name was ripped from her throat as he pressed forward on the bed, covering her with his damp body as he filled her deeper. His hands sought hers, their fingers entwined before he raised her arms above her head, holding her firmly in his grasp, imprisoning her with his strong arms and the weight of his chest on her back as he thrust in and out of her in slow measured strokes that made her want to scream for more. Harder. Faster.

His hips began to push in earnest and soon Anais was moving against him, matching his rhythm. He was totally embedded inside her, yet she couldn't seem to get close enough to him to satisfy her craving for him.

Pressing his mouth to her neck he kissed her, then laid his face in the crook of her neck and breathed against her, whispering sex words in her ear. Words that fuelled her higher and higher. She cried out in protest when he pulled out of her.

Knowing he could not hold on much longer, Lindsay moved away from her and sat against the headboard, motioning her to come to him. He grew harder when he saw that her eyes were glowing and she was smiling. It was a wanton, womanly smile,

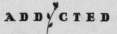

to be sure. It made him so damn aroused as she made a show of sliding her body sensually along his. When she was close enough he caught her breasts in his hands, purposely watching her reaction as he brushed his thumbs along her distended nipples. His hand fisted in her hair when she straddled him. His mouth parted on a silent groan when he felt the wet warmth of her cunt slide along his thighs. It looked so damn good, too good, he thought as he watched her quim graze his skin.

Her face was flushed, as were the tops of her breasts. He wished there was more light so he could see her. But he admitted the lone flickering candle flame had its benefits. There was something erotic about being in bed with silk curtains shimmering around them. The way the shadows licked their way up Anais's curved body was sin incarnate. He was fast losing control, something he didn't want.

Both of their couplings had been heated and frantic—for this one, he wanted to love her slowly and thoroughly.

"Tell me you want this," he asked as she slid her body against him. Her hips undulated beneath his hands, hardening his cock more.

"I want you inside me, Lindsay. Oh, God, how much I want that."

He lifted her onto his arousal. She arched then, the action thrusting her breasts toward him as he filled her.

Good God, he'd never experienced this before, never had lovemaking felt this right, this complete. As he watched her body move atop him, he realized he was at last satisfied, his hunger appeased, his soul fed. He loved her and it was only a matter of time before she realized that it was safe once again to love him back.

Resting her back against his knees while she ground her hips onto him, Lindsay watched her match his rhythm. He would never have enough of her. Never tire of seeing her like this.

"Come for me," he commanded, quickening his pace until they were deep stabs that made her suck in her breath.

Anais thought she might die of pleasure. With her nails she dug into his shoulders, crying out for the release only he could provide. She gave no thought to protection or anything other than the pleasure he was giving her.

With his fingers he stroked her clitoris until she bucked against him. He waited, bringing her closer and closer until she was wild and crying out. Not until he saw her let go, did he let himself indulge in his own pleasure.

"I love you, Anais," he murmured, as he pressed his face against her, holding her tight until she could hardly breathe.

The euphoria of their coupling deserted her. Silently she answered him. *I wish you wouldn't love me, Lindsay. It would make things so much easier if we could both just hate each other. But then we wouldn't have this.*

His arm reflexively tightened around her waist when she moved away from him. Grumbling in his sleep, he pulled her atop him and covered them up with the blanket.

"You belong to me, Anais," he murmured. "And you're not leaving my bed tonight, or any other night for that matter."

18

Anais awoke early and brushed the sleep from her eyes. Turning her head on the pillow, her gaze slipped to the person beside her. Ann was sleeping like a baby.

She should return to her room before the servants arose to start their daily duties. Would Lindsay be gone? she wondered, remembering how she had left him in bed, sleeping heavily. She hoped so. She also hoped that Louisa had not already arrived in her room to wake her.

The pounding of hooves above the dim chatter of birds made Anais jump out of bed. Anais ran to the window in time to see Lindsay galloping down the lane atop Sultan. The view of him melting into the gray-blue light of the dawning morn made her heart ache. Gone was the night of loving and open emotions. With the dawn came the return of her secrets and the full realization that she was treading dangerous waters.

Tying the sash of her wrapper tight around her middle, Anais tossed her hair over her shoulder and looked back at her sister, who was still asleep. Tiptoeing back to her chamber, Anais let herself inside and breathed a huge sigh of relief. Neither Louisa nor the chambermaid had been in yet, and she saw that Lindsay had haphazardly made the bed, covering any evidence of their lovemaking. The pillow was still indented from his head, and Anais found herself brushing her fingers along the spot, feeling the warmth that still lingered on the crisp linen.

Slipping back the covers, she discovered a folded piece of vellum tucked beneath her pillow. Opening it, she saw Lindsay's bold handwriting scrawled across the letter.

No more secrets. I spoke of mine last night. It is time for you to speak of yours.

The note fluttered from her fingers, landing atop the wrinkled bedsheet. Did he know? No, she was being nonsensical. How could he possibly know? It was impossible that he had uncovered her secret. Perhaps he just assumed that she was keeping something from him.

Good God, she thought in panic, what if he did find out? What was she to do then? She didn't want to hurt him, especially after last night. He would be destroyed if he discovered how she and Garrett had betrayed him.

Jumping up from bed, she hurriedly penned a letter to Garrett. She had to see him. She needed Garrett's steady nerves. Together they could come up with a plan to keep Lindsay from learning their dark secret.

A fat log cracked in the hearth as Lindsay took a chair close to the fire, settling his chilled body into the warm leather. It was

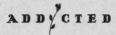

bloody cold and the wind was up, sending drafts through every room in the house.

He'd ridden long and hard, breaking a sweat in an attempt to outrun his thoughts, but they had chased him through the forest and down the paths that led to Bewdley. He was cold and tired from his ride, but the fatigue did not stamp out what he really felt— unease. The disturbing sensation had been gripping him since awakening all alone in Anais's bed that morning. Instead of relenting as it should after his ride, the sensation only curled tighter.

Was Anais's eagerness for his bed nothing more than the hunger for sex? Did what they find together mean nothing more to her than carnal pleasures? He feared the answer, knowing it was not difficult to confuse lust with love. In his case, he knew where his heart lay; he loved Anais. To him they had made love. But what did it mean to her?

She had left him sometime during the night, and awakening alone in the bed was one of the most gut-wrenching kicks in the stomach he had ever felt.

"Your tea, my lord," the parlor maid murmured as she set the silver tea tray on the desk and poured him a steaming cup.

"Thank you." He took the cup from her thin fingers and sipped it carefully. "Where is everyone? The house is rather quiet."

"Lady Weatherby and Lady Darnby have returned to the modiste to outfit Lady Ann with another dress."

He wanted to ask where Anais was, but he refrained and instead asked after Lord Darnby's health.

"He is better, I think, my lord," she said as she passed him a silver plate loaded with fruitcake and biscuits. "He sat for a few minutes this morning in this very room. His color was high and he seemed in good spirits."

Nodding, he bit into a piece of cake covered in marzipan. "And what of Lady Anais?" he finally asked.

"I have not seen her today. Shall I make inquiries with her maid?"

"No. That will not be necessary. I was only making conversation."

"I see, my lord," Mary said politely, despite the quizzical expression on her face. "Shall you be attending the Duke of Torrington's New Year's Eve ball tonight, my lord? I believe Lord and Lady Weatherby have accepted the invitation."

"Oh, I'm sure," he drawled. "My father is never one to look down his nose at an invitation. And New Year's Eve is akin to my father what a feast day is to a patron saint."

The maid flushed and lowered her head, although he saw a hint of a smile before she hid it from him. "Well, then, my lord, if that is all, I shall return to the kitchen to help Cook with supper."

"Good day," he said with a nod, watching as she curtsied and inclined her head, which was covered in a white lace mop cap.

The door closed behind the maid and he let his head rest back against the leather. Was Anais upstairs avoiding him? Had she any idea what thoughts were running rampant through his mind—*what utterly terrifying thoughts?*

No, she could have no idea. He scarcely believed them himself. Yet he could not bring himself to discount the niggling feeling in his gut. And that had been the reason he had stopped by William Crosby's bookshop and purchased a medical manual.

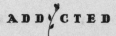

He peered down at the black-and-gilt cover. *A Dissertation on the Human Anatomy; Its Parts and Functions, Failings and Maladies, by Dr. Samuel Stuart.*

He barely knew where to start. How would he begin researching the myriad of afflictions the human soul could succumb to? How would he know if his research was leading him down the right path, and furthermore, did he really want to know what it was she was keeping from him?

"Bloody damn cold, wouldn't you say?"

Lindsay looked up from a diagram of a cross section of the female body, only to see his father slide into the chair opposite him. "Makes my bones ache, this weather," his father grumbled as he reached for the wool plaid that was draped over the back of the chair.

"It is indeed rather chilly," he replied, watching his father arrange the blanket over his legs and wondering when it was the Marquis of Weatherby had turned into an old man.

"What is it?" his father grunted as he poured himself a cup of tea. "Why do you look at me like that?"

"Like what?"

"Like a doddering old fool," his father thundered in a throaty snarl.

Returning his gaze back to the diagram, Lindsay mumbled, "Forgive me. I did not mean to make you feel as though you were an invalid."

"Hmph. The only invalid in this house is that pain in the arse lounging about upstairs. It's high time he started getting on the mend. I'm bloody sick and tired of having so many people around all the time. It interferes with a man's routine."

Despite his own foul mood, Lindsay found himself grinning. Just last night his father had proclaimed to everyone who would listen in the assembly rooms that he had never had more enjoyment than the past sennight when his home was overflowing with guests and evening entertainments. But then, he'd been three sheets to the wind when he had said it.

"What do you have there?" his father asked. "Not some drivel written by Scott or Keats, I hope. You should be brushing up on your equine knowledge if you've a mind to breed that beauty you brought back with you from Turkey."

Lindsay had all but forgotten the fact he had returned home with the intention of starting an Arabian breeding program at Eden Park. Returning home to find Anais was going to be his houseguest for an extended period of time had done little to motivate him to begin. Hell, he'd been far too occupied with making plans to get Anais back, that he hadn't given a fleeting thought for his breeding program. Hell, it had hardly even registered in his brain it was the Christmas season.

"Well, what is it?" his father grumbled. "A tome on breeding practices?"

"Actually, it is a medical text."

His father's eyelids narrowed and something flickered across his yellowed orbs before he looked away and peered into the flames. His father remained quiet—almost pensive as he watched the flames flicker in the hearth. Lindsay was about to excuse himself, when his father's eyes swung to his. "Always liked the fire a good log produces over coal. Used to sit here for hours during the night watching the flames."

"And what did you see in them?"

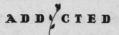

"Ghosts. Many of them."

Lindsay swallowed hard, wanting to break the intimacy of their locked gazes, but he could not. He had never seen his father in such a state. He had been a young boy the last time he witnessed his father this sober and somber.

"You're on a dangerous path, boy. I know. I've traveled it before." Lindsay looked away and pretended interest in his teacup, but his father kept talking. "You're gaunt. You've circles under your eyes like you haven't slept in weeks."

"It's nothing—"

"Don't lie to me," his father spat. "You've never had the kindness of heart to lie to me before, so don't start now. You've never spared my feelings and I shall return the favor in kind. You're killing yourself over this girl and it pains me to see it. I know that you've been deadening yer pain with opium."

Lindsay looked at his father in horror. "Just what the devil do you think, that I've gotten myself into a…a *dependency?* I have dabbled in opium, nothing more. I don't *need* to have it."

"That's what I told myself, too, in the beginning. And it was true, I didn't have to have it, but before I knew it, I'd given my body up to the alcohol. I thought I didn't need it, but my body disagreed with my mind."

"I am not dependent upon it. I am not *you!*"

"It was your greatest wish in life, wasn't it, to not become like me. I knew it all along—all those years you were a small boy, I felt it—your disgust, your disapproval—*your fear.*"

I don't want to be like him, Anais. I don't want to hurt everyone I love and not care about anything but my own needs. He was sixteen when he had blurted that out. And she had reached for his hand

and clasped it tightly in hers. *You won't Lindsay. You're nothing like him. You'll never be like him.*

"I know I was never the father to you that Broughton's father was to him, or even the sort Darnby is to his chits. I know I wasn't what your sensitive nature needed in a sire, but I swear to you, I never wanted this for you. I never wanted you to walk in my shoes. I may not have grown to love your mother, but I always loved you."

Never had his father admitted any affection for him. Lindsay found himself speechless, staring at the man he barely knew.

"I was once like you, boy. I, too, loved and lost. I, too, have been consumed by demons. I turned to drink when the woman I loved betrayed me. It was the only thing that deadened the pain. It was the only thing that could stop me from thinking about her day and night, and week after week. You have discovered the same cure."

"That's not why—"

"Then why have you taken it up? Why can't you put it down?"

Lindsay looked away, ashamed of what he wanted to say, but knowing that there was no other truth. "Because all my life I've been weak. I feared your fate would befall me because I always felt the niggling of temptation nipping at my heels and I fought so hard to ignore it, and there were some days I thought I wouldn't be successful because it was so damn hard to resist. I never wanted to be you, falling down drunk and groping women. I didn't want to hear my wife crying in the middle of the night because she had caught me in bed with one of the maids or dallying with her friend."

Lindsay squeezed his eyes shut and pressed his fingers farther

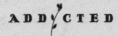

into his palm, attempting to control the sudden rage and emotion that threatened to spill from the pit of his gut. "I couldn't bear the thought of Anais looking at me like she looked at you when you were stumbling drunk. I never wanted to see disgust in her eyes. I never, *never*," he roared, pounding his fist on the arm of his chair, "wanted to turn her away from me the way you turned Mother from you."

His eyes flew open and he met his father's hard stare. "So, I discovered the opium and I thought that if I wasn't drinking like you, and I wasn't chasing anything in a skirt like you, that I would be safe from my fate of becoming you. I truly believed that one day I would be worthy of her and I would outrun the craving for temptation. I thought of opium as a lark, something we all partook in to have some laughs and relaxation. I didn't realize till too late that I used it to control what I really am— your son."

His father blinked once, then again, slowly, as if he was trying to stem the moisture Lindsay suddenly saw spring into his father's eyes before looking away and back to the fire. "It will no doubt come as a shock to you, but I despise what you've had to see. I hate that the model for a gentleman you had in your life was me. But I can't change any of that, can I?" he muttered as he lifted his teacup to his lips. "I can't change my path in life. But I sure as hell can set you on the right way." His father set his cup down on its saucer with a clang. "Let me tell you something about women like Anais. Women like her are a man's dream. I know I've professed she's a nothing little baggage, but the truth is, if I were your age and I had someone hanging on my every word and looking at me with those big, blue eyes as though I were a god, I'd be as smitten as you are. What man doesn't want the demure little paragon that pants hot for us? What man doesn't want the lady by day and the temptress by night? I'm no different. I fell in love with a woman like Anais. I wanted her. I loved her and she told me she wanted me, too. She gave me everything, then she told her papa that I had forced her. She lied and she devastated me in the process when she turned something I had never experienced before, into something ugly and hateful. And she made her circumstances in life better when she married a duke and forgot all about me. But I didn't forget her—I couldn't. Every time I closed my eyes I saw her. I felt her touch, and damn me it was more than I could bear." His father was breathing heavy and his big hand was fisted tight in his lap. "Your Anais is just like her, boy. She'll tell you 'no we shouldn't' even as she's raising her skirt for you. And after the deed is done and the passion subsides and she's left with the memories, she'll cast you aside because you can't be what she wants. You can't be the man she has created in her mind. And she'll torture you with the memories. I know your torture," he grunted as he shook a finger at him. "She is making your life a living hell. Forget her!" he roared, smacking the arm of the chair. "Forget that night in the stables because it is obvious she has. You may have lost your heart to her that night, but she didn't lose hers to you. I'll tell you, life with that one will only make your days hell."

"My life is hell without her."

"Have you not heard a damned word that I've said? She was never yours. You only thought you could have her, but you can't. Let her go before she kills you."

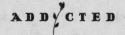
"You're overwrought, Father. This outburst cannot be good for you."

"*Goddamn you!* Must you make me say it? Very well," he huffed. "Broughton and the Darnby chit are keeping secrets from you!"

Lindsay felt as though he'd taken a blow to his middle as he stared at his father. The longer he looked at his father, the more wild and rampant his thoughts were, and they flooded his brain like water rushing through a dam.

"I'm sorry," his father grumbled, rising from the chair. "I know what she means to you, I've known since I found you in the stable doing your best to make me think that you were not there with her. You wore your heart on your sleeve, but when I turned and saw her, I knew, *knew* she didn't love you as you loved her."

"That's a damned lie!"

"Her affections come with conditions, boy! That isn't love. You've never seen her faults, you've always been blinded to her imperfections because you always wanted to worship the ground she walked on. Damn me, I cannot stand by and watch you kill yourself over someone who is so undeserving of the sacrifice. She is not the woman you think she is and it is time you learned the truth of it."

His father took an unsteady step toward him. "People think I'm a drunkard, and I am, but I tell you, I have eyes, and I see things that people don't think I do. Ask her about her secrets, and remember, Lindsay, that you've always been a gentleman with her."

The door of the study closed with a bang and Lindsay was left with the gruff words of his father reverberating around his head. What secrets could he mean? What had he seen? No, the old man was not in his right mind. Alcohol had poisoned his thoughts—he couldn't be trusted. There was only one thing in life he could count on, and that was Anais's goodness and her unfailing ability to tell the truth.

And yet he had purchased the medical text in order to discover what her condition was—the condition she wished to hide from him. The secret, he was certain, that could be answered if he would only believe in his instincts.

With an oath, he hefted the book from the table and flipped through it for what felt like hours. Page after page he read the words until they blurred into a black string of ink. Finally, he came to a chapter that read, *Disorders of the Blood; A Comprehensive Study.* He skimmed the paragraphs and found something that struck a chord with him.

Anaemia: the deficiency of blood and its life forces in the body. Symptoms include frank bleeding, occult bleeding, inability to catch one's breath—pallor, malaise, and if left uncorrected, irreparable damage to the heart and subsequent death. Treatment is with meats—eaten rare...

He looked up from the page and felt slightly ill. She had all the symptoms, including the heart damage. How many times had she looked unnaturally white, like she had no blood at all flowing through her veins? How many times had she sounded winded? Suddenly, the image of Anais choking down kidneys and rare pieces of beef swimming in juices came to him and he read on, needing to know how a person became so anaemic that their heart was damaged from lack of blood.

The malady is most commonly found amongst women of childbearing years. Excessive flow of the monthly fluxes as well as the result of miscarriage and birth. Confinement is the main causative reason for women who were normally well prior to conception.

Broughton and the Darnby chit have been keeping secrets from you.... His insides curled as if a hand had reached into his belly and was twisting his guts. A wave of nausea washed over him, threatening to spill the contents of his lunch up when he thought of Anais's softly rounded belly. *Confinement is the main causative reason...* The words tortured him. What was he to think? He wasn't even certain he was up to the task of thinking with any clarity.

"My lord," Worthing, their butler, said discreetly. "Lady Anais has requested that one of the footmen take a message to Lord Broughton. I've come to inform you that the lady has asked that a mount be saddled within the hour. I, er..." the butler said awkwardly, color painting his cheeks an unbecoming scarlet, "I thought you would want to know."

"Thank you, Worthing," he said automatically, feeling like an automaton grinding forward without any purpose or feeling. "I do, indeed."

"Shall I have the Arabian readied for you, my lord?"

Lindsay tapped his fingertips against the book in his lap as he continued to stare into the fire. "Yes," he murmured rising from his chair.

Yes, it is time to discover your secrets, Anais.

19

"What is it?" Garrett asked as he brought Anais into his arms. "I've been worried sick ever since I received your summons. Have you begun bleeding again?"

"It is nothing like that," she murmured, sniffing into her hand-kerchief. "I think he knows. Oh, God, Garrett, I do believe Lindsay has somehow found out."

Relief flooded his face and he ran a soothing hand down her spine. "Impossible," Garrett scoffed. "You're worrying over noth-ing, Anais. Your emotions are fragile, that is all. My brother tells me that this is all very normal for a woman in your condition."

"You don't understand. I don't want to hurt him."

"I know," he whispered. Anais heard the sadness in his voice.

"I don't want to hurt you, either," she sobbed. "I swear it, Garrett, I never, ever wanted to hurt you or use you to lessen the pain of what Lindsay did to me."

"Shh, sweeting, you're distraught. It isn't good for you. Here, give me your hands." Anais allowed Garrett to guide her farther into the cottage. "Now then, shall I make you a cup of tea? You

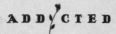

could use a cup, your hands are cold. You look very pale. Have you not been sleeping?" Fresh tears leaked from her eyes and cascaded down her cheeks. Garrett's expression softened and he reached for her. "Do not worry. Before you leave here this afternoon, we will have a plan in place. I swear to you, just as I swore to you months ago, I will stand by you and whatever decisions you make."

Saddle leather creaked in the cold as Lindsay swung his leg around and dismounted Sultan. The animal snorted and tossed his head high into the air. Reaching into his jacket, Lindsay removed three cubes of sugar and fitted them into his gloved palm. Sultan ran his muzzle along the leather, wetting it before taking the sugar. Now quiet, Lindsay left the horse and trudged silently through the snow.

Stealth was the order of the day. He had come to spy on the woman he loved. As he followed her through the woods to this little cottage at the edge of Broughton's estate, it had taken every ounce of self-control not to charge Sultan ahead and overtake her, demanding to know what the hell she was doing meeting Broughton in such a secluded place. But he knew if he handled her in that manner he might never learn what secrets she was keeping from him.

Reaching for the branches that hung low before him, he swung them up in the air then stooped beneath, letting them fall back into place. Two steps farther, he found himself before a frosted windowpane.

His heart couldn't seem to find a steady rhythm. He wasn't ashamed to admit his weakness. He was terrified of what was going to greet him once he wiped his hand against the glass, removing the dirt and grime and seeing for himself what lay beyond the frost.

He heard them before he could see them. Anais's gentle voice suddenly rose above Broughton's baritone rumble. She sounded as though she was weeping. Unable to stand it a second longer, Lindsay put his gloved fist to the window and swirled his hand in a circle. Slowly, as if by magic, the image of Anais greeted him.

Seeing her here now, with Broughton, in Broughton's cozy, secluded cottage made him shake. So many emotions, swirling like tempests, ate at him—anger, frustration, desire, love—violent emotions, every one of them. He had not lied to her last night when he told her he was consumed by her, for he was consumed. He was an empty shell of himself without her in his life.

Out of the corner of his eye, Lindsay saw Broughton move toward her, his hands, ungloved, stretched out to her and he caught her easily about the shoulders. Just as easily, she stepped into his embrace and wrapped her pale hands around Broughton's shoulders. Lindsay could not breathe as he watched her nestle her face against Broughton's chest and close her eyes as if Garrett's arms brought her the safest of harbors.

This is how she used to come to him. But she had not allowed him to hold her in such a way since he'd returned. She had shared her body, her weakness for passion, but she had not shared her vulnerability or her fears. She gave those, as well as her trust, to Broughton.

His breath, coming in rapid fire, clouded the glass and with a violent oath Lindsay swirled the edge of his fist once more

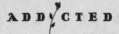

against the window, enlarging the circle so that he could see more of the cottage.

Broughton was leading Anais by the hand to the bed. Lindsay could not move, could not blink, nor could he breathe. He could only watch in perverse horror as she willingly followed Broughton and sat down beside him, allowing him to remove her bonnet and skim his fingertips along her alabaster cheek. He saw their lips move and would have paid anything to hear what they said to one another. Was Broughton confessing his love? Was she accepting it?

He saw a tear trickle from Anais's eye and streak down her cheek. He imagined himself chasing away the wetness with his thumb, kissing away her tears until they were ones of utter satiation. Like the tears she shed when he brought her to climax. Happy tears. Beautiful tears. He could not stop from asking himself what sort of tears these were that she was giving Broughton.

Broughton's dark head tilted to the side and Lindsay watched, jealousy jabbing him, as the man who had once been his close friend closed his eyes and gently kissed her chin. This was a man in love, Lindsay realized, and it took every ounce of his control not to go bursting into the cottage and pummel Broughton until he was nothing but a bloody, broken heap.

Anais's head tipped back and he watched her lips part—a sob? A cry of pleasure? Of need? Of pain? And then suddenly her shoulders were shaking and her face was pressed tightly against Broughton's neck. She had wound herself so tightly against him that Broughton was compelled to lift his face from her hair, struggling to draw breath. *Drowning in her.*

They sat, meshed tightly, their arms wrapped around the

other as Broughton held tight, rocking her, allowing Anais to give vent to whatever feelings were coursing so violently through her.

There was something profoundly intimate in their embrace. Lindsay could not help but wonder at it. Had she ever come to him so willingly? Had she ever offered so much of herself to him, or had it merely been him taking her succor? *Him needing her?*

He tried to think of the times he had held her. He could not recall an occasion in which she had wept this unbridled before him. No, she had never been this vulnerable with him. She had never needed him as much as she now needed Broughton.

For the first time since returning home, Lindsay allowed himself to fully believe that perhaps it was true, she had forgiven him and moved on with her life while he had done neither. He could not forgive himself for what he had done, nor could he go on with his life. Life was not worth living if it did not contain Anais's smiles, or her warm body against his.

A gentle sound reached his ears, part sob, part sad laughter. He looked up from his hands and saw that Anais and Broughton were now standing, her beautiful face clutched in his palms. Tenderly Broughton dried her cheeks before taking her hand in his. The cottage door opened and the rusty hinges creaked in the quiet as the sound of their boots upon the wooden porch echoed off the leafless trees. Lindsay waited, breath held, heart immobile in his chest for the sound of their retreating footsteps.

"I will see you at The Lodge tonight, then?" Broughton asked. "A quiet dinner will set you to rights."

"I will be there," she murmured through delicate sniffs.

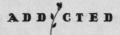

"All will be well, Anais. He will not discover our secret—I promise you that."

"I'm sorry I dragged you away from your work, I know how busy you are. It was just..." She sniffled.

"Leave Raeburn to me. Do not worry so much. You need to take care of yourself. You need your strength."

The hair on Lindsay's nape bristled. His insides clenched and twisted as the page in Dr. Stuart's medical text flashed before him. Good God, he could go no longer denying his instincts.

Closing his eyes, he willed the image of Anais to come forward. He saw her with her rounded belly, which was slightly bigger than it had been the first time he saw her naked in the stable. And her breasts, which were always large, were firmer—fuller. The nausea at the breakfast table? The paleness of her skin?

How could he continue to remain blind?

"Thank you, Garrett—for everything."

"Shh. We are beyond this now, you and I. We have a tie that binds, do we not?"

He did not hear her reply, nor the sound of them walking to their mounts. He did not even feel the earth shake beneath him as the horses pounded along the path. The only sound that registered in his brain was the sound of his blood rushing violently through his ears. Damn him, his father was right. They were keeping secrets from him.

The cottage door swung open. Lindsay took one step forward, his boot pressing into the uneven floorboard that creaked beneath his weight. The cottage smelled of her—of country flowers and Anais. He wondered if Broughton was aware of it, the way her scent clung to her hair and clothes. The way it cloaked the air when she was in the room, the way it lingered, caressing his flesh when she left.

He had expected the cottage to smell musty. After all, Broughton hadn't kept a gatekeeper for nearly three years. It should have been dusty and full of cobwebs, but the sight that greeted him was not ramshackle neglect, but one of recent improvements.

No gatekeeper would ever have slept in such a magnificent bed. Broughton was generous with his servants, but not to this extent. The bed was constructed of expensive mahogany and the posters were heavily carved—the style was the height of fashion. The coverings were of brocade velvet and silks.

Hell, his own bed at home was not covered in something as costly as this. No, the bed was not that of a gatekeeper, but it was certainly in the keeping of female taste.

Lindsay's mouth curved in distaste as he stalked to the bed and ran his gloved hand along the sage-green brocade, watching as the black kid leather disappeared amongst the crème bullion fringe. This was the bed of a woman—*a kept woman*. A bed designed to tease and titillate. This was a bed designed for fucking.

With a vicious growl, he fisted the bullion in his glove. Is that what the cottage was, a place to tryst? A place where Broughton brought Anais to fuck her?

Rage, seething and impetuous, flared to life and he flung the coverlet to the ground, searching the expensive silk sheets, for what, he wondered, his gaze searching blindly. For signs of lovemaking? What did he expect to see?

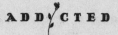

Had she been entertaining Broughton here while she was living at Eden Park? Had she been entertaining his friend in bed in the manner she had entertained him?

Unable to look at the bed any longer he stalked to the hearth and rested his arm on the mantel, trying to rein in his wild thoughts and raging blood. What purpose was this serving? He already had his answers. She'd been meeting Broughton in secret here—God only knew how long she'd been spreading her thighs for him—God only knew how far along with child she was— for he realized that now, could admit the god-awful truth. Anais was carrying Broughton's child.

Your courses should be coming soon, miss. The servant's words rang in his head. He recalled the day he stood in the hall, outside her bedchamber and listened to Anais with her maid. He had not intended to eavesdrop, but he had been unable to move after he heard Louisa's next words. *Although, I thought they should have been here a few weeks ago, but of course, you haven't been well. It's not uncommon to miss a few months altogether after going through a bad patch such as you've gone through.*

Lindsay pounded the thick walnut mantel with his fist and pressed his head to his forearm, cursing himself for failing to see the signs. He laughed at the absurdity of his predicament. Damn her, last night she had pleasured him as he had never been pleasured in his life, and all the time she had been carrying Broughton's child within her.

He gagged, disgusted—*sickened*—at the image of his hands caressing her belly—his lips grazing that gently mounded flesh. Squeezing his eyes shut he fought the image of her atop him, struggled not to hear her breath against him or the feel of her breasts pressed to his chest. *Breath for breath, mouth to mouth, breast to breast...*

Pushing himself away from the hearth, he blindly swept the room with his gaze. A table sat beside the bed and he strolled over to it. A book lay atop the table and he picked it up, turning it over in his hands. A book of Lord Byron's poems. No doubt Broughton had read to her while they reclined in this bed, spent from exuberant bouts of sexual congress.

Swearing a vicious litany, Lindsay pulled the drawer open to fling the book inside, but he spotted another book, half-hidden beneath a sheaf of papers. He did not bother to listen to his conscience. He didn't give a damn that he was invading her privacy. He deserved the truth. He had given her nothing but the truth—every painful bit of it. And she had given him nothing but lies.

Pulling the ribbon that secured the front and back covers, he flipped through the pages and realized that it was Anais's diary. He turned to the last page and looked down at her confession.

Why did you have to betray me with Broughton? Why did you give him what I wanted so desperately from you?

20

Seated at her dressing table wearing nothing but her corset and petticoats, Anais waited for her maid to finish pinning up her hair. As she sat before the mirror, the oil lamp casting shadows along her neck and décolletage, Anais noticed that for the first time in more than a month her cheeks had color.

Physically she felt better than she had; mentally however, she was distraught. Her meeting with Garrett that afternoon had done little to rid her of her fears and nagging doubts.

"Shall you wear pearls in your hair this evening, Lady Anais?" Louisa asked as she twirled and pinned up a segment of her hair. "It is New Year's Eve, perhaps a bit of a splash is in order to ring in the new year the right way."

"I don't think so, Louisa. It is only supper after all."

"If you say so, miss."

"Perhaps, though, I will wear the blue ribbon tonight."

"Shall I add feathers, miss? A braided bun looks quite lovely worn with feathers."

"Feathers would be nice."

"Are you planning on wearing the blue silk, then?" Anais let her gaze slide to the bed, where the turquoise gown lay spread out on the counterpane. "Lady Ann has some peacock feathers that would look lovely with that shade of blue. Very Oriental if you don't mind my saying so, miss."

"Yes," Anais murmured. His Eastern houri, Lindsay had once called her. And how she had wanted to be that woman for him. It seemed ages ago that he'd said those things to her, and yet, it was not even a year. So much had happened in that short time— so much was different now.

She closed her eyes as Louisa wound another wedge of hair up into a knot. Garrett's face flashed before her—handsome, loyal, trusting. Then Lindsay's face appeared and she opened her eyes to drive away the image, but she still saw him, the picture of him naked in her bed, pleasuring her.

She had allowed herself too many nights of pleasure with Lindsay. Even though she loved him—would always love him— they could have no future, not when the past was fraught with lies. She could not do that to him, betray him a second time. It was best to believe that sometimes love just wasn't enough to carry two people through life. A marriage needed to be founded on more than love and mutual passion. It needed honesty, trust, openness—all things Anais knew she was too cowardly to give him.

"Well, then, miss, before I finish your hair shall I ask Lady Ann if she would mind sharing her feathers?"

Drawing her gaze away from the gown, Anais looked into the mirror and saw Louisa watching her intently. "That would be fine, Louisa."

"I shan't be a minute, miss," the maid said before curtsying. Anais followed the maid's retreat in the mirror before her gaze strayed to her breasts that rose above the ruffled corset. The image of Lindsay tracing the blue vein that arose from her breast as it climbed to her neck appeared before her eyes. Shivering, she felt his touch all over again. Remembered his glittering gaze in the muted candlelight. He had devoured her with that gaze, especially when she had offered him her breast for his pleasure.

With a shudder, she smoothed her hands down her arms as the flames in the hearth flickered and licked their way up the flue. Heat radiated from the blaze, yet still she trembled. She knew it was not from cold, but from the sensation—the remembered feel of Lindsay's lips drawing her nipple into his mouth and suckling her till her womb clenched.

She looked away from the mirror, no longer able to see her breasts in the reflection without thinking of Lindsay with his dark head bent to them. Her chamber door opened as she fought to stem the illicit images running wild in her mind—she sought composure, fearing Louisa would see and understand her state. The door closed then, with an abruptness that made her breath catch and her eyes dart to the mirror.

She gasped at the image that greeted her in the glass. Lindsay—beautiful, virile Lindsay standing against the door, his black jacket slung over his sleeve, his white linen shirt, devoid of waistcoat and cravat, lay open at the throat, revealing a tanned patch of skin and a hint of the silky dark hair that covered his chest and belly. His trousers, formfitting and tucked into black glossy boots, revealed the muscled contours of his thighs.

His curling hair was windswept, wild and untamed—utterly masculine—as it molded along his forehead only to hang in loose waves around his neck. She could almost see him lounging on his silk cushions in his Turkish tent room, reclining in Eastern indolence as he inhaled the perfumed vapors of opium.

He looked every inch the libertine standing before her the way he was, and she saw for the first time the curious shimmer in his eyes. They were glittering, but in a way she had never seen before.

Had he been dabbling in opium? Was that the reason behind the queer gleam she saw?

"Good evening, madam. I am thrilled to have found you alone. It has saved me a considerable deal of trouble." A soft but interminable click echoed off the walls. He had locked the door.

His voice was different—distant somehow, and she felt a tremor of unease slither down her spine. He stalked lazily into her room, his eyes slowly perusing the walls, jumping from lamp to lamp that were lit on the tables. She followed their trail, wondering what thoughts were running through his mind— wondering why the oil lamps were of such interest to him. Then she saw how his eyes rested on her, how they slid down to her décolletage and belly, and she knew then that he was seeing her—seeing things she had made every attempt to hide from him.

When his gaze slid up to meet hers, his eyes were darker, more green—more glittering, but with what emotion, she did not know.

"You have lit the lamps, how very kind of you. However, I thought you preferred the subtlety of candlelight?"

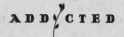

"One cannot dress by the light of one candle."

"No, but one can dally by the light of it—quite effectively, in fact."

Anais swallowed hard, knowing that the moment she had feared was upon her.

"Beautiful, beautiful, angel," he whispered as he slowly shook his head.

"I am not an angel."

"No, you are not. You are a fallen angel."

"What is your purpose here, Lindsay?" she asked quietly as she studied her shaking fingers that rested on her lap.

"What do you think it is?"

She looked up from her hands and met his gaze that was boring into her. She glanced away, unable to hold his unwavering, hard expression. "I do not know, but I pray that you will not torment me much longer."

"Torment you?" he mocked with a hollow laugh. "You don't know the meaning of the word. You have never felt the claws of torture ripping into your soul. You have never been to hell."

"And you have?"

"Yes." He kept his eyes trained on her while he tossed his coat onto the bed. "Stand up, please."

"This isn't the time, Lindsay."

"I said—" He stopped, pressed his eyes as he appeared to gather his control. "Please indulge me, Anais. Stand up."

"My chamber is the last place you should be found. I am only half-dressed," she replied. She had never dealt with Lindsay in a rage. In fact she did not know to what extent his temper ranged.

"Get up!"

Anais found herself jumping to do his bidding when she saw the veins in his neck distend with blood and anger. "Lindsay, you are not yourself. Have you taken opium and come up here to fight with me?"

"Don't you dare speak to me of *my* failings," he growled, taking one predatory step closer. *"Don't you dare!"*

"You said you wouldn't—"

"You impugn what honor I have left when you accuse me of coming to you after taking opium." He smiled, but there was no mirth, no warmth to it, but rather what she imagined a panther might look like after cornering an innocent doe that was to be its next meal.

"All this time, you sermonizing. You finding fault in me. I cannot live with the type of man you are, Lindsay," he said in a falsetto voice that mocked hers. "I cannot be a party to vice— I cannot watch you turn into your father. Well, do you know what I see standing before me? I see your mother."

She gasped, cut to the quick. He knew where to aim his arrows.

"Hypocrite, that is what you are, Anais. You tell me that I am flawed? You have the audacity to act as though your family is above such failings—that you and your father are above succumbing to weakness and vice? Of course we cannot include your mother in your exalted company. We both know what she is."

"Stop that talk!"

"You whored yourself last night, didn't you? I should have left you some banknotes on the bedside table for your remarkable performance. Did you mean any of it, Anais?

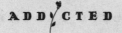

Because I believed you did, or was it just an act? Was it just fucking to you?"

"Stop it," she cried, feeling tears spring to her eyes at his cruelty. "Say what you have come here to say and leave. Whatever issue it is that is making you this cruel can only stem from me—*my actions.* You mentioned my father, well, leave him out of this. He is a good man. His only crime is that he had the misfortune to be taken in by my duplicitous mother."

Lindsay laughed. The sound made the hair on her arms rise. "Your father is no more moral than your mother—in fact he is no better than my father—the man you take delight in looking down your nose at. You want honesty, Anais? Well, you shall have it—your father's sickbed confession to me that afternoon you found us talking. I didn't want to tell you. I didn't want to destroy your faith in your father— or me. But what a damned fool I was. You were no green girl. In fact, you are just as cunning as Rebecca."

"Get on with it," she cried, hating the mockery in his voice.

His eyes narrowed and his lips parted in a dark, empty smile. "Your father, that good honest man you put on a pedestal, has been tupping Rebecca behind your back. *He's* her rich protector. Yes, Anais," he said, pushing on, despite the fact she was fumbling on weak knees.

"No, it's not possible—"

"Oh, anything is possible, angel, I've learned that, and in the most painful way possible. What stealthy little connivers women are."

"Rebecca and my father," she gasped, unable to credit the thought.

"She was after money and security. She couldn't get it with me, so she turned to someone much more willing to part with his pocketbook."

Anais had to sit before she fell down from sheer shock. She could hardly breathe, couldn't think, but Lindsay ruthlessly carried on, refusing to aid her in the slightest.

"That's right, Anais. And your father couldn't stand it, couldn't bear the shame and the pressure that Rebecca was putting upon him, so he took the coward's way out and decided to put a bullet in his head and leave you with the mess. But he botched that up, didn't he? He managed to bugger up his suicide and instead set the whole bloody house on fire. Your father couldn't wait to confide in me. He wanted to be absolved of his crimes and I told him I would never tell you. I told him I would protect you from the ugly truth. And you thought me weak?" he growled. "I have never met a more spineless man than I did the day I stood looking down upon your father. All I could think about as I gave him my word was at least my father admits to his debauches. He does not hide behind the Bible and a deceitful cloak of piety and goodness—he admits to them and invites the scathing contempt of people—*you,* your contempt and ridicule. And I am just like him. I admitted it. I am weak. You have shunned me for it. You have made me feel dirty and vile because I could not resist the lure. All the time you acted superior I thought I deserved it because it was coming from you—you who were always good. You who would never lie. You who knew right from wrong."

Anais didn't say anything, she just stared at him. She was

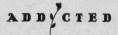

afraid—afraid of looking too deep and what she might find lurking beneath his skin. What would she find there? She feared the question even though she knew the answer.

"I have not fallen far from my father's loins, Anais. What of you? How far have you fallen from the antics of both your mother and father?"

Silence stretched on until a soft knock echoed through the room "Miss." Louisa called, rapping on the door. "Miss?"

"Go away, Louisa," Lindsay demanded. "If you want to retain your post in this house you will go below stairs and not breathe a word of what you have heard in this chamber."

"Lord Raeburn?" the maid asked and Anais heard the astonishment in Louisa's timid voice.

"Go, now."

"Aye, your lordship," Louisa replied obediently. The sound of the maid's half boots beating a hasty retreat down the stairs echoed in the hall.

"How far have you fallen, Anais?"

"I have no idea what you are going on about—"

He took a step toward her then stopped. "You should not leave your things laying about Anais. You never know who will come across them."

Her gaze flew to the bed. A million thoughts ran rampant in her mind and she gripped the mahogany table to support her.

"Don't you want to know what I found?"

He could have found many things. So many things she couldn't explain—things she was afraid to tell him.

"I found a cottage, and it was done up in the most decadent of styles. Not at all in keeping with a gatekeeper's requirements. No, I would say more in line with a mistress. Perhaps even the sort of abode your father keeps Rebecca in. It was very feminine, very refined in elegance. The colors were soft. Sage-greens and golds and crèmes." He turned and glared at her. "Your type of colors, Anais. *Your* type of elegance."

She made to shake her head to deny him, but he narrowed his eyes.

"Don't."

His voice resembled the sound of a cracking whip and she flinched at the coldness of it. Never in all the years she had known him had Lindsay been this angry.

"It smelled of you, Anais. Inside I could smell country flowers and woman—your scent." She shrunk back from his blistering gaze, unable to do anything else but part her lips on a whispered denial she knew was futile. "Inside were two people—a man I used to call friend, and a woman whom I call lover. I also found a book."

Her knees buckled and she sank onto the chair. What had he found? Which of her lies had he uncovered?

"Right and wrong, good and evil," he whispered, reaching into the pocket of his jacket and dragging a brown leather volume out from the black fabric. "No shades of gray. No faults. No weaknesses. Just a perfect angel."

"That is not possible for anyone—"

"But you did your damndest didn't you? You did everything to make me believe—make me want that perfect soul. *I* believed you were an angel. I believed in your goodness." He laughed, a bitter sound that slithered along her skin. "It was the *only* thing I believed in. I bared my soul to you. I cataloged my weakness

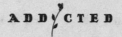

before you, laying my fears before your feet and begging you for your forgiveness and understanding. It disgusts me now, because you ate it up. You allowed it—encouraged it—you," he murmured as he wheeled upon her, "you stood before me and acted like an angel of mercy when you were really betraying me with my friend."

Her head snapped back as if he had slapped her. "That's right, Anais," he said holding the book up in the light so that the gilt edges of the paper glimmered in the golden light. "I've read it. All of it."

"You had no right!" Her words were cut short when he wheeled the book into the hearth. The flames hungrily devoured the paper, sending black smoke up the flue along with her confessions.

He watched the flames as he spoke. "I don't know why I am so surprised by what you have written. You tried often this past week to tell me that it was over. Even as you were lying with me in bed you tried to tell me, but like a blind fool I could not see past my desire, my love—a love that has never, ever wavered in its constancy. A love I believed could never die. I didn't want to see the truth, I know that now."

She tried to speak, but her jumbled thoughts prevented her from making a sound. Her mind was jumping, searching, trying to decipher which of her lies Lindsay had discovered.

"Had I not betrayed your trust, had I not used opium when I had planned on coming to you, we would not be here now. I all but pushed you into Broughton's arms, didn't I? I can hardly blame you for that. As much as I want to, as angry as I want to be with you for turning to another, I cannot fault you. I will accept the blame for that, Anais. Opium came between us. That is my shame. I admit it. Now it is time to admit to yours."

She watched him walk toward her with steely determination in his eyes. He reached for her wrist and pulled her up from the chair.

"What are you doing?" she whispered, meeting his gaze.

"How much longer did you expect me to play the fool?"

"Lindsay, don't—*please.*" But he was beyond listening and instead turned her around so that her hands and face were pressed to the wall and his fingers, fierce and quick, began to unlace her corset. With one tug, he pulled the lacings from the silver eyes and tossed the cord to the ground. Then his hands came around her waist and searched for the ties of her pantalets before roughly shoving them down her hips and along her thighs.

"Please," she whimpered when he reached for the hem of her chemise and raised it along her body. He stopped, pressed his face into her neck and breathed unsteadily against her. He was shaking, as if he just realized what he was doing.

"I am crazed, Anais. I can't think. I can only see you in his arms, loving him. Please, end this. I deserve to know, don't you think?"

She felt the harsh brush of his breath against her neck and then he turned her to face him. He looked as though he was ready to weep. There was desolation, despair in his eyes, and it destroyed her to know she was the cause of it.

"Do I not deserve to know your secrets, Anais?"

She shook her head, tears clouding her vision. No, she could not. He would know, but then his fingers touched the edge of her chemise to where the angry red marks on her breasts were illuminated by the lights. She knew then it was too late. He already knew.

"This is what you've been trying to hide from me. This is why you never allowed me to see you by lamplight—why you intentionally made it dark in our bed last night."

She allowed him to lift the hem of her chemise and pull it over her head. He did deserve to know, however much it pained her to admit to her failings. Lindsay deserved the truth.

She stood naked in front of him, allowed his hands to reach up and cup her swollen breasts, his fingers tracing the red slash-like marks at the side of her bosom. He tested their weight in his palms before using his fingertip to trace the vein that disappeared beneath her rose-colored areola.

"You didn't want me to see this—see you."

She knew he required no answer. He knew what she would say. She had wanted to hide her body from him—every scrap of evidence, far away from his knowing eyes.

He fell to his knees as his fingers sought her rounded belly. He traced the shape of it, running his mouth along her stretched skin which bore angry red marks. "Oh, God, you have murdered what remains of my soul."

Anais closed her eyes, hating the pain she heard in his voice. Tears cascaded down her cheeks as she let her head rest against the wall. She wept, fearing his questions, fearing her answers. She was weak. So damn weak.

"You've had a child," he whispered, but it was more a choked sob and she fought back her own cry. It would be so easy to lie. Lies had never tripped so easily from her tongue than they had since Lindsay had returned to her life. But she was sick of the lies. She was tired of fearing his discovery and his reaction and subsequent repulsion. She was heartsick of being weak.

"Tell me, Anais," he begged, his eyes were scouring every inch of her body. She could not hide from the truth any longer.

"Damn you!" he cried. "You gave Broughton a child!"

Anais smothered her own cry. Self-preservation, the fallen angel inside her screamed. *Lie, deny.* By rights she should be furious with him, he had left her alone after taking her innocence. He had betrayed her. Forgotten her. He deserved to suffer, to know that his actions and choices that night had set this moment into motion.

He thought her Broughton's lover, and the accusation stung. But what other choice had she given him? Her lies had led him to the only logical conclusion that was left.

He was looking at her with his green eyes—eyes that reflected tears and pain and betrayal. And from somewhere deep inside her, the woman she had once been, the honest, upright woman, resurfaced. She reached for his face and cupping it in her hands, she ran her thumbs along his cheeks. "No, Lindsay," she whispered, her voice broken and quiet. "I gave *you* a child."

21

Dazed, Lindsay looked up into Anais's face and thanked God he was on his knees. The room began to spin, and he felt himself sway as shock and disbelief flooded his body.

He was breathing hard, as if he'd been running. He couldn't think, could only say over and over in his mind that he could not have heard her correctly. He was simply overwrought.

It was Broughton's child she had bore. Hadn't she taken up with Broughton after she had witnessed him with Rebecca? Of course it was Broughton's...

But the questioning voice in his head reasoned differently. *It could have been his.*

His mind drifted and he saw the vision of Anais lying beneath him on top of the haystack. He knew it was more than possible he might have given her his child that night—that beautiful, magical night in the stable...

As if she could read his mind, she reached for him. "I carried your child," she whispered tremulously, taking his unsteady hand and moving it along her belly. A belly that still carried the marks of being stretched with life.

"No," he mumbled—confused, mute, impotent of forming any cohesive thoughts or questions. Numbness was quickly replaced with a cold anger that spread out to his limbs. "No!" he growled, louder, as if by yelling he could denounce her words, could erase the sound of her voice ringing in his head.

Her lashes lowered, shielding the emotion in her eyes. Only then did he see a glistening tear shimmer on the golden tips, then it dropped, only to splash and then trickle down the pale curve of her cheek. "Yes, Lindsay."

His hands shook and he pushed away from her as if she were anathema. No, she could not have done such a thing. She was lying. Anais would never be so deceitful, would never do something so heartless as to conceal such a thing from him. But as he looked up at her, at her stricken expression, at the way she could not hold his gaze, he knew he was only fooling himself.

She had betrayed him in the cruelest of ways and his mind began to race as thought after thought, denial after denial, tripped through his mind until he couldn't stand to consider the possibilities anymore.

He stood up, wavering—reeling—with rage and shock. Disillusioned and hurt by the woman he thought incapable of duplicity.

He stared at her, disbelieving everything he had heard, everything he was seeing. His hands flew to his hair and he gripped the sides of his head, fisting his fingers tighter and tighter into his hair in an attempt to think, to push the sound of her words from his head with the pain of his hands. *No, no, no, this could not be happening.*

"Lindsay, say something."

"All this time," he murmured, bewildered. "I've imagined every sort of hell, you with Broughton, loving him, giving him your body…but you didn't. It wasn't—" He stopped, the horror of it all suddenly registering in his brain. "You hid this from me. Why?"

"You left me!"

"No!" he roared. "I searched for you. I went to your house. To London. I was turned away without seeing you. I tried, Anais, I tried to find you. I tried to apologize. When you went to France, I followed you. I searched for weeks."

Her face paled. "You left the country?"

"To find you!"

Her fingers flew to her mouth where they trembled against her lips. "I…I didn't know, didn't think you would follow." She looked at him with horror. "I thought you left the country because you were done with me."

"Why wouldn't I have followed you? Christ, Anais, I loved you. I wanted to marry you. I told you that, the night in the stable."

"I didn't plan…" She stopped and reached out with her hand to steady herself on the edge of the dressing table. "I lost my faith in you, Lindsay. After finding you with Rebecca…I…I couldn't see you again. Don't you see? It…it could never be. Oh, God, it might have been all different."

The stricken sob that came from her cut him to the quick and suddenly he stopped and faced her, clarity at last beginning to chase the chaos in his head away.

Incredulity was swiftly replaced with dawning horror. "Where is the child?"

He had yelled that, unable to control his emotions and the frenzied anger that began to erupt like a volcano within him. She flinched and pressed her naked body against the wall, her head lowering, her gaze unable to meet his. *What had she done with his child?*

Filled with utter terror, he stalked to her and took her about the shoulders. "Damn you, Anais, what have you done? Where is it?"

"She is safe."

He fell back a step. *A daughter...a father...* He looked about the room, stunned, shocked. Anais giving birth to his child— *his daughter.*

Anais slid along the wall until she was within reach of the pile of underthings he had carelessly discarded into a heap. He watched as she bent at the knees and retrieved her chemise, immediately covering her lush breasts and fertile belly.

"What have you done with our daughter?" he asked on a strangled whisper. Damn her, he had a child—a child she had hidden from him. He had the right to know. He had the right to be a father, to claim this babe, a babe he had known nothing about.

"You needn't worry. She is safe and loved."

A terrifying fear began to grip him. "What do you mean?" he thundered.

"I have seen to her safekeeping—I..." She looked away and sniffed back her tears. "Surely you understand that I...I couldn't keep her."

With a cry of horror he released her, shoving her away. "What have you done?" he asked, the whispered sound filled with horror.

"The only thing I could have done as an unmarried woman who found herself with child."

"I wanted to marry you——" he ground out "——I wanted you. I wanted that child. I did not leave you, Anais. You hid from me when I was trying so desperately to find you."

She covered her face with her hands and sobbed. "I didn't know."

"Where is my child?" he roared, beginning to lose control of the anger and pain that was slashing like a knife through his chest.

"You don't understand…I had no choice…I had to make a decision, it is too late to change what has already been done."

Emotions tripped through him, ripping him apart, destroying his ability to think with anything that resembled rationality. He was confused, lost. The voices in his head taunted him like hecklers jeering the actors in Drury Lane.

Broughton and the Darnby chit have been keeping secrets from you. Over and over again, he heard his father's gravelly voice. The phrase was now like a goddamned mantra in his mind.

"So you refuse to tell me?" he asked incredulously. "I am not meant to learn of my child's fate, is that it? I have no rights?"

"If you would only hear me——"

"Oh, I hear you. I am to have no rights because I betrayed you, because you deem me worthless because of the opium. I am meant to have no heart, to not give a damn that my daughter is somewhere out in the world, and I was never meant to know about her. What do you think I am, Anais? A monster? Did you think I wouldn't care? Did you think to hide this from me… forever?"

"Garrett said——" She stopped, shook her head.

"Garrett said what?"

She would not answer him, leaving him to reflect on everything he had learned. "What is done is done, Lindsay. There is no return, for either of us."

Thank you, Garrett. Thank you for everything ... Anais's words to Broughton at the cottage came to him. His head snapped up and he searched Anais's face, dread dawning in his mind as the clues rushed in like high tide, overwhelming him as wave after wave of realizations came rushing in his mind, sucking him under until he thought he would drown.

Traveling so far and so close to your day, Mrs. Middleton, and in such weather?

She was born early, neither of us expected, that is, er...well, Robert was with me you see...

We have a tie that binds us, Anais. A tie that binds forever....

He thought of Margaret Middleton's unease that night in the salon when he peered down at her child. Remembered the shared look of uncertainty that flashed between Middleton and his wife. Had Anais looked nervous? Had she even looked at the child?

The thought just wouldn't let go. He couldn't shake it, and the longer he thought about it—about the injustice, the impotence of the whole thing, he became angrier and angrier, until he saw only red and roared, "You gave my daughter to Robert Middleton and his wife!"

She did not need to say anything. The shock and mortification on her face told him what he needed to know and he staggered back, far away from her. The heel of his boot hit the edge of the bed and he fell against the mattress, shocked, sickened.

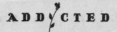

"Let me explain," she said, rallying her spirits.

He looked up at her through a blurred cloud—tears. He had not openly wept since he'd been a beardless boy. Mist had gathered in his eyes the morning he awoke after his betrayal of Anais—he had snuffed the tears with opium. He had always killed the pain with opium. But he didn't have the opium now— he didn't have its safety infusing his veins. He was on his own— alone to suffer through this gut-wrenching agony.

"Lindsay, please hear me," she pleaded as tears streaked down her cheeks.

"You gave my child—*my daughter*—away," he mumbled, his voice filled with disbelief. And suddenly he could not look at her. Could not stand to be near her.

Jumping up from the bed, he stalked to the door, his long legs hungrily eating up the space between the bed and the door.

"Where are you going?" she cried, running for him, preventing him from grasping the doorknob by clinging wildly to his hand. He brushed her puny attempts aside and flung the door wide-open—hard—so hard it reverberated against the wall, sending a picture crashing to the floor. Lindsay bolted into the hall, shaking her grasping hands from his shoulders.

"Don't do this, you will ruin everything."

He stopped at the bottom of the stairs and turned slowly on his heel to look up at her. He had left her standing in her chemise and stockings at the top of the stairs. As he looked up at her, nothing but pain coursed in his blood.

"No, Anais," he said, pointing his finger in the air. "*You* have ruined everything."

* * *

Within minutes, Lindsay left the house for the stables. Furiously, his fingers maneuvered the bridle and bit into Sultan's mouth. Seconds later the Arabian was saddled and charging out the stable doors.

It was twilight. Lindsay ran the stallion hard through the snowy paths in the woods, heedless of the low-hanging branches and the patches of ice that littered the twisting paths. The beating of hooves pounding on the packed snow and the rhythmic grunts from deep within the Arabian's heaving chest filled Lindsay's ears, driving out the other thoughts that were threatening to turn him into a raving lunatic.

Anger drove him on, and harder he ran his mount, his body now one with the stallion as he guided Sultan with ease through the winding curves until they cleared the trees and Broughton's estates loomed ahead of them. Pushing Sultan on, Lindsay bent low over the saddle, his greatcoat whipping violently behind him as the stallion's long legs devoured the remaining distance. The animal's snorting, heavy breaths rushed out of its flaring nostrils, painting the darkening night air in gray clouds.

"Walk him," he ordered in a chilling voice as he brought Sultan to a prancing halt and tossed his reins to a servant in Broughton's stable yard.

Pulling his gloves from his hands, Lindsay stalked with ruthless determination up the stairs of The Lodge and let himself in. Sands, Broughton's butler, in the midst of reaching for the door latch, shrieked in surprise, but recovered with aplomb, masking his shock and distaste behind an inscrutable mask of propriety.

"Oh, good evening, my lord. It is good to see you again."

Sands studied him from the top of his windblown hair to his chest, which was covered in only a shirt and an open greatcoat. With an arch of a haughty brow, the servant raised his gaze. "You appear to have forgotten to dress for tonight's dinner, my lord."

"Where is Broughton?" he growled, slapping his gloves down atop the hall table. He didn't wait for Sands to assist him with his coat. Instead, Lindsay tossed it atop his gloves before turning his head and glaring at the servant. "Get him. We have business."

Sands swallowed hard and blinked back his surprise. "I'm afraid his lordship is busy at the moment. He has asked not to be disturbed."

"Out of my way. I'll announce myself."

With his boots ringing on the marble tiles, Lindsay made his way to Broughton's study. Trying the knob, he found it locked. "Broughton," he snarled after pounding his fist against the wood. "Broughton, open up this goddamned door! *Now!*"

"I am busy at the moment," came the cool, controlled response.

With a vicious kick, Lindsay rammed the toe of his boot beneath the door and tried to shoulder it open. It didn't budge. Red mist gathered behind his eyes until all he saw before him was rage. "I said open this goddamned door or every servant in this house will be privy to what I have to say!"

Lindsay's fist was poised to strike the door again when it suddenly opened. Barging through, he found Broughton standing in the middle of the room, eyeing him with open hauteur.

Everything inside Lindsay went to hell. Charging in like a snarling bull, he went to Broughton, prepared to slam his fist in his face. "You goddamned bastard," he snarled, breathless with rage. "I'll kill you for this."

"Shut the door, Raeburn," Broughton snapped as he walked around his desk.

"You stole her. You stole my daughter."

"So you did find out, did you? How did you decipher it all, when your head is usually filled with opium?"

"I'm going to let you live long enough to tell me all I want to know, and then," Lindsay said with frigid preciseness, "I'm going to gut you and make you suffer for what you have done."

Broughton's lips turned into a half smile and he turned away, giving Lindsay his back. "What have I done that is so abhorrent? I saved Anais from certain shame and humiliation. I saved the babe and gave her a home in which she will be safe and loved and have a prominent place in society. So tell me," Broughton roared, whirling on him, "why am I the damned villain when you have done nothing but frig off to the ends of the world while I was cleaning up your mistake?"

"Shut your mouth!" Lindsay ground out through set teeth. "The conception of that child was *not* a mistake, damn you!"

Broughton stepped forward. "Where were you, Raeburn, when she was throwing up every morning? Where were you when Anais was out in the garden weeping because she was alone and with child and so close to having her secret discovered? Where were you when Anais needed someone to help her plan for her and the child's future? I'll tell you where, you were nowhere to be found. You were off with your opium and your pipe. And I was here to pick up the pieces. Here to console a woman you left pregnant. Here to protect the reputation of a friend."

"I was in France, searching for her."

"She wasn't bloody in France, was she?" Broughton shot back. "She was here all along, where you left her, pregnant with your child."

Broughton was a liar. Anais had told him she had gone to France. He had told her that he had followed her there. Unless of course, going to France was just another one of her lies.

"I told you to have a care for her, but you knew better. You and your damn opium—"

"My bad choices do not give you the right to do what you've done. You gave *my* child to your brother."

"That's right. I would have taken the babe for mine," he taunted, and smiled when Lindsay's eyes narrowed. "Oh, that's right. I wanted to marry her, even if that meant claiming your son as the next Earl of Broughton. I was prepared to give your babe more than my surname, I was prepared to bequeath him my title. But she wouldn't marry me. Even though you had betrayed her with Rebecca and left, leaving her with child. Even though it became more and more apparent that you would not return before the child was born, she still remained faithful, hoping against hope that you would come back and do the right thing."

"I didn't know!"

"Why didn't you write? I went nearly every day to Eden Park to see if you had written your mother. I was hoping that you would have at least notified her of your whereabouts. I had every intention of writing to you then, to tell you of Anais's condition. But you were too damn busy indulging in your addiction to bother putting a quill to paper. Every day, Raeburn, I made the trek to your home to inquire whether or not someone had learned of your whereabouts. *Every damn day* I had to go back to Anais and tell her that there was still no news from you. And every day, I would try to reason with her. Would try to make her see that marrying me and allowing me to give the child the protection of my name was the right thing to do. But she could not do it. She loved you, despite it all. Despite everything you'd done, she could not bring herself to love me enough to marry me. Instead, she wept and pined for a selfish prick that got what he wanted from her and dithered with her friend the first chance he got."

Guilt, shame, reality began to override his anger. "You did this to spite me! You did this to revenge yourself upon me. You always wanted her for yourself and now you've found a way to bind her to you."

"She won't have me!" Broughton fisted his hands at his sides. "I bet you take delight in the fact, don't you? I wager you love knowing that despite everything I've done for her, she still cannot bring herself to marry me. Oh, she clings to the story that it's uncertain if she will ever bear another child. She tries to make me believe she is thinking of me and my heir, but I know that she uses that excuse as a crutch, a way to keep me at arm's length."

"Regardless, you still betrayed me."

"It was about protecting Anais and the babe. It was never about you."

"Where is the child?"

"Safe."

"Where is she?" Lindsay roared.

"If you think you can stride in here and destroy everything I

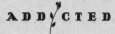

have worked hard to make right, then you are utterly mad. I will not let you simply take the babe from my brother and his wife. I will not let you harm that babe's reputation, nor Anais's. You're too late, Raeburn, to claim your paternal rights. You should have done that months ago. You should have been enough of a man to offer marriage after you took her virginity in a goddamned stable. If you had, then none of this would be happening now."

Lindsay shoved aside the niggling of guilt that pierced through his considerable anger. He did not need to explain himself to Broughton. He knew he had not intended to leave Anais with child. It had always been his plan to wed her—he'd never have spilled his seed in her if he had only been out to slake his lust. No, he was guilty of many things, but never of defiling Anais and leaving her to suffer alone.

"I will ask only once more, where is the child?"

"I am expecting company this evening. I'm afraid I will have to ask you to leave, Raeburn."

"The hell you will dismiss me like I'm a bloody servant. You think this is a little matter you can sweep under the carpet? Well, I assure you, I won't be going away."

"What the devil is going on?"

Lindsay swung around and saw Robert Middleton standing in the doorway of the study. Middleton looked between Broughton and Lindsay. The ashen color of Middleton's cheeks made Lindsay realize that Robert knew exactly what was going on between Broughton and him.

"I have come for my daughter," Lindsay said in an utterly cold and demanding voice. A feminine sob sliced the taut quiet and Lindsay's gaze narrowed as he saw Margaret Middleton cling to her husband's arm. "Tell me where she is before I tear this house apart."

"I'm not sure what you think—"

"I know you have taken my daughter from me," Lindsay thundered. "I know you have given her your name. I also know that she will not spend another night in this house. Now, get out of my way."

Shouldering past Middleton and his sobbing wife, Lindsay stalked across the hall and reached for the banister. Taking the stairs two at a time, he climbed the steps in pursuit of the nursery, heedless of the sounds of Broughton's threats and Robert Middleton's wife's cries of despair.

"You cannot come into my home and threaten me, Raeburn," Broughton called from the hall. "Furthermore, you cannot just search my home on a whim."

"Watch me," Lindsay grunted.

"He's going to take her away, isn't he?" Margaret Middleton sobbed into her lace handkerchief. "He's going to take my baby."

"Hush now, Margaret," Robert whispered. "Hush now."

"Get down here this second, Raeburn!"

He heard the pounding of Garrett's boots on the stairs behind him, and he curled his fingers into fists at his sides. "Sod you."

"Send the servants below stairs," Robert ordered Broughton, "the less they hear the better. Margaret, compose yourself. Raeburn, a minute, if you please."

Lindsay ignored Robert's demand and instead headed down the hall, counting the doors, knowing the nursery was coming closer with every hurried step. In the end he needn't have bothered to count, for the nursery door opened and an anxious-looking maid peeked out at him. She tried to close the door in

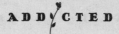

his face, but he reached for the latch at the same time Robert Middleton clasped his wrist, stilling him from entering.

"A moment if you please, Raeburn."

Unable to look at the man who was fathering his daughter, Lindsay instead made a grunt deep in his throat as he looked at the toe of his boot.

"The child is innocent. I hope you have not come up here in anger."

"I have not come to hurt the child. Have you come up here to prevent me from seeing her?"

Robert released his hold and stepped back. "No, I have not. You have every right to see the babe. I trust, however, for the babe's sake that we can keep our voices down and prevent the servants from overhearing us. It is not my pride or yours that concerns me now. It is the child's future I am worried about."

"My anger is under control, Robert. You have my word I will do nothing to undermine the future of the babe. I only want some time alone with her."

Robert nodded. "I understand. You only have to ring if you need something."

"What I need is for you to keep Broughton and Anais away from me. I cannot imagine she will be stupid enough to follow me here, but she is desperate and desperation calls for many things. While my anger is under control now, I fear it will erupt if I have to face the two of them before I am ready. I know that I am to blame for much of this, my poor choices in life have got us here. But I am only human, Robert, and right now, right or wrong, I am livid with both of them. This punishment they have sentenced me with is, in my opinion, disproportionate to my crimes."

"Raeburn, understand—"

"I ask for your understanding, Robert. Put yourself in my place. The woman you have loved your whole life has your child without your knowledge, she gives that child away to another man to raise, and you find out when it is too late to do anything about it. Tell me, how would you feel?"

Robert looked away and glanced down the stairs. "You are right. It is any man's nightmare. But my wife, she's distraught. You will have a care for her feelings also, won't you?"

Lindsay allowed himself to see the woman who stood at the bottom of the stairs, clutching her handkerchief to her bosom. Her eyes were bright with tears, and when she saw him looking down at her, she burst into shrieking cries. He had left Anais looking much like this, crying and weeping.

What did they see, he wondered as the anger slowly left when they looked at him. A monster? A crazed lunatic?

What did he see looming before him?

Margaret Middleton looked up at him through her tears, and he realized what he saw. Finality. Resignation. The anger that had ruled him in Broughton's study was gone, replaced by a haunting sense that he was looking at the end before it had really started. It was made all the more unbearable when he finally acknowledged that he had played a significant part in this painful tableau.

He watched Margaret as he addressed her husband. "I will be mindful of her feelings, but she has to realize—"

"I realize, Raeburn, even if my wife does not. I can only begin to fathom your shock and your pain. When you are ready, come to me, I will tell you what I can. For now, go and see her and know that you shall have all the time you need." Robert

reached for the latch. "Molly, you may come out, if you please, and retire for the night."

The young maid peeked around the door and stepped cautiously out, dropping a curtsy and trying valiantly not to look bewildered before she stepped between them and vaulted down the stairs.

"Take your time, Raeburn."

Robert turned and strode down the stairs, catching his wife in his arms and hugging her to his chest. "It is all right, love, she will be safe with him. Give him a chance, love, that is all he wants."

Looking away from Robert and his sobbing wife, Lindsay opened the door. What was he doing? He knew nothing of infants. Had never even held one. But this was his child—his daughter.

He stepped into the room that was bathed in rose light from the pink glass oil lamp that sat atop a table in the corner of the room. Beside the table was a rocking chair, with a set of knitting needles attached to a half-completed pink baby blanket that rested atop the chair cushion. A rosewood cradle with ivory lace curtains draped over the frame sat beside the chair. In the opposite corner, a bed was pressed against the wall.

Silently Lindsay took a step forward and his heart faltered with nervousness and uncertainty. What would he see lying in the bassinette? What would he say? He almost turned to leave until he heard a soft whimper and saw a swath of white lace peek out from beneath a mountain of blankets. His heart began beating again—a mad, frantic pace. He took another step and peeked down, searching through the layers of silk and lace to the plump, pink cheeks that were nestled lovingly in the Broughton family linens.

With shaking fingers he pulled back the corner of the blanket and saw what he had created with Anais.

Tears stung his eyes and he pressed his fingers to his lids, stemming the tears that sprung up with urgency. Such beauty. Such innocent wonder. Tears spilled freely from his eyes as he looked down at the sleeping baby, and he could not keep from staring at her or stem his tears. His arms ached to hold his daughter and his heart felt as if it were breaking into a million little pieces because she did not know him.

22

"May I get her for you?"

Lindsay straightened and saw Margaret Middleton standing in the doorway. She was still clutching her square of Nottingham lace, but she had composed herself and only the faintest sound of a distant hiccup remained. He tried to speak, but it came out as a harsh and strangled "please."

Margaret stepped into the room and padded softly across the carpet until she was standing over the cradle. With an ease that amazed him, she swooped down and lifted his daughter from the silk linens, covering her pink cheeks with butterfly kisses and murmured endearments that came naturally to a mother's lips. And then she turned and presented him with a sleeping cherub—an angel he could not take his eyes off of.

Margaret placed his daughter in his arms and he continued to stare down at the babe in wonder. A life. He had created a life!

His gaze, blurry, roved over her chubby cheeks and red bow mouth, hungrily cataloging her features, embedding them for eternity in his mind. Margaret removed the lace bonnet that shielded the babe's head and he sank, almost unthinking, onto the chair.

Beautiful black curls, which were in the image of him, covered her small, round head. The profoundness of what he was seeing stunned him and his arms began to tremble as the full realization of what he was seeing began to sink in.

"Call if you need me. She may need to be fed," Margaret said, running her fingers through the babe's locks. As she did, the child stirred and opened one eye that was edged with long, sooty lashes, and then she looked up at him, seeing him—*her father*—for the first time.

"Her name?" he asked in a hoarse whisper.

"Mina is her name, my lord. Anais named her. We did not change it."

"Mina," he repeated.

Margaret left, closing the door so that a sliver of light from the oil lamp in the hall filtered into the nursery. He looked down at the sleeping bundle in his arms and marveled at the beauty— the perfection of his daughter.

She squirmed in his arms and he saw her pink little toes curl when they met the cold air. He smiled, such perfect little toes, all five of them. He counted her fingers next—all there. His hand, large and tanned, ran over the silky curls. She pressed her cheek into his arm and he felt her heat sear him through his linen shirt.

She had his dark hair, his lashes, and from the glimpse he had, she bore his eyes, as well. But the shape of her face, a perfect oval, was her mother's. She had Anais's cheeks. Anais's lovely mouth and proud chin. He kissed her chin, feeling the softest of fluttering against his cheek—baby's breath. There was

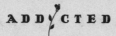

nothing sweeter than the feel of an innocent child's breath against one's cheek—nothing more wondrous than knowing that the baby was your own flesh and blood.

Mina stretched against him, yawning widely and throwing her arms up wide alongside her head. He laughed through his tears and reached for her little fist and brought it to his mouth, kissing her with such love he thought he would die of it. "You will consume me, little Mina, just as your mother has."

She yawned again and he released her hand, allowing his fingers to trace the delicate blue veins on her wrist. His blood. Anais's blood. The blood that now swam in Mina's veins.

He looked down at his child and squeezed her to him. Mina was a beautiful visual of his love for Anais. It was out of love that Mina had been born. But Anais had not wanted that love — the life they had created.

But he wanted it. God, how he wanted this child. He closed his eyes and brought her to his chest, not caring that his movements were awkward and stiff. This was his child. This was his right.

He rose from the chair and walked to the bed. Reclining, he brought Mina's chest to his chest, and he slipped her inside the opening of his shirt so that she was lying against his skin and she could hear his heart beating beneath her ear. He hugged her and cupped her head in his palm, loving her as she breathed her innocent baby's breath against his chest.

"She never gave us a chance—gave *me* a chance," he said to his sleeping daughter. "She never allowed me the opportunity to show you how very well I could love you—how well I could love you both. I could have stopped. If only I had known, Mina. I would have been a good husband and a good papa. If only I'd known..."

The sound of pounding feet on the stairs made his arms tense. Instinctively he held Mina tighter to his chest. Feminine weeping echoed along the walls, and he braced himself to see Anais—to see the woman he had loved so desperately; the woman who had betrayed him so mercilessly.

She appeared in the door, the warm light from the oil lamp illuminated her from behind, and her golden curls, which were spilling from her coiffure, glistened like a halo around her head. At one time he thought of her as an angel; now he could not even bring himself to look at her.

Heavy silence made the atmosphere taut, and he did nothing to relieve the obvious strain she was feeling. He did not comfort her as she sagged against the door and wept. Instead, he looked down at his sleeping daughter and willed himself to maintain some semblance of calm.

"Your revenge upon me has been complete, Anais," he said, his voice hoarse with pent-up emotion. "I trust you are well-satisfied with the events. We are even now, are we not? I have broken your heart, and you have destroyed mine."

She flew from the door to stand beside the bed in a whirl of blue satin. Her eyes were puffy and red-rimmed, as if she had been sobbing for hours. "I didn't plan it this way."

"How could you?" He reached for her wrist and brought her forward so that she could see Mina lying against him. "How could you have done this to me—to us—to our daughter? How could you not love her enough to fight for her?"

A strangled gasp whispered past Anais's lips, and Lindsay

saw how she stared at their daughter as if she were seeing Mina for the first time. Anais's trembling hand reached out to touch the babe, but she snatched it back as if she were afraid to touch her.

"You don't understand, Lindsay...." Anais's voice trailed off as Mina began to squirm against him. "I never meant for any of this to happen. You weren't supposed to find out—"

"And that's what hurts so damned much—that you would deliberately hide this baby from me. I have rights, Anais, but you took those away from me. You never gave me a chance."

"My pride ruined everything," she whispered. "Had I not allowed my vanity to rule my mind I would not have had to make this choice. But I was so angry with you and hurt. I wasn't thinking rationally. I was thinking only with my heart, and it was broken into a thousand pieces after I found you with Rebecca. But despite that, I knew if I saw you again, I would be just as much in danger as I ever was—for I knew I loved you, despite everything that Garrett had told me, despite what I had seen. I didn't want that, Lindsay. I didn't want to be weak. I didn't want you to think that you could do anything you wanted and I would always be there waiting for you, ready to take you back. I didn't..." She choked on a sob and brushed the back of her hand across her eyes, wiping away her tears. "I feared you would think you could always placate me with a smile and an empty compliment."

She sobbed a loud, choking sound that seemed to come from some well deep inside her. "Oh, God, I never wanted to have to make up excuses for you the way you made up excuses for your father. I didn't want you to think that the words *I'm sorry* would be enough."

"So you wanted to punish me."

"In the beginning my pride was wounded. I felt betrayed and used and a part of me did want you to suffer. I know that it is childish, but God help me, it was never my intent to make you suffer like this. But that is all in the past, we cannot change the past."

"So you allowed your pride to destroy us?" He looked up at her expectantly and she crumpled to the ground, weeping. He felt the urge to cup her face in his hand and brush her tears away with his thumbs as if he could make everything all right with a soft touch and a whispered word.

"Yes, I suppose you're right. I allowed my pride and anger to ruin everything we had—everything we might have had. I have no justification for my actions, only that I feared that I could so easily become your mother and that you would be like your father. I didn't want that, you see, to be someone you thought you could walk all over. I wanted to be strong, to prove to myself that I was strong."

She rose from her knees and placed her shaking hand along her midriff. "I know you will not believe me, but it is the truth that I never meant to deny you your child."

"I no longer know what to believe," he mumbled. "I only know that what I have truly longed for is no longer mine." She nodded and turned away from him. When she reached for the door, he called, "You will not run away again, Anais, not before I have the answers to all my questions. Be waiting when I come to find you."

"I do owe you that much, do I not?" She looked over her shoulder at him and he saw her gaze slip down to Mina, who

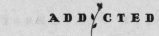

remained contented in his arms. "Perhaps one day you will begin to see things from where I stand, Lindsay. Perhaps one day, you will understand and you will forgive me. We, both of us, have failings. I have forgiven you. Will you not forgive me?"

New Year's Day passed very quietly at Eden Park. Lord Weatherby spent the day recovering from his drunkenness while everyone else in the house seemed to lounge about on settees, reading and napping and generally attempting to recover from the Christmas festivities. Lindsay's whereabouts remained unknown and Anais worried for him—fearing that perhaps he was indulging in behavior that was not good for him. Herself, she had decided it prudent not to join the rest of the family below stairs, fearing an unexpected meeting with Lindsay.

For the next two days, Anais kept herself hidden inside her chamber, lest she come face-to-face with Lindsay. The truth was, she was terrified to see him. No one knew what sort of mood he would be in, and she feared she would only make his demeanor more foul if he were to set eyes on her.

Feeling stifled and confined after two days of solitude, Anais reached for the shawl that was draped over her window bench and left her chamber. It was late, nearly midnight, and the house had long settled down for the night. The lure of a quiet walk through the halls called to her if for nothing other than a change of view, and perhaps a clearing of her increasingly anxious thoughts.

Anais padded down the stairs and headed to the ballroom where she intended to slip through the French doors and out onto the balcony to look at the stars in the cold night air. She wanted to clear her head, to formulate a plan or at least some semblance of an explanation of her actions for when Lindsay came to call upon her.

He had left her stewing in her juices, making her contemplate and worry over when he would come for his answers. But he had not come, and it had left her feeling befuddled. She had even sought him out in his private den, fully prepared to discover him smoking opium. But he had not been there.

Striding to the terrace doors, Anais felt a gust of frigid air swirl beneath her gown. It was then that she noticed the doors were already partially opened. Wrapping her paisley shawl about her shoulders, Anais reached for the latch and peered up at the full moon and the smoky clouds. Another gust of wind rose up, causing snow to swirl in circles along the terrace floor.

Shivering, Anais let her gaze drop from the sky as she gathered the woolen shawl tighter around her. As she reached to swing the door closed, she saw Lindsay standing alone at the balustrade with his back to her, his ungloved hands gripping the icy stone.

How lonely and bereft he looked standing alone with his head bent. How her heart ached to see him this way, to know that she, and she alone, was the cause of his misery.

The wind howled and the air billowed in, lifting her shawl from her shoulders and carrying it outside on the breeze. The wool tangled between Lindsay's legs and he bent down to retrieve it. He looked back, and before she could escape his notice, he pinned her with his gaze. He said nothing, but held the shawl out to her. Stepping quietly onto the terrace, she reached for it, whispering her thanks as she flung it around her shoulders.

"You should go back inside," he muttered, turning from her. "It's cold tonight."

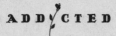

She stood behind him, watching his shoulders tense further beneath his black evening jacket. How she wished she could reach out and touch him, to run her hand along his back. She once would have thought nothing of doing such a thing. And now things were so very different between them.

"I've been looking for you."

"Oh?"

"Your valet says you have not been home these past two days."

"I did not wish to be found."

"I was worried."

"You needn't have bothered."

"The opium——"

"Is no longer your concern. I know your feelings about it. And you know mine."

Which meant he was still using it. In all likelihood he was probably under its influence even now. She wanted to beg him to stop, but what right had she to ask anything of him, especially now?

"We have received word from my aunt," she said awkwardly as she twined her fingers around the fringe of her shawl. "She is sending us a carriage. It should arrive within a sennight to take us back to London."

"Make certain your father is ready for travel. There is no need to leave before his health permits it."

Silence stretched on and Anais struggled to find the words to tell him what he wanted to know. Why wouldn't he ask her?

Unable to find the words needed to start the conversation, she took a step back, her boot heel sliding against the stone. His shoulders tensed at the sound, and he looked back at her, his face etched with fatigue.

"I can go no longer not knowing. What were your thoughts when you first discovered you were carrying my child?" he asked quietly.

Anais gripped the wool shawl tighter, as if it were a shield. How she dreaded this conversation, despite the fact she wished for nothing more than getting it over and done with. What a coward she was.

"Did you weep when you realized you were with child?"

"Yes." He would know if she lied. He had always expected the truth from her and she had failed him miserably these past weeks. She could not fail him now.

"What was it like, having a part of me inside you?"

The pain in his voice whipped at her flesh, stinging her. These were not the questions she had expected from him. She found she could not answer them. She could not bear to think of when she was pregnant, let alone talk of it. The memory of carrying Lindsay's child alone was enough to bear without having to feel those emotions all over again.

"Did you hate the babe, Anais? Did you wish to rid yourself of your shameful secret?"

She reached out a trembling hand to him, but dropped it and looked away from his set shoulders. No, she had never wished anything to happen to the child. She had loved their babe and it had nearly killed her to let their daughter go to another. But he could not see beyond his own pain to understand her turmoil. And she suspected that he would not be able to for a long while.

"What was it like?" he asked again when she didn't answer him. "Could you feel her growing, moving inside you?"

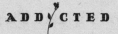

Anais's eyes welled with hot tears as her lips trembled with barely controlled sobs. "Yes."

He lowered his head and exhaled. "Did you ever think I might have wanted to do the same?"

The wind rose up again and Anais's eyes blurred and stung in the cold. The blustery air stung her cheeks as the crystal drops trickled from her eyes, freezing the tears onto her skin.

"I would have given my soul to watch you grow round with my babe. I would have been awed and humbled by the life we had created and the changes in your body. I would have whispered to her that I loved her, that I wanted her."

She was biting her lips now, trying to stem the flow of tears and the flood of pain. The full realization of what she had done hit her full force. How would she ever make amends for what she had done to him? How would this horrible pain, this hurtful betrayal, ever subside for him? What kind of a selfish, prideful creature had she become?

"Did you know that I was looking for you, here and in London?"

"Yes." There was no point in lying now. Her secrets were out.

"But you purposely hid from me. Why?"

"I did not want to hear your excuses. I was heartbroken that you chose the opium over me, that you could so easily mistake another woman for me, especially after what we had shared in the stable. You destroyed my belief in you, Lindsay."

He nodded. "I know I did, and I am sorry, Anais."

"My pride was pricked. My heart broken. I sought to lash out in the only way I knew how, and that was to hide from you. I was afraid that if I saw you again, I would weaken. I...I've never had the strength to deny you, Lindsay, and I knew that if you asked for forgiveness I would grant it."

"And France? Please tell me that was not a lie. Tell me that you did go there. That I was not a fool..."

"I did not think you cared enough to follow. I...just wanted a reprieve from you, from hearing your voice in my father's study."

"You sent me on a wild-goose chase," he said, shaking his head. "You were never even there."

"I didn't think you would follow—"

"Why? Because I didn't want you? Because you thought I had gotten what I wanted out of you and couldn't be bothered to find you? What did you think my visits were about, Anais—all those demands to find you? What did you think when I looked you in the eye after I had made you mine and told you that we were going to be man and wife?"

"I thought them lies, just opium-induced dreams that I couldn't allow myself to believe in."

"So, you said you were going to France hoping to gain what?"

"A few weeks to think. Some time away from you. I knew that if you thought I had left, you wouldn't come by. I would be free of you, at least until I had figured out what to do. I truly believed that once you discovered that I had left for France, that you would leave for London."

"You thought to punish me."

Anais looked down at the swirling snow on the stones. "Yes," she said, her voice barely above a whisper.

"You said you didn't know you were with child, was that the truth?"

"When I came up with the idea to say I had gone abroad, I

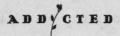

did not know about the babe. I discovered the truth later, but by then it was too late. You had already left, and no one knew where you were, or when you would return."

"I cannot believe you didn't think I would follow you to France. The minute I learned you had left for the continent, I went to find you—I *had* to find you."

She felt sick at the thought of Lindsay searching through Paris for her. What a fool she had been. What a prideful, vain idiot she was.

"You must know, Lindsay, that I loved the baby," she said through trembling lips. "From the moment I discovered I was carrying your child, I loved it. I wept for it, knowing that its life would be filled with shame and scandal."

"It didn't have to be."

Anais looked away, ashamed, her heart breaking and crumbling the longer she looked at him.

"Tell me about the day our daughter was born," he asked, his voice cracking with emotion. "The details of that event have plagued me for days."

She wanted to tell him, to reach out and enfold him in her arms. She wanted to take in his warmth through her cold limbs, but she stayed where she was and allowed the words to fall softly from her lips.

"It was night, and I had been staying in the cottage at the edge of Garrett's estate." She noticed how his jaw clenched, but she looked away and recounted the memories. It was the first time she had since the night she had given birth to Lindsay's child.

"I had been in labor most of the day and Garrett sent for his brother."

"So Broughton stayed with you?" he snapped, anger erupting in his voice.

"I was alone, Lindsay. Only Garrett, Robert and Margaret knew I was there. Mama and Papa thought I was touring the continent with my aunt Millie. Millie knew that I was staying with Garrett and his family—she did not press me for answers. She knew that I was…" she trailed off. "She knew I was hurt over you, but she did not know that I was with child. She agreed to the sham because she thought I needed time to mend my heart. She left for France with her companion, and I left for Garrett's estate. Papa was very distracted at the time—no doubt this was when his affair with Rebecca began. Mama did not care what I did. It was not difficult to deceive them. Jane, my aunt's companion, mailed the letters I sent to her for my parents from Paris. They didn't know I was living less than a mile away from them. We were very careful to keep out of Society. I never left the cottage except for the odd horseback ride in the forest at night. Garrett was the only person to visit me. I relied on him. He didn't trust anyone, most especially the village midwife. I…I needed someone, I was so afraid," she uttered quietly, choking back a sob as she relived the pain of her contractions.

"Did he comfort you?"

"He was very kind. He held my hand and put cold cloths on my forehead. He told me that everything was going to be all right."

"I would have done that. I would have defied convention and stayed with you as you gave birth to our baby. I would have done anything to take your pain away." He paused and then searched the sky. "Was it long for you?"

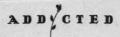

"Not overly."

He nodded and looked down at his hands, which chafed red from the cold and wind. "I would not want to think of you in such agony. I hope Broughton brought his brother to you when you needed him."

"He did. Robert arrived quickly and he delivered the baby shortly after." She bit her lip, remembering the sound of Mina's lusty cry, recalled watching the emergence of Mina's black head sliding out of her body. How beautiful and perfect she had been. How she had been filled with a sense of profound love as Robert lifted Mina high in the air, turning the babe so she could see what her pain had wrought.

"What was it like, to see her being born?" His back was to her, but Anais knew by the sound of his voice that he was quietly weeping.

"Beautiful. To finally see the life that was inside you all those months is beyond words. To see what you created..." she trailed off, swallowing hard. "Her cry, it was the most beautiful sound in the world."

"Did you put her to your breast and whisper to her?"

"Yes."

"I should have liked to have seen you with her at your breast. I would have sat beside you and stroked her head and counted her little fingers while she suckled from you. I would have liked to have watched you give birth to her, to feel what it is like to see something that you created being born into the world. I would have kissed you and thanked you for giving me such a gift, such a beautiful, perfect child."

Anais covered a sob with her shaking hand. She was dying

inside, knowing and sharing the agony that Lindsay was now feeling. "My heart overflowed with love for her."

"And yet you gave her away."

The words were uttered in such a soft, broken whisper that Anais felt as though a knife were cleaving her heart in two.

"You will never know the pain that caused me," she cried, fisting her hand so that she would not run to him and touch him and beg him to forgive her.

"I know the pain. I feel it. I feel it now, coursing through me, eating away at me."

"I hemorrhaged after delivering her. I was sick with the fever and weak from the blood loss. I do not even remember the days—the week—after giving birth to her. I heard Robert telling Garrett that I was going to die. I did not want to die and leave Mina alone. All I can recall is listening to her cries, her screams of hunger. But Margaret saved her. I wept as I watched Margaret feed my child. My heart broke when I saw Mina lying contented and full against Margaret's breast. You know not how I felt when I knew that I could not give our daughter the sustenance she needed. But Margaret could give her what I couldn't, and she adored her. I knew then, watching Mina with Margaret and Robert, that she was meant for them. They love her. They've made her a part of their family. *She has a name,*" she whispered at last, reaching out and touching his hand, only to have him pull his away from hers.

"She always had a name. She had *my* name. I would have given her everything. I would have given you everything, but you took that chance away from me when you sent me to France when you weren't even there. You never let me show you what I could be. And do you know what hurts most?" he asked, stepping

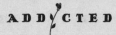

toward her. "What hurts most is the fact I used to lie awake at nights and think of you with my children surrounding you. I wanted nothing more in life than to be your husband, your lover, the father of your children. How is that for irony? The only dream I've ever had and you snatched it from me."

He reached out and clutched her face roughly in his ice-cold hands. "Would you have ever told me, Anais? Would you have told me that we created a life? Or would you have gone to your grave with this secret?"

She could not hold his gaze and he swore, letting her go. "I would never have believed that you had it in you to be this cruel. Do you know how this will haunt me forever? I have a child, Anais, *a child* that I cannot claim. That I must love in secret from afar. A child that bears another man's name."

His hands dropped from her face to rest at his sides. "All those times I begged you to let me in. I pled with you to allow me inside, and you allowed me in, but you made me crawl, made me beg—"

"I'm sorry," she sobbed. "I did not purposely conceal my pregnancy from you."

He straightened and his eyes dulled. "I'm sorry, too, Anais. So sorry for all the bad decisions I've made. I'm sorry that I cannot forgive you, or myself. I'm sorry that I was not a better man for you, the type of man you and our child needed."

She reached out to him, gripping the sleeve of his coat. "Where are you going, Lindsay?"

"Away. Isn't that what you've been trying to tell me? You want me away from you so you won't have to be confronted with the memories of what you've done. What I've done."

"Don't walk away like this, *please.*"

"There is nothing left, Anais. All you have to offer is pain and hurt. All I can give you is the same. There can be nothing but regrets between us now. Regrets and sorrows and tears of pain. As you've tried to tell me, it truly is over. Goodbye, Anais."

And then he stalked off and disappeared down the terrace steps and into the night.

23

The stinging rap of the brass knocker tapping against wood rang out in the crisp night air. Burying his face in his greatcoat, Lindsay waited for Thomas, Wallingford's aging, austere butler.

The click of the lock bolt drew his gaze and within seconds he found himself looking down into the pale, rheumy eyes of Thomas.

"Good evening, Lord Raeburn."

"Evening, Thomas, is Wallingford in?"

"I am afraid his lordship is indisposed."

Lindsay scanned the foyer, and noticed numerous cloaks and umbrellas hanging on the coatrack. Wallingford was indeed not available to entertain him if the number of frilly, feminine fripperies littering the hall was any indication. He felt himself scowling. He had not wanted Wallingford to be occupied. He'd already spent nearly three days alone in London. Three days that he had lost to the red smoke. He did not want to be alone with his thoughts any longer.

"Shall I see if his lordship is at home?" Thomas asked, scouring him with his unreadable eyes.

"Please." He desperately needed to talk with someone.

"Very well, then. Come in, please."

Lindsay stepped over the threshold and cupped his hands, blowing his hot breath into them. He had forgotten his gloves and hat in his preoccupation. He had not even bothered to order his carriage around, and instead walked the twenty-minute route to Wallingford's town house in Berkley Square.

Thomas suddenly emerged from the salon Lindsay knew Wallingford used as a studio. "His lordship will see you. Please await him in the study."

Passing the butler his greatcoat, Lindsay shook off the cold and headed for Wallingford's study and the warmth of a fire. As he stalked into the room he heard the shrill laughter and twitters of numerous women. He turned away from the hearth in time to count seven women, giddy and flushed, tiptoeing their way past the study door. Good Lord, Wallingford was actually seeing his vision to fruition.

"Evening, Raeburn," Wallingford grumbled, closing the door on the women. "An unexpected pleasure."

"Sorry to disturb you with your harem," he replied, turning his attention back to the orange flames that flickered in the hearth.

"I was finished with them anyway," Wallingford drawled. Lindsay heard the crystal stopper from the brandy decanter pop open, followed by the sound of the golden liquid spilling out into a cut glass tumbler.

"A drink?"

"No, thank you," he replied, rubbing his hands together more in anxiety than cold.

"So what brings you to London? Out on the prowl tonight,

are you? Come by for some company on your adventures? Where shall we go? Do you fancy a seedy whorehouse or an elegant brothel? Shall we get ripping drunk at the theater and then crash Lady Moncton's soiree? God, I'd love to shock that old dragon. Maybe I'll piss in her prized potted bird of paradise again this year. Christ, to see that old bird's face when I let my prick out of my trousers," Wallingford chuckled. "Made quite an impression on many ladies that night, or at least I assume it was my ten inches that caught their eye."

"I'm not seeking a cohort to share a night of debauchery."

"Pity," Wallingford said, gazing into the tumbler. "It's been a while since I've spent a night in debauched excess. I think I've forgotten its pleasures."

"You call having seven young women in your studio doing God knows what not debauchery?" Lindsay asked gruffly.

Wallingford arched one sardonic brow. "Clearly you are not yourself tonight."

"What do you think your father will do once he learns what you've been up to?" he blurted, unable to stop himself. Wallingford only shrugged and studied his brandy in the firelight.

"Probably piss himself then promptly expire with righteous mortification," Wallingford stated baldly as he lowered his tall frame into the leather wingback chair that sat to one side of the hearth. "Or at least one can dream of such a scenario."

"You don't care what anyone thinks, do you?"

Wallingford's gaze met his over the top of the tumbler. "No, I do not. I stopped caring when I was ten." Wallingford took a sip and studied him with dark eyes. "As interesting as this conversation is, I hope you did not disturb me with my seven nubile nymphs to discuss me and my follies."

Lindsay felt his face flush. "No, I did not."

"Have a seat," Wallingford commanded, motioning to the matching chair that sat opposite him. Lindsay did as his friend bade and stretched his legs out before the fire, crossing them at the ankle. "You are far from Worcestershire and your beloved Anais. Tell me, why are you here?"

He stared into the dancing flames and saw how they burned a brilliant blue at the base—blue that resembled Anais's eyes. He could not stop thinking of her. Could not push the image of her out of his mind. How he had been tormented these past days by his thoughts—his visions. Not even the opium had released the pain and longing in his breast.

"You truly are consumed, are you not?" Wallingford said without a trace of amusement.

"That is what happens when you lose yourself in a woman," Lindsay murmured, finally looking away from the flames.

"I would not know, I have never lost myself in a woman."

Lindsay studied him, amazed at his friend's revelation. "Never?"

"Never."

"Of all the women you've taken to bed, you have never experienced becoming one with a woman? Never felt the pulse of her heart deep inside you? Never absorbed her into your blood and your soul?"

Wallingford's eyes flickered to meet his. "I have never allowed a woman to touch me with anything more meaningful than sexual superficiality. I fuck women, Raeburn. I do not make love

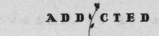

to them. I do not let them into my soul. I do not feel them creep into my heart. Women are for physical release, nothing more."

"Have you never been tempted?" Lindsay asked, feeling sympathy for his friend. "Have you never been close to allowing yourself to be lost in the feel of a woman?"

"No," Wallingford answered without blinking. "I believe that few men do experience what you have. I do not think that what the poets describe with such beauty and wonder is easily found between two people. It is bodies in motion, panting and sweating and grunting. Each are searching for their own needs—satisfying their own yearnings and not giving a damn about the other person. I have never felt more than that. Whenever I am inside a woman I am thinking of my pleasure. I couldn't give a fucking toss about anything else but slaking my needs and spending myself on their willing bodies. Whatever connection I may feel when I am driving inside a woman ceases to exist when my cock slides out of her body."

Lindsay gazed back into the fire, feeling cold after listening to Wallingford's perfunctory description of the sex act. It was not that way for him. It had never been just sex with Anais.

"I can still feel her," Lindsay found himself muttering. "I smell her. I can hear the sound of her heart beating in my ears. I can still feel her nails scraping along my shoulders and the sound of my name on her lips."

"Then why are you here?"

"She has betrayed me."

Wallingford steepled his fingers and tapped them across his lip. "I am sorry, Raeburn."

"No, you're not. You're the most cynical man I know. You're

not surprised she has betrayed me, you expect betrayal from women. You think of them as nothing but deceitful manipulators who are only after a title and a fortune."

"I am sorry that Anais has meddled with your heart. The feeling cannot be at all pleasant, I'm sure."

Lindsay closed his eyes, shoving the pain away, but Anais's image flashed before him, followed by the image of his child. "I wanted more than this!" he cried, shoving himself up from the chair and pacing before the hearth. "I wanted more than memories of her. I wanted a *life*—and she has taken it from me."

Wallingford followed him with his dark, fathomless eyes, not commenting, only watching—absorbing.

"It hurts to breathe. It hurts to live. I hate her, yet I do not think I can exist without her."

"There is a very fine line between love and hate, my friend, and that gray area is usually desire."

Lindsay closed his eyes, fearing the visions while at the same time welcoming them. Visions of Anais in his bed. Anais beneath him. His daughter lying content against his chest, sleeping in innocent wonder. *Love, desire, anger, hate.*

"Are you surprised by her betrayal? Did you think Anais not capable of deceit?" Wallingford asked.

"Not of this magnitude. Not something this cruel."

Wallingford nodded and reached for his tumbler. "Women, like men, are capable of unspeakable cruelty—never forget it. It is the human condition to hurt and destroy. It is our compulsion—our fate, to devastate those we love most."

Lindsay looked up at the painted ceiling of Wallingford's study and saw the image of plump women with long, unbound

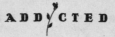

curls cavorting in clouds as if they were angels. He closed his eyes, blocking the images. "I never thought her capable of destroying me."

"Who is it you love with such passion and fervor?" Wallingford asked. "Anais the paragon or Anais the woman she is now? Who is it your body cries out for, Anais the woman who stands upon a pedestal in her mantle of idyllic womanhood or the woman who has sinned?"

Lindsay's eyes snapped open and he saw that Wallingford was pressing forward, watching him with unreadable eyes. "In the seconds before you climax with her and you look down into her face and you see yourself in her eyes, and you feel your hearts become one, who is it you lose yourself in, Raeburn? Anais, the childhood friend who could do no wrong or Anais, the girl you made a woman?"

The ticking of the clock sliced the taut silence, *tick, tick, tick*.

"Both."

Wallingford smiled almost cruelly. "You cannot have both. One of them must die. One of them is surely dying now. She can only be one person to you. She cannot be your angel and your mistress. She cannot save you and fuck you."

"No."

"Yes," Wallingford hissed. "She can no longer be the Anais we knew as boys—the girl who was never tempted to be anything but good. She has been tempted—tempted by you, and she is no longer pure and untainted. You have given her the taste of pleasure and sin. You have made her mortal and now you wish to punish her for what you yourself have done to her."

"No," he cried.

"She is no longer your angel, Raeburn. She is your Eve."

"You don't understand—"

"I understand more than you think. You want the demure little angel, you want her to save you from your demons and your opium habit. You need her kindness and understanding. Yet you want the little minx she's become. You've become addicted to her cries of pleasure. You want the fucking. But angels don't do that, do they?"

"Stop referring to it in such a coarse way!" he roared. "She does not fuck me like your dalliances fuck you." The atmosphere became taut and both men stared at each other, chests heaving. "I make love to her," he growled.

"Beautiful, passionate love," Wallingford drawled as he waved his hand in a mocking manner. "Your souls intermingle and you become one, and yet despite this connection, this morphing of two into one, you cannot offer her your forgiveness even when you have demanded that she forgive you."

Lindsay narrowed his gaze. "Her transgression far outweighs mine."

Wallingford smiled smugly. "How very human you are. Instead of forgiving and moving on with the one person who shall haunt you for the rest of your days, you stand here before me, cataloging and weighing her trespasses and reasoning that because hers are more weighty, you are justified in your indignation and your self-righteous behavior. You should be at home loving her, forgiving her, losing yourself in her mercy and sweeping her up in yours."

"How can you say that when you do not know what she has done? I never expected *this* out of *you*."

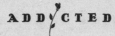

"So that is the way of it!" Wallingford vaulted up from his chair. "You've come here so that I can mollify you and share in your belittling of Anais? Well, you've knocked on the wrong bloody door, Raeburn, because I will not join you in disparaging Anais. I will not! Not when I know what sort of woman she is—she is better than either of us deserves. Damn you, I know what she means to you. I know how you've suffered. You want her and you're going to let a mistake ruin what you told me only months ago you would die for. Ask yourself if it is worth it. Is your pride worth all the pain you will make your heart suffer through? Christ," Wallingford growled, "if I had a woman who was willing to overlook everything I'd done in my life, every wrong deed I had done to her or others, I would be choking back my pride so damn fast I wouldn't even taste it."

Lindsay glared at Wallingford, galled by the fact his friend—the one person on earth he believed would understand his feelings—kept chastising him for his anger, which, he believed, was natural and just.

"If I had someone like Anais in my life," Wallingford continued, blithely ignoring Lindsay's glares, "I would ride back to Bewdley with my tail between my legs and I would do whatever I had to do in order to get her back."

"You're a goddamned liar! You've never been anything but a selfish prick!" Lindsay thundered. "What woman would you deign to lower yourself in front of? What woman could you imagine doing anything more to than fucking?"

Wallingford's right eye twitched and Lindsay wondered if his friend would plant his large fist into his face. He was mad enough for it, Lindsay realized, but so, too, was he. He was mad, angry—all but consumed with rage, but the bluster went out of him when Wallingford spoke.

"I've never bothered to get to know the women I've been with. Perhaps if I had, I would have found one I could have loved—one I could have allowed myself to be open with. But out of the scores of women I've pleasured, I've only ever been the notorious, unfeeling and callous libertine—that is my shame. Your shame is finding that woman who would love you no matter what and letting her slip through your fingers because she is not the woman your mind made her out to be. You have found something most men only dream of. Things that *I* have dreamed of and coveted for myself. The angel is dead. It is time to embrace the sinner, for if you do not, I shall expect to see you in hell with me. And let me inform you, it's a burning, lonely place that once it has its hold on you, will never let you go. Think twice before you allow pride to rule your heart."

"What do you know about love and souls?" Lindsay growled as he stalked to the study door.

"I know that a soul is something I don't have, and love," Wallingford said softly before he downed the contents of his brandy, "love is like ghosts, something that everyone talks of but few have seen. You are one of the few who have seen it and sometimes I hate you for it. If I were you, I'd think twice about throwing something like that away, but of course, I'm a selfish prick and do as I damn well please."

"You do indeed."

Wallingford's only response was to raise his crystal glass in a mock salute. "To hell," he muttered, "make certain you bring your pride. It is the only thing that makes the monotony bearable."

* * *

Slamming the door shut, Lindsay stepped out into the dark night and pulled the collar of his greatcoat around his ears. With one last glare at Wallingford's front door, he snarled and turned to walk down the gaslit street, wandering along as if he was in a dream.

Goddamned selfish bastard! Wallingford choking back his pride for a woman? *Damned liar,* Lindsay scoffed. Wallingford wouldn't choke back anything if it were in aid of a woman. The man was a misogynist. To Wallingford, women were good for one thing and one thing only.

Damn Wallingford for saying those things to him. For forcing him to confront what he feared—that he wanted Anais to be the two women he loved. He wanted his angel and he wanted his sinner. And both were now out of his reach.

Damn her, she had kept his child from him! Had given his own flesh and blood away as if it were nothing more than an outdated dress a lady would pass on to a maid. Didn't she realize that Mina was a part of him? The creation out of their love and shared passion? The product of that night in the stable where he had given everything of himself to her?

Stalking along the cobbles, he felt a snort of indignation creep into his throat. She had denied him the one thing he wanted more than her love—her child—*their child.* And he could never forgive her that. Even now, his body burning for her, he could not erase the anger he felt when he thought of what she had done.

Rounding the corner he saw that he was no longer in Mayfair. Ahead was Soho—the dividing line between the pleasant, well-ordered West End and the seedy, dark East End. It wasn't always safe to be traveling in a coach in the East End let alone on foot, but he had become something of a regular in the dregs of the eastern parishes. He could handle himself and whatever trouble came his way.

Feeling the familiar hunger awaken in his belly, Lindsay continued ahead, waiting to find the little alley, rife with rats and rubbish and overflowing cesspools. And through this little alley he would find himself in St. Giles Parish where vice of any kind was available for purchase—bodies—dead or alive. Women, or even more abhorrent, young girls. Ale and gin. Fenced items and even murder could all be purchased from the many rookery rats lurking about the dark streets. But what he wanted, what he came to St. Giles to purchase, was not sex or drink, but opium.

Skirting to the left, he found the dank, narrow alleyway off Petticoat Lane. Ignoring the whistles from the whores who gathered in the corner of the crumbling brick buildings, warming themselves by a fire that had been lit in an iron pot, Lindsay stalked on.

"Oh, gov'ner, I've got just what ye need."

"A case of the pox, or the clap, I should imagine," he grumbled. Christ, he was in a mood. Normally when he traveled this path, he tossed the whores pound notes and continued on his way, but tonight he was not feeling charitable.

"C'mon, gov, give 'ol Bess a try. Let me see what ye got hidin' in those fancy trousers of yers. I bet ye've got lots for Bess to play with. I'm good on me knees, lovey. I bet your fancy lady back 'ome don't take your lovely cock in 'er mouth."

Fishing through his waistcoat, he pulled out a fiver and tossed

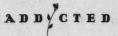

it to the women. "Purchase a room and some food," he snapped, then continued past the whores until he could see the ramshackle houses of St. Giles. Lord, had he ever really noticed the despair before?

Of course he had, in some part of his mind it had registered in his brain that these people lived in reprehensible conditions. Had he not spoken of the filth and squalor and the multitudes of homeless children to parliament? Had he not petitioned Russell's Whig government to set about change and clean up the East End so that these people might have some dignity and basic human rights?

But he had never really seen the extent of the waste, the pain, the unending hardship that loomed before him. Until today. Every other time he had journeyed here, his mind had been clouded with opium, or the lure of procuring the opium.

Christ, opium had blinded him to so many things.

Standing before the door of his preferred smoking den, Lindsay looked through the windows that were covered with smoke grime. Taking the door latch in hand, he let himself in. No such thing as a butler or porter in this establishment. Not here in Tran's seedy Oriental opium den.

"Meester, sir," Tran murmured as he bowed over and over again. "You come back. You spot is here."

"Good," Lindsay replied. As he followed Tran to the back of the den, Lindsay picked his way through the crude hard pallets where the poor and down on their luck lay on their sides, smoking their pipes. Soldiers and sailors, whores and criminals were strewn about, some conscious, some just beginning to feel the effects of the drug.

In the back of Tran's establishment, through a low-beamed arch, the silk cushions that were plump and embroidered with dragons and cherry blossoms awaited. This was where the elite came to smoke their opium—far away from Mayfair. Far away from discovery. These were not dilettantes out for a lark, but habitués, like himself. Disciples, he admitted, blind followers to the powers of the sinister beauty of opium.

"You sit," Tran said. "I will get servant."

"No, no," he murmured, holding Tran by his coarse jacket. "I will do it myself."

Tran nodded. "I get pipe."

Lindsay lowered himself to the cushion and removed his greatcoat and jacket. One needed to be comfortable when one was indulging in the pipe. As he waited for Tran to bring him his pipe and the weigh scale along with the decorative box that held the opium, Lindsay looked out upon the floor and allowed his gaze to linger over the others who had come to indulge themselves in the heavenly demon that was opium.

He felt slightly ill when he took in their situations. Some were nothing but walking skeletons, and others, just new to smoking opium, struggled to create an effective vapor to inhale.

In the corner beside him, some young men, obviously well-to-do and of the burgeoning middling class, laughed and giggled as they shared a pipe around a circle of friends. That had been what it was like in Cambridge. Except Broughton had always vomited from the taste and Wallingford had more often than not passed out after one or two inhalations, leaving him free to smoke as much as he liked.

There were always whores in an opium den, and Tran's was

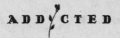

no different. Tran was a man of discriminating taste. Only the finest Oriental beauties with their black shining hair and exotic eyes were employed by him. On occasion, Tran was able to procure local London girls with their famed peach-colored skin and ample bosoms.

"Here is pipe," Tran said, holding out the bamboo stick. Bending down, Tran placed a brazier at Lindsay's feet and lit it with a sulphur match. "You want girl this time?"

Lindsay looked about and saw a petite Asian girl eyeing him intently. She was lovely and exotic with long, straight, black hair that would wrap nicely around his hands and his body, and perhaps, in the days before he knew Anais carnally, he might have motioned her over to him. There they would have shared the pipe and shed their clothes in front of everyone. Sex was out in the open in a den, so that one could fuck and smoke at the same time. It had never bothered him before, but it disturbed him now. He couldn't imagine anyone seeing Anais beneath him as he made love to her. He couldn't imagine smoking opium while Anais watched him.

Suddenly he felt dirty and shameful, like a leper begging in the streets. He never wanted Anais to find him here. Never wanted her to see him smoking opium.

Not before tonight had he felt any shame in smoking. So what was different now? What made the very thought of lying down on this cushion and smoking the pipe so unpalatable?

"That girl?" Tran asked as he broke into a smile and pointed at the woman on the other side of the den. "Pretty girl. She please you."

"Not tonight, Tran."

Tran bowed and left him to prepare his pipe. Most men of Lindsay's class preferred to have a servant sit with them and prepare the opium while they lounged about. He, on the other hand, preferred to do it himself. He enjoyed the slow seduction, the allure of preparing it, waiting for it, hearing it calling to him.

Crouching on his feet, he opened the tin that housed the opium and pinched some of the aromatic black strands that resembled tea leaves. Weighing it, he was satisfied he was using just the right amount to produce the desired effects. Placing the opium in the warming pan, he poured some water in the reservoir of the pipe and waved it over the heated brazier.

This was where the opium became a mistress. This was when she was to be coaxed and coddled so that she would produce a satisfying round of intercourse.

As he waited, Lindsay continued to look around and noticed that the once-giggling and boisterous young men were now sleeping deeply on their sides. One of Tran's servants was blowing out the flame of the brazier while the Asian beauty he had seen earlier was busy rifling through the sleeping men's pockets. Lindsay wondered how many times his own pockets had been picked while he lay in an opium-induced dream.

Below him, a sailor made a gurgling sound and flopped onto his back. Lindsay waited to see the rise and fall of his chest, but it remained utterly still. Another soul lost to the opium den, he thought with his characteristic detachment.

He had seen many die from smoking too much. He had seen many—men and women—sell everything, even themselves, for just another chance at the pipe. And as if to prove himself right, a young man barely into his twenties crouched beside him.

"Some company, guv'ner?" he asked. "I can do anything you want, if you'll only share what yer havin'."

Lindsay looked at the man and saw that his body was wasted and thin. The boy was dying and opium was his disease.

"Well, guv? How about it? A little pleasure, for a little opium?" The man—a boy, really—leaned forward and whispered, "I can give you mouth play. And from the looks of yer trousers, yev got something big beneath that fancy fabric."

Lindsay dropped the pipe to the ground. He stood and saw the boy's eyes go wide and begin to shine. "I knew that's what ye wanted, guv'ner. A strong man likes to have his cock mouthed from time to time, isn't that right?"

"Have it," Lindsay growled and turned away to reach for his jacket.

"What's that, guv?"

"You may have it. I'll fix another."

Lindsay left his spot and motioned for Tran to set him up with another kit.

"How about back room?" Tran motioned to a pair of crimson satin curtains with gold embroidered dragons. He had never gone to the back room, preferring the decadence of his own opulent den. Smoking with others had never been a priority to him. For so many, the company of other habitués is what drove people to the dens. For him, he had never wanted to be bothered by other people. It was the solitary moments of dreams and blissful surrender to the opium that seduced him.

Tran parted the curtain, and Lindsay followed him through. It was another world. One of Eastern decadence. There was flesh everywhere, writhing and moving. Smoke tendrils rose and danced, curling along bodies. The scent of the alluring vapors drew him in.

This is what he wanted. Escape. To run and never feel. The back of his brain throbbed with the need for opium. The smell of it had raised his pulse made his breathing harsh and short.

A black-haired beauty, naked, walked toward him with her hand outstretched. "Come. I take care of you."

Blindly, Lindsay followed her, obeying the call of the opium.

24

"Vallery, go to bloody hell," Lindsay snarled as he pressed his face into the pillow, trying to shut out the lights and sounds of life that surrounded him.

"I've been there for the past three days, with you."

"That's what I pay you for," he grumbled. "Now get me another pipe. *Please,*" he added when he peered through his lashes and saw his valet scowling.

"You're killing yourself," Vallery grunted beneath Lindsay's weight as he rolled him onto his back.

"Good. P'raps the memories will finally die, too."

"Listen to me," Vallery spat, taking Lindsay's face in his big, leathery hands and giving him a good shake. "You do not want to die. You might think so now, but you'll regret it when the deed's done."

"Not likely. I've other regrets I find more pressing, I'm afraid."

Vallery glared at him as he pulled him up from the pillows to stand. "I find your humor lacking, milord."

"Do you? I thought I was lightening the mood. It's gotten

rather morose in here, what with you constantly prophesizing about my bad end."

"What other end can come out of this?" Vallery snapped.

"I'm not trying to do myself in, if that is what you're insinuating. Good God, that's far too dramatic for me. Besides, it reeks of a bad opera that one might see in Covent Garden. *Tortured Aristocrat Turned Opium Fiend,*" Lindsay drawled with a dramatic flare, "it's like those Minerva novels my mother used to read, all melodrama and more hype than content."

"If you're not trying to kill yourself, then what the bloody devil are you doing?"

"Trying to survive, Vallery," he murmured, "the only way I know how."

"I've never seen you in such a bad way with the opium before."

"That is because I've never used this much before. I believe this is what is meant by the downward spiral. I'm spinning in a vortex, Vallery, and it feels so bloody good. So good that I can't stand to think about not having it."

"A truly disconcerting notion, milord."

Lindsay eyed his valet. "Did you ever just stand in the grass with your feet bare and the sun shining upon your face as you held your arms out wide and spun until you were so dizzy that you fell to the ground? And when you opened your eyes the blue sky was above you swirling, so, too, were the treetops and the clouds. And you would just lay there, watching the world go by in a pleasant twirl that made you smile. God, I remember such peace when I did that. And that, Vallery, is what the opium gives to me. Tranquility. A sense that everything is innocent and uncomplicated."

Lindsay smiled faintly, remembering those days of ease. There was no opium, no regrets, no betrayals between them. There had only been him and Anais. He had been much too old to keep spinning beneath the sun, but he kept indulging in the activity because Anais would laugh and squeal, and he would watch her, then she would tumble to the ground—on top of him—and he would lie beneath her, pretending to be watching the sky, when really, he watched her and felt his body come alive beneath her lush form. She had thought him a knight in shining armor, a slayer of dragons.

Innocence and wonder. It was all lost now, save for the times when the opium ruled him. More and more, he allowed his mistress to govern his mind and body. He was dependent upon her to take the pain away. He needed her, not to die, but to live—or at the very least—exist.

Gone was the shining knight, replaced with a tarnished dragon chaser.

"You're treading very deep and dangerous water, milord. You need to get yerself out of this."

"Never tell an addict what he needs, Vallery, unless it is to tell him he needs more of his fix," he snapped, irritated with Vallery and his lack of understanding of just how much Lindsay needed the opium. Not just mentally, but physically, as well. "Which, by the way, is exactly what *I* need. Now get me my opium or sod off and find yourself another job. I can have a Chinaman in here to do the task faster than you can say yen-shee boy."

"You don't need any more of that Shanghai poison. Now get cleaned up and clear yer head."

"How the bloody hell do you know what I need?"

"I know you don't need any more of that. You've been chasing the dragon for days."

"And I still haven't caught him."

"Milord—"

"Vallery." Lindsay placed his hands on his valet's wide shoulders and stared down at him. "I *need* more opium."

"No, you do not."

"The price of my mistress's pleasure is a complete and utter rapture. She has my mind and now she rules my body. She is calling me forth, Vallery, and she's a painful little bitch when she doesn't get her way."

Vallery's expression saddened. Lindsay looked away from it, not wanting to see his pitiful reflection in the dark brown gaze of his valet. "I feel ill, my friend. The effects of it are waning, and now I need more to feel good, to feel at least that my bones will stay within my skin and that my tremors will melt away. I need a little more. Just enough to take the edge away."

"Not now, milord. Lord Wallingford is here."

Lindsay shut his eyes and prayed for patience. In a few minutes the point would be moot, for he would be able to light his own spirit lamp, and heat the black gum on the silver needle. He could fix his own pipe, like he normally did. He did not know when it was that he had started to need Vallery to sit with him and fix his pipe so he had a steady supply of smoke.

"Did you hear me, milord? Lord Wallingford is here."

"I heard you.'"

So Wallingford was still around, was he? Lindsay had done his damndest to turn his longtime friend away. Pity was some-

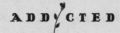

thing he abhorred. He didn't want anyone's trifling pity. He didn't want any speeches, or bloody heroics or cajoling demands to clean himself up. All he desired was a well-seasoned pipe, a never-ending supply of red smoke, and to drift off to the heavens where he didn't have to think or feel anymore. And Christ above, he didn't want an audience as he did it.

"It was Wallingford who helped me get you out of that rat hole in order to bring you home."

"He needn't have bothered," Lindsay groaned. Scrubbing his face with shaking hands, Lindsay eyed the bamboo pipe with the jade inlay handle. His brain was throbbing, firing in pulsations that screamed, *I need opium—now.*

"That hedonistic den will be the death of you."

"As far as opium dens go, Tran's is a virtual paradise. Have you not seen the pleasure to be found beyond those crimson-colored curtains? What a Garden of Eden. You can smoke, be fucked by an Asian whore and robbed while you idle away the hours in a fog, although I do not partake of the whores. The pickpockets, I cannot say."

"I don't let anyone near you," Vallery said, "even though the women want you enough. Found one climbing on top of you the other night, her greedy little hands were in your pockets, and it wasn't a six pence she was looking for."

"Really?" How disturbing. He didn't remember a blasted thing. But then, that was the point of smoking until he passed out—nothingness. Numbness. Had he been aware of her, he doubted he would have been able to rise to the occasion. He had never been one for whores.

Still, after all this time and everything that had happened, there was only one woman he wanted crawling all over him, and that was Anais. God help him, he was a reprobate, but he could not stop thinking of how damn exciting it would be to be high on opium while he fucked her. Oh, yes, it would be beautiful to take her like that, endless hours of loving her body. Smoking and stroking, his body on top of hers, hers on top of his. His hips moving slowly at first, then with determined strokes. What a beautiful rhapsody it could be watching her back arch, seeing her expression as she came for him. She would look utterly stunning coming and shivering as he watched her through the smoky vapors that would curl around them like a gossamer cocoon.

Christ, he needed another hit of the pipe. He was beginning to feel, to experience the thaw around his heart, the heart that still beat with the faintest glimmer of hope that one day things might be like they once were.

"Lord Wallingford brings a letter from Lady Anais. She is in the district once again. Home from her aunt's."

Lindsay froze. It had been weeks since he had seen Anais. No, that wasn't entirely correct. He saw her every night in his opium-fueled dreams. She was a vision, a fantasy come to life amongst the curling smoke. His dreams were all he had now. The opium was all he had.

How dramatic his fall had been. To sink so low. To actually physically tremble with the need to take his pipe in hand and obliterate himself in a haze of vignettes that involved Anais and him, and a physical joining that could never be.

"No doubt she is staying at The Lodge with Broughton and his family?" he asked, venom dripping in his voice.

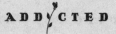

"I do not know, milord. Lord Wallingford has the news."

"Tell him I don't want it. Send him away, Vallery."

"I'm not going anywhere, old boy."

Lindsay whirled around and saw Wallingford standing before him, holding a letter out to him. "Drop the missive and leave. I'm busy."

"Busy doing what? Sinking deeper into an addiction that will leave you broken?"

"As a matter of fact, yes."

Wallingford shook his head. Lindsay saw disgust in his eyes. "I can't stand to see you destroy yourself like this."

"Then don't watch."

"Damn you, Raeburn, you selfish bastard!"

Lindsay blinked, startled by the outrage he heard. "If you came here to preach about the opium, you can save your breath. I'm not giving it up. Ours is an equitable love affair, my friend. I understand her and she understands me."

"And no else does, is that it?"

"That is correct."

"What do you think Anais would do if she saw you like this?"

"She won't, will she? She's gone. It's over."

"It doesn't have to be."

"Piss off, Wallingford. You don't know anything about what passed between us. Stick to your absinthe and leave me the hell alone."

"I've been by your side in that godforsaken den, Raeburn. I've watched as women have crawled over to you, desiring you, their hands all over your body. And all you care about is the pipe. You don't even glance at them. There is only one woman you see. One woman whom your body will come alive for. It's not over."

"If I could get hard," he sneered, "I'd have an orgy with those women, but the opium—my mistress—doesn't allow for fornication with others. That is the cost of being her disciple."

That wasn't true. He could still get aroused. And while he hadn't been physically aware of the whores in the den, he'd been aware of the sexual desire in his blood. But only one woman could fulfill those needs, however much Lindsay hated to admit it.

There had been one night, however, right after he had left Anais, with a beautiful Asian woman at Tran's. She had been delightfully curved and seductively naked. Her long black hair had skated over his naked chest as she lowered herself down the length of his body. He'd been so high from the opium, flying above the clouds, waiting to feel her mouth on his cock.

It wouldn't get hard.

"It's no good, darling," he had said, pulling her away from him. "He knows what he wants, and as lovely as you are, you aren't what he needs."

He had cried then. He was completely ruined. Physically. Mentally. Spiritually.

He hadn't bothered with the women at the opium dens after that. Instead, he concentrated on his visions of Anais and pleasured himself in the temporal plane while the physical plane withered away.

"You truly are beyond help now, aren't you? You're lost to it. You've let it beat you."

"If I wanted to hear a goddamned sermon, I would go to

church," Lindsay snarled as he turned back to the silver tray that housed his elaborate opium spread.

"That, Raeburn, is precisely where you are going."

"What the devil do you mean?"

Wallingford broke the wax seal and opened the letter before handing it to him. "I promised Anais I would make certain you read this. Now, read it and get yourself into some semblance of shape. Smoke whatever you're going to need to sit through an hour of church, and don't argue with me any further."

Lindsay looked at his friend with raised brows. "You think communion and prayers for redemption are going to save me now?"

Wallingford snorted, "I don't know what the hell will save you, Raeburn. I don't know what can open your eyes to the life surrounding you. I just pray that when we find it, it is not too late."

"De Quincey was in his late teens when he started using opium, he lived to be seventy. I have a few years yet. It's a bit premature to be picking out my casket and tombstone."

"*Confessions of an English Opium Eater,*" Wallingford said with a shake of his head. "De Quincey's great claim to fame, other than his opium habit. I hope you don't think that book an exemplary way of life. He struggled with that addiction his entire life, Raeburn. Is that really what you want, to live your life like this day in and day out?"

Lindsay looked up from Anais's letter. "Do you want the truth?"

"Of course."

"Then, yes. Yes, this is how I want to live. Not feeling a damn thing. Not caring about anyone or anything. Now, leave me alone. I need two pipes before I can even think of getting dressed."

* * *

Slamming the carriage door shut, the cracking sound echoed through the crisp morning air. Lindsay sprawled out on the velvet bench, his gloved hand curling into a fist as it lay upon his lap. His gaze stayed transfixed on the snow that was slowly beginning to melt. Occasionally, he would see the lure of green beneath the white stuff, teasing him with the idea that spring and warmth were not too far away. The naked branches, which a fortnight ago bowed with the weight of ice and snow, were now upright. He could see the faintest beginnings of leaf buds swelling along the wooden stalks. Soon the vale would be in bloom. Everything would be green and alive—full of wonder and life. He half wondered if he would live to see it.

The carriage wheels rolled along the roads, which were thawing and filling with mud and snowy slush. Soon they would be traveling over the bridge that crossed the Severn River, bringing them to the village.

"When was the last time you slept?"

"I sleep every night."

"Without the opium drugging you."

Lindsay did not glance at his traveling companion and instead kept his gaze on the scenery outside the carriage window. When *was* the last time he had slept the night through, and without opium? The night he'd slept with Anais, in his bed. They'd made love. Passionate, beautiful love.

"You look like hell, you know," Wallingford mumbled as he reached inside his jacket for a cheroot.

"I'm fine."

He saw the bridge directly ahead and mentally calculated

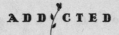

how many minutes he had left before he found himself in church, suffering through a ceremony he had no wish to witness. Bloody hell, why had he even bothered to read the letter from Anais?

"You don't look fine to me," Wallingford said between a cloud of smoke. "You look as if you have not slept in weeks. You're gaunt. When was the last meal you took?"

He rounded on Wallingford who sat opposite him, leisurely enjoying his smoke. Wallingford's fathomless eyes studied him intently from beneath the rim of his beaver hat and Lindsay had the irrational urge to plant a punch on Wallingford's handsome visage. "I don't want to hear another word! Do you understand? *I'm fine!*"

"If you say so," he shrugged. "But you are only lying to yourself. Any fool with eyes can see that you are not." Walling ford exhaled, blowing a cloud of smoke between them. "Perhaps it is not wise for you to go to this…this service, after all. I might have erred, insisting you go."

"I must," he whispered, averting his gaze so he was once again seeing beyond the glass to the outside.

"Why must you? Because Anais will be there?"

"It is personal "

"Why is this particular Sunday so damn important? Why, when you have not stepped foot in a religious house since you arrived back in England?"

"Because I must," he said, finally meeting his friend's shrewd gaze.

"I can't quite figure it out. What has prompted you to get off your divan? Nothing else has worked these past weeks, so why would a church service inspire such energy? Do you mean to patch things up with Broughton by attending his niece's baptism, then? Is that the reason you have dragged yourself out of your opium haze?"

Lindsay let go of his tightly held facade for the first time in weeks. "Surely you can reason why I must do this. You of all people must know. Or have I been so brilliant at hiding what I fear I wear on my sleeve?"

Recognition flashed in Wallingford's blue eyes, then he sat forward and wrapped his arm around his shoulder in a very caring, very un-Wallingford manner.

"I am so very, very sorry, Raeburn," his friend murmured and Lindsay could hear the sincerity in his voice. "So sorry."

He nodded and looked down at his gloved hands. "Thank you for not asking me to say the words. I...I can't say the words. They hurt too much."

Wallingford sat back against the squabs. "Words aren't necessary. I see the truth in your eyes. I have only to think back to our conversation to know the truth and the depths of your agony."

"I thought you might have dragged the truth out of me that night I went to see you," Lindsay muttered, looking up from his hands.

"I wanted to, but I knew that you would tell me if you wanted me to know. You have my sincerest, most profound sympathies. I cannot imagine what it must be like, what you must be feeling right now—"

"Rage. Pain. Hate," he looked at his friend and his mouth twisted in a deprecating smile. "Lust, desire. I want to hate her for what she has done. I want to make her pay. Yet whenever I close my eyes I can think of nothing other than pleasure—the pleasure I find only with her. What hold has she over me, Wallingford, that I should wish to forgive her so easily, that I can forget that she has given my child to another man to raise?"

"I can think of only one thing that could make a man forgive such a thing. Love, Raeburn, love is what hold she has over you. The same sort of elemental passion the poets talk of. The same, passionate, violent emotion that most men can only dream of finding."

"I did have that with her."

"You still have it, else you would not be trying to hate her, you *would* hate her."

"It was all I ever wanted from her—her love and our child. She deprived me of a chance. I should despise her for it, yet all I can think about is my future, and how bleak and utterly black it will be without her in it. The whole matter is perverse, is it not? What the hell can be the reason for such depredation?"

"'Be kind and compassionate to one another, forgiving each other, just as in Christ God forgave you,'" Wallingford said quietly and Lindsay saw that his friend was looking out the window at a place far, far away from the road they were traveling. "It is from Ephesians and the only passage of the Bible that I can recall. Perhaps I remember it because my grandmother would repeat it to me day after day as she fought tirelessly to reconcile me to my father. And to some extent, my stepmother. She failed in that. I cannot forgive. But perhaps you have done just that. In your heart you have forgiven her. You have offered her the compassion of your soul. You share a pure love with her. A love that is so rare, so perfect, that it can survive anything—even betrayal. Even," Wallingford said as he looked at him with eyes that shone sadness, "opium."

The church bells rang, heralding the flock to the fold. The carriage rounded the bend and St. Ann's Church loomed to their right. People dressed in their Sunday best were climbing the steps where the arched doors were opened and the welcoming glimmer of candles could be seen flickering from the ceiling of the nave.

Forgive and you shall be forgiven. For the first time, Anais's quiet words had new meaning for him. She had forgiven him for everything he had done. The question now was could he forgive her?

He must have spoke aloud, for Wallingford pressed forward and clasped a strong hand on his shoulder. "No, Raeburn, the question is, can you forgive yourself?"

Lindsay looked away, back to the church steps and the couples climbing them. "I...don't know."

"You must. To forgive is to free yourself from this opium prison you have built for yourself."

"I have nothing without opium."

Wallingford squeezed his shoulder. "Don't you see? You have nothing with it, my friend."

25

The choir sang the opening hymn as Anais ran her fingers along the gilded edge of her prayer book. Refusing to look up, she stared at the words before her, fearing that if she raised her chin and sang the words she would meet Lindsay's green gaze from where he sat in his family pew ahead of her. He sat to her left, leaving her with a perfect view of his strong profile. He had only to glance over his right shoulder to find her. She could not look up, for she knew if she did, she would not be able to keep her eyes from the face that had once been so dear to her. That same, beautiful face was now the ghost of a man who haunted her dreams and plagued her thoughts.

How ill he looked. How tired. It was the opium, it was killing him, and so, too, was what she had done to him. When he had walked away from her that night, he had turned his back on her and welcomed another woman into his life. Opium was now his lover and her clutches were deep. So deep that Anais feared he was lost to her forever.

Her fingers shook slightly and Garrett, who was seated beside her, reached out and settled his hand atop hers. She felt him looking at her, but she did not return his gaze. She could not hurt him any more than she already had. They had made their peace with one another. Garrett accepted her friendship, as she accepted his. There was love between them, but not the physical love that Anais felt—would always feel—for Lindsay.

As if knowing her thoughts, Garrett squeezed her fingers, giving her hand a reassuring shake, a silent acknowledgment that he was, and always would be, there for her. Her rock. Her pillar of strength when she was weak. She wondered who Lindsay had to cling to. How would he weather the storm?

The answer was etched on his face. Opium would be his safe harbor.

The choir had stopped and Mr. Pratt, the vicar of St. Ann's, stood at the pulpit, smiling down upon the faces of his faithful flock. Anais met his gaze and she saw a glimmer in his normally sedate brown eyes. The church was full and she could tell that Mr. Pratt was overjoyed to have the four aristocratic families of Bewdley taking up their family pews as they once had, many long years before.

"Good day to you all," he called, his melodic voice echoed from the plaster ceiling. "Today we welcome a new member to our church family."

As if on cue, little Mina squirmed in Margaret's arms and let out a lusty, and a not at all dignified yawn. Anais's gaze darted to Mina, who was stretching, then up to Lindsay, who was watching the babe. His mouth quirked in a lopsided grin when Wallingford pressed beside him and whispered in his ear. Looking away, she was not quick enough to escape detection

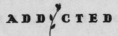

from Lindsay's knowing eyes. His gaze found hers and rested upon her until she could not bear the intensity a moment longer.

Jane, her aunt's companion, pressed against her and took her arm in hers. "Never mind him," she whispered. "Pretend he doesn't exist."

How in the world was such a thing to be achieved when her whole being was infused with the awareness of him? Her body was alive with memories of his heat against hers, his lips pressed to hers…pretend he didn't exist? It was an utterly futile task when she could feel him in every corner of her soul.

"Mr. Pratt is motioning for me to come up to the front," Garrett murmured in her ear. "You will be all right, won't you?"

"Of course." She attempted a smile. A smile she knew was sad and almost pathetic-looking.

Mr. Pratt motioned Robert and Margaret to the front, and her heart squeezed painfully in her chest as she watched Margaret pass the squirming bundle in her arms to Robert. She noticed how Lindsay went rigid as Robert pressed a kiss to Mina's plump cheek. She also saw how Wallingford placed a comforting hand on Lindsay's shoulder and she knew then, that Wallingford was Lindsay's confidant.

And then, as if he could feel the weight of her stare, Lindsay looked at her—those green eyes pierced her to her very soul and she saw the hurt and pain in them.

"Who gives this child to God?"

"We do, her parents," Margaret and Robert replied in unison, and Anais could not conceal the gasp of pain that escaped through her pursed lips as scalding tears dropped from her eyes to roll along her cheeks.

"Shh, dearest," Jane purred softly. "It will soon be over. Put on your brave face, my dear. That's it," she whispered. "You are a very strong woman, Anais. You can do this. Show him he hasn't broken you. Show him that you are not doubting your decision."

Ann, who was seated beside Jane, leaned forward and placed a protective hand on Anais's knee, but kept quiet, as if her innate intuition told her the secret Anais was trying valiantly to hide.

"Heavens!" her mother chastised in a low hiss. "What are you carrying on for? You'll only make your eyes puffy and your complexion blotched."

"Be quiet, Mother," Ann snapped while Mr. Pratt continued with his baptismal blessing. Ann sent her a look that spoke of her sadness and worry, and Anais gripped her sister's hand and hoped that one day Ann would find it in her to understand the reasons Anais was unable to confide her secret to her.

"I baptise you, Mina Gabriella Middleton——"

Anais's head came up. She saw Lindsay's eyes narrow and Wallingford's hand press into his shoulder at the same time Jane gripped her arm. It was the first time Anais had ever heard her child's full name spoken aloud—a name that was foreign to her ears. A name that should have been Mina Gabriella Markam, daughter of the Viscount and Viscountess Raeburn. The enormity—the *finality* of it all hit her and she let out a broken sob that she attempted to cover with her trembling fingers.

It was like giving her up all over again. Anais bit her lip, trying to prevent herself from breaking out in uncontrollable sobs. She wanted to run up to the front of the church and proclaim that she was not Mina Middleton, but the daughter of the Viscount

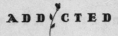

Raeburn. That she had been conceived during a night of incredible passion and love, that it was not a night of regret, but of rejoicing.

No, Mina's conception had been out of beauty and passion.

Blinking back her rapidly falling tears, Anais suddenly found herself back in the cottage, standing over Mina's bassinet, watching her sleep, allowing her tears to fall down her cheeks and land atop the lace blankets that covered her daughter. She had not allowed herself to hold Mina. She had not permitted herself to touch her or whisper to her for fear that she would never be able to let go of the child she loved so desperately— the piece of Lindsay that was so very dear to her. She had only allowed herself to look at her innocent daughter and weep for what she was about to do and for what might have been.

Her arms had ached to hold her, her heart had throbbed with the desire to tell her child how much she was loved and adored. Only she knew how she had lain awake at nights crying as she smoothed her hand down her empty belly, trying to relive the time when Mina had been a part of her. How she ached with the memories, how her body was shaking with the desire to run up and take Mina out of Mr. Pratt's hands and run with her, stealing her away from everyone.

"Oh, dearest," Jane murmured, rifling through her reticule for a kerchief. "Please don't cry, please don't— "

"Allow me," a deep voice murmured ahead of them and she saw that Lord Weatherby, Lindsay's father, was reaching out to her, his handkerchief in his hand.

"Thank you," Jane whispered before pressing the white linen into Anais's hand. "These ceremonies tend to make the fairer sex quite emotional, I fear. Why, I think even I might be succumb-ing to tears," Jane mumbled as she waved a hand before her face.

"I understand," Weatherby said as he looked at Anais. His yellow eyes were watery, but not from drink. "They can be quite emotional for what some might term the stronger sex, as well."

"Thank you, my lord," Anais mumbled before a fresh crop of tears sprung to her eyes.

"You are welcome. I pray you will find relief for your tears quite soon."

Lindsay caught her gaze and she looked away, ashamed of how she was acting, afraid that her behavior was going to cause un-necessary speculation upon her. She could not bear to look at Lindsay and know that it was over between them, to know that she, and she alone, was responsible for killing the love he once had for her. She could not stand the torture of seeing her daughter lowered to Margaret's arms and Robert placing a pro-tective arm around his wife's waist as the three of them—a family—huddled lovingly together.

Mr. Pratt smiled widely and addressed the congregation with his arms spread wide. "From a letter to the Corinthians. 'If I speak in human and angelic tongues but do not have love, I am a resounding gong or a clashing cymbal. And if I have the gift of prophecy and comprehend all mysteries and all knowledge; if I have all faith so as to move mountains, but do not have love, I am nothing.'"

The ripple of movement and sound from the congregation quieted—an unnatural calm that unnerved Anais settled over the church. It was so eerily peaceful and quiet that she feared

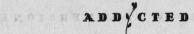

her rampant thoughts and dark secret that shouted in her brain may be discovered at any second by the entire church.

"'Love is patient, love is kind,'" Mr. Pratt continued and she saw his gaze stray to her, then to the pew before her where it rested upon Lindsay. "'It is not jealous, love is not pompous, it is not inflated. It is not rude, it does not seek its own interest, it is not quick tempered, it does not brood over injury. It does not rejoice over wrongdoing but rejoices in the truth. It bears all things.'"

And then she felt Lindsay's burning green gaze upon her and she lifted her face to meet his.

"'Love believes all things. Hopes all things. Endures all things—'"

Anais smothered a gasp as Lindsay's eyes darkened and she felt him reach out to her with a penetrating look that had consumed her so many times before.

"'Love never dies,'" Mr. Pratt said emphatically as he looked out upon his congregation.

Love never dies...but it does, Anais wanted to cry. It does die. It withers and dies on the stalk of betrayal.

"In Psalms we are told, 'When the just cry out, the Lord hears them, and from all their distress he rescues them.'"

She wanted to be rescued from this pain, from this heartbreak that made her unable to sleep or eat or to think of anything other than the man she had loved so desperately and had betrayed so abominably. She wanted to be saved from the hell she had been living in these past weeks, knowing that Lindsay hated her and knowing that she deserved nothing less from him. She wanted to be absolved from this unbearable state of loving and never having, of dreaming and praying that a miracle—however small—might happen and bring Lindsay back to her life.

"Let us proclaim peace unto our neighbors," Mr. Pratt announced. "Let us shake the hands of the people around us."

"I can't do this," she all but cried as she shook off Jane's hold.

"What are you doing, child?" her mother snarled, reaching for her skirt to prevent her from going anywhere. "Stop it at once, you're making a spectacle of yourself and your family."

Ann pried her mother's fingers from Anais's dress. "For heaven's sake, Mother, let her go. For once in your life care about something—*someone*—other than your own consequence."

Reaching for her reticule, Anais stood, her prayer book falling from her lap to the floor as everyone around her was standing and smiling and offering hands to be shook along with murmurings of "peace be with you."

Thank you, she mouthed to her sister and turned to file out of the pew before running down the aisle, knowing she was making a scene and not caring, because she could not sit there a second longer and feel like a fraud—like a failure as a woman, a lover.

As Anais's half boots carried her down the long aisle, she was aware that the sunlight was shining through the glass windows and that it had been weeks that it had shone so brilliantly. She was aware of the stares and the hushed whispers and the sound of feet behind and her name being called in Lindsay's baritone voice. And still she ran, trying to outrun her demons.

Flinging open the church doors, her bonnet askew and her skirts raised well above her ankles, she ran down the steps onto the empty sidewalk. Stopping, she gasped for breath as the tears

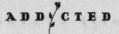

streamed down her cheeks, the pain making it almost impossible to breathe.

"Anais, wait," Lindsay cried, following her down the stairs. Shielding her face with her hands, she gave him her back.

"Don't run, not again," he said, his voice full of raw emotion. Then she saw him extend his hand, his fingers trembling. "Peace, Anais."

"There is no peace!" she cried, slapping his hand away and wrapping her arms around her waist, hugging herself. "I wish I had died after giving birth to her," she spat, giving vent to every thought and feeling she had ever had. "I wish I would never have awakened to see her clutched in Margaret's arms. You think that it was easy for me to give her up?" she spat angrily. "That I just tossed her aside without a thought or care as if she were as insignificant as a peach pit. But you know nothing," she spewed, heedless that someone passing by might hear her. "You don't know the pain I have. *I didn't even get to hold her!*"

His mouth opened then closed and she jumped in before he could say anything. "That's right, I lied to you that night on the terrace. I did not clasp her to my breast. I said that because I knew you wanted to hear those things and somehow I thought if I said the words aloud that maybe—*just maybe*—the memory might be created. I *wanted* to believe those things. But the truth is I slipped into unconsciousness before I could even touch her. And I could not bring myself to hold her when I left the cottage because I knew that if I did I would never be able to go through with my plans. I hadn't even *seen* her till the night I found you clutching her. I had not even permitted myself that small luxury."

She glared at him through tear-filled eyes. "You talk of your pain? You cannot even begin to understand the sacrifice I have made. I gave away a piece of myself, my soul! But I did it out of love, never think otherwise. I made the choice to live my life without her because I knew in my heart she would be better off without me and I could not bear to know that a life created out of such perfect love would be forced to live with the ugly truth of her birth. I thought," she sobbed, breaking down before him. "I thought...I did the right thing."

"Oh, God, Anais," he groaned stepping toward her.

"Don't," she begged through a choking gasp. "Please don't say anything. Just...go away."

"I don't think I'll ever be able to leave you, Anais."

Her heart squeezed as she listened to the hope, the longing in his words. Her own hope flared, thinking of what-if. Could it be? Then she looked at him, a shell of the man he once was, an empty husk that had once held so much potential. "You've already left, Lindsay. You just don't realize it yet."

26

The early spring wind had turned cold. Dampness settled around him, but Lindsay felt none of it. As he watched Anais walk away toward the waiting carriages her words rang loud in his ears.

Was it true? Was he already dead to her? Had he lost himself so quickly?

He knew the answer to that when he felt his body begin a series of fine shivers, felt his head begin to throb with the need to be filled with smoke.

Opium had been a means to resist drink and women, a way to prevent becoming his father. What a treacherous demon it was, for it had turned him into something worse than the person he feared most. He had destroyed the woman he loved, ruined her life, and his own. He had even altered the future of a child. And all for the sinister seductions of a drug he no longer even liked, but needed.

"Son," he heard his father say in a voice that wavered with emotion.

He could not turn around, could not look away from the corner where Anais had disappeared.

"Lindsay, please, come into the carriage with us and we'll go to the baptismal luncheon together."

It was his mother's voice, so kind and soft. He remembered that comforting voice from his childhood when she would tuck him into bed and tell him what a fine man he was growing up to be.

He was a wreck, now. The furthest thing from a gentleman.

"Please, Lindsay, come away—"

Shaking off his mother's hold he snapped, "For Christ's sake, not now, Mother."

The shock he heard in her gasp made him reach for what little control remained in him. He turned, only to find her right behind him, standing on the stairs. She was crying, and he reached for her hand, grasping it hard in his, bringing it to his mouth and pressing a kiss to her knuckles.

"Forgive me," he begged. He never wanted to hurt anyone, least of all the woman who had raised him, loved him, taught him how to be a man of worth—a man worthy of a woman like Anais. And he had failed her. Miserably.

"I…I am not myself," he told her as he let her hand fall away. "My head aches. A nap will set me to rights. An hour, Mother. Then I shall be able to meet you at The Lodge."

"My beautiful boy," she whispered through trembling lips. He allowed her to cup his face in her gloved hands and tilt his chin until he was looking at her. "What have you done to yourself, Lindsay? Where has my son gone?"

"He's lost, Mother."

The sight of her tears undid him. He had only ever seen his

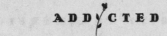

mother cry because of his father. Never had he or his actions brought sadness to her, and knowing he had at last accomplished that killed whatever flicker of life remained in him.

"Can you not find him?" she asked. "I...we," she said, glancing at his father. "We want him back so terribly bad."

"I will try," he said, stepping back from her, lying to her. The truth was, even if he wanted to quit, he couldn't. He was no longer just a disciple following the path of his mistress. He was addicted. Wholly dependent. His body now needed opium like it required food and water.

"An hour, Mother, or perhaps two," he said, walking backward, away from her. "I just need to sleep. Just for a short time."

Draping his coat along the seat of a chair, Lindsay turned his attention to the silver tray that sat atop the hall table. A missive had arrived. His heart faltered a beat and he found himself illogically hoping that it was a letter from Anais. It was not.

Breaking the seal, he read the missive that had been sent by Robert Middleton. He walked the distance to the conservatory. His harem, he thought absently. A forbidden place to do forbidden things.

As he walked, he ignored the rush of anticipation that quickened his steps and instead read the letter in his hands.

Raeburn,

I was not certain you would attend Mina's baptism, so I decided to write to inform you that I shall be taking Mina and Margaret back to Edinburgh within a fortnight. I'm certain you shall agree that it is best for all concerned.

Now alone in his den, Lindsay closed his eyes and sunk down onto the red velvet divan. *Dear God, no.* What bloody right had Middleton to squander off with a child that was not rightfully his own? But Mina was Robert's child now, he reminded himself. She was only flesh of *his* flesh, nothing more. Mina was not, nor would she ever be, his daughter in more ways than blood.

The paper trembled in his hand and he peered down at the scrolled words through eyes that burned.

You must understand there is nothing that can be done. We have introduced her to the world as our daughter and I may assure you that to Margaret and myself, she is our daughter. No one will question her legitimacy as it was common knowledge that Margaret was nearing her date before we left for Bewdley. The child will enjoy everything we have to give her. I vow she will be—and is—loved and cherished.

I have taken a position as a professor at the university. My post shall keep me in the north. I'm certain you will find these arrangements satisfactory as it will dramatically reduce the chance for awkward, and admittedly, unpleasant surprise encounters.

You will find in this packet another letter, concerning information that I thought you should know. You will recall that I made every attempt to inform you of the facts prior to your departure to London. Since I was not successful in that, I will take the opportunity now, to write them down for you.

Lindsay crumpled the letter in his hand. Anger raced through his blood and he spat a foul oath as he stood up from the divan.

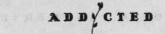

Bending to pick up the folded letter that Middleton had tucked inside the missive, he headed away from the spring bath that steamed so invitingly beside him, and made his way to the curtain partition that housed another divan. There, the silver tray awaited him. So, too, did the lacquered box that housed the opium.

Dropping the last of Middleton's missive onto the divan, he pulled the lid of the box off and rifled through its contents, searching for the Constantinople pats that would bring him solace. Finding the yellow cake he broke it in two, pulling out the black, seedlike pieces. He stared down at them lying in his palm, hating them—needing them.

Bloody hell, was this what he truly needed?

In truth it was now all he could think of. He was afraid that it was the only thing he wanted, maybe even over Anais.

Glancing up from the opium cake, his gaze sought the mother-of-pearl-and-jade pipe that sat atop the tray. Would the opium be enough to replace the empty spot in his soul that Anais had left?

He spied the letter and he wrestled with the idea of reading it or smoking the entire cake and sleeping for days, only to awaken without any memory of the past weeks.

Should he read the letter and inflict more pain, or should he shut himself off from the world and feel nothing?

Shut everything out, his mind shouted. Reaching for the pipe so that he could send himself to oblivion, his hands fumbled with the opium, but it was not eagerness that made him clumsy. It was fear. He knew what he was doing. He was trudging down the path to destruction, following his father's boot steps down a dark and muddy path. Step for step he was right behind his father, sinking into vice. Submerging any emotions in a substance that prevented any feelings at all.

His fingers faltered with a sulphur match and he burnt his fingertip before he could light the wick that would heat the burner. Shoving aside every thought and feeling he had, Lindsay reached for the opium and put it on the needle, heating it until it began to bubble. When it was at the right stage of softness, he pulled it off, rolling it between his fingers until the consistency was perfect.

There had been a time when this was a ritual for him. A game of seduction. He had thought it amusing. A lark. A dream on a cloud of sensuality. Now it was a necessity. There was no beauty in feeling the opium warming between his fingers. No seduction in waiting for the feel of the first rush, warming his blood. Now there was impatience. Anger. He could not wait to feel the opium. Could not bear to seduce it into working.

At last the first few tendrils began to rise from the brass burner of the pipe. With impatience, Lindsay pulled the cravat from his neck and tore at the buttons of his shirt. Reclining on the divan, he reached for the pipe, bringing it to his mouth, he felt the warmth of the vapor on his cheeks. With a great pull, he inhaled the smoke, filling his lungs until he thought they might burst. With a slow exhale he let a minimum of the smoke out, watching it rise up to the ceiling of his tented pleasure den.

His gaze found Robert Middleton's missive, and he wondered what it could contain. Certainly nothing that could salvage the events of the past weeks.

Taking two more pulls on the pipe, he steadied himself and

reached for the letter. With the steadying influence of the opium, he could read the missive.

Breaking open the seal, he scanned Robert Middleton's hurried scrawl.

> She had labored the entire day on her own without anyone to help her or offer her encouragement. That is my first regret.

His heart sank. Another lie. She had said that the ordeal wasn't overly long. That Broughton had stayed and cared for her. Why had she lied? Why had she thought she needed to make it easier for him to hear? Did she think him that weak and fragile? Christ, was he that weak?

He looked at the burner and the opium. He told his mother he would try, and yet here he was, lighting up once again because he couldn't deal with the emotions—the pain that coursed inside him. Yes, he was weak, he could no longer deny that.

> My brother arrived at the cottage to check in on her, it was then that he found her in the latter stages of labor. He raced back to the house to retrieve me, and when we arrived it was apparent the birth was imminent. She was brave and made nary a sound while she delivered your daughter, and I could not help but be awed by her calm control.
>
> All went exceedingly well until the time that the afterbirth failed to detach from the womb. It was then that she began to bleed brightly and profusely. There was so much

blood—much more than I had ever seen in my life. I began to fret and wasted much valuable time in panic when I should have been using the skills that were taught to me. That is my second regret. In my defense, I will say that I had never encountered a complication upon birthing as the one Anais presented me with. So much blood—flowing blood—that overwhelmed me and left me feeling helpless.

His lips wrapped around the pipe, and he inhaled again, then again, until images of blood swarmed before him. Of their own accord, his eyes found the letter and he began reading once again.

After struggling to manually remove the afterbirth, it was apparent that Anais had lost a vast quantity of blood— I fear that her entire body of fluid was pooling about me. I can still hear her life's blood rolling from the sides of the bed, tapping against the wooden floorboards.

Although I was successful in removing the afterbirth and stemming the bleeding, I thought little could be done to restore the quantity of life's blood she had lost.

Thankfully, Anais was unconscious for the majority of this ordeal. And I would take the time to tell you now, that her last words to me as she looked up into my face with her wide, frightened eyes—eyes that saw her impending death—were "take care of my baby."

Fearing I failed her in life, I resolved not to do the same in death. I had my brother retrieve my wife and not caring about the trauma she, herself, had suffered not more than a fortnight before, bade her to feed Anais's babe.

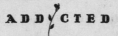

Owing to her advanced pregnancy, my wife had milk in her breasts to feed the babe. It was then that our days and nights were filled with caring for the babe and seeing to the needs of my patient who had not regained consciousness. I feared the worst when the fever set in almost two days later. I was convinced Anais would surely not cling to life much longer.

Pressing his shaking fingers to his eyes, Lindsay stemmed the tears that began to gather amongst the opium mist. She had needed him and he had left her bereft and alone. He had wasted away his days in idleness and self-pity while Anais had been struggling to bring his child into the world.

We cared for the child since the night of her birth. It was not too difficult to pretend to the servants that Margaret had delivered the child. We had not shared the despair of losing our own with anyone other than my brother. After losing two previous babes, we wanted the loss of our third to be kept between us. Since no one realized that Margaret had lost the babe, they all assumed that the child they suddenly heard crying in our chamber was our own.

Despite the fever and gross blood loss, Anais awoke, clear-minded and free of fever on the sixth day. I needn't tell you how many tears were shed upon seeing her with her eyes open. Nor do I need to tell you the anguish felt by all when she realized that she could not care for the child in the way a mother must.

I will never forget the look of her when, two weeks after

giving birth, she bade my brother to take her home. The parting look she gave her baby will haunt me forever. Never think that what she did was for the ease of her circumstances. Never think that what she did was an act of a spoiled woman, for what it was, was an act of an angel.

We shall never forget our angel. We shall never forget that it was the two of you who made our fondest wish come true.

May you one day find peace with what has happened, and learn to be content in the knowledge that your love for each other has made our life rich beyond measure.

The letter slipped from his hands. He had one of two choices. Weep as he hadn't allowed himself to weep in years, or pick up the pipe. It was not a difficult decision. The pipe felt familiar in his hands. The tears did not.

Anais strolled down the long marble hall and stopped before the heavily paneled wooden door. She knocked and waited for a response. None came. Opening the door, she saw Lord Weatherby asleep on a settee, his wife's head was resting on his shoulder. They were holding each other.

As if in slow motion, she turned around, realizing that something was wrong. The house was too quiet. The servants too still. There was a pall over the house that was heavy and dark.

Lindsay.

Lifting her skirts, she ran from the room and down the hall. It was raining outside and the butler had left her parasol and coat on a hook to dry. She passed the coat tree, skidded in a puddle

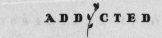

of rainwater and ran into a pair of strong arms that wrapped tightly around her.

"Lindsay?" she asked breathlessly as she held on. When she looked up, it was into the grave face of Wallingford.

"Take me to him," she demanded, pulling away from him, but he reached for her and held her tightly about the wrist.

"He would never want you to see him this way, Anais. I promised—"

"I don't give a bloody damn what you've promised him. I will go myself. I know where to look."

Releasing her, Wallingford motioned her ahead. They both knew where they were going. When Anais opened the door of the conservatory, it was to see it bathed in candlelight, the gentle glow flickering off the orange and pink silks.

"Back there," Wallingford indicated. "Behind the curtain."

Summoning her strength, Anais walked to the back of Lindsay's harem. With a hand that trembled like a leaf, she pulled back the cover and gasped, covering her mouth.

"He is only sleeping," his valet reassured as he packed up a silver tray and the items surrounding it. "He should awaken in a few hours."

"H-how long?" she asked, stepping into the room. Her gaze had not strayed from his body. His breaths were slow and shallow, she could barely tell he breathed at all.

"I do not know, my lady. I was not here when he arrived."

It was dark outside—hours since she had left him that morning standing in front of St. Ann's.

"He has been known to be gone for days, Lady Anais. Do not look so stricken. He will awaken."

Days? Anais fell to her knees in a crinkle of taffeta beside Lindsay's limp body. Good God, he looked to be in death's sleep. When she reached for his hand and gripped it, holding it between her breasts, he didn't move. Didn't even flicker in acknowledgment.

"I...I had to see him," she whispered, as she gazed upon him. "Somehow I knew that my place was here, between him and the opium."

She looked up and saw Vallery watching her. Tears spilled from her cheeks, and she reached out and ran a shaking hand through Lindsay's black curls, and the hair he had let grow long.

"He will not thank you for it, my lady. In fact, you'll see another side of the man you thought you've always known."

"He won't hurt me," she whispered, conviction in every word as she looked down upon the man she would never stop loving or wanting in her life. "He would never lay a hand on me in anger." *Just in passion,* she silently added.

"The red smoke rules him now."

"No," she murmured, swiping at her tears. "It does not. He is more than this, sir. He is a man of intelligence, of sensitivity. He's done so many wonderful things for others, including myself and my family. He has been the provider for his mother, his father. He has carried the burden of responsibilities from a young age, and shouldered them without complaint. No, sir," she cried, squeezing Lindsay's hand, "there is so much more to him than anyone knows. I know that. I've always known it. I just temporarily forced myself not to remember those attributes."

This bond we have, it must never be broken. Promise me, he'd asked

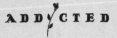

her that night in the stable. *Promise me that this chain that binds us will never come unlinked.*

She had told him that she would always be bound to him. That her heart would forever belong to him.

That afternoon she had told herself she was done watching Lindsay kill himself with opium. She had tried to convince herself that she wanted to start anew. To break away from the past. To live without Lindsay.

It had worked, too. For a few hours. Until she began to think of her future, which naturally progressed to thoughts of Lindsay.

He was so much more than this, this opium-smoking ghost. He was flawed, yes, but beneath the mistakes was a man who would do anything for anyone. A man who would cherish her, protect her—love her—as she was. He was a beautiful man, inside and out. And it was with that realization that Anais knew she would never love another like she loved Lindsay.

He was worth the fight, the tears, the heartache. They had traveled so far, too far to turn their backs on each other.

"This chain that binds us will not come unlinked," she vowed to him. "It will not, Lindsay, I swear it."

She looked up at him through a lock of her hair and saw that he still slept. She clutched his hand to her breasts and held on to it with everything she had. "Together, we will conquer this demon. You must believe that. You must."

27

Through the fog, he heard her rise from the divan, the rustle of silk cascading over velvet. Through the smoke, he heard the snapping of buttons being set free from their closures. His blood ran hot as he thought of the dress being shed from her body. The crinkling of silk once again drew his attention, rousing his desires.

Peering through the rising vapors of the pipe, he watched the silk gown skim down along her back and over her waist until it fell onto the floor. Her arms rose up over her head, so that he could see the side of her breast, full and soft, as she wound her hair up into a bun, securing it with pins. She turned then, gracefully walking through the curtain of opium to kneel before him. She still looked like an angel to him. She probably always would.

"I knew if I smoked enough you would return to me," he murmured as he caught a loose lock of her hair on his finger. "Why do you weep, angel?" He brushed away the tear that had crept out of her eye. She didn't say anything. She never did in his opium dreams. There was no talking. Only loving. What could be said with words, was spoken instead with their bodies.

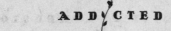

"Your tears pain me. Let me take them all away and replace them with tears of pleasure."

He touched her, felt her body jolt then soften beneath the gentle grazing of his fingertips. She wore only a thin chemise, plain, unadorned, nothing to distract from the enticing view of her breasts pressing against the soft cotton. With his palm, he felt her skin; warm, supple. Her heart beat steadily against his hand as he reached for the strap of her shift and pulled it down along her shoulder, baring her milk-white skin.

"How is it you grow more beautiful?" he asked as her breast filled his hand. "How is it possible to keep wanting you more than the time before?" She smiled, blooming under his appraisal, making his heart ache. How he wished this was really her he saw amidst the smoke. Yet, he smelled her, the scent of the French perfume she had worn that night he had made love to her for the first time. Even amongst the opium fumes he could decipher the delicate floral mix with her own unique scent.

He recalled through his fuzzy mind how he had envisioned the perfume gliding down between her breasts, the memory inspired him, and reaching for the hem of her chemise he raised it over her head and discarded it. She was naked, bared completely to him and he studied her like a slave at a bazaar. She did not complain. She never did, not in his dreams.

Guided by his hand, she lay down on her side, her spine facing him. He studied her skin, the way she glowed in the candlelight. He followed the flickering shadows, trailing his fingers along her back, down to her hip and the curve of her luscious buttock. The sounds of pleasure coming from her spurred him on, and he pressed her forward so that she was on her belly and he was straddling her. Perfumed smoke came from his mouth and he watched as it curled over her neck and shoulder, bleeding onto her skin. The sight aroused him and his cock pulsed, finding home between the cleft of her bottom.

With his mouth, he trailed his lips along her skin as the smoke continued to cover her body like a swath of gray silk. The sight was so erotic, so hedonistic, that he picked up the pipe, inhaled deeply, then exhaled. The curling tendrils floated over her hips, caressing her bottom, escaping between the folds of her quim.

As she moaned and moved her hips in invitation, he stroked her with his hands and mouth, loving her through the smoke as he exhaled the very last of the opium from his lungs. He was ruled by twin cravings, oblivion and passion. Opium and Anais. But here, in his fantasies, the two became one.

His blood was thick, his body languid; he was high on opium, floating above the clouds. He was drunk on Anais and the pleasures waiting to be explored. He could last for hours like this, in this pleasurable plane of sensuality.

There was no need to rush. So he took his time, touching her, trailing his fingers down her legs and the inner facings of her thighs. He parted the globes of her bottom and stroked her sex, sliding his cock along the trail of wetness he had spread. She was begging him to join her as he trailed his tongue down her spine while his cock slid along her skin, mimicking the sex she longed for.

His name, said in a pleading, husky whisper, was an alluring enticement, but he resisted the urge to penetrate her. No, he needed to build her up, so that she was at least half as high as himself. He wanted Anais adrift in lust and longing.

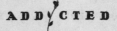

Pulling the pins free, he undid the bun, letting her hair fall down over her shoulders. He picked up handfuls of the silken mass and touched it, then let it fall back over her shoulder. He wanted to feel all that hair draped over him, wanted to clutch it as he cried out in orgasm.

"How badly I want you, Anais," he murmured as he turned her over onto her back. When he looked down into her beautiful face she was smiling up at him and holding out her arms to him. "I need to feel your heat, my body in yours."

"Beautiful, Lindsay. Don't you know that I would give you anything you desired?"

"Anything?"

She nodded, giving him free rein over her body. His own tightened in reaction as she ran her hands through his hair.

"You have such beautiful skin," he murmured before his lips brushed the nape of her neck. "So soft, so responsive to my touch." His lips captured her nipple, which was hard and pink. He suckled it, bringing it into his mouth, then tonguing the tip to make it even harder. "Your skin tastes like opium and woman—ambrosia," he said as his hand skated down her belly to her parted thighs where she was wet. "You taste of desire here. You always do." He pressed his fingers against her, brushing her clitoris. He watched her response through the smoke that escaped the abandoned pipe. "I love your sounds of pleasure," he told her as he passed his thumb once more over her clitoris. "I want to hear you gasp that way when I am inside you."

When she tilted up her face, he couldn't stop himself from clutching her face in his hands and lowering his mouth to hers. His kiss was slow and provocative, his tongue mimicking what his cock was straining to do. She moaned and he deepened it. When her hands trailed down his belly, he didn't pull away. He needed her touch. Her mouth. In his dreams, she always knew what he needed, and this one was no different. She captured him in her hand, stroking him. He was hard, ready to be inside her, fucking her for hours.

Breaking the kiss, Anais moved her mouth lower, down his neck, his shoulder, his nipple, which she circled and laved with her tongue. Currents of electricity ran through his body as she flicked his nipples once more. Filling his hands with her breasts, he pleasured her until her mouth reached his belly. Without warning, she captured the swollen tip of him between her pouting lips. Sucking in a ragged breath, he reached for her hair, holding it back so he could watch her as he thrust his hips forward, filling her mouth over and over with his length. She looked so lovely, here in his opium den, on her knees taking him deeply.

"I want to come like this," he said fiercely while watching her tongue flick up the length of him. His hand fisted tighter in her hair as his strokes became harder. Then suddenly he was pulling away and reaching for her. "Not yet, angel. We've got hours left before you'll leave me."

She looked confused, but he ignored it as he took her hand and helped her to lie on her side. "Simultaneous pleasure," he explained as he parted her thighs and kissed her glistening sex. He parted her with one hand, stroking his tongue along her folds. Then she was there with him, in this decadent position, pleasuring his cock with her luscious mouth.

It was a heady, hedonistic visual, Anais lovely and naked,

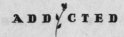

sucking him as the opium vapors shimmered between them. How long they pleasured one another, he could not say, but he came like that, their bodies entwined, Anais loving his cock, and him her glistening quim.

He had no sooner spent himself, before he hardened again. It was always like this when he dreamed of her while under the effects of the opium. Pulling her up from where her face rested on his thighs, he lay back, his head cushioned on the pillows. He had dreamed of her like this once before, sitting on his chest while he tasted her. She had loved it then, she loved it now, he realized as he heard her moan and felt her shudders. She looked beautiful and wanton, her breasts heavy and inviting. He brought her to orgasm with his tongue, two, perhaps three times before he released her and allowed her to finally slide onto his cock. He was kneeling, rocking into her as he cupped her buttocks in his hands. His penetration was deep, slow, enough to make her gasp with each stroke. Their bodies were slick with sweat. Anais's damp hair bound them together, clinging to his skin like her arms clung to his neck. Together they rocked, their bodies in perfect rhythm, their breaths evenly matched. The feel of her breasts, the scrape of her nipples against his chest completed the perfection of their union.

She was as high as he now, drunk on the passion, the pleasure he was giving her as she held on to him as if she would never let go.

Hours later, opium smoke continued to fill the room. His brain was clouded, fogged, his body on fire. Opening his eyes, he saw that Anais was beneath him, lying on her belly as he ran his hand along her back, his hips pressing into her. He was slowly giving her his cock…in and out…in and out in a slow, lazy rhythm. His finger had found its way between her bottom, rubbing and circling the little puckered opening that beckoned him to explore what he had never dared to before.

He had been doing this for hours, taking her in every position, and still he could not get enough of her moans and cries, the look of her taking his cock, the feel of her cunt.

Rocking against her, he reached for her wrists, wrapped his hands around the delicate bones and held her so that her arms were above her head and his body was flush atop hers as his cock drove in and out of her.

"I can go longer, Anais," he whispered against her neck. "I could take you like this all night."

Her lashes fluttered and her mouth parted as he penetrated her deeply. "You have been."

He was rocking hard now, taking her as the pressure of his hold on her wrists increased. "I don't want to give you up…never want to give you up," he said through gritted teeth as he pumped harder into her.

He didn't spill inside, but instead pulled out and allowed his seed to splash onto her bottom. He watched his cock pulse against the cleft of her derriere and he rocked against her as he slid the head of his cock between the globes of her bottom, sliding up and down as he held himself above her, watching as he branded her. He was hardening again, he thought in wonder, but she was already asleep, their entwined hands clutched her chest.

Lying down beside her, he brushed her damp hair away from

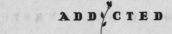

her forehead, her beauty, and his love for her nearly overwhelming him. An angel lying with the devil. He really was nothing but a beast when he raised her leg and let it drape over his thigh. He slid into her, slowly, gliding himself inside her pink quim. Holding her close, he rocked against her only occasionally, allowing her to sleep. He drifted off that way, too, buried deep inside her, their bodies pressed together, the last remnants of his mistress cloaking them.

Twin cravings, he reminded himself. Oblivion and passion. Stirring, Anais brushed against him, her lashes flickering until she was looking up at him. Her eyes were glazed, glassy with passion. He pressed forward, letting her feel his cock. His finger pressed in, filling the alluring bud between her plump buttocks. Her eyes went round as he matched the rhythm of his cock and finger. Taking her nipple into his mouth, he suckled her, building her up once more. He stroked her hard, filled her up with his finger. She arched and scratched her nails down his shoulders as she cried out in pleasure.

Beautiful fallen angel, he thought, watching her fall apart in his arms. Won't you stay with me forever?

The sun shone in through the bank of windows. Lindsay winced at the brightness. Why had Vallery not closed the drapes this morning? Bloody hell, he tried to move, but his limbs felt like gelatine, and his head swam with the lingering effects of the opium.

Christ, the sunshine was doing nothing to help his physical misery. His head hurt and his fingers were shaking. He needed more opium.

"Vallery!" he roared for his valet. The stubborn man did not come to his aid. Instead, Lindsay was left alone to fend for himself. Grumbling, he wiped his face and noticed how sated his body felt. He normally felt very relaxed after a night indulging in opium, but this satiation was something completely different.

He was naked, he realized as he looked down at his body and saw with surprise that he was fully erect this morning. His body was covered in sweat, and the scent of sex along with opium lingered on his skin. Bloody hell, what the devil had gone on last night?

His vision had at last cleared and he turned his head on the pillows only to see a mass of golden hair tangled beneath his arm. His mind blanked and he suddenly couldn't seem to breathe. As he sat up, he noticed the woman was naked, too, her delightfully rounded bottom calling to his hand.

With shaking fingers, he reached out and touched the woman who lay so still beside him. "Oh, God," he cried, suddenly moving—thinking.

"Anais!" Pulling her hair away from her face, he revealed her familiar features. "What have I done?" he asked over and over as he searched her body for any signs that he had hurt her. "Christ, what did I do to you?"

He couldn't bear to think of it. Had that dream of her last night, the hours of lovemaking been real? How could it have happened? Had she been here the whole time, while he had been smoking?

The thought made him bilious. She had seen him at his absolute worst, and he had treated her as though she was one of the whores who worked at Tran's den.

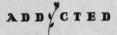
"Anais, open your eyes, angel," he pleaded. He noticed how badly his fingers were trembling and wondered if it was the need for opium or fear that had made them shake so badly they were useless to him. She was still sound asleep, even though he cradled her shoulders in his arms. The smoke had made her this way. His habit had done this to her. He held her, watching the slow rise and fall of her chest. He lay with her, holding her, realizing the worst. Opium had at last won out over Anais.

28

"Why did you do it?"

Anais glanced over her shoulder at Lindsay, who was resting against the wall. He had not used opium since last night, and now, late in the afternoon, he was feeling the effects.

She wondered at his question. Did he want to know why she had made love with him last night, or did he wish to know why she had returned to his house when there had been such a sense of finality between them at the church?

Holding his gaze, she walked to him, dressed in only her chemise. Vallery had sent them in a tea tray with some sandwiches and biscuits. Anais had eaten, but Lindsay had not taken anything, not even a cup of tea.

She poured him a cup, held it out to him. He reached for it, but shackled her wrist, drawing her down so that he could take the cup from her hand and set it aside.

"Why, Anais?"

"Because I promised you to never let the bond that links us

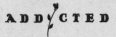

come unchained. Because there are no more secrets between us, Lindsay. Nothing to hide from. Nothing to be ashamed of."

"Did I hurt you? Your wrists are red where I held you. I was...rough. Inconsiderate."

"No, you were passionate. I gave myself to you knowing the depths of your passion while acknowledging mine."

"You shouldn't have seen me that way—Christ—"

"Were your desires just the effect of opium, Lindsay," she asked as she brushed his hair out of his eyes, "or were those true desires for me?"

His gaze lifted to hers. "Do you have to ask? Can you not tell, Anais?"

"That is why I came to you, Lindsay. Because I am drawn to you like a moth is to a flame. My passion for you was real and I knew your feelings were for me, because of what you truly feel, not because the opium rules you. You were so honest in your passion, Lindsay, and you needed it, to be with someone who cares. Someone who desires the man you are."

He closed his eyes, his hand fisted against his bent knee. "I never, ever wanted you to see me like that. If I could, I would take it all back, even sacrifice those hours we spent loving each other, if I could just wash those memories of me out of your mind."

"Don't," she pleaded, reaching for his hand. "Do not worry about me, Lindsay. Please—"

"I want to stop," he blurted, "but I...I can't," he said, his voice catching. "I can't stop. Even now, knowing you've seen me at my worst, knowing how ashamed it makes me feel, I still find myself looking at the tray, at the pipe. I'm craving it, Anais. Dying for it, that feel of the pipe in my mouth and the smoke in my lungs."

The honesty he spoke with tore at her heart. When she had told Wallingford and Vallery to lock her in the conservatory with Lindsay, she thought she knew what she was dealing with. Now she wasn't so certain.

"I need it," he said through trembling lips. "It's gone from my body and now I'm shivering and my nose is running," he sniffed. "I no longer rule the opium, Anais. It rules me. I have to have it."

"Then have it."

He looked up at her, his eyes glowing with tears. "You have to leave."

"I'm not leaving, Lindsay. I promised you."

"Why do this when there is nothing left?" he roared. Jumping up, he paced the width of the room like a caged animal. "Why make me quit when there is nothing to live for?"

"What do you mean? You have a full life ahead of you. A brilliant future in finances and parliament and bettering the country for those who are not as fortunate as us to be born into the aristocracy."

"Why can't you see," he raged, "that the only thing I could possibly quit for is you?"

Silence hung heavy between them. "Do not stop for me. Quit for you, Lindsay."

"I can't. Not right now, Anais. I know I have no right to say this to you, not after what I've done, but the truth is, the only thing that could possibly bring me out of the darkness is a chance that at the end of the tunnel I might find you waiting there in the light."

Anais cupped his face, forcing him to look at her. "I will be there, Lindsay. I swear to you, I'll be there, waiting."

* * *

His bones felt as though they were trying to escape the confines of his skin. He was sweating, yawning, his skin was covered in goose bumps. And the cramps, Christ, his stomach was roiling, the pain a constant reminder of what he needed.

He was restless, his mind churning with the craving for opium.

"Tell me how it will happen," Anais asked.

Lindsay closed his eyes as she threaded her fingers in his hair. He was lying with his head in her lap, trying to stave off the ever-increasing need for opium.

"It will peak in about three days," he mumbled, trying not to think of the hell awaiting him. "It will not be pretty, Anais. I am regretting my selfish actions now. You should not be here."

"Don't be silly," she whispered. "Why don't you try to sleep, Lindsay?" she suggested as she rubbed his temples in soothing circles. "I will be here, whenever you need me."

"I need you now," he said, feeling another ache in his gut that brought tears to his eyes. "Yet I am afraid of what I might do. I have not been without the opium for many years, Anais. I...I don't even know who I am without it."

He reached for her hand and held it in his trembling one. She had bathed in the spring bath, in a soap scented with jasmine. Her skin was soft, fragrant, and he held her palm to his chest, holding her so tight he was certain her skin would be red. With his fingers, he traced the delicate veins of her hand, watching as her fingers laced with his.

"Can you endure this, Anais?" he asked, looking up at her. He was crying, silent tears that trickled down his cheeks. "Christ, can you stand to see me like this, pathetic and weak?"

She brushed the tears away, her strength never wavering as she held on to his hand. "I believe in you, Lindsay."

He cried in earnest then. Wrapping his arms around her waist, he buried his face into her belly and cried like an infant. "I'm so sorry, Anais, that I am this sort of man. You deserve so much better, and to hold you hostage like this, to force you to stay, to make you promise—"

"Shh," she whispered, rubbing his back. "I am not a hostage here."

He looked up at her through the shimmering tears in his eyes. "I do not deserve you, but I know I cannot endure this without you."

"Lindsay, you deserve so much more. In time you'll realize that."

He didn't believe her, but he didn't argue with her, either. He just lay there with his head in her lap, the feel of her fingers raking through his hair as he looked up at her. He tried to think of the future and couldn't even begin to see that far. He saw only as far as the table beside the divan that had once housed his opium.

"I wish I could take back that night, Anais, when I used the hashish."

She covered his mouth with her fingers. "I wish I could take back my rash decision to lie about going to France. But thinking that way will only eat us up inside."

He nodded, looked away. They were silent a long while when Anais finally looked down at him and asked, "What are you thinking of?"

His gaze flickered to hers. "Truth?" She nodded. "Opium." Her eyes saddened, even as he felt the resolve in her strengthen.

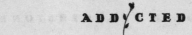

"I can't speak false words to you, Anais. The opium, procuring, smoking it, being lost in its powers is never far from my mind. No matter how enticing the thought of you might be, it is never enough to completely drive away the craving."

"I understand."

He nodded, knowing she did understand. He was tired, his mind active with the need to smoke. She was rubbing his temples, and her belly cushioned him. He snuggled deeply into her and closed his eyes, trying to find the inner strength and conviction he had once possessed.

Then he drifted off, trying not to fear what would be lying in wait for him when he awoke.

Anais awoke in the dark to the sound of Lindsay pacing along the tile floor. He was breathing hard and swearing as he stopped to rifle through the drawers of the table.

"What have they done with the opium?" he growled, tossing the empty canister to the floor. It landed with a crack on the tiles. "Gone. All gone," he growled.

"Lindsay, come back to bed."

"Where is the goddamn opium?" He had all but roared that question. "Jesus Christ, you cannot expect me to just stop," he panted. "Please," he begged, coming to her, pulling her from the divan where they had slept. "It's not safe, Anais, to just stop. I'm crawling out of my skin with wont for it."

"It is the only way."

"It's not the only way," he cried. He pushed her aside and started searching through the drawers once more. The delirium was setting in. It was far more frightening than Anais had thought. What was even more alarming was the fact that she knew it was just the beginning.

"Let me out," he commanded as he whirled on her. "Just for a few minutes. I need out, need air."

"There is plenty of air in this room, Lindsay." She went to light the candlewick so she could see him.

"Don't." His voice seemed disembodied in the darkness. "I don't want you to see me like this...hungry, needy, feral," he growled as he resumed his pacing. "Just...call for Vallery and let me out. I won't be gone long. I swear it. I'll come back."

"Lindsay, you said you would try."

"I will. Tomorrow. But tonight...tonight I need it, Anais. I...I can taper off. Come off it slowly. You can't expect me to just stop like this, Anais. I'm going out of my damned mind! I need opium and I need it *now!*"

"If you walk away from this, Lindsay, you'll lose everything."

"Including you, I suppose," he snapped as he threaded his hands through his hair and resumed his pacing. "Is that what you mean by that? You'll walk away and never look back. So I am to choose," he snarled, "which one I need most. You or opium."

"Lindsay, if you let it win tonight, you'll never conquer it."

"I don't want to conquer it," he yelled, whirling on her. "Don't you understand? I want it. I want it in my mouth, coursing through my blood. *I need it!*"

"I know it's hard—"

"Hard? Christ, what the hell do you know about it? You're not the one suffering through it. Oh, God, Anais, please. Don't you understand? Don't you know how much my body cries out for it?"

"I understand, Lindsay."

"Then call for Vallery. Please. Call him."

She nearly caved in when she heard the pain, the anguish in his voice. He was hurting, physically and emotionally, and she didn't know how to help him.

"Anais?"

"No, Lindsay."

He stormed over to the door and rattled the handle. "Call him."

Anais strode to the door and reached his hand. "No, Lindsay."

"I said, call Vallery," he shouted.

"Come away, Lindsay."

"I said call Vallery, Anais, or...or I will..."

"You will not hurt me," she murmured, taking his hand and easing it from the doorknob.

"I want out of this fucking room!"

"I know," she said, taking him into her arms.

"Oh, God, it hurts," he cried, holding on to her as he let his head drop against her shoulder. "You have no idea how much, Anais."

If it was anything like watching him go through it, Anais thought, it was more pain than the devil himself could inflict.

Suddenly, she felt hot tears against her collarbone. "I can't do this."

"Yes, you can, Lindsay."

"No," he said, shaking his head. "It hurts too much. My head...it screams for it. I...I could have hurt you, Anais. I wanted to, just for a chance to get my hands on the opium."

"You would never hurt me, Lindsay, I know that."

"I already have, though, haven't I?"

"Shh," she whispered as he held him tight. "This storm will pass."

"I cannot endure another."

"Yes, you will, you can. I have never seen you stronger, Lindsay. You can beat this. *You will beat this.*"

He shuddered against her, pressing his body into hers. "Don't leave me, Anais."

"Never. When you open your eyes, Lindsay, I will be there."

His fingers, trembling uncontrollably, caressed her mouth. "Promise, angel?"

She kissed his fingers. "Promise."

"Come into the bath with me, Anais," he asked. He took her by the hand and walked them over to the spring bath. She watched as he removed his trousers. Then he reached for her and pulled her chemise up and over her head.

"Maybe the water will take away the pain in my body. And your arms, Anais," he said, lifting her up and carrying her into the bath, "will take away the pain in my soul."

Together they slipped into the warm water. Anais held him, locking her arms and legs around him so that she could caress him and whisper into his ear.

"You are very strong, Lindsay. You will do this. I believe that."

He looked up at her, caught her gaze through the moonlight that had crept in through the windows. He captured her lips with his. "Take me away from all this," he begged. "Make me forget everything but you."

Her mouth, gentle, caressed his jaw where it was stubbled with growth. Her lips sought his neck, his Adam's apple bobbed as he swallowed hard—she kissed it, and he felt himself go boneless against her, the water lapping around them as he held tightly on to her waist. Her hands smoothed down his shoul-

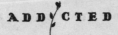

ders and arms, which he knew still trembled, before wrapping
around to the muscles of his chest, soothing him, loving him.

She knew what he needed, and she gave it to him so easily,
so perfectly. Without question or reservation.

Christ, he needed this, he thought as he closed his eyes and
allowed her to touch him. He needed her caresses, to feel her
strength so he could absorb it, could steal it from her to shore
up his own faltering resolve. He needed to be part of her, to
know that he still held some piece of her, a piece that was his
alone.

He knew she did not do this out of pity. She did it out of love,
out of the passion they had for one another. And he was weak
enough to allow her—no, he would beg her for it if she stopped
her touches, and the trail of her lips on his throat. He was not
beneath begging Anais. But she didn't make him plead. She knew
that at this time, what he needed, almost as much as he needed
the opium, was her touch to take away the pain in his body and
the ache in his heart.

He wanted to show her pleasure, to bury his mouth in her
sex and taste her, to feel her fingers pulling at his hair as she
came, but he was weak, and he was selfish. He wanted, for just
this once, to have Anais show him her physical love. To take
his body into her own hands and show him what he meant to
her.

Her lips were gliding down his throat, her fingers playing
with his nipples, which were hard and tingling. His body was
ready, greedy to take everything she was offering him. Restless,
he moved his hips against hers, nudging his cock between the
apex of her thights. The need to be buried in her was primal,

almost overpowering, and he nudged harder, seeking entrance into her cunt, which was tight and warm and waiting to accept him.

"Let me give you this," she whispered against his cheek as she reached for his bollocks and cupped them in her hand. He moaned, the feeling at once so perfect, yet not enough. She played with him, teased him, made him burn, then reached for his cock and stroked him up and down in a lazy fashion that had him gritting his teeth, trying to reach for something that was harder, faster, that would have him spilling into her palm. Yet he didn't want to demand or dictate. He wanted her to explore him, to love him just as she desired.

"Let me try to take the pain away," she murmured as she passed her fingertip over the head of his cock, which was already leaking with anticipation.

"You are, angel," he said on a sigh as she suckled his nipple. "I feel nothing but you now. I want nothing but you and the pleasure you give me."

Christ, she made the ache in his body leave as she laved his nipples and stroked his cock with firmer strokes that had him growing thicker. His cock lay between their bodies, he felt her quim, wet with desire, brush against his thigh, and he shoved it between her silky thighs, letting her ride him as his hands made sweeping motions down her back, to her lush bottom, which he softly grazed with his fingetips. The water was warm, but despite that, he felt goose bumps rise on her flesh as she rode aginst him, pleasuring herself while pleasuring him.

She gave him everything. Her whispered words of love, her curved body as she pressed into him. She brought him up until

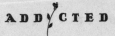
he thought he would spill into her hand, then brought him back down, only to bring him to the brink of orgasm once again.

It was slow and beautiful. The first time she had ever taken him on her own. She knew how to touch him, how to make him moan, but did she know how much he needed her now? How he needed to be inside her to fill the empty spot in his soul— the one she had left when they had parted ways. Did she know he needed her to join with him to keep the heavenly demon from screaming in his head?

"I need you, angel," he pleaded next to her ear. "Keep me safe, won't you?"

He begged her as he felt her fingers swirl against the swollen head, spreading the seed that had seeped out. He begged again as her sex slipped over his thigh, rubbing in time to her stroking hand.

Christ, his voice was weak, full of pain and eagerness. He thought he might have been weeping, knew he was when she kissed the corner of his eye, taking the droplet away on her lips.

She knew what he needed, knew what that one broken word—*please*—meant.

She opened to him and guided his cock into her quim, slowly giving herself to him to hold, to fill.

He buried his face into her hair and allowed her to love him as he so desperately needed.

There were no words, just shaky breaths and clutching hands and mouths hungrily seeking each other. She was riding him slowly, the pace intentionally slow so he could feel every quiver, every shudder of her body as she held him safe. And then he was spilling into her, his body trembling, his voice crying out—

but not in need for opium. She had made him forget about that. Now, all he could see was her. All he wanted in his life was the woman who clutched him to her and allowed him to silently weep against her. He felt no shame at his tears, just relief knowing his secret was out, that the demon who held him was slowly being exorcised out of him, but made more bearable by Anais, a woman who owed him nothing. A woman who loved him despite his flaws. There had been other passionate couplings between them, but never one as beautiful and humbling as this one. As he clutched her in his shaking hands and wept against her, he whispered into her ear, the words that made him believe.

"Love bears all things. Endures all things," he said. "Ours has, hasn't it?" She nodded and held him tighter. "But can it endure this, Anais? This demon who holds me so mercilessly in its claws?"

She touched his face and kissed him. "My love can and will, Lindsay. I will be here when you open your eyes. I will give you whatever you need to make it more bearable."

29

Two days later, the withdrawal from the opium overtook Lindsay. He was constantly trembling and shaking. He couldn't keep fluids or food down, and even when his stomach was empty he still purged into the chamber pot. Anais was always there, rubbing his back, wiping his brow with cool cloths. There had not been any further scenes like the one where he had demanded she let him out of the room. But there were still moments when she thought Lindsay would go mad with longing for the opium. Other times he separated himself from her. She couldn't reach him then, could only pray that he would emerge from the darkness that gripped him. There were other times when he would break down and cry, in pain, the physical and emotional kind. It was these moments that Anais knew he got lost inside himself and the pain of the past few weeks. She feared he might never come back, but he did—and always to her.

He spat into the bowl, coughing up the last of the bile. Anais wiped his mouth and covered his brow with a clean cloth. He was sweating profusely. But she didn't care. She took him into

her arms and held him to her. He fell peacefully back to sleep ·
in her embrace.

He slept most of the day, only waking to be sick. Sometimes
he moaned in his sleep and thrashed around. Anais knew then
that his body ached. So she would either rub his limbs, or, if he
was steady enough, she would help him into the spring bath,
which seemed to help him the most.

She had even shaved him in the bath. "Angel of mercy," he said,
with the first smile she had seen in weeks from him. Shaving him
had been an intimate act, bringing them closer than they ever
had been. Afterward, they had relaxed in the water, touching
and whispering and taking support from one another. That hour
in the water had sapped Lindsay of his energy, and she'd helped
him back to bed where he slept peacefully beneath a sheet.

There were no more secrets, nothing to hide behind. They
loved one another, despite what they had done to each other. They
had asked for forgiveness from each other in the quiet of the dark.

The future, while fraught with uncertainty, held a glimmer
of light, a light that had not been present four days ago.

"My love?" Lindsay asked, as he swallowed, his throat dry. The
room was quiet and he raised his head, looking for Anais. He
found her, asleep in a chair. Dark circles were beneath her eyes
and she looked as though she had lost weight. He frowned at that
thought. He liked her plump and luscious. She had seen to his
needs to the cost of her own. It was now time he repaid the favor.

Rising from the divan, his body still hurt, but his head felt
better. The craving for opium was now only a little whisper, not
the roar that it had been. He was hungry, he realized as his belly
grumbled loudly for the first time in months.

He walked the short distance to Anais, and picked her up. She didn't move, didn't even flutter her lashes. She was exhausted, his angel. As she should be. She had been the one, the only one, to see him through the hell of these past days and nights. She had never left his side. True to her words, she had always been there whenever he opened his eyes. There were times when he hated to see her, times when he wished that she were replaced by an opium pipe. Yet there had been other times when Anais's arms and body had been the only thing keeping him sane.

The words they had repeated while holding each other in the baths, their mantra that had given them both the strength to see this through came to his lips.

He kissed her brow. "My love for you will never die, Anais. Never."

He had at last made peace with himself. It was a good start.

"You wanted to speak with me?"

Lindsay looked over his shoulder to see Broughton standing in the doorway of the study. With a nod, he ushered his friend in and waved to an empty chair by the hearth.

"I..." Lindsay swallowed hard and gazed out the window, gathering the courage to speak. "I must beg your forgiveness, Garrett," he said, using his friend's Christian name for the first time ever. "The way I charged into your house, the way I spoke to you—the accusations," he said, turning at last to look at his friend. "I was wrong. So wrong to treat you like I did. I know, and knew then, that you had only tried to do what was right. It was just..."

"The opium ruled then."

Lindsay nodded. "In part, but I cannot always blame my behavior on the opium. As much as I want opium to take the fall for this, I cannot. It was me. I am responsible for the way I treated you. I was angry, disillusioned, hurt," he said. "I had a child. A child I wanted, and couldn't have. A child I lost through my own faults. I was lashing out, trying to hurt everyone around me. I saw everyone's culpability except my own. I didn't want to see it or acknowledge that I had been partly responsible. I know now that I must accept that blame. What I said to you was inexcusable."

Broughton nodded and rose from the chair. Lindsay extended his hand. "Thank you, Garrett, for protecting my daughter and Anais when I should have. My gratitude knows no bounds. You are the very best of friends. A better friend to me, than I have been to you."

Broughton grasped his hand and tugged him into a hug. "Good God, you've done it," he said, "you've licked this addiction and come back to us."

Lindsay clapped Broughton's back. "Not fully back yet, but soon, I hope. I will not lie, I've thought of opium twice since I began speaking to you."

"You'll fight this," Broughton grumbled. "And you'll win, too. Bloody hell, Raeburn, I never wanted to hurt you."

"I know that now. It just took time and a harsh look within to realize it."

Broughton shook his hand, pumping it up and down with exuberance. "Let us speak no more against each other."

"Agreed." His friend was about to leave when Lindsay stopped

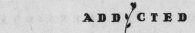

him. "I realize it's a bit premature to be asking favors, but I wonder if I might beg of your indulgence?"

With a nod, Broughton regained his seat, listening to Lindsay's request.

Anais stepped into the cottage and closed the door. The wick was burning in the oil lamp on the commode and a fire was roaring in the brick hearth. "Garrett? I received your note. You wished to see me?"

Looking around the cottage, she saw no sign of Garrett. Frowning, she pulled her gloves from her hands and untied the satin ribbons securing her bonnet.

"Are you here?" she asked again as she folded her cape and placed it over the arms of the rattan chair that sat by the door.

"I am here."

Anais whirled around and saw Lindsay standing in the door that led from the water closet. In his arms was Mina, snuggled up against his chest, her sweet face pressed into his neck. He looked so strong, so noble standing there. She realized she was looking upon the old Lindsay, the one of her youth, the one who held the world in his palm.

Every minute locked in the room with him was worth it, if only to see him looking like this.

"I had Garrett write the missive, Anais. It was me—us—who needed to see you."

"What purpose... for wh...wh..." she stuttered like a simpleton as he stepped closer to her with the baby.

"You said you never got to hold her. That confession broke my heart."

He stood before her and brushed her hair away from her face before tucking some curls behind her ear. "I was such a selfish bastard. I just barged into Broughton's home and demanded to see her. I never dreamed you had not been able to touch her."

"I must go," she murmured and she cursed herself when she allowed her gaze to drop from Lindsay's face to rest upon Mina's pink cheek that rested against the naked skin of Lindsay's throat.

He reached for her wrist and held her. "Don't leave. There is no point in running. We—both of us—are through running from our demons."

She tried to shake her head but he *shhed* her and drew her over to the bed where he had her sit and lean back against the pillows. He looked down at her, his eyes glowing a brilliant shade of green, and placed Mina in her arms.

"This is how it should have been, me placing our daughter in your arms."

She gasped, sobbed, cried out and smiled all at once when she felt the weight of Mina in her arms. When she looked down at the tousled mop of black curls, she cried, fat, scalding tears that slid down her cheeks.

"Are you crying or laughing?" he asked as he stretched out beside her. "I see tears, but I see a big smile, too."

"Oh, God, Lindsay, she's beautiful. I never...I didn't know she was this perfect. She looks like you." She grinned, looking at him. "She has your wild hair and your eyes."

"I see you in her, too. She has the shape of your face and your cheeks."

"Oh, God, I cannot believe we made her."

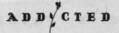

Lindsay laughed. "We did indeed. I remember the night very well. It was perfect. Beautiful."

"Thank you," she whispered as she continued to cradle Mina in her arms. "Thank you for this."

"Thank you for her, Anais. Even though she cannot be a part of our lives in any true sense, I am thankful for her. I am happy that I had this time with her—and I am happy that we have this time to share together."

Anais nodded and rocked Mina back and forth in her arms, her gaze cataloging Mina's features and implanting them in her memory.

Lindsay nodded and trailed his fingertips along Mina's little hand that was pressed against Anais's breasts. "I have made my peace with Broughton. I thanked him for taking care of you and Mina when it should have been up to me to see to both of your safety."

"I am glad you've made peace. You were always good friends. I wouldn't want to come between the two of you."

"You were always between us, Anais. I knew that. I had known for a long time that Broughton held a special affection for you. I suppose that is why I believed it so easily that you chose to be with him."

"Garrett loves me, Lindsay, but not in the way you think."

"Why didn't you marry him?"

"Because what Garrett and I have is special. It is a very deep friendship, but it is not a physical one. I could have grown to love him, I suppose, but I could not have felt for Garrett what I physically feel for you. I could not cheat him out of a passionate marriage. I couldn't do that."

He nodded and motioned for her to hand him Mina. "You look tired, Anais. I know these days have been hard on you. I put you through hell. Why don't you get undressed and slip beneath the covers. I will give Mina to you and you can both sleep."

"I shouldn't—"

"Just down to your chemise, Anais. You can trust me."

Sleep. The word sounded like heaven and Anais easily gave in to the lure of the thick coverlet and the beckoning sheets.

"We have a few hours yet with her, Anais. Sleep for a bit and I will wake you."

Dressed in her chemise, Anais pulled back the corner of the quilt and slipped beneath. True to his word, Lindsay placed Mina in the crook of her arm. She smiled and traced the chubby contours of Mina's cheeks.

"Sleep," he whispered as he brushed her hair away from her cheeks. "Sleep."

Lindsay watched as Anais's eyes grew heavy and finally closed. He lay there for some time, his head propped in his hand, just watching Anais and his daughter sleeping together. It was as perfect a picture as he could ever imagine.

A profound sense of rightness settled into his chest. He loved this woman. He loved this babe. He would fight for them and the future that hung in the balance.

"Lindsay?" Anais murmured sleepily as her eyelids slowly lifted.

"I'm here." Unable to stand it any longer he leaned down and brushed his mouth against hers. "I'm here—forever, Anais."

Her lashes fluttered and she looked up at him with wide blue eyes.

"Forgive and you will be forgiven," he said, his voice cracking. "Is that true?"

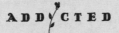

She nodded and reached for him. "I lied when I told you the love was gone, Lindsay. It has never left. It has only grown stronger. These past days with you have made me realize it. I love you. We are destined to be together in good times and bad."

"I don't need to hide anymore, do I, Anais?"

"No, Lindsay. No more hiding. We are both as we ever were, I think. Faults and all."

"Can you believe in me again, Anais?"

"Yes. Can you forgive me?"

"I already have. Anais, I love you so damn much."

"Kiss me, Lindsay," she purred and he cupped her chin in his hand and gazed into her eyes. "Love me."

"Forever. With everything I have, I will love you." He slipped a plain gold band around her finger. "I had bought you something big and expensive, then realized it wasn't right. We don't need anything flashy to tell the world of our love and commitment. Just this simple band, with no beginning or end. Like my love for you."

"Lindsay," she said, looking up at him through her tears. "You have come back to be the man of my dreams. My commitment to you has never been stronger. I know the days, the weeks ahead will be a struggle for you. But I am here. Every step of the way."

He squeezed her hand and kissed Mina's head. "The world looks different to me now, Anais. The future is bright. I can't wait to start it. It was so beautiful this day, to awaken and find you at the end of the tunnel standing in a ray of light. I have hope now, where I only ever had fear. Thank you for that, angel."

Pressing her head to his, they looked down at their daughter, peace stealing over them. Lindsay was right. The future was theirs.

Epilogue

"Oh my God!" Lindsay cried. "I swear I shall practice celibacy, every day for the rest of my life! I swear it, Anais."

Anais drew in a long breath and held it before pushing with all her might.

"Very good, Anais," Dr. Thornley muttered. "Now, you will want to push longer the next time. You are almost there. You, Lord Raeburn, might wish to quit your caterwauling and assist your wife by supporting her legs."

Anais, sweating and tired, lay limp against Lindsay's chest. He was on his knees, supporting her weight and insisting that she allow him to do everything required of a man who was about to become a father.

"Another one," she panted, drawing her breath as she pushed again.

"Oh my God," Lindsay said over and over as their baby's head crowned.

"Yes, well, God is not here at the moment, Raeburn, so you might act in his stead and ready that towel beside you."

"Right," Lindsay grumbled and Anais felt his shaking, panicking hands searching the bedcovers for the towel.

"Now, a nice slow, steady push, Lady Raeburn. This should be the last one."

And with a little push, a screaming babe was pulled from her womb.

"A boy!" Lindsay cried as the doctor placed the bellowing baby onto the towel that Lindsay held. Immediately he wrapped the babe in the towel and clutched the squirming newborn to his chest.

"Look," he whispered and Anais could hear his voice shaking. "Our son, Anais. He's so beautiful—you're beautiful."

"And this is why," the doctor said to the student he was training, "husbands routinely assisting their wives in childbirth will never come into fashion. They are a damned nuisance if you ask me. They require more assurance than the mother."

"Not even your ribbing," he said with a glare to the doctor, "is enough to mar this moment. It was absolutely incredible," Lindsay said, kissing her brow. "Utterly amazing. I think I shall deliver the next one myself."

"Ugh," Anais groaned as another contraction seized her.

"What is it, love? What's wrong?" Lindsay asked, panic seizing his voice.

"Ah, here comes the afterbirth," Thornley announced. "No problems with it at all. Now, lad," he said to his assistant, "you've seen your first babe being birthed, what do you think? Lad?" The doctor looked over his shoulder then dropped his gaze to the carpet.

"I think," Lindsay said with a laugh as he rocked his son, "that the lad should choose another line of work."

"Bloody hell," he snapped as he bent down and waved his hand above the pale face of his student. "Damned afterbirth gets them every time."

Lindsay smiled and bent down to kiss Anais and placed his son in her arms. "Thank you, Anais, for our son."

She smiled and cupped his cheek. "Will you give me a few minutes and then come back?"

Lindsay saw that the nurse was carrying a bowl of water and a pile of linens were draped over her arm. Thornley was dragging a still swooning student from the room, and he could hear his father grumbling loudly in the hall.

"I'll go tell Mother and Father the news, then I'll return."

"Here," she laughed. "Don't you want to take him and show him off?"

Lindsay grabbed his son from her arms and kissed her hard before striding to the door.

"About bloody time!" Weatherby snapped and then Anais heard his voice soften and break with emotion. "Damn me, boy, he's all you. Our blood runs true, does it not?"

"It does, indeed, Father." And a few tears crept out of Anais's eyes when she heard the pride and love in Lindsay's voice.

Hours later, after the sun had set and the oil lamps had been lit, Anais sat up in bed with her son at her breast and her husband at her side. She watched Lindsay's long fingers stroking the black curls on their son's head as the babe suckled eagerly.

"I received a letter from Middleton today. We did the right thing, allowing Mina to go to Robert and Margaret," Lindsay murmured as he watched his son nursing. "She's as happy as a clam. And Middleton is clearly besotted with her." Anais smiled

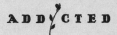

and brushed her fingertips along his whiskered cheek. "He says she's walking now, such a precocious little thing. I wonder where she inherited that from?" he teased before kissing her soundly. "We shall have to purchase her a pony. Riding will be in her blood."

"She is a bit young for a pony, don't you think?"

He grinned up at her and winked. "Never too young for horses, my love."

"True," she said, looking down at her son.

"Anais?" Lindsay asked softly as he brushed a lock of her hair behind her ear. "Have you gotten everything you wanted? I mean…are you happy?"

"Happy enough that I didn't kick you when you mentioned having another child."

"So, *very* happy then?"

"Blissfully happy and completely in love."

"Me, too," he whispered. "I could not imagine a life more perfect than the one I'm living at this very moment."

ABOUT THE AUTHOR

Charlotte Featherstone is the multipublished author of sensual historical and contemporary paranormal novels, e-books and short stories. An avid reader, she counts among her vices good chocolate, her husband's coffee and dark, brooding alpha heroes. Charlotte lives in Ontario, Canada, with her husband and young daughter and is currently working on her next novel for Spice Books.

Please feel free to drop Charlotte a line at:
www.CharlotteFeatherstone.net

ACKNOWLEDGMENTS

A book is never simply written. It is rewritten until it comes together as it is meant to be, and *Addicted* is no exception. I have so many people to thank for their belief in this book.

My agent, Mary Louise Schwartz, has always been there for me with hand-holding when needed and butt kicking when required. Your enthusiastic "there's no way this isn't going to sell," still makes me smile. Thank you for taking on this project with me and for always being there through panicked phone calls and e-mails.

To the art department at Harlequin for giving me such a stunning cover and for using the red smoke idea. I adore it and couldn't imagine anything more perfect.

To Kristina Cook (Kristi Astor) my longtime critique partner who has been with me from the very beginning. Where would I be without you? You truly are my rock in good times and bad. I know *Addicted* wouldn't be here if it hadn't been for you encouraging me along the way. I value your insight, your skills and friendship. There are no words that begin to express how instrumental you have been in helping me get here. I thank you a hundred times over.

And last but most certainly not least, to my editor, Susan Swinwood, for allowing me to write this book as I had originally intended. Your edits empowered me to stretch myself as an author and take chances. Thank you for allowing me to keep Lindsay as he truly is, scarred, dark, flawed and so very human. You "got him" and that really is a dream come true.

FROM THE BESTSELLING AUTHOR OF
DIRTY, BROKEN AND *TEMPTED*

MEGAN HART

I pay strangers to sleep with me.
I have my reasons…but they're
not the ones you'd expect.
Looking at me you wouldn't
have a clue I carry this little
secret so close it creases up like
the folds of a fan. Tight. Personal.
Ready to unravel in the heat of
the moment.

Then one day I signed on to "pick
up" a stranger at a bar, but took
Sam home instead. And now that
I've felt his heat, his sweat and
everything else, can I really go
back to impersonal?

"…sensual and graphic, as a whole [it's] about so much
more than sex…I wasn't ready for the story to end."

—*A Romance Review* on *Tempted*

Available the first week of January 2009!

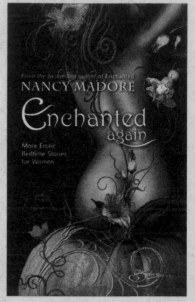